"I am sorry Lord Hereford has your brother. You must know it would not be in the warden's political interest to harm the boy," said Rose.

Roxburghe set down the bottle of whisky. "You are familiar with Hereford enough to make that manner of observation?"

"I know that such kidnappings are the backbone of much of the power wielded in the borderlands. A dead hostage is useless to him when most people just give him what he wants." Tension tightened her chest. "But then I imagine you are not most people."

She didn't move as he lifted her braid and wrapped it around his fist, ever so gently, his dark eyes dancing with amusement. "What else do you know about me?"

She knew he was dangerous.

Sliding her hair from his hand, she tilted her chin. "I know you are a hunter." Her words came out in a heated rush. "But I am not your prey."

"But then I am not hunting tonight," he said in a low voice. "If I were, you would already be mine."

Claimed By A Scottish Lord

MELODY THOMAS

AVON

An Imprint of HarperCollinsPublishers

This is a work of fiction. Names, characters, places, and incidents are products of the author's imagination or are used fictitiously and are not to be construed as real. Any resemblance to actual events, locales, organizations, or persons, living or dead, is entirely coincidental.

AVON BOOKS
An Imprint of HarperCollins*Publishers*
10 East 53rd Street
New York, New York 10022-5299

Copyright © 2010 by Laura Renken
ISBN 978-0-06-189870-9
www.avonromance.com

First Avon Books paperback printing: July 2010

Avon Trademark Reg. U.S. Pat. Off. and in Other Countries, Marca Registrada, Hecho en U.S.A.
HarperCollins® is a registered trademark of HarperCollins Publishers.

Printed in the U.S.A.

10 9 8 7 6 5 4 3 2 1

To my gal pals past and present who have given me the gift of their knowledge and the treasure of friendship: my daughter, Shari, my mom, Faye Joann. To Marlene Carroll (thank you for all your support). Betsy Bickenbach & Lois Molidor (remember Hawaii ladies). Jeffery McClanahan & Jean Newlin (my critique partners). To my LionHearted ladies (and for the two of our courageous own who lost their lives to cancer these past years).

Finally, to my Windy City Romance Writer family and those I have known for over ten years: Anita Baker, Elysa Hendricks, Kelle Riley, Chris Foutris, Haley Hughs, Fredericka Meiners, Dyanne Davis, Julie Wachowski, Allie Pleiter, Terri Stone, Debbie Pfeiffer, Denise Swanson, Lyndsay Longford, Cathie Linz, and Susan Elizabeth Phillips. You have all in some way touched my life and made me a better person for it. Thank you so much.

Claimed By A Scottish Lord

Chapter 1

The Borders, Scotland
Summer 1755

Rose Lancaster jumped back from the cobbled street barely escaping being run down by the village crier mounted on a shaggy horse.

"Hear ye, here ye! The Black Dragon has returned! Lord Roxburghe has come home!"

Despite the unusual heat of the day, the streets and narrow alleyways of Castleton were filled with people as if it were an autumn country-fair day. The village's younger maidens and children lined the cobbled streets nearer to the square. They carried flowers, now wilted from the uncommon heat. Some had been here for hours.

Rose stood taller than most surrounding and jostling her. Shading her eyes with a hand, she peered in the direction from where the crier had come. Her height was God's gift or curse, depending on the day—and the company. She glimpsed the growing wall of dust approaching the village.

Since half of the surrounding lands around Castleton lay on the Scottish side of the border, many of the town's residents called themselves Scots. But in a place where skirmishes had been fought over stolen sheep and women, religion and politics since before the Roman emperor Hadrian built his infamous wall to separate England from the northern hordes, a man's loyalty oft depended upon who was visiting on any given day.

Not this day.

For as long as she remembered, she had heard grand stories about the Roxburghe heir, the Borders' native son, a former privateer and smuggler. Now, after a thirteen-year absence and the murder of his father, Ruark Kerr, the border lord had come home to procure his place as head of the Kerr clan.

Though no one knew for certain what had driven him from Scotland those long years ago, everyone seemed to understand and appreciate what brought him back. Shortly after his father's death earlier this year, the king's warden arrested and imprisoned Roxburghe's twelve-year-old half brother. The boy had been languishing in a prison for weeks. Rose had listened all morning to speculation that Roxburghe's long-awaited homecoming would bring war down upon the hated English warden, a man Rose also hated since his return to England a year ago.

But she could not think about the world's problems as she set her sights on a way to cross the street. Taking this main road leading through the village square had turned out to be a mistake only amplified as the crowd surged against her. If she did not make it back to the abbey before nightfall, Friar Tucker would return and discover her gone. She disliked deceiving him. Having raised her since she was three, he was dearer than her father.

Angry for allowing herself to be trapped in the impassable human current, she clasped a collection of books to her chest and continued to shoulder her way through the press of people, feeling like a salmon fighting an upstream current. "Pardon. I need to squeeze through. Pardon."

A woman's voice suddenly stopped her. "Rose, child. Whatever are you doing in Castleton? What have you there in your arms?"

Rose patiently smiled at the aged shopkeeper who was also the village postmaster. Silver sausage ringlets peaked out from beneath the calash of a stiff white bonnet framing her face. Rose bobbed a polite curtsey. "Good afternoon, Mrs. Graham. I am taking these books to the abbey. Mrs. Simpson found them in her husband's collection and loaned them to me."

Mrs. Graham's ample bosom rose and pressed against a red apron. "Och, child. I have never known a person what spent more time with books than you do. You need to find yerself a man and settle down. Now, me Geddes is a strappin' lad and will inherit my shop one day."

Geddes Graham was also a malefactor whose loyalty to any cause could be bought for a stipend. Rose peered at the quaint little boutique over the elder's shoulder, its bric-a-brac decorating the brightly painted shelves behind the large window recently installed. She wondered sadly how a kind woman like Mrs. Graham could birth a weasel like Geddes. Rose's longing for a family was a subject she rarely broached with anyone, but she had bigger dreams than to live out her life with any man she did not love or who did not love her in return.

"Thank you, Mrs. Graham." She kissed the woman's cheek. "If I should wed, I could not want for a better mother-in-law than someone like you."

The matron pressed a palm to her cheek and blushed. "Pish-posh, child." She giggled and pulled a folded missive from her pocket, sealed with a wafer impressed with a cross and a sword, Friar Tucker's signet. "This came for the abbey this morning," she said over the low din. "Jack has no' been by to fetch the mail."

Rose shifted the books in her arms and popped the wax seal. With the abbey's prioress nearly blind, Rose managed the daily business and correspondence for Sister Nessa. "Jack is with me." She skimmed the page.

Friar Tucker had gone to Redesdale some days ago to attend the funeral of an uncle. Now something of utmost importance took him to Carlisle. He would return by the end of the month. A postscript read that they were not to worry.

Why would he say that? The very dictate caused apprehension. Why would he go to Carlisle? "Thank you, Mrs. Graham."

She started to turn when a shout from farther up the road brought the crowd to life.

As if it were one beast, the throng seemed to awaken and move, dragging Rose forward. Until now, she had kept her fiery hair hidden beneath its purple-and-green plaid wrap that even though it did not complement her simple yellow dress she cherished all the same. It was all she had left of a mother she remembered only in vignettes. Clutching the books in her arms, she struggled to pull her scarf tighter around her shoulders, afraid it would be torn from her and crushed beneath careless feet.

The ground beneath Rose began to rumble. An overpowering curiosity captured her and caused her to remain and watch the procession through town.

"Roxburghe always was a wild one," Mrs. Graham said, clearly relishing the delicious horror of it all, while craning her short neck to see over the crowd. "We were surprised 'e didn't end up at the bottom of the sea or hanged from the gallows, him leaving the way he did those years ago. Now they say he's here to exact revenge on the warden for holding Roxburghe's brother for ransom. Hereford will start a war over that lad. Roxburghe is no' a man to sit back and do anyone's bidding." Mrs Graham leaned nearer. "Lord love us, Rose," she shouted above the growing din. "Do ye see him yet?"

Rose's gaze riveted to the summit as two dozen horsemen poured into the crowded marketplace at a full gallop. Briefly silhouetted against a turbulent afternoon sky, neither men nor horses showed any sign of slowing for the eager crowd that suddenly silenced and parted like the great Red Sea.

"There he be!" a man yelled from the rooftop behind her.

The earl of Roxburghe, distinguishable by his dark blue jacket, sat atop a red Irish hunter, riding at the head of his men. Even as she found herself holding her breath, watching as he drew nearer, Rose did not know if she should admire the Black Dragon or fear him. But for the first time in her life, her heartbeat quickened at the sight of a man. And unlike the dragons of old made up of only myth and legend, this one was real.

He was tall with strong shoulders. Unlike most men of his rank, he wore no wig. His hair was nearly black and queued at his nape. A wide leather belt with two ivory-handled pistols tucked inside cinched his jacket but did not hide the patterned crimson-and-hunter-green waistcoat beneath. Unshaven and hatless, his leather trews and spurred boots dulled by dust, he looked like the freebooter some claimed him to be, the same man who'd made his name and fortune as an infamous privateer—a quintessential predator.

People living on the borderlands did not readily give their loyalty. But she knew most of Castleton and the surrounding farms would not have survived last winter if not for the extra goods Friar Tucker had got his hands on because of Roxburghe's efforts.

The thunder of horses' hooves grew deafening. Then the Roxburghe laird was rumbling past her, followed closely by his armed retainers, the draft of their passing catching her hair and skirts in a whirlwind of dust and debris. Beside Rose, a young woman pressed her palms to her ears against the din and laughed aloud, her voice carried upward like a bright red pennant in the wind. The pandemonium seemed to go on forever, until amid the fading metallic clang of bridles and spurs and the ringing in her ears, someone behind her shouted, "Godspeed, Ruark." A round of "ayes" followed the pronouncement.

Lord Roxburghe had not so much as slowed.

If Rose hadn't been so sure she'd have been trampled to dust, she would have leapt into the street and forced him to stop just so he would at least acknowledge the little girls who carried the flowers for him. But the riders were already passing through the square and moving away from the village before she could catch her breath and still the strange fluttering in the pit of her stomach.

A hush crawled through the crowd, broken only by an occasional cough as dust settled over them.

"Must be in a hurry," the bearded blacksmith behind Rose said.

"Would no' you be?" another shouted from across the street. "Hereford will pay for taking the laird's brother to be sure."

The Honorable Macfayden, Castleton's burly mayor, cleared his throat. In his official capacity as village spokesman and advocate of good causes he pronounced, "'Tis good the new Kerr laird has returned. The English warden will have his hands full. Maybe he'll be leavin' the rest of us alone now."

"Hear, hear!" Enthusiasm mounted and a call to celebrate all future success for the Roxburghe heir rang out.

"To the Boar's Inn, men!" The battle cry sounded.

Restored to their previous vigor, the crowd began to disperse. But watching the townspeople lumber away, Rose felt only disappointment that their returning hero had lacked the courtesy to acknowledge those lining the streets to pay him homage.

"His lordship is bound to pass near Hope Abbey to get to the river crossing," Mrs. Graham said from beside her, peering at the sky. "If it rains, he may seek shelter."

Startled at the unpleasant notion, Rose lifted her gaze to the darker clouds roiling on the horizon. 'Twas not uncommon that travelers stopped at Hope Abbey for food and rest. With Friar Tucker absent and Rose away from the abbey, Sister Nessa would panic.

Rose bid Mrs. Graham farewell and escaped down a backstreet that followed the turnip fields to the stable. Viewing the open road beyond, relieved to see only remnants of a lingering dust cloud where the Black Dragon had been, Rose was confident that he would be across the river by the time the storm broke.

"'Tis a strained tendon." Ruark rubbed his palm gingerly along the stallion's foreleg. "This horse is not traveling farther or I risk permanently damaging him."

His ship's former second in command, Bryce Colum, knelt beside him. "A week or two at least," he concurred. "Bloody hell."

Ruark peered up at the sky. Amber tinged the red sky just in front of the storm that had been following them for the five miles since leaving the village. The wind in the trees had picked up considerably in the last fifteen minutes. "Hope Abbey is just beyond the woods," Ruark said. "They have a stable. I know the prior."

Most of his men sat around eating while talking in low tones. The pace he had driven them these days had allowed little time for food or rest. Like him, each of them had a lawless quality about him. He looked back over the road they'd just traveled, then scanned the surrounding area. "Take all but four men and go north to Stonehaven. Leave one of the packhorses," he said.

Colum rose. He was not as tall as Ruark. With Ruark standing five inches over six feet, few men were. "Hereford's men are probably watching the road," Colum said. I will remain with the stallion. He's a fine horse—"

"Worth killing for? I want anyone watching this road to see this pack crossing the bridge. No purpose will be served if the warden's men learn any of us has been here. Give me your jacket."

Colum ran an impatient hand through his hair. He slipped out of his jacket and took Ruark's. "You would leave that stallion to Hereford's men?"

The question triggered an arched brow and the barest hint of a grin. "I am disappointed in your lack of faith in me," Ruark said, as he shoved his arms into the sleeves of Colum's jacket, testing the fit. "There is nothing Hereford can take from me that I will not eventually reclaim. But I would rather lose a horse than give our good warden a reason to hang you as well. Besides, I have another reason to stay. Take the men and go now. I will be a day behind you."

Colum ordered all but four men to mount and ride. Amid the near silent commotion, another man approached carrying coffee. "Here ye be," McBain said. "Thought ye might enjoy a refresher even on a blistering day like this."

"Thank you." Ruark took a swallow of the coffee and smiled inwardly for it was blacker than hell, the way no one but McBain could brew it. Powerful and unforgiving. The way Ruark had come to appreciate the world since his years at sea had driven the softness from his life.

He fixed his eyes on the rolling hills. McBain followed his gaze, scrubbing his hand across his bewhiskered face. "It's been a long time. A bluidy long time."

"Not long enough," Ruark said, reflecting McBain's reservations aloud.

"Do ye think there's truth to the rumor that Hereford's daughter is alive?"

"Aye, maybe," Ruark said as he motioned for the remaining men to mount and drank the last of the coffee.

Ruark had not been home in almost thirteen years and he had no idea whom he could trust. But Friar Tucker was one of the few men he knew was not in Hereford's deep pockets. Ruark never understood the source of Tucker's bitter sentiments against Lord Hereford, but he hoped they would serve to ally Ruark and Tucker now against a common foe. If anyone knew the truth of the gossip, 'twould be Tucker.

"If there is a daughter," Ruark said, "I doubt Tucker would appreciate what I have in mind for the girl."

He had never used another man's family to exact retribution, finding the practice repulsive. But watching Colum and the men disappear over the rise, he found himself dwelling on his father's second son. Jamie was a half brother Ruark had never met and knew not, except by the packet of letters he had found awaiting him one year when he had brought the *Black Dragon* into Workington for a refitting. The lad had been only nine at the time and had introduced himself through the writings. For the first time since Ruark had left Scotland, a member of his family had attempted to communicate with him. Ruark had spent that evening reading the letters and every six months afterward for three years, he had sailed into Workington just for those letters.

Their father's death four months ago might have delivered Ruark the Roxburghe earldom, but Jamie's imprisonment had brought Ruark home.

That and the fact that Ruark and the warden were hardly strangers.

Lord Hereford was a former British naval captain who had retired a year ago to his borderland estate to take up the mantle of English warden. He and Ruark had a long history that included Ruark's father murdered and now his half brother arrested for cattle lifting, a hanging offense according to law. Ruark had only just been informed of his half brother's arrest when he landed in Workington a week ago. Hereford held the boy's life for ransom in an attempt to do more than impoverish the Kerr estate.

In Ruark's thinking, a man who would use a boy's life to entrap Ruark was a man who did not value his own life. Ruark would find Hereford's Achilles' heel if it was the last thing he ever did. Vengeance controlled him.

Indeed Ruark rarely left anything to fate.

"They're gone, Miss Rose. They're all gone now."

Jack had run back from the hill overlooking the river and now stood at the cart as Rose held the pony's reins.

Thank heavens. She skimmed the open fields between her and the abbey. Sheer luck had caused her to see the riders in the distance or she would have been caught in the open when they crossed the bridge.

She and Jack had taken the old drover trail out of town,

which shortened the distance to the abbey from town by two miles. But while the trail took her to the backside of the abbey, almost directly to the stables, it also exposed her for a hundred yards to the riverbank.

This was former reiver territory, after all. Exercising caution was always wise in a world where power was its own law, and Lord Roxburghe was more powerful than most. One did not earn the name Black Dragon without cause. "Are you sure it was Lord Roxburghe and his men?"

"Aye, mum," Jack said, excitedly. "They carried a standard all splashed in blood with a fire-breathing monster flappin' in the wind like the tail of a dragon. Is it true he be a pirate, Miss Rose? I heard he's sunk *twenty* ships but that the king won't hang him because he's made the crown rich."

"'Tis a crimson standard, Jack." Her eyes caught a flash of lightning. "Get back on the cart. We don't need to worry about being seen now."

Bright hazel eyes aglow, the boy hopped nimbly into the cart and Rose clicked her tongue. The pony jerked forward.

"Coooee. The Black Dragon." Squinting his eyes, Jack eagerly sought another glimpse of the riverbank, which was in full view as the cart emerged from the woods. "Were we hiding because ye think his lordship would have trussed us like a boar to a spit and tossed us in the river? Ye have yer dirk. Ye wouldna have let anything happen."

"Nay, I would not have," she said, attempting to put his twelve-year-old imagination to rest before he gave himself nightmares. No doubt his mind lingered on the more gruesome details of capture, and though he liked to think himself as Rose's protector, he was still only a boy, recovering from his mam's death last year.

Jack had taken to Rose like a shadow since she'd

defended him from local riffraff some months ago. He followed her everywhere now. She was grateful that Friar Tucker allowed him to stay in the kitchens at the abbey or he'd be sleeping on the ground outside her second-story window.

"Did you get the books ye wanted from Mrs. Simpson?" he asked.

"Yes, I did. And you aren't to tell anyone," she reminded him again, having dragged the oath of secrecy from him before venturing into town. "My visits to Mrs. Simpson are our secret."

He bobbed his blond head in reassurance, the perfect co-conspirator. Jack loved secrets. Last week he had helped her clandestinely bake a strawberry pie for Sister Nessa's birthday, which had required sneaking into the henhouse and stealing two eggs.

Wind gusts lifted her hair. They both looked up at the sky. "Ye best be hurryin', Miss Rose," he encouraged.

She'd wrapped her books in her plaid scarf, but the thin fabric would not protect the leather-bound tomes from rain. She was relieved when they'd finally crossed the open space and entered the woods surrounding the abbey, until the first crack of lightning sounded. A moment later Jack hopped out of the cart. As was their routine, she would take the horse to the stable while Jack slipped through a narrow opening in the stone wall and unlocked the garden gate.

The stable looming ahead of her, she leaped out of the cart and led the pony into the interior out of the storm. The heavy stone walls and thatched roof muffled the thunder, and she was at once met with the pungent smell of straw and aged leather. Her eyes shifted to the stall where Friar Tucker kept the Abbey's prize horse, an aged bay mare. The stall was empty. She still couldn't believe he would be away until the end of the month. He'd said not to worry, but that was like telling the sky not to rain. He rarely left the abbey for more than a few days at a time. Now he would be gone three weeks.

After she unhooked the lead and chains, she housed the pony in the stall beside the plow horse, then scooped grain from the bin and fed both horses. Only after she returned to the cart and removed her books did she realize both oil lanthorns hanging from posts at each end of the stable had been lit. For some reason she had failed to notice this detail when she first entered.

Alarmed, Rose tightened her arms on the books and straightened. She peered up and down the narrow aisle, listening, but heard no one present. It was then she saw another horse, housed in the far stall. Not just any horse either.

The magnificent Irish hunter was a beauty, at least seventeen hands tall, with long legs and a full chest. Though its coat was dusty, she imagined it would shine a glossy red when brushed. Suddenly she had a vague recollection that this stallion looked familiar. Heart pounding, she stepped back and bumped a wooden trestle.

A leather bridle and saddle draped the rack. She traced her finger along the etching of a dragon. A chill coursed down her spine.

Impossible!

Jack had seen Roxburghe and his men cross the bridge.

Rose spun on her heel, swirling straw with her movement, and slammed headlong into a wall.

Or what could have been a wall. Her head smashed against a man's jaw with a blinding *thunk*. Her books flew from her hands, barely missing the water barrel, the impact propelling her backward. She would have fallen had two large hands not grabbed her arms and steadied her.

Her lashes snapped upward as her chin tilted and she stared into a pair of eyes, not quite black but indigo. Sensation bolted down her spine. Then just that fast, as if he felt it too, the expression of annoyance on his face vanished and her own alarm melded with something more pliable than fear.

Shock perhaps, for she would admit to nothing else.

Close up, Lord Roxburghe was even taller and more solidly built than she'd thought when she saw him atop his horse in the village. But his strength did not come from his appearance as much as it did from some unseen force inside him.

One glance into his unshaven face told her why people called him the Black Dragon. Though it had been the name of his frigate, he wore the mark like a mantle of armor. Heat burned where his hands held her.

"Loose me," she whispered on a caught breath, cleared her throat and said the words again with more authority. "Now, if you will."

His grip loosened. She stepped backward but not so quickly her actions signaled fear or retreat. Her foot bumped one of her precious books that lay scattered in the straw.

"Allow me," he offered and stooped to gather up the books.

She started to protest but he had already knelt at her feet. Instead she let her gaze trace the width of his shoulders beneath his jacket. His hair was nearly black in the shadows that seemed to steal the setting sun's light from the surrounding sky and clubbed back from his face with a leather thong. A small silver hoop pierced his left earlobe and gave him an irrepressibly wicked look. She stole another glance at his face as he rose and had to suppress the urge to step back. She had never met a man taller than she was. Being this close to such a rarity stole her breath.

"You read," he said, turning each leather-bound tome over in his gloved hands. Amusement laced his expression. "*Arthurian Legends? The Myth of Merlin? Metallurgy and Electricity?*"

She removed each book from his hands and held them protectively to her chest, not about to trust *this* stranger with her secrets. She was conscious of a prickling warmth that spread where his fingers had brushed hers as if the books had become electricity themselves. "Is it so strange that a woman should read? Or that I should be interested in science?"

His eyes filled with growing amusement brushed down her, taking in her simple dress and wrap. "Both perhaps." His mouth crooked and revealed white teeth. "Those are very old tomes. Valuable."

She did not dispute that fact. Nor did she explain how she had got her hands on such valuable antiquity. She balked at fearing him. "You are not planning to steal them from me, are you, Lord Roxburghe?"

"You know who I am?" His eyes narrowed perceptively on her hair, then her height. "I would remember if we'd met."

Rose withheld a frown beneath his scrutiny. It was too true that she was memorable to people for all the wrong reasons. He would be no exception. "I was one of your many minions lining the street when you passed through Castleton." She graciously inclined her head in an act only the dimmest would construe as subservient. "No doubt the speed with which you rode through the village, you missed us all standing along the streets cheering your return. 'Tis understandable if you missed the village entirely, small as we are, my lord."

Amusement lifted the corners of his mouth, though his eyes as they peered into hers remained more thoughtful. She wanted to turn away from the disturbing gaze. No one, not even the lowest field hand had ever eyed her thusly, in a way that caused a curious sensation in her stomach.

"A thousand pardons, m'lady. Had I seen you standing there, I would have surely stopped—" His hand motioned to her hair, and she thought he might touch her. "If only to discern the color of your curls. Like a radiant sunset burning against the ocean. The color of warm cinnamon."

Her hair? A radiant sunset? Warm cinnamon indeed. She stared speechless and saw the laughter in his eyes. But before she could give him the rebuke he deserved, he humbled himself with a light bow. "My horse has come up lame," he said with seriousness. "I am seeking shelter for my men and me tonight and a conversation with the prior of this keep."

Rose looked beyond him. The abbey did not have enough food in its stores to feed his small army. Nor did she understand who Jack had seen crossing the bridge.

"There are only four of us," he said, clearly reading her mind. "I will compensate this abbey for its trouble, Miss—"

"Friar Tucker is not yet returned."

If she had not been so intently staring at his face, and noticing the perfect cleft on his chin, she would have missed seeing his lips tighten. "Is there another with whom I can request lodging?"

"You are asking permission to stay here?" she said, surprised that a man as powerful as Lord Roxburghe would seek consent.

"As a mere formality," he said, leaving no doubt he was a man without convention, dangerous, and completely capable of doing as he pleased, yet, still possessed with the illusion of manners.

But in the end, the storm decided for her and she had to get everyone inside. The abbey sat on the highest point in the area. The last lightning storm that struck had burned down the watermill. Friar Tucker already blamed her for that incident, an experiment on electricity gone awry. He would be even more displeased if she allowed similar harm to befall the new Roxburghe laird or his men. Unfortunately, his lordship's rank forbade her from putting him on a pallet in the kitchen or in the stable with his horse where he deserved.

Rose sighed, knowing she would be giving up her much-coveted room to him tonight.

Chapter 2

Unable to sleep for more than a few hours, Rose had risen in the wee hours. At a small desk working in candlelight, she bent over an aged tome, meticulously studying each page.

Sister Nessa slumbered in the bed across the room, her hearty snores vigorously competing with the storm that blew with savage gusts. Thunder fiercely rumbled. Rain battered the rooftop and whipped against the tiny room's dormer window. Rose hated the thought of the storm awakening the nun. With news that Friar Tucker would not be returning for weeks, poor Sister Nessa had taken on the burden, like a mantlet of iron about her shoulders, of caring for everyone at the abbey. His absence weighed heavily on them both, and Lord Roxburghe's presence at the abbey put them all on edge. Rose more than anyone.

She disliked powerful men on principle, and she doubted a lame horse had brought Roxburghe to the abbey. He risked much coming here without his guard. Lord Hereford was not known for even-handed justice. And if the warden suspected Roxburgh of fomenting trouble among the Scots in an effort to rescue his brother, Hereford would have cause to arrest him. She had seen a man hanged once by the warden's order and she shivered instinctively at the thought.

Next to the book Rose studied sat an intricately carved wooden puzzle box she had moved within the amber glow of a half-burnt candle. With reverent care, she turned the artifact over in her palm and traced a blunt-nailed finger over the carvings and symbols she was attempting to decipher.

She had discovered the small ancient relic last month tucked in a larger wooden chest housed in the crypt with a hundred other mildew-encrusted crates. It seemed to be part of an Arthurian legend connected to Merlin and Excalibur. That much she had gleaned from the books Mrs. Simpson had given her. A glance at the eleventh-century author's depiction of Merlin holding the famed sword in one hand and a lightning bolt in the other told her the same markings depicted beneath the drawing were also carved on the box. Interlocking circles of light and darkness and two sideways triangles touching at the corners, marks found on the *Bjarkan* rune, together symbolizing phases of life and great change. But what did they mean?

Rose had spent weeks cataloging the abbey's artifacts. Friar Tucker had handed the directive down to her to keep her out of trouble after last month's unfortunate experiment involving lightning and the new watermill had gone awry. The good Friar did not believe in idle hands and though he did blame her for the loss of their watermill, he had not truly punished her as harshly as he could have.

The task he'd assigned her had been a godsend, not a chore, for the crypt held the most wondrous treasures. Relic-filled chests overflowed with rat-eaten tapestries and old dust-covered manuscripts written in languages older than Latin. Rarely venturing beyond Castleton's borders, Rose lived vicariously through books, seeing the world through words and pictures, always protected behind the abbey's stone walls.

She closed her eyes, tamping down the sudden surge of foreboding, her thoughts restless as they moved away from the puzzle of the sorcerer's box to the abbey's guest.

A lightning flash startled Rose. Heart racing, she looked over at the bed to reassure herself Sister Nessa still slept, before blowing out the candle.

Thunder drummed again, bringing her nervously to her feet. She shoved her arms into the sleeves of her worn woolen wrapper. Working a sash around her waist, she padded barefoot to the window and stared into the Stygian night. With the darkness and heavy rain, she saw nothing but rivulets sliding down the thick lead glass. Surely 'twas near dawn.

She retrieved her slippers from next to the clothes press and slipped them on. She checked the fire in the grate to make sure it would burn for a few hours longer. Then she gathered up the tome and dropped the puzzle box into a pocket she had sewn inside her wrapper. As she eased the door open, the hinges groaned. Sister Nessa's snores stopped abruptly and Rose's hand froze on the latch. She cautiously peered over her shoulder.

A few seconds later, she stepped into the hallway and flinched at the *snick* of the door latch. Sister Nessa could sleep through a storm, but the slightest squeak of a floorboard had been known to bring the woman out of bed wide awake.

At the stairway, Rose leaned over the banister and listened for noise from below. The last thing she wanted was run into the abbey's male guests. Hearing nothing, she flicked her thick braid over her shoulder and started down the stairs. A pair of lamps dimly lit the stairway and her long shadow wobbled like a specter against the wall.

Her soft-soled slippers made no noise as she descended three floors.

Just inside the arched doorway that opened into the main dining hall, she hesitated. Through the centuries, many of the abbey's medieval characteristics had been retained, down to the timber crack frame, waddle-and-daub walls, and gothic stained-glass windows that poured color into the main hall on a sunny day. Tonight lightning punctuated the darkness, casting unfamiliar shadows on the floors. A dying fire was all that remained in the hearth from last night.

Seeing no sleeping forms on the ground, she strode to the hearth, set down the book and lit a lamp to take downstairs. These early-morning hours belonged to her and she usually spent them in her special workroom in the crypt, one that she had made for herself, with wooden shelves to house her collection of books. Her sanctuary was where she kept all of her tomes and where she never worried that she would be disturbed. Only ghosts lived down there. Everyone but her claimed to have seen one.

She had just closed the metal lid when a rasp of cloth whispered from the shadows behind her. She was not alone.

She spun so quickly that her woolen robe swirled around her, then rippled softly against her legs. "Jack?" she whispered.

The boy disliked storms. She worried he might be huddling in some corner, but she could see nothing in the darkness. "Jack? Are you in here?"

Lightning briefly illuminated the room, revealing a bottle of whisky on the dining table to her right. And it was open. She lifted the lamp.

Lord Roxburghe leaned with his back against the wall not six feet from where she stood. His dark hair hung wet and unbound past his shoulders. The damp cloth of his fine white linen shirt defined the braided muscles of his arms and chest and opened in a "V" that showed a mat of dark hair. He'd been outside in the storm. What fool would go outside on a night like this?

She had to have walked directly past him when she'd entered the room. How could she have missed him? She had so skillfully avoided him all last night, even volunteered for scullery duty while the other older girls served him and his men their meals.

Her panic momentarily subsided with the cock of his brow. "Jack?" The question was asked with amusement. "Am I intruding on a lover's assignation?"

"Lover? Jack?" She laughed outright at his conclusion.

"A pet perhaps."

"What sort of pet would I have named Jack?"

"A bird? Rabbit? A cow?"

"Jack is a boy," she said, after a moment's silence, "though I do not understand why it is any of your concern who I should be meeting."

His contemplation of her remained steady. He was toying with her, she realized. But as another flash of lightning lit the room, she noted something in his expression that surprised her, a moment of vulnerability unlike the fierce image she had of him, and she wondered what had brought him out of a warm bed on such a wretched night as this.

Then he stepped toward her. She stepped backward and bumped into the chair. The movement drew his attention. His eyes paused on her face and made her suddenly conscious of how she must look dressed in her nightclothes, the hem of her robe several inches too short, showing off her thin ankles and slipper-clad feet. To her horror he laughed. Then he reached for the whisky bottle, and she felt foolish for her initial reaction.

"Do you oft venture about at night in a state of undress seeking out boys?" Light glinted from the tiny silver ring in his ear as he brought the bottle to his lips.

She should walk away, except that he stood between her and the door. She held the lamp away from her face to better see his. "Do you oft stand outside during thunderstorms?" she countered.

He lowered his voice as if they were sharing a secret. "I asked my question first."

She tasted the warm scent of whisky on his breath and resisted licking her lips. "Jack sometimes sleeps in here. I thought the noise I heard might be him. But I was not seeking him out. I am on my way to the crypt."

He leaned a hip against the back of the aged Tudor chair, one of sixteen around the table. "The crypt?" His eyes swept her. "Why am I not surprised? Any woman who braves books about Arthurian legends, metallurgy and electricity cannot be afraid of something as insignificant as moldering corpses. Please tell me you are not attempting to bring some poor soul back to life."

Rose barely stifled a laugh. "And if I were?"

He studied her. "Then I would wonder how one so innocent could look upon a long-dead corpse and not feel horror by the stench alone. Death is not a becoming sight." He took another sip from the bottle.

"I've seen death," she told him. "Not so long ago a battle took place near here between the English and the Scots, a battle later decided on the hallowed grounds of Culloden. The cemetery is a mile from here."

"Twelve years ago, you would surely have been a child," he said quietly as if children did not witness death.

She stole a glance at the half-empty bottle of whisky

in his hand. "I have been at this abbey since I was three. I have witnessed much in seventeen years. Nor do storms make me nervous. Yet, I would never go outside during one. Do you fear death? Or defy it, my lord?"

He peered at her with amusement. "You tell me."

Tilting her head to one side, she studied the parts of him not hidden in the shadows. For a moment, she was back on the street, watching him ride past, a sea of dust rising around her and her heart pounding against her ribs like a tabor. A suppressed wildness about him made a mockery of his refined manners. "You are down here because you cannot sleep," she said quietly. "Drinking but not drunk. On first glance, one would think you were afraid of lightning storms."

"And on second glance?"

She measured him for the space of one breath. Two. Three. His lack of a riposte gave her the answer she sought. Aye, the Black Dragon had a human side. One that she doubted few people ever saw. "I would conclude the opposite, but not for reasons you might think. Lightning is the most powerful force on earth. It intrigues, tempts, and taunts you. You cannot master it but it makes you feel something powerful. Only a man who cannot feel life seeks to find ways to destroy his own, if only to define his own existence."

One corner of his mouth crooked. For a pair of heartbeats he said nothing. Then, "Are you suggesting I am suicidal?"

She shrugged, for it was possible she had not read him correctly, though she doubted it. She possessed a gift for reading people's hearts and Ruark Kerr's was dark. This man had killed. Yet, he was troubled by death.

"I am suggesting you are a man unsure of his purpose. Or you are afraid of storms. Either way you are a fool to stand outside in one. This abbey sits on high ground."

"Aye . . . that it does." She almost jumped when he touched her cheek as if to brush away tendrils that had fallen from her braid. "You have not told me your name."

Certain that she was flushed, she lowered the lamp. For if she could see his face, then he could surely see hers. "Rose. My name is Rose."

His gaze touched the thick rope of her hair lying over her shoulder. "A rose that smells like lilacs. It must be your room I was given earlier this evening. The linens smell like you."

No one had ever told her she smelled like lilacs and it came as a shock to feel another nervous flutter in her stomach. "Yes, the room is mine."

Next to Sister Nessa, she had been at Hope Abbey the longest. Sister Nessa had not wanted the room nearest to the hall, but Rose had. It faced south and was the warmest in winter when the trees were barren of leaves. In the summer, shade cooled the room. But it was late springtime, the season Rose loved the most for the lilacs bloomed and she spent weeks making her soaps from the flowering vines outside her window.

He offered her whisky. "Would you care to join me, m'lady Rose?"

Common sense told her to go. "I don't drink."

"Anything?" His devilish eyes raked her. He was baiting her now. "I had not believed Tucker gave up his taste for spirits but I have seen nothing here."

Only Friar Tucker's closest friends knew that he no longer drank spirits. "You have known each other long?"

"Long enough to be aghast he has left his flock to the wolves."

She scoffed at his sarcasm. "The presence of one male at this abbey would hardly keep wolves at bay, my lord.

We live in the borderlands. Friar Tucker has not abandoned us. He will be back the end of the month. His uncle passed away. He has gone to Redesdale."

Roxburghe's expression altered minutely. "Redesdale? Near Kirkland Park? Lord Hereford's lands?"

"If you know Friar Tucker then you know he lived in the area long before Lord Hereford's return last year. You need not worry that he holds allegiance to Hereford. He does not."

Roxburghe seemed to study the bottle in his hand. "Did he know Countess Hereford and her daughter then?"

His tone as much as the query gave Rose more than pause. She now understood Roxburghe's reasons for coming to the abbey.

He was following rumors that Lord Hereford's wife and child might be alive. Believing that the daughter might hold some value, he was looking for a way to rescue the half brother Hereford had incarcerated. If Roxburghe and Friar Tucker were friends, then his lordship had come here for help. Rose also knew Friar Tucker would not help him.

She didn't want the earl of Roxburghe's problems to be her concern. Not now. Looking down at the lamp sputtering against the draft, she cast about for a way to change the topic but could find nothing to ease the tension in her heart. "I am sorry Lord Hereford has your brother. You must know 'twould not be in the warden's political interest to harm the boy. I cannot believe he would."

Roxburghe set down the bottle. "You are familiar with Hereford enough to make that manner of observation?"

"I know that he came home a hero, too. He was once a captain in the Royal Navy. He has medals for valor. I know that your brother was caught cattle lifting along with two of his cousins. I know that no one is without blame." She awaited some hint of Roxburghe's reaction. When she saw nothing, she added, "I also know a dead hostage is useless to everyone, and that most people in your position would just surrender to the ransom demands. But then I imagine you are not most people."

He lifted her thick braid and wrapped it around his fist, ever so gently. "What else do you know about me?"

Rose knew he was dangerous. She'd once heard he'd left Scotland because of a woman when she married another, and that gossip linked him to beautiful women across Britain, France and Italy. He'd left a trail of broken hearts and shattered marital aspirations that kept most noblemen with unmarried daughters and sisters far away from him.

Divided between wariness and curiosity, she slid her braid from his hand and tilted her chin. It was a rare man who forced her to tilt her chin. "I know you are a hunter at heart and you are no longer attempting to disguise your intentions toward me behind casual conversation. But I am not your prey."

"I am not hunting tonight," he said in a low voice. "If I were, you would already be mine."

She held back a gasp, yet she made no effort to escape him. "You . . . you overreach yourself, my lord."

He made no effort to move either. The ever-present smile on his lips remained, but something had changed between them. Something as imperceptible as a hawk's path through a current of air, yet, there all the same between them. "How so?" he asked. He reached in slow motion to ease the braid from her shoulder, and his featherlike touch suddenly filled her with inexplicable emotion. "Does a virgin stand before me, Rose?"

The man was outrageous. No one had ever asked her anything so utterly private and intimate, or so erotic her entire body reacted.

No proper lady would have stood for such impropriety. But then no one had ever accused her of being proper, and she was no coward to retreat on the first salvo. She was, after all, self-reliant, driven as much by curiosity as she was by her passions. "I am not ignorant of such things. I have read many a conspectus of the medical sciences, my lord. This is farming land with horses and cows and pigs. I know the names of body parts no one speaks of in polite company."

Amusement shone in his eyes as he pointed out, "That was not my question."

"You will receive no other answer." She met his gaze and knew he was gauging her. "You are quite at your leisure to conclude what you will. But I assure you, I am no lady." She had not meant the statement as it sounded. "What I mean is that ladies are frail creatures . . ."

He laughed a clear baritone sound that startled her with its temerity. He was a rogue, and to the devil with you if you didn't like it.

She understood now what attracted her to him, something even more compelling than his looks. She could admire a man who thumbed his nose at conventional mores, who defied authority with the courage of his convictions. His gaze fastened on her mouth and, from the lazy-lidded heat in his eyes, he must have recognized the same passions deep inside her as lived inside him. And just that fast in the cold, dark cavernous dining hall with the world asleep around them, they were two people quite different from what the world saw.

"You are not coy or pretentious. A commoner . . . maybe.

But not at all common. What family would give someone like you to a convent?"

"My mother died when I was young. I . . . I barely remember my father."

"I remember mine. I have forgotten what it is like to be so innocent."

The trod of boots coming from down the corridor suddenly inserted itself into the heated silence. The mood shattered. Panicked that someone would see her alone in the night with a man—this man—in her sleeping clothes, she stepped around the chair just as Roxburghe moved to intercept her. She landed against his chest. His hands went to her waist to steady her.

"What are you doing?" she breathed out in a rush. "Someone will see us."

But someone had already seen them.

A man stood in the archway backlit by lamplight. Only then, did she realize Roxburghe's body shielded her face from the visitor's sight. If she had gone running from the room a moment ago, she would have collided with the hapless fellow. She hid her face near his chest, feeling absurdly safe in his shadow.

"The storm is passing." The man's voice carried to the shadows where she stood. "Dawn is on the horizon."

"I'll be outside in a moment," he said, the warm breath from his words rippling her hair.

The man hesitated. "Aye, captain. We will be awaiting your orders."

Rose listened to his steps fade like the storm that had surrounded the abbey most of the night. But the silence brought another storm to bear on her, one far more perilous. She slowly raised her chin and found Roxburghe's eyes on her face with unmistakable attention, a look he instantly shuttered as he eased his hands from her waist. The heat where his palms had shaped to the slim curvature of her waist lingered as she watched him walk to the end of the table and drag a jacket from the back of the chair.

She set the lamp on the table. "You are leaving the abbey before daybreak?"

He shoved his arms into the sleeves and turned, his eyes going over her. The stubble shadowing his jaw seemed to darken his gaze. "It is best if no one knows we were here. I will return for my horse when it is safe to do so."

"You would risk your life coming back here for your horse?"

"If not a horse then what is worth dying for?"

Rose frowned. "That reeks of cynicism. Have you no care for your life?"

He laughed. "My life is of utmost importance to me. So is my horse."

He clasped on a wide leather belt as he watched her with a predatory readiness in his movements and smiled lightly as if she were a curiosity encased behind glass. It was an action borne of a man comfortable in his own skin no matter his faults or his sins. Or hers.

And for some reason his self-possession unsettled her more.

"His name is Loki," Roxburghe said.

The meaning was not lost on Rose. Loki was the Norse God of destruction, an ironic name for the gentle horse she had briefly glimpsed last night, but not incongruous when one considered the stallion belonged to the Black Dragon.

"It is not safe to cross the bridge while the river is high," she said, walking around the table to face him at the other end. "There is another rarely used crossing two miles west.

The bridge is older but on higher ground. Only the locals use it. You should be able to cross unseen."

He picked up two pistols and shoved them into his leather belt. He truly did look like a freebooter as he approached her from around the table's head, his boot spurs jangling. "I am relieved," he said.

Rose had always thought herself to be sensible and levelheaded, but this man had worn on her nerves. "For what?"

"You do not wish me to drown."

"Do not be so confident of that. This is former reiver country. Lord Hereford's men are not the only ones you should fear." She straightened before she started retreating from his enormous presence. "I have no desire for anyone to learn you were here either. I would not wish them to steal your horse."

Though it would be less costly to the abbey if someone should, she thought.

"Nor would I wish you to carelessly lose him." Roxburghe reached around her and dropped a bag weighted with coins onto the table. "Tell Friar Tucker this gold is for the abbey's trouble."

Rose was speechless.

"And you, m'lady." He tipped her chin with his cupped hand and traced her bottom lip with his thumb. "Stay away from men in dark corridors and dining halls. Unless you want someone to show you the not-so-proper way to eat on this table."

Indignation surged through her, instantly dissipating any feelings of gratitude she had momentarily felt for his generosity. But before she realized she had no idea what he had just said, except to imply by his tone it must be carnal and therefore not fit for a lady, he grinned and strode from the room, his spurs jingling against the stone floor. The sound followed him into the courtyard and left her prey to unproductive emotions, not the least of which was awareness of him as a man.

She traced a fingertip where his had caressed her sensitive bottom lip, and, even as she wondered how many women he had kissed to know just where to imprint his touch, she wondered more what it would have been like if he had put his mouth on hers instead.

You are a naive girl, Rose Lancaster.

A man like him would not have stopped with a kiss.

An hour later, Rose gave up working in the crypt and put away her books. She went upstairs to her room and changed into a woolen gown. After she dressed, she drew back the faded velvet curtains to let in the dreary, mist-soaked light of dawn and turned.

Her old box bed sat against the wall, the covers thrown over the mattress as if an effort had been made to leave the room as it had been found. The room was no bigger than a large closet but Rose loved the coziness, especially in winter. She had repaired cracks in the wall and along the window frame with plaster and painted the walls the color of sunshine. Though the color came out more like a toasted orange or an over-ripened pumpkin, Friar Tucker had smiled and told her he'd never seen such a unique shade. So she had kept the color.

Unique sounded nice, not ordinary . . . or common. Lord Roxburghe had told her she wasn't common.

Like her unique height and the color of her russet hair, once compared to the copper of a fresh-minted coin. At one time, she would have plucked every red strand from her head if someone could have assured her that her hair would come back blond. She had grown into her body and had come to accept her uniqueness as one accepted an incurable ailment, with as much dignity as she could muster. But this morning, her uniqueness made her feel pretty.

She walked outside into the mist-shrouded courtyard still wet with rain and humidity. A brief lull in the clouds opened a patch of pearl-gray sky to her gaze, but the sky would not remain clear for long. She stepped through the gate.

Jack was already in the stable, diligently bent over a rake, mucking the stalls. With Friar Tucker gone, he had only the abbey's two horses and now the stallion to tend.

A fine regal horse Loki was, too, of stellar bloodstock, with long legs, a full chest and glossy red coat. She leaned against the stall and made a visual inspection of the horse. He favored his right foreleg. She would make a special liniment with herbs grown from the abbey's own hothouse.

The stallion bumped her arm, seeking a pet, and she moved nearer. To assess a horse's personality one must look it in the eyes. Character and temperament were easy to read. Piggy little eyes were sure signs of an untrustworthy beast. Bold but kindly eyes, well proportioned, indicated a good temperament. "No fire-breathing beast are you, Sir Loki," she said, raking her fingers gently through the horse's mane. "You are a handsome devil," she said. "Like your master."

Chapter 3

The storm that had come with the unusual heat of summer rampaged for another day before easing into the steadier, slower rain that filled the rivers and streams and made all the roads around Castleton nearly impassable. As Rose guided the old mare and cart over the neatly manicured drive toward the back of Mrs. Simpson's cottage, she peered up at the welcome break in the sky.

It had taken her over two hours to travel a mere four miles. Even wearing heavy boots, she could have walked the way faster. Once she reached the trough, she jumped out of the cart, careful to avoid the mud as Jack set the brake. Though her breeches and natty tweed jacket had not escaped mud splatter, her boots were not proof against mud, and her stockings were already as soggy as milk-soaked bread.

"Do ye want me to gather the eggs, Miss Rose?"

Rose smiled. "Thank you, Jack. And if you tend to the stalls in the barn as well, I am sure Mrs. Simpson will thank you with your favorite pastries."

She removed the knapsack filled with stores from behind the bench and turned toward the cottage. Today was almost cold in the shade, but the sun felt wondrous. She knocked on the door and, without waiting, entered the cottage.

"Mrs. Simpson?" Rose peered around the cluttered room filled with artifacts and shelves of dusty books that had once belonged to the woman's husband. Sunlight spilled into the room from the windows revealing dust moats dancing in the air. A breeze puffed the yellow curtains and brought with it the scent of mint from the flower box outside the window. A small but comforting fire burned in the stove.

Rose removed her hat and shook out her hair. A black leather tome about sorcery sat upon a table in the kitchen. Her heart gave a thump as she set the knapsack on a chair and picked up the book.

With the exception of maybe Mrs. Graham, most in the village considered Mrs. Simpson a witch. Rose loved that mystique about her.

She had been a skinny six-year-old with tangled hair and skinned knees the first time she'd met Mrs. Simpson. Dressed all in black, the widow had arrived at the abbey in a coach, her husband being a baronet. Friar Tucker had paraded all the girls outside to meet the abbey's new patroness. Mrs. Simpson had taken one look at Rose and clucked her tongue. It wasn't that Rose set out to be a hoyden. It just happened. On that particular day, Rose had been trying to glimpse the new-hatched tits and had fallen from a tree. But Mrs. Simpson had seen something in Rose, an inherent curiosity about the world.

Over the years, the coach had gone the way of the fine clothes as Mrs. Simpson's circumstances changed. But she never ceased sharing the wealth of her books and journals her husband had accumulated through his world travels. She'd taught Rose about herbs and medicinal potions, knowledge that Rose used to make the special liniment now healing Lord Roxburghe's beautiful stallion.

Last month when Rose had discovered her treasure in the abbey's crypts, she'd gone at once to Mrs. Simpson. The discovery was their secret.

"You give an old woman heart palpitations, Rose," Mrs. Simpson said from the doorway leading into her cellar. She wiped her hands on her apron. "With the roads as bad as they are, I didn't know if I should expect you."

Rose looked up from the tome. "You have found another book on Merlin?"

"I've done more than that. You were right. The box contains a wishing ring."

"You have translated the rest of the symbols!"

Mrs. Simpson removed her dingy apron and set it on the stone countertop next to a bucket of soapy dishes. "You might not want to know what I have discovered, dear. Especially since we are studying something unfamiliar and possibly dangerous, in our ignorance."

"Then you believe whatever is inside the puzzle box could be authentic? What have you discovered?"

"Did you bring it?"

Rose dug into the pocket of her woolen jacket and withdrew the small, intricately carved wooden box. Sunlight streaming through the windows in the kitchen warmed the wood and tingled her hands.

"Put it in the sunlight and sit."

Rose set the box on the table, then took her place beside Mrs. Simpson in one of the spindle-back chairs and waited. For what? She didn't know, but Mrs. Simpson watched the box, and so did she.

"Arthurian legend claims Merlin was a metallurgist," Mrs. Simpson said. "The source of King Arthur's power came from his sword Excalibur. Of course, most people consider the entire legend of Camelot and Arthur a myth. But Merlin did exist. And if Merlin somehow forged Excalibur, then it stands to reason the sword was not his only creation."

"How did the box come to the abbey?"

"Merlin hailed from Scotland, which means he could have once visited Hope Abbey. Heaven only knows how many times the abbey keep has been rebuilt over the centuries. The vault itself is centuries old. From your own words most of what is down in the crypt has never been catalogued."

As the widow spoke, the various symbols carved into the box began to darken as if someone put a hot poker to the wood. Rose stared in awe at the transformation. The image of the sun on one side became darker and the full moon on the other lighter. Opposite from what Rose would have expected as the sun usually meant light and the moon darkness.

"The sun and moon represent the continuing cycle of the seasons," Mrs. Simpson said. "Each side opposite the other yet coexisting, like day and night."

"With no beginning and no end. The symbols for infinite or eternity."

"And symbols for happiness and sadness, pleasure and pain, love and hate." Mrs. Simpson cocked a brow. "A warning to the one who opens the box?"

Rose withdrew her hands to her lap, confused by Mrs. Simpson's sudden caution. "Or perhaps the clues are telling us that it takes both sunlight and moonlight to unlock the secrets of the box," she suggested.

"Aye, that as well. From what I can interpret from these other etchings"—her finger traced the *Bjarkan* symbol, the two sideways triangles touching at the corners, symbolizing phases of life and great change—"the ring has power to pull darkness from a man's soul and give it light. But once the ring is on your finger, nothing in your life will ever be the same again. Once the ring is on your finger, it will not come off until your wish is fulfilled."

"Why would Merlin make such a ring?"

"His grandson wanted a child by a wife who had been barren for seven years. Merlin made the ring for him. Unfortunately, the woman died in childbirth."

Rose leaned over to look at the page. "Is that what this says?"

Mrs. Simpson shut the book. "The truth is, we do not know what will happen once you open the box. What you think you want may not be what your heart wants, and nothing great is ever accomplished without sacrifice."

"I am not afraid."

"Perhaps that is your failing, dear. I have learned that it is wise to proceed with one's eyes wide open, especially if you are about to walk into darkness."

"I can take care of myself in the dark."

Mrs. Simpson's tin-gray gaze gentled. "Is it family for which your heart searches, Rose? Or something else? Are you not beloved and needed everywhere you go? Are you so eager to leave us?"

Rising to her feet, Rose folded her arms and walked to the window to look outside. 'Twas not family for whom she searched. How could she explain her heart when she did not understand the thing herself?

She closed her eyes. "I have only a vague memory of my mother. Her softness. The way she smelled—like lilacs. I can almost see her face when I look at my own in the glass. Perhaps I am merely searching for myself."

She laughed at the maudlin sentimentality. "All I know is that ever since I found the puzzle box, the need to be free of the walls surrounding my life has grown into something . . . something almost violent inside me which

I am unable to control. You have lived your life unafraid of who you are. I want . . ."

What? To rid herself of the darkness in her heart? To be loved for herself? Despite herself? To seek retribution against the man ultimately responsible for her mother's death and forcing Rose into hiding for seventeen years? Justice?

The mere thought smoldered inside her like a hot ember burning away at the edges of her soul.

She had never told Mrs. Simpson who she was. Never spoken her father's name aloud. Her very safety had always depended upon secrecy. Friar Tucker had hammered vigilance into her mind from a very young age, so she had lived in silence, never seeking answers to her questions for as long as she could remember, until her father's return to England a year ago.

Most people knew him as the son of an aristocratic family who had made their names as captains and admirals serving in His Majesty's Navy. He had sought the appointment as the king's warden upon his return. The English respected him, while the Scots had great cause to fear and hate him. He showed no mercy to suspected rebels and no tolerance to suspected thieves and lawbreakers. He'd hanged a hundred men in the past year.

Only last month she had asked Friar Tucker why her mother had wed him, why she had been running from him, but the priest had no answer. Rose had wanted to believe that her father could not be so evil. That he could have once loved her mother. That the blood running through her veins was not his.

Rose touched the sorcerer's puzzle box, disturbed by the undeniable shame and need that welled within her. Shame because of who she was. *Need* to be someone who was more than nameless and forgotten by the one to whom she should have held importance.

Once she had dreamed of being an explorer of worlds as her father had been. Now she dreamed only of being free.

By summer's end, she would reach one and twenty. Sister Nessa had once told her that it was not a woman's prerogative to choose her own destiny, but Rose would do exactly that. She refused to be like the other girls at the abbey, confined by the social boundaries of their birth, accepting that their parents had chosen to give them to the church. She accepted nothing.

A part of her felt foolish for believing in such nonsensical rubbish as magic wishing rings. After all, she was an educated woman of twenty. She'd never believed in hobgoblins, fairies, witches or gremlins.

Yet she believed in the legend of Merlin, and if his power had helped guide and protect Arthur, and made him invincible to his enemies, then the ring would be her own Excalibur. Three months and she would change her life forever, break free and make of herself what she would be.

Jack burst through the door at that moment with a basket of eggs, chattering how he had fixed a hole in the coop to keep out the foxes. Mrs. Simpson took him into her kitchen, divided the bounty as she always did to give half to the abbey. Jack devoured a plate of pastries sloshed with strawberries and cream. Rose listened as he recounted his activities of the past week, which included tales of Lord Roxburghe's *secret* visit.

Rose wondered what part of *secret* the boy did not understand. "He came to see Friar Tucker," Rose said when Mrs. Simpson lifted her gaze.

"But Friar Tucker is gone. Vanished!" Jack anxiously

said. "Probably murdered by highwaymen. Or *arrested* and thrown into the gaol for smuggling. Sister Nessa thinks we'll never see him again."

"We need to go," Rose finally said as Jack finished a third glass of milk. "We have more rounds to make on our way back to the abbey."

After Jack hurried outside to tend to the cart and pony, Rose said, "Sister Nessa worries. Friar Tucker has never been away from the abbey for so long. His departure was sudden."

Mrs. Simpson smiled. "He is alive and well in Carlisle. Perhaps 'tis this hostage business that has taken him there. Lord Roxburghe's brother is rumored to be there."

"How do you know this?"

"The mountebank passed through here yesterday. He always stops here to let me look over any tomes he might have picked up."

"You gossip with the mountebank? He is a miscreant."

"But a well-traveled one, dear. He speaks to everyone. 'Twould not be unusual for Friar Tucker to seek some form of mediation between Roxburghe and Hereford, though little good 'twill do." Mrs. Simpson stood with a swish of soft muslin. "So you met the new earl of Roxburghe and you were not going to tell me? Most are curious what kind of man he has turned out to be."

"He is a freebooter," she managed as indifferently as possible, as she walked to the chair to retrieve her hat. "Quite at ease with his sins."

"Most powerful men are, dear. And I assure you, he is not a whimsy to feed a young girl's imagination. His sin goes deeper than most. He once tried to kill his own father."

Rose paused in the middle of stuffing her hair beneath her cocked hat.

"Thirteen years ago, my husband and I were working a site near Chesters, which is very near Roxburghe lands," Mrs. Simpson said. "I became friends with the housekeeper at Stonehaven and heard rumors. All hush-hush. But after the incident, the young lord was gone."

"Why are you telling me this?"

Mrs. Simpson wrapped her leathery hands around Rose's. "Be careful what you bring into your heart, Rose. Hate is a darkness that once acted upon blights the soul. Men such as Roxburghe can turn a young woman's head but beware the demon seed. He is the devil inside like his father before him."

Ruark sat in the noisy dining hall, the early evening sunset slanting through the arched windows at his back. The food had ceased coming an hour ago, though most of the men present had not noticed, the noise of their voices rising and falling as they fiercely argued. No women were present, having been removed when Angus Murdoch returned carrying Hereford's reply to the latest letter of negotiation, a lock of blood-caked hair and a refusal to negotiate. He had arrived that afternoon with Ruark's uncle, Duncan, bringing back Hereford's demands and the grisly momento carried in a box, the current cause for the war cries.

Angus's gaze went to Duncan, who stood with his shoulder braced against the window staring outside. Silence filled the old great hall. Duncan was a russet-haired giant among traditionally tall Kerr men. He had not spoken since his return.

"Hereford left Carlisle five days ago," Duncan said. "He is taking Jamie and Rufus and Gavin to Alnwick Castle."

Alnwick was in Northumberland. Although the castle

had fallen into disrepair since the days that Malcolm III of Scotland was killed there, in all Border warfare Alnwick was still one of the strongest fortresses on the English side. Rufus and Gavin Kerr were the two cousins captured with Jamie.

"The next gift we receive will no' be so benign," Duncan said.

A clansman down the long table slammed his fist down. "And I say Hereford's actions can no' remain unchecked." The speaker was Angus, a bear of a man in his fifties with a scar across his cheek that bespoke of his own years in the earl of Roxburghe's services. "Strike while he thinks we are indecisive."

"Aye!" another shouted. "Enough is enough, I say."

"We can no' give him the ransom he wants," Angus said.

"Ninety thousand pounds Anglish sterling. No one has that kind of wealth," another shouted. "And what of Rufus and Gavin? Will Hereford remove one of their ears to go with that bloody lock of hair?"

Duncan folded his arms. "We can prepare another response and spend yet another month awaiting his and this can go on for a year. I say fight."

Hearty exclamations rose. All eyes turned to Ruark.

Ruark had been listening in quiet fury to the back-and-forth talk, his legs stretched out in front of him, an empty plate to the side of his elbow.

These were his father's allies and friends. Most of them family. Now they looked to him. Not everyone trusted him. His fame might reside in tales of his exploits on the sea, but he had not yet proven himself as their chieftain. If it was a war Hereford sought, then they were all nearly down that road.

"Do you *not* think this is what Hereford wants us to

do?" he asked in the silence now confronting him. "A war, so he will have an excuse to make outlaws of us all? Send dragoons down on your families? Do you not think he will welcome the fight?"

Duncan faced him. "And maybe you've forgotten a Kerr is no coward to run from a fight that began when Hereford killed your father."

"I have forgotten nothing."

Ruark held no illusions about his own character. But his uncle was a fool to think Ruark was anything like the younger man who had left Scotland years ago, or that his loyalties were anywhere but with Stonehaven. Nor was he a novice when it came to sailing into a broadside. Many an opponent had met his fate after lobbing the first salvo from a flawed position of power.

"Hereford's first mistake is in thinking we are weak and without recourse," Ruark said. "Do not let yourselves make the same mistake."

The collective agreement came in mumbled ayes.

"The question is how we retrieve Jamie without more bloodshed. His or ours. I will not allow our actions this day to kill him."

"Aye, but what choice has Hereford given us but to fight?" Angus asked.

"He has given us no choice," Duncan said.

As if on cue, Colum arrived in the arched doorway. For the past few weeks, while negotiations had been going back and forth over the border in a useless time-consuming parley, Ruark had not been idle.

Colum gave Ruark a nod.

"But we are not helpless," he told his men

Two men appeared with an elderly woman between them. It had been Rose who had inadvertently given him the break he had needed the night he had stayed at the abbey, when she had told him that Tucker was in Redesdale to bury an uncle. An uncle Ruark knew Tucker did not have. Ruark had sent a man there the very morning he'd left the abbey. An hour ago, Colum informed Ruark that his man had arrived with Countess Hereford's former handmaiden. They had found her in Carlisle after the disgruntled widow of the recently deceased captain of the guard at Kirkland Park came across an old letter in her husband's effects. After the exchange of a great deal of silver, the woman handed over the letter.

Wearing brown homespun that hung from her small frame and a faded purple-and-green plain wrap, Lady Hereford's former maid looked terrified as she was brought to stand in front of the table, her eyes darting over the unfriendly bearded faces. She clutched the wrap tighter around her shoulders as if the cloth were an iron shield. Something about her seemed familiar . . .

"You are Anaya Fortier, former serving maid to Lady Elena Kirkland Lancaster, Countess Hereford?" Ruark asked over the murmurs of his men.

She hesitated. "What do you want? I have told your man, I know nothing . . . And I am not worth anything to anyone. My husband died years ago—"

"You are from Redesdale, Mrs. Fortier?"

Her knuckles tightened on the plaid wrap. She nodded.

"Are you acquainted with Friar Tucker? He is from Redesdale."

"His father was a vicar living at Kirkland Park for twenty years."

"Then he has family there? An uncle perhaps?"

"Nay, he does not."

"A man recently passed away in Redesdale, a former captain of the guard at Kirkland Park, I believe," he said.

"He served Lady Elena's father. It seems the widow of that man has come across an old letter . . ."

Her expression was one of horror.

"Would you care to read the letter my men were given by the disgruntled wife of that recently deceased guard?"

The woman's next breath brought tears to her eyes. "I do not doubt that woman would trade her soul to the devil for a handful of silver."

"But you will not."

Ruark stood. His own anger, normally subdued, but now barely contained as he leaned his palms against the table and bent toward her. "Then you know something of what happened to Lady Elena's daughter. Is she alive?"

"Nay, I do not know. Her ship perished during a storm seventeen—"

"I have heard the stories. Even those that claim Hereford is keeping his daughter locked away some place on the continent. Is any of it true?"

She began to twist her hands. "Friar Tucker . . . he would know. Please . . . I do not know anything. He swore me to secrecy. I gave my word . . ."

Ruark froze. "Why would he need to do such a thing?"

"Please . . . I know nothing."

Ruark had not come here to frighten old women. But neither would he grant her quarter. He needed answers. "Why would he swear you to secrecy? Tell me, Mrs. Fortier. Far more than your life rests on your next words."

"Oh, please . . ." The woman dropped to her knees. "I was supposed to go with my mistress the night she boarded the ship, but there was a storm. After the departure was delayed, she was terrified that Lord Hereford would find her. She gave little Roselyn into my safekeeping and told me to take the child to Friar Tucker. Her ladyship and

Friar Tucker grew up together. They were always close and she trusted him with her daughter's life until she could return."

For a moment, Ruark did not think he heard correctly. "*What* did you say was the daughter's name?"

"Roselyn, my lord. Lady Roselyn Elena Lancaster. She was three years old the last time I saw her. I swear I don't know if she is still alive."

Roselyn. Rose. . .

I have been at this abbey since I was three. I have witnessed much in seventeen years.

"The plaid you are wearing, Mrs. Fortier. Where is it from?"

Ruark now knew what was so familiar about her. He had seen that plaid or one like it in the abbey's stable, wrapped around tomes about Arthurian legends, metallurgy and electricity—

"It belonged to my lady," Mrs. Fortier said in near hysterics as Ruark walked around the table. She dropped her gaze to the floor. "Please . . ."

He knelt beside her. "Why was the countess running away?"

Again, the woman shook her head. "She and Lord Hereford argued something terribly. 'Twas over the child's inheritance. Lord Hereford thought that by marrying Lady Elena everything would be his upon the grandfather's death. Kirkland Park belongs to my lady's family, my lord. Not Lord Hereford. He was furious when he learned that Lady Elena's grandfather put everything in something called a trust to keep it out of Hereford's hands. The estate will come to the daughter when she reaches the age of majority. If she should die . . . if something were to happen to the child, then the trust . . . everything goes to the church."

"Then if the daughter is dead, Hereford would have no

claim on Kirkland Park. If he believes his daughter dead . . . why is he still at Kirkland Park?"

"I don't know. I don't know. I swear I know nothing more."

"Should we believe her?" Angus asked. No one could be sure that Hereford would exchange Jamie, much less for a daughter most thought dead.

"Bluidy damned Sassenach," someone murmured. "Tucker is as English as Hereford. If the girl is alive, all he has to do is claim she was a foundling left on his doorstep. Who would believe us?"

"Where is Tucker now?" Ruark asked Mrs. Fortier.

"I saw him five days ago. He came to my cottage to tell me that 'twas no longer safe to remain in England. That he had arranged for me to leave . . ."

"Then he must know about the letter," Angus said.

"Do you have anywhere to go, Mrs. Fortier?" Ruark asked.

She shook her head. He looked at the man standing behind the woman. "See that Mary gives her a place to stay here at Stonehaven if she chooses to stay. I do not know how safe it is for her to return to Carlisle."

After the woman was taken from the room, no one spoke. Reality momentarily subdued the initial excitement of those sitting around the table.

Duncan sat on a bench with his elbows on his knees and his head down, and spoke first. "I say, if Tucker does no' cooperate, then his fate should be the same as Hereford's."

"Tucker is no coward," Ruark said. "I have no want to murder a priest when he decides not to cooperate. I will take six men. No more. Give me a week to return with the girl."

"A week," Duncan said. "If you do no' return?"

"*Then* you ride."

"Miss Rose?"

Startling at the small sound of Jack's voice, Rose straightened and stretched to loosen the muscles at her back. She turned her head to see him leaning against the paddock fence looking over the rail at her. Loki stirred beneath her hand. She had been checking for heat and swelling.

The torchlight on the wall of the stable cast Jack's face in an otherworldly orange glow. He could have passed for one of the ghosts that allegedly haunted the crypts. She warmed at the sight of him. "Whatever are you doing awake so late?"

He shrugged, unusually quiet. She had not seen him at supper.

She stood and brushed the dirt off her hands. "What is it?"

He picked up the sorcerer's box she had set on the workbench while waiting for the moon to make an appearance. For five days she had been awaiting the skies to clear. "Is this the magic puzzle box, Miss Rose?"

She latched the stall and approached. "Aye."

And something pulled inside her. Something that pulled constantly at her thoughts waking her up in the night. So powerful that even now, she could feel the low hum in her veins. "This box is part of an Arthurian legend connected in some way to Excalibur. Have you ever heard of Merlin?"

Jack shook his head.

"He was a sorcerer." Edging her thumb along a row of symbols, she held the box out to Jack. "Do you see these markings? The ring inside this box grants its wearer a wish. I intend to find the secret that opens this box. If the moon would ever make an appearance."

"Then what will ye do, Miss Rose?"

She brushed a lock of his stringy blond hair behind one ear. "Then I will close my eyes and make my wish."

"Do ye want to be a king like Arthur?"

She laughed. "Maybe."

"Don't ye want to be rich?"

Who did not wish to be rich? "Sometimes the greatest wealth is not found in your purse, Jack," she said quietly. "I want the freedom to make my own choices. You understand that, don't you?"

"Ye can marry me, and I will give ye freedom to . . . to cook whatever you choose for dinner every night. And I would not complain if ye burned the bread."

Jack was indeed her knight protector. "If you were ten years older, I would marry you, Jack Lowell, and we would travel and see the world. Did you know there are distant lands with trees as large as mountains and skies like warm sapphires? Marco Polo discovered such worlds—"

"Lord Roxburghe has seen distant lands, too," Jack said.

Her dreamy thoughts collapsed like a house of sticks. "Yes, I imagine he has seen much."

The boy suddenly grew quiet. He traced a gauge in the workbench at his hip. "Will Lord Roxburghe be back to the abbey soon, Miss Rose?"

"Why?" She nudged him playfully when he looked dejected. "Have you had enough of mucking Loki's stall?"

Jack shrugged. "He gave me a coin, Miss Rose. In the stables the morning he left. He let me help saddle the horses and told me I was to watch his horse for him."

"You never told me you saw Lord Roxburghe."

Again, Jack shrugged. "He asked if you were a nun." He did? "Oh."

"But I told him the church would no' have you even if ye wanted to be like Sister Nessa."

"Jack!"

"But that's what you're always sayin', Miss Rose. Then Lord Roxburghe gave me a coin and said since ye were so wicked, I was to watch his horse and make sure ye don't sell him afore he returns."

"He said that?"

"Aye." Jack nodded vigorously. "But I told him ye'd never sell what wasn't yers 'less the person owed ye a debt. That you once threatened Geddes Graham with a sword because he stole a cart full of oats from the abbey."

She inwardly groaned. "What did Lord Roxburghe say?"

"He laughed and said it was just like a woman to stab a man in the heart for any reason. What does that mean?"

"It means your affection for him should not be measured by the weight of his gifts, Jack. Your allegiance is yours alone to give and should never be traded for a meager coin."

Jack lowered his chin, and Rose pursed her lips, chastising herself for being so insensitive. A coin was probably everything to a boy like Jack who had nothing—not even family. But the longer she looked at his face, the more he seemed to find interest in the deep gouges at his fingertips, and something else that bothered him. "A coin must seem like a lot," she said, realizing now why he'd ventured into the stable to find her. Something must have happened. "What did you do with all that wealth?"

He studied the scuffed toe of one shoe. "I gave it to the old mountebank what comes past Farmer Herring's every Tuesday. I wanted ye to have a bonnet, seein' as how ye don't have one. Then Rolf, he sees the coin and says I stole it."

Rose slid the lamp nearer to his face. "Look at me, Jack."

The boy refused. Rose tilted his chin toward her and forced his face into the light, shocked that she had not noted his swollen cheek. His eyes blurred with tears, not pity for himself but clearly shame that she should see the bruise. Fury on his behalf burned in her chest. "Someone struck you."

"He accused me of thievin' and we got in a tussle." As Jack spoke the words, his defiance faded. "He told me he'll be fetchin' the sheriff for givin' him a bluidy facer, and the magistrate will transport me away forever."

She looked at the pale-skinned boy whose hazel eyes seemed to fill half his face, and who had given away his single coin to buy a bonnet for her. "No one is transporting you anywhere. Come . . ." She tucked the puzzle box into her pocket. "You need a cooling rag for that bruise on your cheek."

"But what are ye goin' to do, Miss Rose?" He didn't like to see her upset and he clearly worried he was the cause of her anger. "The mountebank be on his way to Chesters. We've no horse what can catch him now."

Two days later, Rose set out of the abbey's gates on the back of Roxburghe's magnificent stallion. Indeed his lordship did know horseflesh. The horse had been restless to escape his paddock for days and, in the mood to oblige him, Rose had taken him out yesterday for a brief stint around the abbey. Today they would travel much farther.

She rode astride, wearing a pair of boy's breeches and a woolen overcoat belted at the waist. She yanked her cocked hat lower over her brow and lifted her face to the sky. Despite her fierce mood, she could not deny the afternoon was beautiful. As a child, she had ridden the empty fields surrounding the abbey at night. With only the moonlight at her back, she'd imagined herself a painted Celtic warrior. Even in the bright sunlight and heat of the day, she felt a vague recollection of the child she'd been. Never afraid. Never alone. Yet restless like this horse—in part due to an imagination that kept constant companion with her want for adventure.

Soon she slowed the stallion to test his gait and high-stepped him in a circle. Leaning over to rub him affectionately, she held tight to the reins and studied his leg to reassure herself that he had healed. She had already ridden six miles from the abbey over dale and hill, through the woods and around fields planted with rye. The high-strung stud pulled restively at his bit, fighting his restraint.

"Take it easy, boy," she said, catching the scent of campfire smoke. She straightened in the saddle and tented a hand over her eyes, locating the ribbon of gray smoke above the trees. "I see the smoke, too."

The corner of her mouth crooked. She had specifically waited two days, when she knew the mountebank would be returning this way on his route back to Chesters. He never ventured far from the border.

The road wound its way another mile around a shallow stream through a tunnel of trees. She followed the scent of cooking fish. The peddler's gayly painted wagon filled with an assortment of wares and pots and pans dangling from the roof sat at the edge of the woods. Two horses chomping on the high grass raised their heads and watched her dismount before deciding she was no threat and returning to eating. She untied the two horses, encouraging them with a *thwack* on the rump to run away.

She tied the stallion reins to the wheel of the wagon and walked into the clearing.

The peddler and another man sat playing a game of dice over coins piled on a rock between them. She recognized the second man sitting with the mountebank as Geddes Graham even before he turned his head.

The peddler jumped to his feet. "Miss Rose," the mountebank said, nervously wiping his greasy hands on his trousers.

He wore a checked waistcoat and greasy leather leggings, the same unwashed clothes she'd seen him wearing the last three times he'd come through Castleton, and for just a moment, she felt sorry for his circumstance, until she reminded herself that he'd cheated Jack of his coin.

"Mr. Rolf," she said.

But it was Geddes whom she watched as his eyes widened a fraction on the stallion. The mountebank might be an opportunist and a cheat, but Geddes was a snake. Unlike most men Rose towered over, Geddes Graham made up for his lack of height in bulk.

"Why, if it isn't our thorny Rose what come to visit us, Rolf," Geddes said, resting his hand above the knife he wore on his hip like a shiny rapier sheathed in gold. "What brings ye to see the mountebank?"

The mountebank stepped eagerly forward. "Ye want a nostrum or other medicines for an ailment, Miss Rose?"

"Jack Lowell gave you a coin for a bonnet he did not receive. I want the coin back."

Geddes snorted as he approached. "Jackie boy is a thievin' scoundrel, Rose. That coin was no' even his."

"You are wrong. He earned that coin. And I want it back. Now."

"Do ye hear that, Rolf? Our thorny Rose wants Jack's coin back."

The mountebank twisted his hands. "Now, ye can no' be grudging any man an honest living, Miss Rose. Even someone as pretty as you—"

Geddes laughed. "Miss Rose, pretty? She's as skinny as a fresh-hatched sardine, Rolf." His leer raked the natty jacket that fell just to the top of her scuffed boots. "A man wants a woman beneath him who is no' afraid of his touch. Look at her, Rolf. One day, she'll be a shriveled old crone like ol' Nessa wonderin' why a real man would never have her."

"I don't see a real man standing in front of me, Geddes. I see an overgrown boy playing at being a man."

Geddes's eyes narrowed. He remained near enough that she smelled his fish breath. "Maybe you stole the coin the same place you stole that stud, Rose. How else would that brat get his hands on a coin?"

He made a move toward the stallion but she stepped into his path, startling him.

Rose slid the knife from its sheath on Geddes's hip and, moving only her hand, inserted the blade between his legs, stopping him cold. "Careful, Geddes. I have never gelded a man. But if you move one inch nearer, I swear on my life, you do so at your own peril."

"Bluidy hell, Rose," he gasped.

"I mean what I say, Geddes." She spoke to the mountebank without turning her attention from Geddes. "Mr. Rolf? I want that coin. Set it on the rock next to me, then move away."

"*Now,* Rolf! Give her the boy's coin. Can't ye see she's got a bloomin' blade to me bollocks?"

The mountebank scurried to do as he'd been told. He put the coin on the rock then hurried to the clearing's edge and stopped. Still holding the knife, Rose backed a step and scraped the coin from the rock. Without taking her eyes from Geddes, she slipped it into a small pocket inside her coat.

Rose narrowed her eyes on Greta Graham's slovenly son as she backed toward the stallion. "The only reason you're still in one piece is because I have a fondness for your mam. For some reason she loves you and I would not be the cause of her broken heart."

"You ain't no saint, Rose," Geddes shouted as she stepped into the stirrups and reined the stallion around to face him. "One of these days you'll regret you weren't nicer to me."

She threw the knife end over end into the ground between his boots. "But not today, Geddes."

The horse sprang forward, clearing a fallen log and scattering the other horses. Behind her, the pair shouted obscenities but Geddes couldn't catch her. She reached flat ground and finally allowed the stallion his head. The distance between them extended until she could no longer hear them.

She had no thought of returning to the abbey yet. She came on the old Roman road and cut through a flock of sheep, sending them scurrying in all directions. A farmer holding a scythe shouted at her, but even then she but waved at him. "Good afternoon, Mr. Herring."

"Are ye daft, girl?" he shouted. "You'll break yer bluidy neck."

Even wearing breeches and a cap with her braided hair tucked beneath, people recognized her. Today, she didn't mind as she skirted the village another pair of miles and left the road, careful not to ride through the vegetable gardens. A warm breeze tugged at her clothes.

She felt as if she were riding Pegasus through the sky. Even while a part of her knew she should not have taken that horse, another part cherished the freedom.

And a sudden memory of her childhood surfaced an impression that had stayed with her despite the years. It confused her for it was from a time before the abbey and the man in her memories was not the evil man her mother was running from but of one who had once set her upon a pony and told her that one day she would know how to ride like the wind.

As Rose galloped Lord Roxburghe's stallion through the high grass toward a crimson sunset, she no longer let herself worry if Mrs. Simpson was right about the wishing ring being dangerous. Tonight was a full moon.

By the time she returned to the abbey and reined in the stallion, her thick hair had unraveled from its plait, and streamed in windblown tangles to her waist.

Having given up on keeping the cocked hat on her head, she'd shoved it in her knapsack miles ago. The thought of spending hours combing out her hair did not make her regret ridding herself of the hat. Some decisions were like that, she realized—like borrowing the stallion for a day.

Yet, a sudden chill went down her spine. The horse tossed his head. She rubbed her hand along his neck. "What is it, boy?"

She looked toward the abbey. The late-afternoon sun shone on its stone walls like a beacon of light—or a warning. The main keep tower, slightly higher than the abbey itself, also seemed to glimmer in the dying sunlight. For a bare fraction of a second, she held the stallion's restless pacing in check.

Friar Tucker lived and worked in the rooms that overlooked the fields. The curtains were opened.

The abbey had guests!

Chapter 4

"**I** *refuse* to listen to a holy man lie to me."

Ruark turned to face the man standing in front of the window. The curtains were partly drawn, but the sun had set and shadows obscured most of the room. One candle burned on the desk. Tucker was a tall man but not big, yet he had always seemed larger to Ruark. He still wore his brown robes, dusty from his journey. A cap covered his short, clipped hair. Ruark had been at the abbey when Tucker returned. Ruark had arrived only to find Loki gone and Rose with him.

Impatience brought Ruark to the window to see what had grabbed Tucker's attention but he saw nothing.

"I can't help you, my lord."

Ruark stepped in his path, his cloak swirling around his calves with the agitated movement. He had not removed the sword or other weaponry upon entering the abbey. The message itself said he had not come as a friend. But it said more. He had come willing to fight for his prize. "Do you think I have been sitting on my arse enjoying my grand homecoming while my brother rots in one of Hereford's hellholes?" he demanded. "Probably to spend the rest of his life imprisoned if I cannot find a way to secure his release."

"I told you, I can't help you," Tucker persisted. "I have no idea what you are talking about!"

Ruark's thoughts crowded around him like brooding buzzards as he focused on Tucker. "I asked you if you knew Countess Hereford. She was from Redesdale. You are from Redesdale. As is the uncle you just buried from Redesdale. Except you have no uncle." He withdrew from his cloak a packet. "My man of affairs has been in Carlisle these past weeks mining for information on Hereford's past. It seems the widow of the man you went to Redesdale to bury is an ungrateful blatherskite with greasy palms and an intent to blackmail you. We found Lady Hereford's maid. She and the child never got on the ship to France."

"Move aside, Roxburghe. Or I will forget we were ever friends."

Ruark grabbed Tucker's wrist and forced the package into his hand. "Your father was a vicar living at Kirkland Park for twenty years. Lady Elena's father was his patron. You grew up with her. When she needed help she came to you."

"Nay." The word came out in a desperate rush.

"Is Rose Lady Roselyn Lancaster? *Is* she?"

"She is like my own bairn', my lord. You can no' have her!"

The revelation struck him like a punch in the gut. He had not known positively until this moment that the daughter lived, that the rumors might be true or that he could feel so betrayed by a man he had considered his friend.

Ruark could not think clearly. "Christ . . . Tucker. How could any man have kept such a secret for seventeen years? Does she know Hereford is her father?"

"Aye, she does." Tucker grabbed Ruark's sleeve. "Wait!"

Ruark had never laid his hands on a woman or child or a

man of cloth, but by God, he was tempted to do so now.

She knew! He'd talked to her less than a month ago in this very abbey.

She'd known about his brother, all along knowing 'twas her own sire that held him imprisoned, and he damned himself now for wasting precious time in finding her. He realized the rage he felt. Rage because of who she was or something else . . .

"You don't understand," Tucker whispered.

Ruark's voice lowered to a rasp. "What I understand is Rose Lancaster is alive. Hereford must know she is alive or he would not still be at Kirkland Park."

"Wed her and Kirkland Park will be yours."

Ruark laughed. Incredulous. "I would not join Kerr and Lancaster blood if we were the last two beings on this earth. She is valuable to me as a hostage."

Tucker grabbed his arm. "I have known you to be an honorable man—"

"Damn you." He shrugged off Tucker's grip. "Do not throw that word in my face. There is no bloody thing as honor when fighting a man who has none." *Christ*, he had learned that much from his own father.

Tucker stepped around Ruark to block him from reaching the door. "She is more valuable than you know. Hereford can't touch her inheritance. Everything is in trust. If something happened to Rose before her twenty-first year, Kirkland Park, her great-grandfather fixed it so that everything goes to the church, which is why Hereford never declared his daughter dead. But upon Rose's marriage, everything goes to her husband. That man can be you, Ruark.

"You've seen Rose. You've met her. She is beautiful and vibrant. She would make a fine wife to any man worthy enough to hold on to her."

Someone pounded on the door. Tucker nearly leapt away.

Colum called from the other side and Ruark opened the door. "The girl returned with your stallion a half hour ago," Colum said. "But no one can find her."

Ruark's eyes narrowed on Tucker as he spoke to Colum. "Is everyone else in the dining hall?" Ruark asked.

"Except for the boy, Jack."

Ruark looked past Tucker to the window where the friar had been standing. Tucker had not moved, but Ruark recognized the truth on his round face. He had sent the boy to wait for Rose's return and warn her. How much time had Ruark given her by remaining here with Tucker?

Ruark pulled on his gloves. "If you see Hereford before I do, give him my regards."

"Sweet Mary, I'm protecting my own."

"And I am trying to save mine."

Ruark removed the key from the door as Tucker grasped his forearm. "If you give her to Hereford, you commit an abomination against that girl. I am sorry I ever knew you."

Tucker was not the first to utter those words. Ruark doubted he would be the last. "I know."

He stepped into the corridor and turned the key in the lock. The door was English oak. The good friar would not be getting out of this room anytime soon.

Ruark turned on his heel. "Unless Lady Roselyn plans to swim across the river, she went into the woods. She is familiar with this area. We are not."

Colum kept pace with him. "I think I might know someone who is equally familiar and will help."

"And who might that be?"

"We met up with a rather talkative mountebank takin' a piss on the riverbank about fifteen minutes ago. He was drunk and rather affable in his desire to sell us his wares. He asked if we were bounty hunters. Seems Hereford put a rather sizable bounty on your head."

That Hereford would put a bounty on his head was not news to Ruark.

"He said if we wanted to know about the goings-on around Castleton, for a coin or two, he could tell us anything." Colum shrugged. "What is a coin or two for a good cause? So I told him we were indeed bounty hunters and paid him. He said he'd heard you'd been to the abbey some weeks ago but not the why of it until he saw a rather fine stallion today, which he himself reported seeing ridden by a flame-haired hoyden he knew to be a thief and a blackmailer. He was quite pleased to offer an extra coin if we might by chance do away with her as well."

"Why is that do you suppose?" Ruark asked with interest as he reached the stairs.

"Seems she threatened to cut the bollocks off one of his best customers. Apparently, this hoyden was under the impression the mountebank had stolen a coin from a young boy living at the abbey, and if he did not hand over his profits to her the other man would be flayed. That flame-haired hoyden wouldn't by chance be your heiress, would she?"

"Will Lord Roxburghe leave now that he has his horse?" Jack's question broke the silence.

Rose leaned with her hand against the thick trunk of a dying oak. Her other hand on Jack's shoulder kept the boy from walking into the field. Behind her, a mile of towering conifers stood as barrier between her and the abbey. "Aye, he will have no reason to stay. He has his horse."

She didn't know if the words rang hollow to her ears

because of the tension inside her or because they were true. Or for something else entirely.

The realization that she had run away from the abbey like a long-eared hare and left Friar Tucker to Roxburghe grated on her like a hot rake. When Jack had met her at the stable, he had told her only that Lord Roxburghe was at the abbey for his horse and Friar Tucker had also arrived. He'd given Jack a message for her: *Go. Now. I will find you at the cemetery.*

Why? Had he been so worried for her safety because she had ridden the stallion without permission? She doubted it.

She should go back.

All these thoughts tumbled through her mind as she took a step backward and leaned against the tree, her heart pounding like the steadily increasing thump of a Gypsy's tabor. Her gut told her something was terribly wrong.

Go, Roselyn. Her mother's long-ago words. *I will find you. I promise.*

She had not come back for Roselyn. She had died.

Jack dropped to the ground. "I'm hungry."

Attempting to quiet her inner turmoil, she sat and tweaked Jack's nose as if that would dissuade her from fear. "You need not worry about supper. Sister Nessa always saves you a plate."

The breeze stirred the grass, and turning her head, she listened to the distant, lonely bark of a fox. All that lay out here among the sod and the sheep was an abandoned cemetery, unmarked graves of fallen English who had died fighting Scots, men on both sides of the border who never made it home to their families. She saw no sign of another's presence, no shadow lurking in the moonlight, and breathing easier, she reached into her pocket and removed the coin she had put there. "Look what I found today," she said.

Excitement banished the worry from his eyes. "Where?"

"Near the crossroads. The mountebank must have dropped it."

Jack laughed and gave her a hug. "Thank you, Miss Rose."

He believed the lie, never thinking she could be dishonest with him. He trusted in all things, which was why that mountebank could take advantage of him. But his unerring faith in her made her question her own character, something she rarely did. A lie was still a lie even if spoken with the best of intention.

She had been living one her entire life.

At the thought, the breeze seemed to strengthen, stirring the treetops. Moonlight washed over her—like the wings of an angel. A strange current of electricity rippled through her body and caused her to pull the sorcerer's puzzle box from her jacket pocket. The wood seemed to absorb the pale light.

"What is it?" asked Jack, leaning over.

"I have no idea."

She walked down the hill to the rusted wrought-iron fence that safeguarded the hallowed grounds of the cemetery.

Holding the puzzle box, she peered up at the sky. The clouds were playing on the wind's invisible currents and the moon had suddenly come out of hiding.

Heart racing, Rose looked for clues on the box similar to what had been revealed when she had set the box in sunlight. The transcriptions on the box began to disappear until only the circle of the sun and the moon remained. The circle depicting the moon had darkened considerably.

As the moonlight grew in strength, heat pooled in her

palms, increasing in intensity. She pressed her thumbs against the sun and moon circlets.

Each side opposite the other yet coexisting. Both shall reveal the path.

"You've been staring at the box a long time," Jack suddenly said from beside her.

She startled. Having not heard his approach, his voice nearly frightened her to death.

"Are ye nervous?" he asked.

"I am more nervous nothing will happen."

"I don't want ye to leave us."

She smiled gently at the anxious boy. "Then perhaps I shall wish only for our happiness."

Maybe that was all a person had a right to ask for.

Rose pressed one thumb first against the sun circlet and then against the moon. "Light to darkness," she said.

To her shock, the pressure she exerted crushed the sides of the box as if it were made of parchment. The wood cracked and the lid sprang open.

She hadn't expected the box to open, much less pop its valuable contents into the air. She gave a low cry as she glimpsed a spot of silver appear in a band of moonlight and then vanish behind her in the grass. She whirled and dropped on all fours only to come to an abrupt stop.

As if she had magically conjured him from her earlier thoughts, Lord Roxburghe was kneeling before her in the mist-washed light, his dark cloak pooling on the ground around his muddy boots. He picked up the ring with his thumb and forefinger and met her gaze over the circlet.

"Yours, I presume?" His eyes went to the ruined antiquity she held crushed in one hand, then to Jack, then returned to settle on her face. "Or not yours?" He held the ring to a beam of moonlight where it seemed to beckon and glow. "It looks to be a man's fit." His eyes slid over her with amusement. "Rather like breeches and jerkins . . . and a certain red stallion."

She reached to take it. "Give it back, my lord."

He closed his fingers over the silver orb, startling her. She realized at once her mistake in appearing so near-sighted and eager. So this was to be her deliverance, she thought, feeling a new rise of panic. She had prayed for something to happen to change her life. But surely this was God's jest upon her.

Anger seized the whole of her body. She could not believe this was happening. "You have to give it back, your lordship," Jack piped up before she could speak. "Miss Rose hasn't made her wish. Tell him, Miss Rose. Tell him you have te make a wish."

A faint flush heated her cheeks. But before she could deny Jack's unwelcome revelation, a horse's low wicker pulled her attention from Roxburghe.

He had not come from Hope Abbey alone. Two men on horseback sat on mounts at the wood's edge beneath the alder and oaks, casually watching their laird. Rising, she swallowed reflexively past the sudden tightness in her throat. Roxburghe followed her to her feet, unfurling his grand height and forcing her to tilt her chin. In a land where lawlessness was a way of life, she realized she was caught in the open with no accessible weapon. Roxburghe would be on her the moment she attempted to go for her dirk.

"I do not think he is interested in anything I have to say, Jack."

"I am very interested in everything you have to say, Lady Roselyn," he said with a hint of steel lining his soft tone. "Lady Roselyn Elena Lancaster. Rose, to those who think of you fondly."

She froze, unable to stop the dizziness washing over her in waves.

A dark brow rose at her silence. "You do not dispute your name," he said, clearly surprised by her lack of outward response.

She saved them both from a tedious lie. "Nay, I do not."

"Then you understand why I am here."

She refused to succumb to panic. The loss of the precious ring faded momentarily as a newer foreboding clutched her gut. If Roxburghe knew her name, then he knew she was Lord Hereford's daughter.

"What have you done with Friar Tucker? How did you find me?"

"Now, that is a story that will take as long to tell as it took me to find you tonight. Take off your boots."

She blanched. Did he mean to strip her naked? And with Jack present?

"Take off your boots, Lady Roselyn, and give them to Jack. I have no intention of chasing you should you decide to run. One of us might get hurt."

Rose sat on a rock wall, the remnant of an ancient foundation to the gatehouse that once guarded the cemetery. She bent her head, and turning her back to Roxburghe, removed each boot, giving first one and then the other to Jack. Fear made her feel weak in front of him. She forced herself past it and stood.

Roxburghe looked down as Jack sidled closer to Rose. Withdrawing a key from beneath his cloak, he said, "Friar Tucker will appreciate being let out of the tower. He might be hungry."

"Go," she told Jack when he failed to move.

He peered up at her. Jack was too young to understand the machinations of border politics and did not seem convinced of her safety. But she could take care of herself and wanted him gone. She gave him what remained of the sorcerer's box. "Take the key. Return to the abbey."

"But Miss Rose—"

"Go, Jack." Sensing his confusion, she placed her palms on each side of his face and forced him to look into her eyes to reassure him. "Friar Tucker will know that I am with Lord Roxburghe. I will be all right."

Jack reluctantly nodded and took the key from Roxburghe's hand. He walked to the edge of the cemetery, looked back at her once, then ran across the glade into the woods.

When he was gone, Rose faced Roxburghe and met his assessing eyes coolly. He was frowning. Just a slight crease in his brow. The moonlight gleamed off his raven-dark hair, giving it the sheen of silk. Her mistake was that she had not stepped away from him and the power that emanated from him. An unexpected shiver burned through her and with it came a sudden awareness of her own naiveté and peril.

"Give the ring back, my lord. And . . . I will not fight you."

His brow arched, as if her words forced him to consider her more thoroughly.

"Do women never fight you, my lord?" she asked.

He raised his hand, signaling to someone behind her. Two men with horses stood thirty feet away in the mist-shrouded grass and approached.

He held up the ring to light. "What is this to you?" he asked.

Only my dreams and my future.

"A sentimental trinket I found in the abbey crypt."

He deflected the half-truth with a grin that did not reach his eyes. He slipped the braided band of silver on his finger. "Then you will understand if I find the ring equally sentimental—if only to keep you near."

There had been no time to think or to respond. "Nooo," sounded weak against the frantic beating of her heart.

He did not even know what he had done.

Ruark felt a moment's dizziness that almost made him stumble, and the heel of his palm went to his temple as he opened his eyes and peered at Rose narrowly, wondering what the hell kind of curse she had just put on him. He had been half expecting that she would have taken off running. The instant the thought had also seemed to occur to her, he recovered enough to grab her arm.

"Too late, my lady."

She gasped as he pulled her to where his men waited. "Let go of me! What are you doing?"

She shoved against him as he felt the pockets of her jacket and her calves for any weapons, stopping short of running his hands over her bosom and backside. But as he rose in front of her, his eyes told her he would strip her bloody naked if she gave him cause.

One of his men held Loki's reins. The horse carried no saddle. Ruark lifted Rose to the red stallion and hoped she could ride bareback.

"You assume I am more valuable to Hereford than your brother," she said.

"You are a treasure to any man, Lady Roselyn." He grinned, for indeed she was like silver in moonlight. "More than you know."

The sound of a horse at a gallop intruded. A large bay crested the rise in front of him. "Jason's coomin'," one of his men called.

A moment later, the lad reined in his horse in front of Ruark.

"Raiders, my lord." Sound carried in the glade. He could hear the distant thunder of horses. "At least two dozen."

"Friends of yours?" he asked Rose.

"Geddes Graham leads those miscreants," she said. "It is like him to be out on a full moon causing mischief. I would say that he is harmless, but it would be a lie. Still, I would not wish for you to kill him. I am friends with his mother."

He signaled another rider some distance down the road behind him. "I have no desire for a bloodbath, Jason. Make sure the others know. Warn Colum he will probably be having guests," he said.

Ruark had left Colum to watch the abbey in case Rose returned there while he and his men had spoken to the mountebank and learned that there was cemetery not far from the woods. With Rose's love for the macabre and crypts, Ruark deduced she would come here. He had been right. But the presence of the raiders concerned him.

"Geddes will not harm Friar Tucker," Rose said. "Even he would not dare."

Ruark mounted his own horse and pulled on Loki's reins. He moved off the road and into the woods. As he rode past his men awaiting him at the cemetery's edge, they fell in behind him. He kept to the trees as best as the landscape allowed and rode quickly.

Rose rode just behind and to the left of him. An occasional glance over his shoulder told him she was still on the horse, though he didn't have to look to know. He could feel her. Smell the lilac encasing his senses. Her docility should have made him suspicious for she was the least submissive woman he had ever known, but it was enough just to keep her out of his head.

He clenched and unclenched his gloved fist on the reins trying to ease the tension from his body, annoyed that he could not. A mile later, his small party of riders joined two more of his men awaiting him. The moon remained ghostly bright, skimming the treetops, and soon Ruark was concentrating on the thin ribbon of trail.

Traveling for a half hour, he followed a path parallel to the river before he broke into the open. Except for Colum, the rest of his men were there. They fell in behind him as he rode his horse down the loamy bank and into the river. A cold spray of water leaped to life around him and slowly rose to his calves. His men had worked two days to find a place shallow enough to traverse the river without using the public crossing north of here. To his left, the river's rocky bed dropped and the fast-moving current would grab a person. A two day's ride away laid Kerr land, and safety.

In that instant, the stallion's reins went slack. He twisted in the saddle. Somehow, Rose had cut the reins. Ruark cursed. He swung his horse around and grabbed the stallion's bridle, barely ducking in time as she made the horse rear. Throwing her leg over the horse, she slipped from the back of the stallion and into the rapidly moving current. For a moment, she disappeared into the swirling blackness only to bob up ten feet away. Even as he heard someone shouting in the darkness, Ruark had already removed his boots and jumped into the river after her.

Chapter 5

Rose didn't know how long she had been in the water. She had swum maybe a hundred yards when the icy current grabbed her hard and would not relinquish its fierce grip, even after she found purchase in the rocks. The undertow pulled at her, thrashed her to and fro. Driftwood wedged between the rocks pressed against her.

Somehow, she'd managed to remove her jacket, nearly drowned attempting the feat, but her jerkin and breeches still weighed her down. She lost her grip on the jacket and watched it sail away, lashed and tangled by the boiling white water. She had learned to swim in this river, knew it well, had not for one moment thought that escaping into it could actually kill her. When she slid from the stallion's back into the water, she had not considered that the recent rains had swollen the river to its outer banks.

With the moon having gone behind the clouds, she struggled to see. She could hear shouting behind her. She looked back over her shoulder just in time to see Roxburghe slide from his horse and push off into the river after her. Panic struck her. She struggled to pull herself onto the slick rocks at the water's edge, but her hands slipped, the current jerked her backward and swept her along like human flotsam.

The river's rolling banks became cliffs that began to rise on either side of her, creating a shadowed narrow channel. The passage became a black abyss. The current picked up speed and power. She was headed straight for a waterfall! She swam harder at an angle, fighting to reach the shallower water.

She made it to the other side and with all her strength, grabbed a projecting tree branch covered with debris. A backwash spun in a monstrous whirlpool only feet away. She knew craggy boulders hid underneath. Over the water's roar, she heard the thunder of the waterfall, and couldn't believe she had traveled so far. Her heart hammered, her chest ached. No wonder she could no longer feel her fingers. She gasped for breath, water roiling over her.

Inching her hands one over the other, she sought a stronger grip, found one, and held on for life. If she let go she would be sucked into the whorl of white water and spit out over the waterfall. She didn't know which was worse—to have gone willingly with Roxburghe or be dashed against the rocks in a foamy, pulpy end.

Then Roxburghe was suddenly behind her, his arm wrapped tightly around her waist and lifting her out of the current. "Let go," she heard him yell over the roar of water. "I've got you!"

Squeezing her eyes shut, she shook her head. She could not do it. She could not trust him. She could not go back! "You let go!"

His arm tightened on her waist. Somewhere in her brain, she knew he was standing in the water. "You need me to get to shore. We can no' stay here. The water is too damn cold. Let go, Rose."

His body prevented her from slipping back into the current. Yet it was that very strength and power that dissuaded her from trusting her life to him. She clenched her hands tighter, terrified of letting go of the tree branch, a lifeline in the murky depths that had become her life. Fate had taken away her rainbows and her dreams and now it would drag her the rest of the way down.

Over the roar of water, she screamed. "I will not go back with you. I—"

"You can not return to the abbey," he shouted near her ear. "There is no place in Britain or France you will be able to hide from your father now. That is the way it is, Rose. But if you go over the falls, I go with you."

The thought gave her pause. The idea that she might die with him, might have to spend eternity bound in death to him, sharing the black waters of an abyss or the flames of hell together, was too horrible to contemplate.

But the choice to go to her father should have been her own to make, just as the choice to let go of the branch was now. In any case, they would soon both be too weak to fight the current. Roxburghe was right about the danger. She could fight him and end up too weak to pull herself from the water before they went over the waterfall.

She loosened her lifesaving grip and he caught her in his arms. Together they struggled to the bank and crawled out of the water exhausted and half drowned. She collapsed to her knees next to him. He rolled onto his back and placed one forearm over his eyes. Over the river's roar, she heard his labored gasps as she sucked in her own lifesaving breath. His Holland shirt had been torn across one shoulder. Like her, he wore nothing on his feet. She could still escape him.

Somehow, she still possessed the strength to make a dash for the rocks, but his hand shot out, grabbed her ankle like an iron vise and she slammed to the ground against her palms. She twisted around, ready to kick him, but he was already upon her, holding her down with one thigh insinuating itself between her knees. She launched a dazzling attack of her own, withdrawing the dirk from a slim sheath on her hip and laying it against his throat. The action had been so clean and swift she felt a moment's satisfaction. She met his narrowed eyes, even as her mind was immobilized by the terrifying idea he would strike her.

"I see now I erred in playing the gentleman and should have frisked you more thoroughly," he said and spit blood. She must have hit him in the mouth.

"Gentleman indeed! I refuse to be your hostage."

His breath brushed her cheek, but that was not all she felt of him heavy against her. "Have you ever cut a man's throat, Rose? 'Tis messy."

She had never maliciously harmed any creature, yet her hand tightened on the blade.

"I would not die instantly," he continued as if to convey there was a chill in the air. "I would still have time to snap your neck. Such a lovely neck, too."

"Do not try to be charming, Roxburghe. I am extremely angry."

And she was cold and trembling. And frightened. She didn't want to kill him. She wanted only to escape. As if to confirm her intention, she tightened her grip on the blade. "Do you doubt my courage?"

If he had been angry before, something else had replaced the emotion. "Nay, love. I am only debating how best to disarm you without getting my throat cut."

He made no attempt to remove the blade from her hand. He was smart, she realized. If he disarmed her by brute force alone, he would have given her psyche room to retreat. Surrender became a powerful tool of defeat if given by choice, even if that choice was an illusion.

She didn't resist when he finally eased the knife from

his throat and pressed her wrist to the soft ground, into the mud and pine needles. His weight rested on his arms positioned now on either side of her head. Neither moved. They were wet and covered in slime. But it didn't veil the heat of him. Her shirt sucked to the crevices and curves of her body, and she may as well have been naked beneath him for all the protection the thin fabric provided her. Though she was frightened, something melted inside her.

The dirk fell sideways next to her hand.

The tips of his damp hair brushed her cheeks. "I concede you handle a blade well. An interesting pastime for a sister of the abbey. Would you have really used it?"

She fixed her gaze on his face. "I . . . no one has ever tested me that far."

He frightened her and infuriated her, and she knew she should fear him. He did not move as she'd expected. Lord above, now that the shock of nearly drowning and going over the falls was wearing away, she felt a moment's faintness. There was nothing casual in the way his eyes touched hers. She didn't know what emotion it was he caused to rise in her.

She'd heard accounts where women were abused and violated by their captors. The infamous Kerr laird would know of such stories, too.

"Please," she murmured, aware of her own weak response.

"Please, what?" he said in a low voice.

She stared into eyes that were wild and dangerous. She remembered in sunlight they were the color of a twilight sky. "I want you to get off me. You are . . . heavy."

He laughed. Rose thought she hated him at that moment. She wanted to buck and dislodge him. But his chest already flattened her breasts and she dared not move. His face held no emotion, as if he could read her thoughts. "If I wanted to rape you, love, the deed would already have been done."

Pushing away from her supine body, he stood and wiped the back of his hand across his mouth. Stunned, she stared up at the black velvet sky filled with stars and took her first deep breath. But without his body heat, the night air had chilled in the fine mist. After a moment, she propped herself on her elbows. Her wet hair fell over eyes like reeds. She shoved it back with her hand and flinched. Her entire body hurt. Especially her leg.

Roxburghe was squatting in ankle-deep water rinsing mud and blood off the back of one hand. He had injured himself on the rocks as well.

He watched her from beneath half-lowered lids. After a moment's pause, he returned to tending the cut. For a man with such large hands, he worked quickly and efficiently. He appeared to have a familiarity with cleaning wounds. Her gaze dropped to the ring on his hand before she caught herself and looked away.

"Do you always wear breeches?" he asked.

She endured the amusement she glimpsed as his eyes went over her and slowly returned to rest on her face, and accepted the question as rhetorical.

"Why were you hiding at the cemetery?" he asked.

She pressed a thumb against her temple. "I go to the cemetery often when I wish to . . . pray. Everyone knows that."

"Including those border raiders?"

She turned her head startled and alarmed. "What makes you think they were not after you?"

He propped an elbow on his knee. "Because the abbey is in the opposite direction of the border crossing. And a conversation with the mountebank told me otherwise. No . . . I suspect your man, Geddes Graham, was after you. Not to play nice, either."

A heavy silence fell between them. If only she could think clearly. Roxburghe was right. She could never go back to the abbey. "Geddes is a weasel. He is an informant for . . ." She refused to say *my father.* "For the king's warden," she said, the most hated man in all Scotland.

People would despise her, too, when they learned his daughter still lived. Her life as she had known it was forever at an end. A part of her wanted to laugh at the absurdity and utter irony.

Instead, she started to shiver from the combination of wet, cold, and pain and wrapped her arms about her torso. "Geddes and I have never got along. I took money from him that belonged to Jack."

Wrapping a torn piece of fabric from his shirt around his palm, Roxburghe returned to her side and knelt on one knee. Hard muscles encased not just his arms but his legs. She had so desperately wanted to find a weakness in him, yet his strength overwhelmed all impressions.

"You need to dry out. We cannot remain here. Can you walk?"

He was asking if she could walk barefoot in the woods. The soles of her feet were as callused as cow's hide. She'd grown up barefoot. But she had injured her thigh. She could feel warmth pooling against the cloth of her breeches. "Wouldn't it be better to await your men to find us?"

"Lest you have not noticed, we are on the wrong side of the river. I doubt even you have a taste for raider company, dressed as you are." With care, he gently tilted her chin. "I don't want to kill anyone over you tonight, Rose."

She pulled from his grip. Her ring on his finger, like the small earring in his ear, flickered in the moonlight.

And fueled the pace of her thoughts.

What manner of man would not be afraid of border raiders when he was but one against many? A border raider himself. The same kind of man who had let her keep her weapon—who would risk death to jump into a raging river after her.

That he had done so for the life of his brother only made her own actions and defiance less clear in her mind.

Ruark ascended the path that let away from the river, a small winding trail more suitable for goats than humans. The sound of rushing water still roared in his ears. Twice while climbing, he'd stopped to hand Rose up the slippery boulders.

The trek had been treacherous for half a mile as the crude path narrowed upward through moss-covered rocks into woods of rowan, ash, and tall pine. Barefooted, the path was even worse. He'd noted blood on one of Rose's feet. But there was nothing to be done at this moment. It was the only trail out of the wash.

Neither of them spoke until they reached the woods and the noise of the river faded. Without asking her permission, he sat her on an old rotten log to rest and reached for the torn hem of her breeches.

She misunderstood his intent and caught his hand to stop him.

"Easy, Rose. You have to allow me to look. You are bleeding." He sat her foot in his lap and followed the trail of blood with his fingers up the slim curvature of her calf.

She squirmed. "You do not need to touch me . . ."

He noticed that about her: she disliked being touched, or perhaps only his touch disturbed her, for she seemed consumed with tenderness for others.

It was not her foot that was injured, he realized. The

blood came from a jagged gash on her thigh that he could see through a tear in her breeches. He silently swore. She had attempted to bind it with torn cloth from her shirt. He rent one of his sleeves, then rose and knelt in a shallow stream to rinse the cloth. He returned to her side. "Why didn't you tell me you were injured?"

"What would we have done? Hailed a carriage and ridden out?"

He suspected Rose was the type of person who could be bleeding from an artery and still would not open her mouth in complaint or ask for help. She intended to carry her own burden whether she be his hostage or nay. So it surprised him when she squeezed her eyes shut, clearly afraid of what he saw.

"Is it . . . horrible?"

He could see it was deep but she had done a fair job of stopping the bleeding. "I will know more when I see the injury in the light of day."

"Bind it tightly, but not so tight you cut off the circulation to my leg."

Though he knew quite well what he was doing, he did not mind her instruction if it gave her the illusion that she held some power over her life.

Conscious of how she looked, her eyes and hair awash in a checkered patch of moonlight, and wearing a nearly transparent shirt, more undressed than other women he'd bedded, he concentrated on applying the cloth firmly to her thigh and wrapping the makeshift bandage around the wound. And for one moment, decency reared its symbolic head, denouncing him for a bastard.

"Between what remains of my shirt and yours, we are running out of medical supplies," he said. "At this rate we will both be down to our breeches."

"Then 'tis fortunate you allowed me to keep my dirk."

The tendons stood out on his arms as he leaned forward. "Indeed."

He peered at her, reminding himself she was cold and in pain, and then suddenly looked past her down the narrow trail.

Something, a noise, voices in the night, touched the periphery of his senses. But he heard nothing now. "What is it?" Rose asked.

He didn't answer. His body tensed. He stood. "Remain here."

The path hooked sharply just ahead, and he walked toward an outcrop of rocks. Farther from the invading sound of the river, he could hear voices. Torchlight glow speckled a hollow below. He crouched behind the rocks and scrub. It was a group of some twenty or thirty redcoats bivouacked for the night.

Bloody Sassenach soldiers.

The flames from a central fire flickered over their faces and red coats and knee breeches. Some of the men were drunk. Others played dice. The late-evening breeze carried the sounds of their subdued laughter and voices as they sat around the fire. All, without exception, were well armed.

Rose suddenly came up behind him. "Dragoons—"

He clapped his palm over her mouth and dropped to the ground on his belly beside her, looking back down at the hollow. One of the men made a searching glance toward the rocky ledge but returned his attention to the tin plate in his hands as the bloke beside him said something that caused laughter.

Ruark pulled back slightly and peered at Rose, who glared back at him from over the rim of his hand. "A scream carries too easily," he said softly against her ear. "If you make a sound, Rose . . ."

He meant the threat in his words. "This is a well-armed British detachment and by the looks of it they have been drinking. Trust me. I can guarantee they will not treat you nearly as kindly as I have thus far."

She nodded in understanding, and he eased the pressure of his hand. The ferocity in her eyes dimmed only slightly as she spit dirt from her mouth.

"I do *not* trust you." But her anger with him did not preclude her recognition of the danger she also faced. "What are we going to do?"

They'd followed the only trail out of the wash. Rose was physically unable to go back the way they'd just come. He studied the hollow and found a row of tents at the wood's edge, and he smiled to himself.

"We steal a horse."

"Are you insane?"

The wind was rising and the sound of restless trees replaced that of the river. He could always count on rain in Scotland. Tonight he wouldn't mind. "The patrol has bivouacked for the evening," he said.

Careful not to dislodge any stones, he edged them down the trail, helping Rose walk with one arm beneath her shoulders. He could have slung her over his shoulder like a sack of oats and been done with it but he saved her the indignity. Much to her dislike some moments later, he borrowed her dirk. The thing was bloody convenient to have, and he didn't know when he'd have use of a weapon. He wouldn't have allowed her to keep it otherwise.

An hour later, he had secured himself a fine black horse belonging to the officer in charge, and a pair of boots that actually fit. He had also acquired a knapsack and a cloak, which he gave to Rose when he returned to where he had left her, gagged and tied to a thick exposed tree root. He hadn't trusted her not to crawl away while he hunted down a horse and food, and the moment he'd come across rope, he'd used it. As he knelt in front of her, he warned her again of the consequences if she should cause him any more strife. Then he lifted her onto the saddle and climbed behind her. Only after they'd ridden a distance from the Sassenach camp did he remove the gag, which was all that had been left of his other sleeve.

"You are an ogre, Roxburghe. The French pox is too good for you!"

He laughed and gathered her closer with one arm, liking the warm feel of her between his thighs. "What do you know about the French pox?"

"I know that nothing cures it."

With that pronouncement, he grinned. A faint clink of the bridle and her firm bottom pressed intimately between his legs, he turned the horse south. "You are a lot of trouble, Lady Roselyn."

Chapter 6

Ruark carefully finished binding the wound on Rose's thigh as she slept. She laid on her back perfectly still, her hair spread around her head like a sunset halo and, despite himself, he lifted a strand and rubbed it between his calloused fingers. She wore only her white shirt and the cloak beneath her that he had unwrapped from around her unclad form to tend her injury. She may as well have been naked.

Aye, she was temptation itself.

Full breasts crested with dark nipples pressed against the thin fabric of her shirt, the kind of breasts that fit perfectly into a man's hands with nothing left over to waste, flat stomach, the beckoning flair of her hips and narrow tuft of pale hair between impossibly long legs. The whole of her nothing but softness and curves. He'd already spent half the morning watching her as she slept, and reluctantly, he edged the cloak over her. He hadn't liked where his mind was heading and didn't know what to do about it. He had sworn no oath of protection to her, owed no one but his people his allegiance.

But it was not just her beauty that had kept him by her side contemplating the daughter of his Sassenach foe. Not for the first time did he wonder how Friar Tucker had kept her hidden all these years. Or why Lord Hereford had ever stopped looking for her. Tucker had not told him everything.

Perhaps had she shown less courage, he would be less invested in her and more inclined to ignore the extent of his desire.

He wanted her. And he did not think he would.

For desire it was, like watching Venus in the night-time sky so close he'd oft stood on the deck of his ship and wondered what it would be like to touch that light. But he'd always had the power to temper his wants with restraint.

A whisper of movement alerted him that Rose was awake, and it was as if something warmed inside him as she stirred. Her lashes fluttered open and he was caught in her verdant gaze. Still half asleep, she stared up at him, before she blinked as if in confusion. She peered around her at the mist-soaked glade, slowly becoming aware of a crackling fire and a shelter of pine covering her.

Her hand went to her hip to find her dirk gone. Noting her lack of apparel, she pulled the cloak around her and sat up, spilling her hair around her shoulders. The amused light in his eyes caused her to frown. She should feel grateful he'd allowed her to keep the shirt she still wore.

"Where are my clothes?" she demanded.

"You will get them back when we are ready to leave. After your defiance yesterday, I can see removing your boots was not enough. I will take no chances. Not with that injury you have on your leg."

She looked around the glade. "How long have I been asleep?"

Strangely, her ire only served to confirm his admiration of her. "Long enough to decide it is far more perilous for me at this moment than you."

Alarmed, she peered past him. "Have you seen dragoons?"

"Oh, aye." He laughed, in good humor. "Dragoons are everywhere." She observed his warm scrutiny with a frown. "You have been asleep for five hours," he said on a more sobering note. "We traveled through the night. I stopped because the horse needs rest, as do you. How is your leg?"

" 'Tis attached," she murmured.

He crouched beside the fire with his elbow against one knee. She stole a closer look at him only to discover him staring at her.

"That wound needs to be sutured," he said.

She looked as if she wanted to tuck her leg somewhere safe from his scrutiny, but knew he was correct. "How will you do that?"

"I took an officer's field kit along with that horse. There will be a needle and thread inside. Or I could cauterize it."

He considered the pain either procedure would inflict, and looked away to tend to the meal. McBain had sutured more than one injury on his body. He had more scars than years . . .

"Have you ever mended flesh?" she asked.

"I lived on a ship for nearly thirteen years. I can mend anything." His gaze suddenly softened. " 'Tisn't that difficult, love."

She sighed. "Then I have not dreamed this nightmare about ogres, magic spells, and fire-breathing dragons," she said. "You are real."

"Aye, I am real, Sassenach."

"*Sassenach* . . ." His tone as much as the single word caught her attention. "Do you despise the English or just Lord Hereford? Did you not yourself hire out to the Crown? Were you not allied to his Royal Navy?"

"Only in so far as it proved profitable." And until his father died.

"The authorities would hang you if they knew you were a smuggler."

"Aye, they might, if such crimes could be proven." He spoke with no small amount of amusement, considering that Friar Tucker could be hanged for the very same transgressions, along with half the borderland lords with him. "My conscience has already settled the fact in my mind that I am a criminal at heart."

He gave her what was left of a stale oatcake from the knapsack he'd stolen along with the horse. "You are not eating?" she asked, hesitantly.

"I ate while you slept."

If she'd been less starved, he suspected she would have denied him the satisfaction of accepting his hospitality. But she was so hungry she even ate the crumbs that fell on her lap. Accepting his generosity should have been the worst of her sins, he realized, as she swallowed the last bite and he met the awareness in her eyes.

So she feels it, too.

He offered her the whisky flask and was surprised when she took it. He watched as she carefully sipped.

Sunlight cast a golden glow over her skin and hair and her impossibly full mouth, over the full mounds of her breast visible beneath the thin cloth of her shirt. He did not understand the connection between them and his lasciviousness began to irritate him.

And she was a virgin, no less.

"Thank you," she rasped.

Hardly expecting the sentiment, he laughed. "For what exactly am I being thanked?"

Her attention paused on his mouth where she had knocked him with her elbow last night. He could still feel the tenderness. "For saving me in the river last night. I hope you were not too wounded."

The corner of his mouth turned up at the blatant lie. "What is a bit of blood shared between intimate enemies? Hmm? I still have my tongue."

" 'Tis a shame. Tongues can be rather useless in the wrong mouth."

This time he did laugh aloud. "An empirical statement coming from you, Rose." She suddenly slid away. But he was ever quick to block her with his arm. "Especially from someone who has probably only used hers for eating and saying all the wrong things."

"I do not want to be attracted to you," she said bluntly.

"Duly noted."

He did not want to be attracted to her either.

And there it was. The reality of it as vexing as a splinter beneath his flesh, as if the thought had plagued him all along but had only taken shape now for what it was. As if her beauty was not enough to admire or endure without also enduring his own honesty and the reason she was with him now.

He needed her.

Without Rose, he did not have enough with which to bargain for his brother's life.

But even were he not in her life, she would still not be free.

She must have recognized this.

His chest suddenly moved with silent laughter at the utter absurdity of his lust. He crossed his wrists and returned his attention to Rose, his control tenuous at best.

"You may find all of this amusing. I do not." Her chin lifted. "I have spent most of my life at the abbey and among the people of Castleton," she said. "I may not be a sterling example of female gentility, but I have always tried to treat people fairly and with kindness, believing that one's actions would lend to a like treatment in return."

"Then you expect payment for good behavior?" He purposefully misconstrued her words.

Her gaze widened. "Most certainly not." She brushed crumbs from the cloak as if casting about for a way to better frame her thoughts. "I have little memory of my father," she said after a moment.

Some of the verve left her tone as if she sought to remember what she could of the man who was her sire. "I know people despise him. Even as I know he once served the admiralty as a decorated war hero. Now he is returned to Kirkland Park, the hated king's warden, for he dares enforce laws in the borderlands to rein in certain lawless elements."

"Is that who you think he is?"

She blinked and looked away. "How can I know the character of a man I do not remember? Mayhap I need to believe he is more decent than others say. I only know he has left Hope Abbey alone."

"Why is that, do you suppose?"

She scraped the moisture from her cheeks with the heel of her hand and glared. "You ask a lot of questions for someone who should know the answers. Perhaps Friar Tucker paid the proper taxes and has done nothing so outwardly untoward as to attract the warden's wrath. How should I know Hereford's mind?"

"Has he ever been to the abbey?"

"Nay. And I wish you never had been either. For you are as autocratic as he must be. As are all men. A *fish* serves a more useful purpose on this earth than do men.

At least I can eat a fish. I am not responsible for what happened to your brother."

"The boy to whom you so casually refer is James Marcus Kerr," he said. "My father's son by his second wife. She calls him Jamie. I have never met the boy. I was gone from Scotland 'ere he was born and did not return for thirteen years because my father beat the living hell out of me, claimed me unworthy as his heir, and hoped I would die on the sea. I did not. Jamie shares my sire's blood through no fault of his own. He is twelve."

He laid his palm against her cheek and turned her face into the sunlight. "I do not take my actions lightly," he said. "Some would go to war over what Lord Hereford has done to my family. A month ago, before my return, I was one of those men. But in the end, my brother would still be dead." He lowered his hand. "I wish things could be different but they are not."

She did not pull away from his gaze as he had expected, and instead he was the one who broke contact as he bent to return her plate to the top of the knapsack.

He did not want to see Rose as anything more than political currency. He was a pragmatist, a man at ease with his duty with no qualms doing what was necessary to secure his brother. He'd never had much of a conscience when it came to life's ambiguous moral choices. So he did not understand his feelings now.

"I fear I am far braver dealing with another's ailment than my own," she said, returning his attention to the task at hand.

She had lifted part of the bandage and was studying the injury on her thigh. She wrapped her hand around the whisky flask as if considering its contents, then offered it back. "I know this is sacrilegious for me to say to a Scotsman, but whisky is nauseating. If I must get myself drunk to endure sutures, I prefer wine as my anesthetic of choice. I . . . I can do this without intoxicating myself." She squeezed her eyes shut and said bravely. "I am ready."

Ruark edged the flask back to her. "Drink, Rose. A sip. You might be ready, but I am not. I can knock you out and you'll feel nothing or you can drink . . . or both."

And strangely, the fact that Ruark Kerr, the infamous Black Dragon, did not seem bent on intentional cruelty toward her seemed to soften her eyes as if his actions somehow gave her hope that in the end he would find a way to free his brother without sacrificing her.

She was wrong. More than she could possibly know.

"My apologies, Rose."

He could endure his own pain more than he could suffer hers. Before she could respond, he clipped her head with his fist, and darkness mercifully claimed her.

Rose dreamed in a landscape barren of color and light, gliding on wings of shadow. Pain came and went with the darkness that weighted her like lead in water and she struggled to rise from the depths consuming her. She could not breathe. She fought to loosen the ties that bound her before she drowned.

Cold, wet, and shuddering, Rose was not remembering the river's rage that had nearly taken her over the falls. She was remembering the storm that would take her mother out to sea. She heard the seagulls screaming and wheeling above her head and the strain of battened-down canvas in the rush of wind. People standing in the rain on the docks. The scent of lilac, faint in the fine mist of dawn. The warmth as someone carried her and held her, and Rose knew it was her mother.

"*Roselyn . . .*"

With a gasp, she opened her eyes and sat up.

Arms had come around her almost at once, gently pulling her back into a protective embrace, promising she would be safe.

In the somber shadows, she recognized nothing. Rain fell in the darkness beyond and she was cold. Roxburghe's voice came to her. He lay between her and the way out of the shelter. As if to guard her . . . or protect her. She had not realized how close in meaning the two actions were. There was a narrow divide between being imprisoned and safekeeping. Tonight she felt safe.

"You are dreaming, Rose."

She splayed her fingers over his chest if only to test that he was real and not a figment of a dream, knowing she should never test boundaries.

His heartbeat was steady against her palm, like the sound of rain outside their shelter. The heat from his body warmed hers. "I . . . I am sorry," she whispered.

His arm tightened around her, and at once, the dream of moments ago began to fade back into the darkness. "Why?"

Blinking moisture from her eyes, Rose drew in a breath. "She died alone in an angry sea. She died because of me, my lord. I want to know why."

He pushed up on his elbow and she felt his hand go to her forehead. But she could have told him she had no fever. Even the throb in her thigh had faded to the background of her thoughts.

She could feel his gaze on her face, a palpable touch. "Who died, Rose?"

But she was emerging from her dream world now as if she had stepped from the icy mist that would drown her and into Roxburghe's arms.

She had awakened once earlier in the day and he had

given her supper and told her the weather had worsened. But in the darkness, the rain and the rest of the world faded with the dream. In the darkness, her senses hummed. Only in the darkness did she truly feel free.

He didn't kiss her, but still she could feel his lips as he spoke so near her own, and she was suddenly remembering the way he touched her mouth at the abbey, imprinting himself on her memory like a brand.

She felt the strangest urge to be touched again. "Shh, love," he said as if reading her thoughts.

The pads of his thumbs stroked her lower lip, his touch feathering across her face. "*Bòidheach.*" His head lowered and his lips brushed hers. "You are beautiful, Rose."

She held her hands to his chest as if to push him away. Muscles constricted. A pulse beat against the heart of her hand. Hers. His. Did it matter?

His pause was infinitesimal but she could feel every sinuous detail of his conflict. She denied the urge to venture beyond, and yet . . .

He hadn't moved from her. His hand tightened in the thick fall of her damp hair. His breath touched her lips. And as the silence lengthened between them, she resisted the impulse to turn away from him. She didn't understand what was happening to her.

Something seemed to burn the air between them. She tried to be bold in the wake of this sensual incursion against her soul. But she found she could not, and lost herself in the swirling contradiction of her emotions.

In a measure to catch the race of her confusion and desire that suddenly spun about her like a child's top, she raised her palms to cup his face as if to slow it instead. Understand it by its shape. His face was rough, his lips warm and his breath moist against her thumbs.

He dipped his dark head, taking her mouth in a slow kiss that melted the final remnants of her dream world and became reality. His muscles were tense, rippling as he trailed his mouth down the column of her neck. She lay absorbing the sensation. Her head tilted back and his lips suckled the pulse beating wildly at her throat. With an oath, he touched his forehead to hers, pulling air into his lungs as if he'd been in a brawl. She pulled back only to have him close his palm around her nape. He cupped her face and lifted it to his, his breath a sultry caress on her lips.

A subtle change in his touch where his tongue had quested. "Open your mouth for me, Rose. Let me inside, love."

The words were like drinking a heady glass of wine but his kiss was like the burn of scotch whisky as he joined his mouth seamlessly to hers. His tongue now invading as he dragged her into a long deep kiss, no longer gentle as raw, hot sensations washed over her.

And she kissed him because suddenly she could not help herself and wanting him was like wanting to breathe. And as he lowered his weight and pressed her to the soft ground beneath her, she inhaled against the shock of his body against hers, restless as he cupped her breast and awakened her passion, as if she drew some portion of him up into herself with every breath they shared.

As if the darkness had conjured him from the shadows and given him wings to glide.

The kiss went on and on. He tasted alive. Life-giving. Like the rain that drummed in a restless cadence on the canopy of branches above their heads.

It was too late to reconcile the woman she was with what she was doing now. *Too late* . . .

Not even the ache on her thigh could vanquish the

sweet fire of sensations. She had never felt anything so sweet touch all of her senses at once. Her palm grazed his upper arm and shoulder and discovered where braided muscles tightened beneath flesh. His hand traced the curve of her waist and he pulled her against him so that her breasts flattened against his chest. The quiver that vibrated through her body sent a corresponding response through his. She could feel the beat of his pulse as if it were her own. His fingers splayed the round curve of her bottom and brought her more fully against his arousal. Little separated them from full contact but the leather of his breeches. Her fingers tangled in his thick course hair. He smelled of earth and rain and sweat, an utterly male essence foreign to her.

'Twas not at all unpleasant. Her breathing had slowed as she followed his lead. Where his hands and mouth went on her body, hers followed on his.

In the darkness, nothing mattered but that he made her feel alive and free.

She was safe in the darkness.

His presence surrounded her.

Sliding her palms over his shoulders and down the slope of his back, she melted against him and met the plunder of his tongue. His clothes were damp, the linen of his shirt rasping against her more tender flesh, but she did not care.

He lowered his mouth to her breasts. The graze of his teeth brushed her nipples and she murmured incoherently. His hand moved between her thighs and with the gentlest of pressure nudged her legs apart. She was hot and damp. His fingers played upon her intimately, teased her until she was anxious, doing things that made her forget everything but the moment at hand. His finger pushed into her, then pulled out, in and out, pushing upward in the most exquisite way. He knew just where to touch her. How much to give before she asked for more. The pressure in her womb became insistent, spreading up through her body from his fingertips. He was fire, touching her.

It did not matter that she could not see him working his fingers and mouth over her. She had closed her eyes.

He did not seduce. He conquered with an expertise she would never have.

And she let him.

From somewhere a voice cried out . . . her own.

His mouth was still on her breast, laving her with liquid heat, but he had moved over her body. Then his hand was gone, and he was replacing his fingers with something much, much larger, to probe the edges of her softness. Throbbing recognition pulsed through her body. She felt discomfort as he entered her . . . and something strange and burning.

He softly swore on a suffocated breath.

And despite her want not to, she also gasped.

She grasped his head, and pulled him into a kiss that asked for nothing, but would demand everything. She would not allow this moment to be more than what it was.

"What are you doing, Rose?"

"Do . . . *not* stop."

Their breaths mingling in the darkness, she tasted blood on her lip where she had bitten down. Not to displace the pain but to welcome it. She set her heels into the soft ground and lifted her hips to push against him, forcing him deeper. Pain anchored her. Reminded her who she was.

His breathing had slowed. He raised his head slowly.

His features were lost in the darkness.

Perhaps for just a moment he had forgotten she was Lord Hereford's daughter. But she had forgotten nothing.

That it should hurt. That it should be Roxburghe who hurt her was just in her mind.

She would not make herself vulnerable.

But she was.

He proved that much as his body began to move, filling her completely, and he took her, lifting and stoking the fire. And then they were each taking from the other.

And the humming grew louder in her head. Did he not feel it, too?

Beneath her fingers, his shoulders bunched with his movements. Her nails dug into his back. There was no proof against the pleasure he gave her. She could not turn it away.

No words were spoken between them. There didn't need to be.

Only the sound of their breathing answered their need. His possession burned unchecked through her body.

She did not want to be vulnerable. But in the end, it was her very vulnerability that made her shatter. But it was still dark.

And for her, darkness had always been safe.

By the time pale shafts of light penetrated Rose's consciousness, she was already half awake. She awoke to a burning soreness between her thighs and the smell of him on her body. The place beside her was empty.

Only the sound of a rushing stream and birdsong intruded on her thoughts. That and the rough abrasion against her skin where Roxburghe had scraped her tender flesh with his kiss. A cloak lay over her. She still wore her shirt, and it covered her to mid-thigh. But she was still practically naked, and in daylight, she felt more vulnerable than ever before.

She pushed up on her elbow. A low-hanging mist hovered over the ground making the trees ghostly in the morning light. She looked for Roxburghe, half holding her breath.

She could see neither him nor the horse he'd stolen from the dragoons. Her hand went to her thigh.

He had done a fine job stitching the ugly gash. The scar would be thin. Though why should she care? She expected no man would ever see her legs.

She crawled out of the shelter, dragging the cloak, and limped to some dense brush to relieve herself, watching the camp through wispy willow branches surrounding her for any sign of Roxburghe. She was tender in the most private of places where he had touched and done things . . . impossible things that made her cry out with the pleasure of it. She closed her eyes.

Nothing had ever consumed her so utterly as last night. She should be more shocked at herself than she was, and wondered if something was wrong with her that even now her heart tripped. She wanted a cold bath, as if clean water could scrub away the passion as easily as it could the blood. There was a tremor in the cadence of her thoughts.

Blackbirds circled the treetops and she had the sudden unpleasant image of carrion-eating crows. She combed her fingers through her hair. She began to feel like the only surviving human in a world gone insane, completely alone in this foreign wilderness forest. She recognized nothing.

Then the faint wicker of a horse caught her ear and she limped down a path, stepping through the trees to see a stark blue pond as still as glass in the morning sunlight. The black gelding stood hobbled in a patch of grass. She drew a deep breath and started to make her way to the animal, with no thought of where she might go unclad and hunted . . . and lost. Only that she would be free.

Roxburghe suddenly strode into the clearing. He saw her by the rocks and stopped, then wiping his mouth with the back of his hand, looked from her to the horse.

She sensed more than saw the amusement in his eyes as he approached. She had been melded with him all night, perhaps more than his body had imprinted itself upon her senses. She could feel him inside her head.

He held a self-made spear crowned by her dirk tied to the stick with a band of cloth. Three nicely sized trout were impaled on its tip. He wore no shirt, as if he had just come from the water. His wet hair carelessly brushed the tops of his bronze shoulders. The sight of him caused a deep intake of breath.

Fully clothed, Ruark Kerr was impressive. Unclothed, he could stir a rock to life. He was large and strong, wrought from muscle and flesh and a smattering of hair that narrowed like an arrow from his abdomen to disappear into the waistband of his breeches. Hair the shade of the stubble that darkened his jaw.

Last night he had been clothed when he had lain next to her. Then she had awakened in the throes of a dream, and Roxburghe had been there in the darkness. She had found more than succor in his arms.

Now his silence played at the hunger he had awoken in her.

A wolf howled just then. Hugging the cloak to her torso, she diverted her attention to the trees. This place, her feelings, everything was unfamiliar to her.

"These woods are filled with predators," he said, a predator himself who would easily recognize the dangers. His hand was suddenly below her chin and touched the tenderness there. "'Twould be a mistake for you to think you could leave here alone and survive."

"Predators? The two-legged or four-legged kind?"

"Both. You have courage. I would hate to see it all thrown away on an imprudent decision."

Her pulse fluttered beneath his touch. "I want to wash,"

she said bluntly, feeling dizzy as she looked at the pond. "Alone if you will."

"Within sight of the camp." The lack of timbre in his voice pulled her gaze back to his. "I mean what I say, Rose. You are in no condition to go anywhere on your own. And I warn you, the water is cold."

The colder the better, in her mind, Rose thought as she limped down the hill to where water trickled over rocks into the cold pond. When she sensed Ruark had moved away, she stole a glance over her shoulder and watched as he squatted near the fire to tend to the fish. With his elbow braced on his knee, he looked over at her, and she turned abruptly, aware of his interest.

She removed the cloak. Part of her felt emboldened enough to strip away the shirt in defiance of her shyness, and so she did, for the devil had seized her. Only because she knew that he had seen her wariness of him. Let him watch if he chose. She was not afraid of him.

She walked through reeds and mallow ferns and dove into the water, only to come up sputtering as the icy water snatched a gasp from her throat. *Bloody hell!* The pond must be fed by an underground stream.

She forced herself to swim and after a while the cold felt good against her tender flesh if only because she could no longer feel her limbs. Treading water, she looked about her at the open meadow, escape always on her mind. Then she turned on her back to enjoy the rare bout of sunlight warming her face before she forced herself to return. If he could withstand the pond long enough to fish, then so could she. Being a proficient swimmer helped, and with deep strokes, she waded farther out and floated on her back. Finally, she swam back to the bank.

A shadow fell over her. She looked up to see Ruark standing near the rock where she had laid her cloak. Fully dressed now, he held the rest of her clothing balled up in his hand. He'd tied back his dark hair with a leather strip. His earring glistened silver in the sunlight and momentarily drew her attention.

"Breakfast is ready," he said, amused and clearly recognizing her quandary. She would have to climb out before she turned blue.

She wished now she hadn't been so eager to shed her shirt.

"Turn around."

"And give you my back? Not on your life, love."

Damn him. She rose out of the water feeling like a mermaid with her wet hair hanging like reeds to her hips. She struggled up the embankment and snatched up her cloak. Then faltered and would have fallen to her knees had he not grabbed her arm. He set the cloak around her shoulders and handed her her clothes.

"I can walk without aid," she said weakly.

Ignoring her, he lifted her into his arms. "No doubt you have become accustomed to your own independence, love. But not today."

He brought her into the camp and set her down beside the fire. Forced by weakness and the need to sit, she dropped on a dead worm-eaten log, feeling like one of the scaly, tattered lichen she'd dislodged with her ankle.

He bent and retrieved the tin cup on the fire-warmed stones next to the cooking trout. He pressed the rim to her lips. "Drink. You will feel better."

Pushing the cup away, she turned her head. "I would beg to differ, my lord. I already feel like a foxed sailor."

His mouth crooked. "A foxed sailor? You mean a drunken jack-tar. Aye. The English cannot hold their spirits."

He was teasing though he may as well not have been. He

had no great fondness for anything Sassenach. "Drink. 'Tis hot willow-bark tea. Breakfast will be ready shortly."

Unlike the heated passion of last night that left an indelible tenderness between her legs, his touch remained gentle, and to her, his kindness made a paradox of his absolute disreputableness.

She held the warm cup in her palms and looked over the rim at the willow trees as she sipped. The taste was astringent and bitter and the tea would work to help alleviate pain and swelling in her leg. The bark was obtained in the thin channeled pieces between the slight downy and serrated leaves. He would have had to have gathered the bark earlier and dried it on the rocks.

"Did you learn about willow-bark tea during your time at sea as well?"

"One learns something about medicine if one wishes to keep his crew alive. But McBain is the expert. I was merely the patient most of the time."

She peered down at his back as he bent to slide the fish on the tin plate that went with the cup she held. "You have been injured?"

"I have seen my fair share of battle," he said without looking at her. "A broadside can destroy a man in more ways than you can imagine."

She could not imagine standing on the quarterdeck of any ship facing cannon fire. Or giving the order to fire. That he had done so only brought home to her the manner of man she found herself against.

She scraped her finger idly over the cup's rim. "Last night . . ."

He lifted his gaze and the words froze in her throat. She remembered how he had withdrawn from her and spilled his seed outside her body. "You were careful to see that there would be no child between us . . ."

Even as his expression remained unchanged, he said, "Nothing is ever certain."

Jack was a bastard child, she thought, hoping that Friar Tucker had taken him under his wing until she could somehow return and claim him.

"Do you have children?" she asked.

'Twas a blatantly intimate question, and brought on a bout of self-consciousness. "No one has come forward to claim me as their father yet, if that is what you are asking."

"I could not care less if you have populated the world."

He braced his wrist on his knee, amusement in his eyes. "What of you?" he asked after a moment. "How is it someone of your . . . not so virginal passions managed to remain untouched for twenty years?"

She barely swallowed the sip of tea before she coughed. "No one has ever interested me . . . in *that* way. And even if I had been interested, I have bigger dreams than to find myself someone's wife . . ." her voice faded.

"A young girl's dreams found in the magic of a wishing ring?" he asked and her gaze dropped to the ring on his hand. "Now that I know something about you, I am even more curious by Jack's statement when I came upon you in the cemetery. He said you had not made a wish upon this ring."

"You know that 'tis a wishing ring?"

"The Gypsies sell these at country fairs from Carlisle to Wick. You can buy one for a halfpenny and have more than one wish in the bargain."

His mockery insulted her and made her feel foolish. "Do you believe in magic?"

Clearly, he was a man who believed in very little and trusted his survival to few. "Maybe when I was five, when my uncle pulled a coin from my ear."

"Then what does it matter what I think the ring is or

was to me? 'Twas probably all twaddle anyway, as you say. I do not believe in fairy tales and I have never cared what faults people find in my traits and appearance. I have never aspired to be a princess."

She finished the tea and licked the moisture from her lips with the tip of her tongue before handing the cup back to Roxburghe. The flush on her cheeks deepened as she realized he was watching her in disbelief.

"Sweet Jesu, Rose." He raised his eyes to the heavens and spread his arms. "Lord, save me from my idiocy before I do something else I will regret."

Then on a note of laughter that did not quite reach his eyes he said, "Do you not see yourself as a man sees you?"

She swallowed against the tightness in her throat. "I have not known many men," was all she could think to say. Then with more brevity, "I find the male species to be much like fleas. Bothersome at best. I avoid them when I can. You have not given me a reason to reform my opinion, sir."

He laughed, entirely unaffected by the insult. She wondered if anything she could say would affect him. He was like a tall stone pillar who should have left her feeling cold, not hot and flushed with a restless fever raging in her veins.

She probably did suffer a fever.

"When will we be to Stonehaven?" she asked.

"By nightfall," he said.

"Do you plan to keep me chained in the lower bowels of your castle?"

"Considering your penchant for enjoying basements and crypts, even if I had a castle, which I do not, I wonder why that would scare you." He touched her hair. "You are more suited to sunlight than darkness. I would chain you in the tower."

"Now you are baiting me," she said.

"Am I?"

He brushed his fingertips across the wild fluttering pulse at the base of her throat, and lifted her face with his palm. For tense seconds, as she stared into his eyes and, dear Lord, at that mouth—curved down just slightly at the corners as if some perplexing quandary lurked just beyond—a shiver rocked her.

She knew he was going to kiss her again, and it was not fear she felt. Her lips already felt thick and hot as if in anticipation.

And then he did kiss her, but not like a man who was hungry with passion like the mating of mouths that left her hovering between terror and bliss. He did not plunder her mouth as he had last night, yet it left her weak all the same. She managed the slightest protest but because he had kissed her or because his mouth left her lips and trailed down the curve of her neck, she didn't know.

"What are you doing?" she rasped.

"I could ask you the same thing. What are you doing?" His thumbs brushed the bottoms of her breasts. "'Tis one thing to be a virgin and another entirely to have never been kissed before last night. Yet, you played the seductress with skill, love."

"Me?" She pushed him away and he sat back in the grass. "Why did you kiss me just now?"

His chest suddenly moved as if with silent laughter. He leaned on his forearms and looked up at her. "I kissed you because I could," he said.

He was not braced for the fist that struck him on the chin. A whisper of movement that had alerted him just as he glimpsed a facer coming his way. With lightning-quick reflexes, he caught her other hand, which held a rock. His senses had been so ill tuned that it took him that long to realize how far he'd let down his guard. It took him another breath to realize what had just happened before he had the foresight to wrestle her to the ground.

Rose couldn't believe it as her cloak entangled around his limbs. "Get off me! Bastard!"

"My God, Rose." For all his fury at that moment, his was a gentler hold than she deserved. "Tell me you did not just attempt to bash me in the head with that stone."

"I have every right to kill you for what you have done to me! You would do the same. Tell me you would not!"

Glaring into his eyes, she could only wonder whose heroism was being tested more as he held himself against her. "Do not tempt me to take more of what you already lament losing, Rose. Be thankful I am such a saint."

"You are the devil! Do not think that last night will ever happen again."

"Ah, so you got what ye wanted from me, did you, love?"

She stilled beneath him. "I have no idea what you are speaking—"

"Look into your soul and ask yourself why you let me go so far. I am a man, Rose," he said softly, a warning now, for he recognized the danger to her, even if she did not. "An ungodly one at that. You gave me your virtue and I want to know why."

She turned her head. "Would you have preferred that I let you rape me?"

His eyes narrowed as he wrestled his hands around her fists. "Do you think last night was remotely close to rape, love?"

"You *knew* I was an innocent."

"Aye, I did. But did you? And I am not talking in the physical sense. Is it some sort of vengeance against your father you seek? His virtuous, convent-raised daughter sullied by a Kerr." His eyes cut into her like shards of glass. "No doubt 'twill prove a grave dishonor to the noble Lancaster name when people learn the warden's daughter was ravished by a barbaric Scotsman. Your father's humiliation would be complete. All prospects for marriage of his aristocratic daughter will be gone and he will send you away. An interesting scenario, if Hereford cares a whit what state you are in when delivered."

"Get off me!"

"Do you really believe you are worth so little? Look at me, Rose."

Tears sprang to her eyes. "Nay!"

He forced her chin around. "The more I have been considering the problem you present me, the more I have come to realize that if Hereford thought for one moment you were alive, he would never have stopped looking for you."

"If you are implying that he and Friar Tucker are in some kind of unholy alliance . . . you are wrong. Do not dare defame a good man. Do not *dare*!"

"You are worth a great deal to your father. Kirkland Park belonged to your mother's side of the family. You are your great-grandfather's heir, Rose."

"Then perhaps Kirkland Park is important enough to my father that I can trade it all to buy my freedom. And perhaps . . . you are both brigands equally at fault for the events that have transpired. You will probably kill each other and I will be free."

Roxburghe sat back, and she pushed away from him, desperate to scramble from his reach. She could feel the stitches tear, but she didn't care as she backed away.

"You knew about your inheritance," he said. "I thought you did not. I thought you should know the truth, Rose."

"Did you think your revelation would turn me against the only man I truly love and who has protected me?" she said. "Or is kidnapping and . . ." she could not say the word *rape* for the very meaning made a lie of what had happened between them last night. "Is abducting me not enough for you?"

He unfurled to his height and braced his feet as if he faced a broadside. For a tense second he stood there, then the expression left his face, as if it were so easy to toss away his emotions like much unwanted fodder. "Even if you are a 'Fallen Woman,' your fortune is still intact. Papa will welcome you with open arms."

Then he walked past her and out of the glade.

And she hated herself for not hating him.

Chapter 7

Ruark finished saddling the horse. He leaned on his elbows across the top of the saddle and watched Rose. Wrapped in the cloak, as remote as sunlight, she sat stiffly on a rock staring across the meadow. She'd been so still for the past half hour, that a family of gray buntings hopped around her feet pecking in the grass as if she were naught but stone.

He should not have said anything to her, he realized. He should not have cared. He should not care now.

Yet, there had been something in her manner when he had told her about her inheritance, the color that darkened her cheekbones, the wariness in her eyes that did not square with her response. Clearly, she loved Tucker. She would defend him against Ruark no matter what the truth was.

Ruark's gaze lingered on her sunset-colored hair. He could not be near her without experiencing an array of unfamiliar emotions.

Last night she had awakened in a dream, put her hand on his heart, and he had been momentarily lost. He didn't care about the reasons she had turned to him. She may not have even recognized them at first.

He didn't care that she had been a virgin.

Last night nothing else had mattered.

A flash of irritation betrayed itself. Hereford's daughter, of all women, he groaned, and he lusted like a Lothario, forceful and possessive. Lost in the fire between them. Aye, he burned, even now as his gaze fixed on her profile, her tumble-down hair a contradiction of veiled innocence that framed her face and a mouth that tasted better than the finest Scots' whisky.

Now he found himself wanting to protect her the way one safeguarded a fragile treasure that belonged solely to him.

When had she become his responsibility?

The moment she had risked her life to dive into a river rather than come back with him.

Ruark mounted the black and pulled alongside Rose beside the pond. His shadow fell over her and she turned sharply to look up at him. Without a word, he held out his hand, and she stood and faced him. Her hands clutched the edges of her cloak, and his heart thudded at an uneven pace as he awaited her to take his hand. He removed his boot from the tread.

"We have been here long enough," he said.

She laid her small hand in his larger one, lifted her bare foot into the stirrup, and he hoisted her sideways onto his lap, surprising her. Perhaps she had expected him to put her at his back. Readjusting his boot in the tread, he reached around her for the reins. He was not polite enough to keep his body from touching hers as he let his arms brush her breasts, gratified that despite her anger, he could still affect her physically. That despite her silence he was not the only one in torment.

Holding the reins loosely in one hand and steadying her with his other arm, he nudged the horse through a stream and down a gradual incline. Even before he urged the horse into a lope, he was aware of the soft warm bounce of her bottom on his thighs and of her breasts snug against his forearm. The only thing he knew for certain, as he beat down an unseemly arousal, was that he was in danger of embarrassing himself.

Ruark kept the horse off the main road. For three long hours, they saw nothing but open meadows broken intermittently by wooded thickets. The once bright afternoon sky dimmed to gold. Neither he nor Rose broke the silence.

Sunlight warmed the scent of pine and moss and had burned away the mist from the woodland floor by the time the black gelding crested a woodsy hill in late afternoon. Ruark reined in the horse and, with his arm around Rose as she slept with her head against his shoulder, he stopped atop the knoll overlooking the last part of his journey. A number of rabbits looked up from the grass and scattered, along with a pair of speckled does. A chill afternoon breeze washed over him. He felt Rose shiver. Even asleep, she resisted him when he pulled her cloak tighter around her body. He adjusted her on his lap and nudged the horse with his heels.

The last hour had put him in an open meadow where the early summer grass was green and brown cattle grazed. Near a crossroads marked with three weathered stone crosses beneath the branches of a Rowan tree, he turned east and took a little-used road overgrown with oak and scrubby pine. He was familiar with the roads, vales, and hills between the border and Stonehaven. He had traveled this area often as a younger man. He passed the crumbling stone walls of what had once been an old Roman fort. It was a world of contrasts, sitting between splendor and ruin. Death and rebirth. Past and present.

A parallel to his existence. And probably hers, he thought as he glanced at the sleeping woman in his arms.

For his entire life, events or people had tried to dictate or shape the way he lived. Only when he'd been at sea had he truly felt free. He could understand only too well Rose's yearning to be free of society's restraints, for he recognized himself. He was back now in Scotland in a world he'd not known since he was seventeen. For thirteen years, he had lived life like a current of wind caught in the vortex of a storm, as if his next breath would be his last, taunting fate, only to run into headwind now. Here, he was as ruled by the consequences of his station as Rose was by hers.

Again, he pondered how Friar Tucker had kept her hidden all these years, and what he held over Hereford to see it done. It was true Hereford had been away from England for most of Rose's life, but a man like Hereford did nothing that did not first benefit him.

At last, the familiar rush of water sounded from a distance and Ruark shifted his thoughts. Another two miles and he was following the Teviot tributary that would eventually take him home.

They had been riding on the southern edge of Kerr land since earlier that afternoon. He hadn't been back from sea long enough to feel anything but a vague sense of responsibility that this all now belonged to him. Everything that was before him.

His attention on the horizon, Ruark suddenly reined in the horse.

Rose stirred in his arms, drawing his gaze from the distant copse to her face as she opened her eyes. A pheasant suddenly started in the air from the long grass across the vale that edged the thicket below. "What is it?" she whispered, alarmed.

His every sense alert, he walked the horse three paces

and stopped. "This part of our journey together has come to an end."

She turned back to him. A corner of his mouth tipped. "Close your cloak. We are about to have company."

As if on cue, the distant sound of approaching riders carried to them on the late-afternoon breeze, growing more ominous as the first group came into sight over the hill. "Should we not hide?"

"Not from this bunch. You are about to meet the rest of the infamous Kerr clan."

A moment later, a horde of riders thundered over the incline—he couldn't count them all, they were so many—fanning out as they neared. Rose gasped at the fierce sight of them and pressed her back against his chest as if one man could stand against so many. Most were wild-looking, wearing leather trews, or were tartan-clad with their saddles and baldrics dangling with all manner of weaponry and muskets, and looking like the violent revier clans of old. They reined in their mounts and the air filled with the din and dust of their arrival.

Duncan broke rank. His shirt, damp from the mist that clung to the summer air, shaped the weight and height of the man as tall as Ruark himself.

"Did I no' tell ye he would come this way?" someone in the group called. "And with our prize in hand, too."

A ripple of bawdry laughter ran through the ranks as Duncan guided his gray horse through the long grass and scrub and stopped a few feet in front of Ruark. "Our spotters saw the pair of ye come across the glen hours ago."

Duncan shifted his gaze to Rose, who was pressing against Ruark as if that would shield her from the man's perusal. Duncan leaned into the saddle and grinned. "Lady

Roselyn. You're a comely lass for a bluidy Lancaster."

"I need a second horse, Duncan," Ruark said. He *needed* Rose off his lap. He needed his hands free.

Duncan motioned to someone behind him. Jason had been with Ruark and his men at the abbey. Jason must have ridden through the night to get here before him.

"You were no' at the rendezvous point last night, nephew. Jason and the others returned this afternoon with your red stallion and some concern that ye went missing over yonder falls."

"As you can see, I did not."

A moment later, Ruark dismounted and put Rose on the back of a bay gelding behind the younger man.

Ruark lowered his voice and asked the lad, "Where is Colum?"

"He sent us back with the stallion yesterday." Jason also lowered his voice as his gaze found Duncan some paces away speaking to another. "Duncan intended to ride across the border tonight. If we had not seen you . . ." Jason's voice trailed but he didn't have to tell Ruark anything more.

For a moment, he felt fury, but then boxed the anger as his gaze found Rose. Though her green eyes were bright and her shoulders held high, she looked weary and frightened, surrounded as she was by men who would need little provocation to harm Hereford's daughter.

Ruark mounted and reined the horse around until they were thigh to thigh, his fingers fisting around the reins as if that would keep him from touching her, for he recognized only too well the warring faction separating her future from his.

He also recognized that though they might still be adversaries, they had never been enemies.

"We will reach Stonehaven after nightfall," he told her. His impassive glance took in Jason. Then with a nudge of his heels, he lunged past Rose to take his place at the head of his men, leaving her horse to fall into place in the middle of the group.

Whatever else he may have thought, leaving her with Jason, he took no chance she would escape him again.

Stonehaven appeared in the mist-shrouded horizon as the amber-rippled clouds faded to crimson in the western sky. With two tower houses that flanked a baronial hall of gray stone and blue slates, the magnificent house commanded a view of the countryside.

That the place was vast was Rose's first astounded impression. From a dozen chimneys, white wood smoke unfurled into the chilled air. Mullioned casements embellished the structure, the sinking sun touching the myriad of windows and turning the panes amber. A circular carriage sweep joined the road near the front hall, a breathtaking parkland and pine forest at the back. The house was grand and as ostentatious as the oldest baronial estates, an unexpected contrast to the borderland chieftain himself.

She found herself looking for Roxburghe. They had not spoken since he left to ride at the head of his men. One of his men had given him a cloak and with the exception of his height, he looked much like the unshaven bedraggled dozens who surrounded him. She had glimpsed him once as he laughed over something his uncle said, but she had looked away when he glanced over to find her watching him.

Duncan rode beside him now. She had not liked the way his uncle had looked at her in the glade. There had been no gentleness or kindness in his hazel eyes, and the humor briefly glimpsed in his manner had been rooted in something dark and angry. She would not want to be alone in the same room with him, a born-and-bred Scotsman and inherently dangerous to the English.

The troop soon divided and Roxburghe rode with a dozen others into an embellished stone courtyard away from the main entrance of the estate. Within minutes retainers poured outside to meet the heavily armed men. Roxburghe dismounted as two grooms rushed to take the reins of his horse, and after that, she lost him among the confusion and noise as a dozen barking dogs joined in the chorus of male voices.

The man with whom she'd ridden helped her dismount. Barely able to stand, she clasped the edges of the cloak tightly against her as she looked around and awaited instruction. Men were still mounted, armed with swords in their belts, all laughing and in high spirits, and casting her an occasional glance that caused a stab of apprehension in her chest.

"I am to bring you inside, Lady Roselyn," the young man she had ridden with said after speaking to a servant. "If ye can no' walk . . . ?"

The thought that anyone would put his hands on her brought her up. "I can walk. You are Jason, correct?" she asked, remembering the name Roxburghe had called him.

"Aye, mum. Lord Roxburghe's third cousin on our grandfather's side." He executed a brief bow. "This way if ye will, my lady. We are to go through another less-used entrance."

She might be a guest, but she was an unwelcome one.

Once inside, Rose felt the warmth of the entrance hall. She swept her gaze over the tall archway and wood beams that braced the weight of the ceiling and saw it magnificently decorated with flags and the Roxburghe coat of arms, which, ironically, was the mythical beast

Chimera, a fire-breathing dragon with the head of a lioness and the tail of a serpent. The room was a three-story half-timbered hall with lead windows. Flemish tapestries covered the stone walls. A stairway carved from heavy oak led to a second level where a forest of horns, antlers, and stuffed boars' heads glared back at her from amid the aged weaponry on the walls.

Someone came up to Jason and told her he was to take her to the dining hall. "But his lordship told me to take her to her quarters . . ."

"Duncan said to bring her . . ."

She was taken from Jason and escorted through doors down a corridor. The curious unnatural silence that preceded her was worse than the noise in the courtyard. Her breeches were damp where the injury had opened, but she couldn't think of that right now. Her gaze took in the walls and doors as she desperately sought to memorize her surroundings.

The man delivered her into the dining hall. Tall windows reflected back the torchlight flickering on the walls. Dozens of men were there sitting at planked tables as if waiting—for what she didn't know, and she was more frightened because it seemed they awaited her. Hounds lounged around the great hearth and, as if sensing the sudden tension in the room, came to their feet. She took a startled step backward. One command would send them loping across the room and at her throat. But the men, though fierce-looking, did not seem brutal to her as their eyes fell on her—merely hardened. Their voices rose around her.

She tightened her clammy hands in her cloak. She did not see their laird among the men, but she knew he must have come up behind her, for the men's gazes went to the door and a terrible quiet came over the hall.

She stopped her knees from buckling. She stopped herself from stepping near him as if he had the power to protect her. Indeed the only thing that stopped her from turning into his arms was the contemplation of that thought and the realization that she would not be at Stonehaven at all if not for him.

"You had better have a bloody good reason for bringing her in here, Duncan." She heard the quiet fury in Lord Roxburghe's voice.

His uncle stepped forward. He still wore his leather trews and plaid that she had seen him in. Mud caked his boots and woolen hose. He looked even larger in the room that seemed more filled with shadows and ice than warmth from so many bodies. "If this is Hereford's daughter, then we will know it tonight. If no' then some of us are finished with negotiations." His eyes pierced hers. "If ye are innocent, we're no' here to hurt ye, lass."

"Innocent?" she heard herself whisper in panic.

What were her crimes, she wanted to shout at them.

An older woman was brought to stand before Rose. "Do you know who this is?" Duncan asked the woman, and his voice was surprisingly kind, as if he spoke to a child.

A black shawl covered the woman's head and shoulders. She wore black muslin. But her eyes were a kindly blue and did not look as if she meant her harm. Rose did not know the woman. She had never seen her before.

"My name is Anaya Fortier, mum," she said, tears in her eyes. "I was the Countess Hereford's handmaiden."

Rose didn't understand. "My mother? You knew my mother?"

"Aye, mum." Mrs. Fortier looked first at Ruark, then Duncan. "She is the image of her mam. The very image. There is no mistakin'. Beautifil like her, she is. No mistakin'."

Behind the woman, the murmurs grew to a low din. "And her holdin' the Lancaster wealth." Someone shouted something about riding to Alnwick Castle tonight with new terms of trade. "She will no' be any good to Hereford dead. Aye, I swear he'll trade now."

Roxburghe moved behind her. "Are you finished?"

His words effectively shocked the men to silence.

His hands dropped on her shoulders. "You'll swear that Lady Roselyn should pay for her father's sins? With what? Her life?" He moved her behind him. "Aye, we have cause to celebrate tonight. We also have much work to be done."

Roxburghe turned and placed a hand at her arm. "Now, if you don't mind, we can save the questions for later tonight, I need to get our guest to her room."

"Aye, she's a comely lass," a voice called. "Ye can take her to my room."

The men laughed and some of the tension broke. A man in the front raised a mug. "To our laird," he said into the lull. "And to his success."

A sober toast followed, and no one seemed to recognize the tension inside Roxburghe as he took Rose by the elbow, his touch firm yet gentle, and pulled her into the corridor, where Jason was awaiting him.

Roxburghe said nothing to her. What could he say? What could *she* say?

They had reached the entry hall. A woman stood on the bottom stair tread, her hands at her side, her eyes a turbulent blue. She wore burgundy silk trimmed in black lace. Even with red-rimmed eyes, and her hair hanging down her back as if it had not been properly brushed, no one could mistake her for less than a lady. "Then 'twas no rumor . . ." the woman's trembling words stumbled out of her mouth. "Hereford's daughter lives." Her eyes glared accusingly at Roxburghe. "How could you bring her into my house as if she were a guest?"

Rose startled. The woman must be the dowager countess, though she looked too young to be the mother of a twelve-year-old son. Not even the swish of beautiful silk overshadowed the hatred in the woman's eyes as she strode toward Rose, and she stood motionless, saying nothing.

"She is not to be here in my house. Do ye understand?"

Two steps more and Roxburghe was suddenly between them, catching the woman in his arms. "Enough, Julia." He held the woman with gentle strength all the more apparent as she struggled. "Lady Roselyn is my concern, not yours."

"Have ye lived among the Sassenach for so long that ye do not see the grave offense to *me*?" She clasped her fist against her breasts. "Does my son sleep on a soft feather bed with warm blankets, food, and servants to do his bidding? Will he live better now that we have that woman beneath our roof? Where is my justice that you dare bring her into this house?"

"This is not about justice. This is about retrieving Jamie alive. Do not dictate to me again who I can and cannot bring into my house."

"Your house! You have never cared about Stonehaven . . . or this house! Why would you care for my son?"

For a moment, Roxburghe said nothing. Then his hand went to Rose's arm as he handed her over to Jason. "Help Lady Roselyn to her quarters in the east wing. McBain will be by later to tend to her leg. Then bring Anaya Fortier to me. And Jason . . . I am the only person here from whom you receive your orders."

The lad nodded. "Aye, my lord."

Rose felt dizzy and sick, but as Jason's hand came to

her elbow, she drew her arm back with as much dignity as she could manage in her state of exhaustion. She neither wanted nor needed kindness from Ruark Kerr or his minions, and could ascend the stairs on her own.

Ruark waited until Rose was out of sight of the hallway before turning to face Julia. With tears in her eyes, she took a step back as if he would strike her. The action sobered him, perhaps because his father had been known to own a heavy hand on matters of emotional discourse. He was nothing like his father.

"Do you think I am going to hit you, Julia? Is that what you think?"

"Oh, Ruark . . ." She buried her face in her hands. "I don't know what I am thinking or saying any longer. I . . . I don't know. Truly, I am sorry . . ."

"For what? For a mother's anger and frustration? For something that was not your doing to begin with?" He pulled her into his arms. "Christ, Julia . . ."

"I am lost. I thought I was strong. I am not . . . My son is all I have in this life."

She continued to weep. Closing his eyes, Ruark remembered a time in his life when he had always held her thus. She had once been his closest friend . . . before life had changed them both as abruptly as a summer storm changed the landscape after a flood. Yet, thirteen years suddenly did not seem so long ago.

He held his palm to her head. Julia dabbed a tear from her eye with the tip of finger. "Do you trust me?" he asked.

"I have always trusted you."

He tilted her chin and looked into once-familiar blue eyes. "Except when you are frightened."

She pulled away from him. He had not meant the words

to be more than what they were, an attempt to give her hope. But the past lay between them, a memory of the last time he had come to her when she had asked for help.

Aye, they both remembered well enough what she had once cost him, but he felt guilt to realize how soon he had put aside her fate after being banished from Scotland. She had changed much from the girl she had been. He saw the circles beneath her eyes, but he also saw strength in a mother's determination to protect her son.

"There was a time your da would have killed ye for touchin' her as ye are," Duncan said from behind them.

He stood leaning in the entry-hall doorway, a chalice of wine in his hand. Julia stepped around Ruark. "Duncan, please . . ."

Ruark stopped her with his hand on her arm. Then gentled his grip. "Go upstairs, Julia."

She nodded, then, tearing her eyes from Ruark's, looked past him at Duncan before walking up the stairs. When she was out of sight, Ruark faced his uncle. "If you have something on your mind, tell me now, because you and I have had this argument before."

"Jamie is on my mind."

"As he is on mine."

"As long as we are clear aboot your priorities, lad. You've been a mite distracted since ye put that Sassenach wench on the back of Jason's horse."

"Her name is Lady Roselyn."

"I do no' care if she is the good Queen Mary herself come back from the dead. As long as ye remember her purpose here."

Ruark held Duncan's probing gaze. "I do not take my responsibility lightly. Never question my priorities or loyalty to this family again."

"Then while you're fookin' that bonny lass upstairs, do no' be forgettin' her father has been none too kind to those who call themselves Kerr."

For a moment, as Ruark set his hand on the balustrade, he thought he could kill Duncan. "Tell me, Uncle," he said with quiet menace. "Why was Jamie with your crowd, raiding cattle on Hereford's land in the first place? A little bit of mischief and larceny could have been had much nearer without forcing a confrontation with a battalion of English dragoons."

Duncan wiped a sleeve across his mouth, his eyes momentarily shuttered. He set the goblet on the breakfront next to the doorway. "The lad is old enough to learn a Kerr's ways." He walked to the bottom of the stairway. "'Tis my sworn oath to make a man of him, just as it was mine to do the same of you. I'll no' be apologizing to ye or any man."

"Know this now, Uncle! Lady Roselyn is under my protection."

He turned and took two steps up the stairs.

"What has got in your craw?" Duncan carefully asked from behind him. "When ye left here ye were ready to tie the chit to a stake. No man would have argued your right to do so."

Ruark descended a step. "You were about to take raiders over the border today . . . against my explicit order to wait one week. The last I looked, five days does not make a week. Hereford deserves a place in hell for many crimes, but I do not intend to send the rest of this family with him. And that includes Jamie and the two lads with him."

Ruark stared down at his uncle from his place on the stairs, a man he had both loved and hated for most of his life. But Ruark had come to believe of late that it was too simple a thing to throw blame at another for one's ails. Though most would claim the skirmishes started with the English, all of them seemed to forget that it was a bout of cattle raiding that got Jamie caught in the first place.

"A new letter of terms will be drawn up for Jamie's release. You will leave tomorrow to dispatch the terms to Hereford."

Ruark wasn't asking, a fact his uncle recognized and fully appreciated. "I would have gone without your telling me, Ruark. I do not take my responsibility lightly either," Duncan said. "I know that boy is there because of me. Do ye think I would no' trade places with him if I could? With any of those two lads with him? Do ye no' think I blame myself every bluidy day?"

Some of Ruark's anger dissipated and his mind seemed to momentarily clear. Jamie's life needed to be the most important thing between them for now.

Then at the sound of merrymaking in the dining hall down the long corridor, Duncan's mouth tightened, as his eyes revealed a less subtle sentiment. "There's family and friends in the dining hall willin' to give their lives for ye, Ruark," he said. "Do no' be forgettin' that."

Duncan left the entry hall, and watching his uncle go, Ruark swore beneath his breath.

"Duncan means well," Julia said on the landing above him. "He loves this family, and has practically been a father to Jamie, as he was to you. You of all people know the kind of man your father was."

Ruark did not intend to discuss Duncan or his father with anyone. What was between him and his uncle would remain that way.

She reached out her hand to his arm as he ascended the stairs and passed, turning him. "You have risked much bringing Hereford's daughter here . . ."

"Did you think I would do less because the boy is your son, Julia?"

She shook her head. Her wet eyes took in the gallery at the top of the stairs, where nine generations of Roxburghe earls stared down at her from their various places of honor up and down the long antechamber. His father's portrait stood at the other end. With an effort, she finally straightened, her gaze darting to the shadows where Duncan had disappeared.

"He has no' been the same since your father died. Duncan blamed Hereford from the beginning. Duncan was not taking the Kerrs across the Borders for a bit of cattle lifting when Jamie was captured. He was taking them to burn Kirkland Park to the ground. They ran into dragoons."

She wrapped her hand around Ruark's forearm. "Make no mistake, Ruark. Ye may hold the Roxburghe title, but 'tis Duncan's fealty that makes you laird. Or you would no' be so."

Ruark smiled, his eyes softening briefly, for she had meant the warning sincerely. "I know, Julia." Noise from the dining hall drew her up. "Now go to your chambers," he said. "Downstairs is no place for a woman right now."

She nodded. She turned in a swish of silk and expensive French perfume, and he found himself thinking of lilacs and springtime instead.

Turning away to go to his own chambers to wash and change, he sought to unravel emotions that were becoming increasingly complicated in his mind.

Julia had been only partially right when she said that Ruark might hold the Roxburghe title but 'twas Duncan's fealty to him that made him laird.

Except time and the whims of fortune had changed his life. He was not the man he had once been when she had asked his help to save her from a marriage to his father. And Ruark made it a rule never to play another's game again.

As his thoughts turned to Rose, ensconced not so far from his own chambers in the east wing, he knew only that he had already decided the fate of Hereford's beautiful daughter.

Chapter 8

Descending the path to the stable, Ruark still wore a leather jack and the red-and-hunter-green plaid, border-raiding attire, reminiscent of a long night of drinking with his men. The rain had dissipated just after dawn, but under the plum trees, the ground was still damp. Ahead of him, a half dozen stone buildings appeared out of the early-morning mist.

The stable block and distant carriage house was Angus's dominion here at Stonehaven, a man in whose capable hands every Roxburgh earl of the last four decades had entrusted the care and breeding of his horses. Ruark was no different.

As he entered the stable, all around him the air was redolent of sweet hay, saddle soap, and linseed oil, and the ever-present pungency of manure that one found with a careless step. The grooms and younger stable lads mucking the stalls looked up as he strode past them, his thick boot heels echoing on the flagstone floor. He carried a note in his pocket that Colum had delivered to him shortly after Duncan left this morning. Ruark's ally, friend, and second-in-command, Colum was one of the few men Ruark trusted with his life.

Colum had returned during the night. He had a room at the house but rarely used it.

Nor, being British, did he take part in ceremonial or clan activities, preferring to bide his time in more favorable pursuits. Thus, Ruark found him asleep on a pile of straw spooned with a naked woman. They lay tangled in woolen blankets. The light picked out their shoulders and the curve of the woman's breast.

No matter the place or the circumstance, Colum managed to find a woman. But even with his angel's face and crown of golden curls, he looked nothing like the gently born solicitor he was when Ruark rescued him from a press-gang ten years ago near a dockside chophouse in London.

Ruark made no attempt at stealth as he knelt next to the two sleeping forms. Colum slept with a ten-inch dirk beneath his head, and as many a man had discovered, he took exception to being abruptly awakened. But then so did Ruark.

"Bloody hell, Ruark," Colum mumbled without opening his eyes. "You couldn't allow me an hour's respite?"

Ruark rubbed the soft fur of an orange tabby that had run up to him as he crouched in the straw. "I need you to take Friar Tucker a letter."

Colum disengaged himself from the sleeping maid and focused a jaundiced eye on Ruark's face. "Did we not just return from the abbey?" he kept his voice low. "Did I not just spend two days searching the rocks beneath a waterfall for your blood-spattered remains? Did I not just spend those same two days trying to evade a platoon a' dragoons chasing the thief who stole their captain's horse?"

The girl stirred, burrowing her head into the blanket. Ruark picked up the tabby and nodded toward the door. Throwing back the covers, Colum reached for his shirt and breeches. He dressed in seconds, then jerked on his boots. He grabbed his sword and baldric and followed Ruark out of the stall.

Giving the feline one final stroke, Ruark set it down. "Duncan left an hour ago for Alnwick Castle. He is bringing terms to Hereford."

Ruark withdrew a letter from inside his shirt. "With as fast as news travels, Hereford may well know that we have his daughter before our dispatch reaches him. If she is as valuable to him as I think she is, we won't be riding with a contingency of men anywhere. He will be coming to us. I need you to give Tucker this letter before that happens."

Colum reluctantly accepted the letter as one might a smelly boot. "Will Tucker read this before or after he does something contrary to his Christian beliefs, as in, takes a dirk to my heart?" he said in a low voice.

"I suggest you make sure 'tis before. I need to know if what Tucker said to me back at the abbey still stands. He will know to what I refer."

"Aye, your concern for my welfare ever endears you to me." He studied the letter. "Have you had a sudden change of heart?" Colum said, when he recognized Ruark's intent. "The doors at the abbey are not that thick. I heard much of what was said in that room. Including the part where you told Tucker you would never join Kerr and Lancaster blood in marriage. Unless there is something else to which Tucker referred?"

"Give Tucker that letter."

Colum wrapped a hand around Ruark's arm. "'Tis no simple matter here, Ruark." His hushed words came out in a rasp. "The girl is not of age. Hereford will merely have the marriage annulled and gleefully bring you up on charges of rape. She may be long lost, but she is still the daughter of an English earl and 'tis English law that binds you in this matter. You would need Hereford's permissi—"

"Do tell. I do not need a lecture about the marriage act and English edicts. She is valuable to Hereford. Therefore she is valuable to me."

"Bollocks. Gold is valuable to Hereford. This is madness. Make the exchange and be done with this. You never planned to remain at Stonehaven when this was over. By your own words you came back to make Jamie your heir. Why do you care?" Colum's eyes narrowed. "You actually *want* the girl," he said in a loud whisper. "*Christ!* Have you already bedded her? Hell, Ruark . . . What did she do to you when you followed her into that river?" He burst out in a laugh. "I've not seen you hold a *tendre* for a female since that old cat that used to roam the hold and bring mice to your door as an offering of her fondness for you."

"Fook you, Colum. I am in no mood for your humor this day."

Ruark was in no mood for a bloody lecture on his motives. He didn't need to tell Colum a thing. Hell, he couldn't explain half of it to himself, especially after a night of drinking. Except he was coldly sober.

Colum tucked the letter in his shirt. "What if Hereford denies the girl as his daughter?"

"Anaya Fortier saw Roselyn Lancaster last night and confirmed that she is the image of her mother, Elena. We have the right girl. But something does not feel right. I have my suspicions Hereford has known from the beginning where his daughter was. I just don't know what Tucker has over him. Hereford would never have allowed Rose to remain at the abbey."

"He would have if he spent most of his life at sea and

it suited him to let the world think she was dead. Many men send their daughters to convents."

Not Hereford.

Colum left for Hope Abbey and Ruark returned to the manor. Having dismissed the staff earlier, he found the dining hall empty. He walked past tables piled high with plates and glasses, empty whisky bottles, wine, and half-filled mugs of stale ale on his way upstairs to his room. The dull light of a new day pressed against the tall windows in the gallery and somewhere Ruark heard the chime of a clock nine times. But as he entered his chambers, his mind returned to Rose and the problem she presented him.

Maybe Colum was right. He wasn't in his right mind. He had not returned to England to acquire the responsibilities of a wife or an estate.

He had planned to return to the *Black Dragon* and to the sea. He had not wanted Stonehaven's responsibilities.

For his entire life, events and people had dictated and shaped the way he lived. Only when he'd lived on the sea had he truly been free. Now he was back in Scotland, thrust back into a world he'd not known just how much he'd missed until he arrived on her windswept shores. He'd told Rose the truth when he had said he believed in very little, but something had changed inside him since he'd returned to the abbey as old yearnings and wants began to push through the holes in his heart, the way bilge water pushed through rotten oakum that plugged the deck of his ship. He recognized the danger of sinking.

And he recognized that Rose was the lightning rod at the center of gathering storm clouds.

One did not go into a storm with a leaky vessel. The *Black Dragon* had barely survived more than one squall, while under press of canvas, that snapped rigging and nearly laid her on her beam ends like so much flotsam. Until now, he had survived everything fate had thrown at him.

Was he making the wrong choice here?

He walked to the dresser and opened the top drawer. He pulled out the neatly bundled letters tied with blue ribbon, all the letters Jamie had sent him, scribing bits and pieces of his life with boyish pride and how he waited for the day he would be able to join Ruark at sea and be just like his older brother.

What kind of example had he ever been to anyone?

"Does Julia know you've kept Jamie's letters?"

He turned toward the voice. Mary Duff, his housekeeper, stood in the doorway of his bedroom.

Ruark retied the ribbon and replaced the bundle in the upper drawer. "I am sure I have you to thank for seeing that these found me," he said.

"That lad saved every trinket ye ever sent him. Ye can thank Duncan that your father never found out. This whole business has been unnerving fer us all."

Mary was a gray-haired woman, as stout of body as spirit, with a bearing to match the steel in her eyes. She had practically raised him after a long illness killed his mother. She wore a white apron pinned to her woolen plaid skirts, still too clean to have just come from the kitchens. That, and the fact that she had followed him to his dressing room, gave Ruark pause as he dropped into a plum velvet chair to remove his boots.

He leaned an elbow on his knee. "I am bloody weary. If something other than need to turn down my bed has brought you to these chambers, it can wait. I intend to sleep all day and into tomorrow morning."

"I thought ye might have a mind to know, I found some

of your mam's older clothes for Lady Roselyn," Mary said with disapproval in her voice, clearly blaming him for their guest's disheveled state upon her arrival.

Ruark rose to his feet and yanked the loosely knotted cloth from around his neck. "You know enough of a woman's needs to see to hers, Mary."

"'Tis not as if she has an abundance of appropriate clothes."

"Then bring a dressmaker out here," Ruark said. "You have never needed my permission to do what you see fit."

"She has refused to eat."

Ruark did not take Rose for being nonsensical, and perhaps he was too exhausted to worry over her starving herself. Hunger was an ugly, violent thing with which to contend. "She will eat when she is hungry enough."

"Aye, mayhap, she will. Mayhap she won't. She is convinced someone will poison her. I do no' blame her either, seein' as how she was treated last night. She has no' spoken except to ask that we leave her alone. Last night she put a chair to the door only to remove it long enough this morning for me to arrange a tub be delivered. The child is frightened."

Ruark doubted it, but who was he to tell Mary that Rose was no child.

The scent of apple blossoms filled the bathing chamber as steam from a hot bath dissipated in the air. There was one window in the room, high on the wall that was now Rose's prison. She could see a bright patch of blue sky beyond, yet the glittering morning held nothing familiar to her that spoke of home.

She sat on the rim of a beautiful porcelain tub that had been delivered to her room earlier. She had never bathed in anything larger than a wooden hip tub before.

With her calves submerged, she dribbled droplets from a sponge across her arms and breasts, careful of the wound on her outer thigh.

Last night, she had fallen exhausted into bed, curled into a ball, and slept.

She had not cried, and she did not cry now. She sat in the liquid warmth, thinking about her mornings at the abbey and the settled peace and safety of all that she had left behind.

She wanted to slide beneath the surface and experience the sensation of hot water enveloping her. But for her injury, perhaps she would have.

Already she regretted sending supper and breakfast away. With the exception of the bread Rose had taken off the supper tray last night, she'd had very little to eat or drink in days. But there was nothing to be done for it. She had seen the hate in Lady Roxburghe's and Duncan Kerr's eyes.

Knowing something of medicinal herbs, Rose knew of a hundred ways a person could make another suffer without actually killing.

She had never been the object of hatred before. Last night, standing in the dining hall, the object of aversion and scorn, she had hated Roxburghe for bringing her to this point and putting her in a position to feel such wretched shame, when he was the very devil himself all the way up to his silver earring.

As she scrubbed her arms and rinsed the sweet-smelling soap from her limbs, she swore she would not think about the other woman downstairs who said she knew Rose's mother.

Or the way Roxburghe had held her in his arms and why, despite her scrubbing, she could still feel his touch on her body. She dug her blunted fingernails into the sponge, remembering she had dug them into Roxburghe's back that dark, stormy night in the glade as passion had consumed her. Had she left her mark on him? Would he remember her after she had gone from here?

She could not change anything now no matter how she wanted to forget it.

No doubt 'twill prove a grave dishonor to the noble Lancaster name when people learn the warden's daughter was ravished by a barbaric Scotsman.

The terrible words came back to swallow her now in her wretched despair as she struggled to buoy her thoughts and make sense of the last few days.

For she could not deny that Roxburghe had seen something of her heart when she had not. She could not deny that she had known about her inheritance years ago while looking for a book in Friar Tucker's library. Or that there were even darker forces inside her that she did not understand.

Something that was her own brand of vengeance against her father, a man whose actions had sent her mother to a cold, icy grave, and who now drove the passions of those here at Stonehaven.

But whatever her reasons for giving Roxburghe her innocence, he had been perfectly at ease with ravishing her. In her defense, his skillful kisses and hands had wrought the passion she had given him, and she believed that no sane woman could have resisted him. So perhaps, in the end, they had each taken from the other what they wanted, and it did not matter the reasons.

When Rose finished washing, she pulled a fresh-scented linen towel off the stool and stepped out of the tub. Last night she had combed the snarls out of her hair and plaited its length. It fell over her shoulder in a thick rope as she propped a foot on the tub and dried off in front of the stove. The injury had bled much and she was upset that she had somehow managed to tear one of the stitches. She felt dizzy and weak, partially from lack of food. The wound needed light and dry air to heal and so she left it unwrapped as she slid a nightdress over her head and felt it float down her body in a whisper of air.

Rose had met Stonehaven's stout housekeeper only briefly this morning when the footmen had delivered the tub. She had remained long enough to give the servants instructions and promise to find something suitable for her to wear, then Rose had asked them all to go away and leave her alone.

Turning from the tub, she caught her own reflection in the long cheval looking glass as she tied the laces. The garment Mrs. Duff had brought her barely covered the soft swell of her breasts, though it must have belonged to someone else tall, for it reached her ankles and wrists with a brush of white lace. Her pale skin in contrast to the bright green fabric held a beckoning luminosity in the light and Rose ran her palm absently down the smooth, shiny cloth. She had never seen fabric that could catch the firelight yet feel like cool water against her skin. She had not known that something so simple could make her look so astonishingly beautiful, and as she looked at herself in the glass, it was almost an affront to her that she should not look worn and despoiled from the trauma of her abduction and ravishment.

Intent upon the unhappy discourse of her thoughts, she did not at first see that there was someone else in the looking glass with her.

Roxburghe leaned his shoulder against the door connecting the bathing chambers to her bedroom, and she spun around, her first instinct to snatch back the towel, but it lay across the tub.

Even with his face half bathed in the shadows cast by the firelight in the other room, she had the vague impression he had been watching her for some time. He wore the red-and-green plaid she'd seen on his family coat of arms. With a day's growth of beard shadowing his jaw and his silver earing glinting in the light, he looked as disreputable as if he had been up all night plotting and planning murder and mayhem.

He folded his arms. "So you believe my household wishes to poison you."

Freeing herself from his gaze, she tried to step around him only to find his arm blocking her path. "I believe I consider these quarters sacrosanct from your intrusion, my lord."

A corner of his mouth lifted, but his eyes were as somber as night. "Little is sacrosanct at Stonehaven, especially what goes on in these chambers."

Rose attempted to push past him, but it was like trying to move stone. "Move aside."

"Or what?" he said, tilting her face into the light. "You haven't the strength to swat a fly. Have you suddenly decided to surrender the fight? You shock me, love."

"Surrender should make your task easier, should it not?"

He laughed. Hers was a silly remark and she winced at her melodrama, suddenly feeling like some overwrought heroine in the worst sort of book.

"I did not take you for being nonsensical, Rose. Wouldn't killing you rather defeat our purpose for bringing you here?"

A knock sounded on the door. Without moving, he called, "Enter."

The young girl who had helped plait Rose's hair last night pushed a heavily laden trundle cart into the room.

Roxburghe directed her to set the tray on the table nearest the hearth. The maid removed the silver domed lid covering the plate, revealing fruit and cheese and warm bread still steaming, then arranged two cups next to a silver carafe on the trundle cart. She lifted an inquiring gaze to her laird. With a subtle tip of his chin, he nodded and dismissed her.

After the maid left, Rose pressed her thumb to her temple and told his lordship to go away and leave her alone. "You are wasting your time."

But he paid her no heed as he swung her into his arms. "I am not my servants, Rose."

He carried her across the room to the table. She didn't bother protesting as he set her in a chair and then made himself comfortable across from her. She narrowed her eyes. "You cannot force me to eat your food."

He looked offended as he took up the fork and began eating. "Why would I force you to eat? What woman does not wish to have a smaller waist? Though I have seen you. *All of you*. And I think you look rather . . . fine."

It seemed incongruous to her that after everything he had put her through, here he was teasing her while she was half-dressed in her private chambers, and they should be bantering as if they were a married couple sharing intimacies and ways to murder the other.

"Not all poisons kill." She dared him to contradict her, while pride convinced her not to stare at the food or lick her lips. "I've worked with herbs and know certain ones can inflict great agony without causing death."

Visibly savoring a plump strawberry, he watched her watching him. "Then 'tis fortunate for you . . . and probably for us, that our herbal has fallen into disrepair. If someone wanted to make you suffer, they would have to do so with garlic and onions." He casually poured black . . . something into a porcelain cup. "We've an orangery in equal need of restoration if you'd care to see for yourself."

"Are you saying I am free to walk about?"

She watched him tip back the cup and drink. His Adam's apple bobbed with the flex of tendons on his neck as the warm liquid eased down his throat. Afterward, he dabbed the serviette at the corner of his mouth and gave her his full attention. She noted a small wet mark at the corner of his lip.

"I'm saying the incident with Julia was unfortunate, and for that, I apologize," he said. "It will not happen again. Neither will last night." He sat back in the chair. "Duncan departed this morning for Alnwick Castle to deliver new terms of trade to Hereford."

"I see." Now she understood Roxburghe's purpose for coming to her chambers. Her chest tightened. "Then I will soon meet my father? And this entire ordeal will be at an end."

"Aye, it will," he agreed.

"How long before the meeting?"

"Alnwick Castle is five, maybe six days' hard riding from Stonehaven. Two weeks perhaps before we hear," he said. "Then we go to Jedburgh."

Something in the tenor of his voice told her that no semblance of diplomacy remained between the two sides, and battle lines were about to be drawn. So be it.

"I have waited a long time," she said. "No matter what happens in the next few weeks, I would have this done with. But what I do not know and what I would have you answer is what happens to me if my father will not recognize me as his daughter and refuses your terms? Will I be free to leave here?"

Roxburghe was sprawled back in his chair, the cup in his hand, his expression unreadable, but for an instant, she thought she had seen something. "A disavowal from him of your existence? We both know that will not happen."

Damp tendrils of hair fell around her face and she tucked a strand behind her ear. "Until then, will you be testing all my food?"

He leaned forward. "Is that an open invitation to visit this room?"

"Surely, it matters little what I say," she replied in a disinterested voice. "I have no reputation left to lose."

"And after all the effort I have taken to safeguard your morals."

The heat of his gaze flared through her as warm as the air she breathed, as enticing as the scent of apple blossoms and cloves still lingering in her hair, like the scent she had smelled on him, as seductive as the dancing firelight.

Her disinterest in him was a lie. And he knew it.

Strangely, he was the first to look away as he reached for the carafe. "Has the fight gone out of you, Rose?"

She would not be much of an adversary if it had. Yet, perhaps it had gone out of her. She wondered absently what he was drinking, watching as he settled back into the chair and peered at her over the rim of the cup.

Deciding she would not dignify his action with curiosity, she looked away. "I would like to say something," she said.

She supposed it was her mood that was giving her a lofty feeling of detachment, as if she were floating above Roselyn Lancaster as a mere onlooker, indifferent to her emotional agonies. Her future no longer mattered. She would survive. She might be helpless now, but she would not always be so. The man sitting opposite her with the firelight on his face was equally unimportant to her. Except that he had done her a service and he should know.

"That night at the cemetery when you said my name

. . . you were the first person since I was a child who had ever spoken my full name aloud. You freed me," she said. "I no longer live in fear of discovery, of what will happen should my father find me. I no longer fear what people will say when they know the truth. The worst has happened. Someone has discovered the truth and I have survived."

She folded her hands in her lap. "But no matter what has transpired between us, our acquaintance will end soon, and I will be most content to go."

His was a relaxed pose but she could feel the tension inside him. "Indeed."

She narrowed her eyes. "At the very least, the ring you stole from me is valuable. Mayhap you can trade us *both* for your brother."

"Mayhap I will keep both you and the ring, and send Hereford to the devil where he belongs. I could, you know."

"Why?" she asked.

"Why would I keep you? Or why would I kill him?"

"Why would you keep the ring?"

He laughed. "Ah, the deeper, more insightful question." His pause was infinitesimal. "Because it is something of yours, I suppose. And you want it back."

She felt the minutest hint of irritation and something else.

"However . . . I am not as black hearted as 'twould seem," he said quietly, his fingers absently edging the rim of the cup. "You need not be locked in this room. I have a library at your disposal. A large garden if you wish to take your morning and evening constitutionals there. A dining room if you choose to take your meals there. My home is yours."

"You do not ask my parole not to escape?"

The faintest suggestion of humor traced the line of his lips. "Four hundred acres of open parkland surround Stonehaven. Unless you look like a fat wooly sheep, you would have a difficult time blending into the scenery. Nor could I guarantee your safety beyond Stonehaven's borders. Though I suggest you allow your leg to heal before you try. Jason or Mrs. Duff will accompany you wherever you want to go."

As he stood, so did she, but only because he was so tall. He came around the table, sure of himself as she stood before him with bared feet.

No man had ever made her feel feminine and petite. Placing the cup in her hands, he wrapped her fingers around the warmed porcelain where his palm had just been. "Now drink. Eat. No one at Stonehaven will harm you. You have my word."

"The word of an outlaw."

"The word of a border lord, Lady Roselyn."

"A privateer."

"A Scots."

She held the cup between them like a wall, a barrier against her emotions.

He merely sat against the table watching her, and with a twinge of illogic, she wondered why he had not tried to kiss her since coming to her chambers.

She drank from the cup and nearly choked with the fiery heat. "Whisky . . ." she rasped in disbelief. "You lace your coffee with whisky?"

"Chocolate," he casually corrected. "Scotch-laced chocolate."

Rose felt some of the fire return to her. She no longer felt lethargic. She didn't care what the stuff was. "You should have warned me." She frowned as the floor seemed to move up and down in a curious manner.

He laughed. "And would you have heeded my warning."

"Go away," she murmured. "Your chocolate has poisoned me."

She reached out to put the cup back on the table. But for some reason she misjudged the distance and the cup dropped to the carpet and bounced against his boot. "Aye," he agreed much humor in his tone as he bent to retrieve the cup. "You have the most delicate constitution of anyone I know who can hold a dirk to a man's throat."

"I should have known that a man who by his own admission and actions is a smuggler and a libertine would trick me."

He set the cup behind her, leaning into her until he had her pressed her intimately to the table's edge, half sitting and near to sliding the dishes off the table. "I never claimed to be a libertine, love."

And they remained thus thigh to thigh, the thrum of her pulse in her ears. The scratch of his cheek against her tender skin as he slid his lips to the soft shell of her ear. "And I have no reason to trick you, Rose."

She closed her eyes, her heart hammering. Sister Nessa had once warned her about the temptations of the flesh and warned her that she was too free and impenitent with her wild ways. Rose had never appreciated the full import of that lecture until the other night in the glade and the darkness, for she had always considered herself above the inanity that had ruined many a foolish maid in Castleton. But being so close to Roxburghe and remembering his touch like the hottest fire, she recognized temptation in its basest form. Like that sip of scotch-sweetened chocolate. One taste was not enough.

And it frightened her. She was too weak. Or not too weak.

She was beginning to feel much invigorated. She had but to ease her legs apart, she thought, and he would be pressed against her.

Murmuring something inexplicable beneath the hot caress of his breath, Roxburghe pressed his mouth to her ear. "I have no' slept," he said. "You have no' eaten. I can tell ye, *mo leannan falaich*, neither of us is in our right mind."

His dark-lashed eyes were riveting and direct. She had never heard a brogue in his voice or Gaelic from his tongue, and now that she had, she knew that for all his Scot's blood, he had learned the ways of the English very well.

"Is aught amiss, Ruark?" The housekeeper's voice asked evenly from behind them.

Rose looked around Roxburghe. She stood in the doorway behind them, arms akimbo, steel in her eyes as she eyed the laird's back.

"I was just leaving, Mary." He pushed from the table. "Lady Roselyn and I were merely clarifying the terms of her arrangements while she is a guest here."

"Arrangements indeed!" Mrs. Duff snapped at him, the shell earrings she wore bobbing against her cheeks. "Since when have ye behaved yourself less than a gentleman? Out with ye. Now."

Roxburghe spread his arms in surrender. "Who am I to argue your wisdom, Mary Duff? As the dear aunt of my mother's distant cousin, I have always allowed you certain liberties over my welfare and moral education."

"Pish-posh, Ruark Kerr. I swaddled ye when you were a babe. Certain liberties indeed." Mary sniffed. "Out!"

"Is Jason in the corridor?" He asked Mrs. Duff.

"Aye, he is."

He turned to Rose, his manner infinitely courteous, one corner of his mouth turned up slightly. "Mary will see that everything is provided for you. You need only ask. But know the boundaries I have set, Rose. You have free rein outside this room but never alone."

The cool heat of his eyes held her. "Now if you will excuse me. I am to my own bed to sleep."

Chapter 9

Sleep was the farthest thing from Rose's mind as she finished the fruit Roxburghe left on the table. She discarded the cheese and bread, but ate the shelled walnuts. If his visit did anything, it galvanized her to fight. She might currently be helpless but her situation was far from hopeless.

That evening, with her ear pressed to the door, she overheard Jason telling Mrs. Duff that Roxburghe left Stonehaven to go to Hawick, all hush-hush whispers. His lordship's solicitor and banker resided in Hawick, and they concluded that his reasons for leaving must be important or he would not have gone. Jason and Mrs. Duff were *not* to let Rose leave her chambers alone. Not for a moment.

His lairdship was right not to trust her. But if she was to have any chance at all, she first needed to heal the wound on her leg and for that she needed proper food, rest, and light. Not only did she fully intend to recover but also she fully intended to escape. Or if she could not escape, she would meet her father standing tall and proud, not walking with a limp.

To that end, Rose set about facilitating her own recovery, beginning the next morning with a long written list of required items she would need from the kitchen, which included a boiling pot, marigold heads, black willow and wild yam, raw carrots, and meadowsweet, to name a few. Uncooked brown eggs in the shell and honey would also do twice a day and mixed in a glass for her consumption; if the staff would not mind the inconvenience, she would crack the eggs herself.

The fact that Rose merely asked yet demanded nothing of anyone put the onerous burden on the staff to choose whether to comply with her wishes. She had learned through years of managing much of the abbey's internal affairs that people were more apt to cooperate if one merely treated them with respect and honesty and made it seem as if your needs were their needs. Lord Roxburghe wanted her healthy, after all.

Mrs. Duff supplied her with a pot to boil water in the hearth to make a decoction from elm leaves and bark to cleanse the wound, and an infusion from other herbs to ingest for strength. Rose praised the cook's strawberry tarts as the most wondrous ever and sent down a recipe for the strawberry pie that had been Sister Nessa's favorite. Soon the elderly housekeeper and cook were keeping time with her and bringing Rose various garments and apparel, much that needed altering, but a job that Rose did not mind doing.

While Mrs. Duff sat with her, she chatted about how this wing of the house had been built on the foundation of a castle destroyed after the Battle of Stirling Bridge in the thirteenth century, and Rose learned that some of the old corridors were still in use as servants' passageways. All meals were brought up to the floor from the kitchen this way. No detail of Mrs. Duff's conversations went unnoticed, including the fact that his lordship's chambers were somewhere in this wing.

With her collection of scissors, needles, thread, and

cloth, Rose lay in bed at night and worked on sewing special pockets into her clothes and making a knapsack that she would pack with food and other supplies she was collecting for her eventual departure. Already by the week's end, she had collected silver from the food trays delivered to her. A spoon missing hither and thither could be overlooked in the short term, at least until an accounting of the silverware was taken.

Overall, Rose managed to be a model hostage, seemingly too injured to be a threat. It was not a lie that her wound pained her, but she was not crippled and, with some effort, during her first few days at Stonehaven she was able to shove one of the dressers in her bathing chamber below the high window. If she set a chair atop the dresser's surface, she could reach the window's sill chest high, and using a supper knife, she slipped the blade in the crack to unhinge the lock without breaking the glass. The window opened onto a ledge.

That first morning couldn't have been more glorious to her eyes as Rose looked out over the ledge down a beautiful trellis entwined with green and vines and into an empty courtyard, then beyond the peaceful setting to a reflecting pool.

Her breath had caught when she had glimpsed Julia Kerr.

Rose had not let herself think about the woman she had met her first night at Stonehaven. But every morning for the past five days, Rose had seen her by the reflecting pool.

She sat at a table that had been set up on the grass. She ate alone and *looked* alone. And every morning for the past five days, Rose had watched her.

Friar Tucker had once told Rose she was possessed of a soft heart—malleable, as he had called it—easily shaped by the events of a day. She was always trying to mend broken wings on birds only to watch the creatures give up their will to fight, or survive only to be snatched from the air by a hawk. She had befriended an aged shopkeeper in Castleton because her son, Geddes, was heartless and didn't deserve her. She had tried to mend a little boy's heart after his mother died, only to leave him. Even if it was not her fault, she was still gone. Julia looked in need of mending.

But Rose could do nothing for it, she thought. Friar Tucker had warned her she could not fix the ails of the world, and every time she tried, he had proven her right. She had the power to change nothing. The only hope she'd had went the way of her wishing ring. Gone.

Pulling the window shut, she eased her way off the chair to the dresser, wincing as she lowered herself to the ground. She pulled the chair off the dresser without ripping her dress. It was a serviceable green plaid skirt with a yellow bodice that must have once belonged to a tall, skinny waif, evident by the amount of altering Rose had done last night to cover her bosom more fully.

But Mrs. Duff had brought her this ensemble to add to the other odd assortment of attire in her armoire. To complete the outfit with her plaited hair, Rose had thought with some amusement that morning, all she needed was a shepherd's staff and a lamb in her arms.

She wasn't amused now as someone knocked on her chamber door. She walked into her room just as a wizardly old man popped his head around the edge of the door, saw that she was decently attired, then entered. He carried a brown surgeon's box made of oak and pine in one hand and one of the lists she had sent to the kitchen in the other.

"Marigolds aren't in bloom yet," he said, "and I tossed

away the moldy batch we had. We've no wild yam. Though it grows in the hills around the loch. Witch hazel we have but no' mallow root. But the eggs and honey . . . ?"

" 'Tis a rich drink to thicken the blood and hasten healing."

"No wonder ye have caused such an uproar in the kitchen with your menus and wild concoctions." He peered at her with interest. "You are a healer."

Rose dusted off her hands as he approached. "I didn't get a chance to meet you when you arrived," he said. "The name is McBain. His lordship told me I was to see to your leg. But I thought it wise to give ye a few days to work on the matter yourself, seein' as how ye seem to know what ye are doing."

Rose smiled sweetly. "You can tell his lordship when he returns that you saw me and I am well."

"I would, lass, except, when he returned late last night and asked about ye, Mrs. Duff was adamant that ye were still spendin' most of yer time in bed recuperatin'. His lordship being the concerned sort asked if I had checked on ye. I had to tell him I had not."

Rose did not want McBain looking at her leg. He would see that she was far better along than everyone thought. "You can tell him that his concern is unwarranted. I am recovering, but these things take time."

McBain set the box on the table next to a modest arrangement of lilies in a large blue pottery jar. With his short stature and slightly pointy ears, he could have belonged to the fabled fairy people that lived in the forests of Scotland. "That may be so, lass, but ye can no' be expecting me to report to his lordship that you're in the best of health if you're no'. What if you're sufferin' the rot? How would his lordship look if he had to return ye to your da, one legged? Ye can understand his concern. And as I am a man who forms his own opinions about all matters, my lady, I would see to your health myself," he gently replied, then directed her to the chair nearest the fire. "Please. Allow me to have a look at that leg. Those sutures have been in a week."

His gentleness pulled at her defenses and she realized he was using the same tactic on her that she used on others. He merely asked but left the burden of whether to comply with her. She could deny him but then Roxburghe might come to her room and force her to submit to an examination, which would be undignified and humiliating. Then he might decide to search her room and find all his stolen silverware, knives and the scissors she had beneath the bed.

Rose limped to the chair and sat. "You do not plan to give me a bread-and-milk poultice, do you?"

"Nay, and neither will I give ye arsenic, blue vitriol, or white-oak-bark paste. I'm not here to hurt ye or see ye bleed more than you've already done so."

She watched as he opened the box and laid out various medical devices including a screw tourniquet, probe, and a tooth extractor that looked more like a cork opener.

The fire in the hearth suddenly seemed hot at her back. "Are you a surgeon?" she asked nervously. "You have treated many patients?"

"Not many who have lived," he said, moving aside a green jar in his box, his voice muffled as he bent over.

"Are you even a doctor?"

"By necessity," he said, laying a towel next to the box. "Our ship's surgeon was killed my third year at sea. Though his lordship was no' one to tangle spars with, we saw our fair share of action. I learned the trade quickly. If a man was brought to me . . . as ye can guess taking a man's limbs is not an easy thing even if it is meant to save what life he has left."

"That is horrible."

"Oh, aye." He peered at her from beneath bushy brows that looked like aged caterpillars. "You've no idea the courage it takes to look down the black maw of a forty pounder. His lordship did it more times than most. Me? I remained belowdecks and prayed."

She doubted it. He looked like an old curmudgeon capable of freezing the enemy to stone with one look. But at the thought of Ruark standing on the deck of his ship in the midst of battle her heart tripped, and she remembered their conversation in the glade, when he had told her how a broadside can destroy a man in more ways than one can imagine. She had wondered at the time if he had been alluding to more than battle at sea.

"Lord Roxburghe spoke briefly about his time on the *Black Dragon*," she said.

"Did he?" McBain peered over his nose at her with interest. "That is unusual. His lordship rarely speaks of such matters even to friends."

The criticism Rose had wanted to heap on the head of McBain's lordly master suddenly seemed trivial and childish, especially when she wanted to learn more about the man who had come home to Scotland from the sea. "You have known Lord Roxburghe for a long time?"

"Oh, aye. But he wasn't always 'his lordship.'"

McBain finally found what he was searching for. He removed a small tin box and set it next to the folded rag. His eyes twinkling, he peered at her as he removed salve. "Most patients have already fainted by now."

She glanced at the devices on the table. "If you had

pulled out the amputation saw, I would have thrown you out of the room."

He laughed as he shoved a pair of spectacles on his nose. "That be the spirit, lassie."

McBain knelt next to her. Reluctantly, she bent over her knee. She wore a brown stockings and tallow-colored shoes that peaked from beneath the calf-length hem. She eased her dress to her thigh and untied her garter.

She looked away as McBain delicately pressed around the freshly scabbed flesh where she had snipped away the sutures this morning. He made complimentary sounds and grunts about her work, but noted the redness around an area she couldn't see.

Despite the serious slant of his lips, his eyes twinkled as he set down the tin of salve. "Ye were smart to be restin' this week. Meadowsweet will help with itching as it begins to scab more. We've no' much in the way of an herbal here but you are welcome to visit when you are up to the walk and see what we have. Maybe ye can teach me a thing or two about what is there on the shelves."

"I do not think so." She smoothed her hands over her skirts. "I mean I cannot see how I can help you." It wouldn't do her any good to involve herself with the people here at Stonehaven. She didn't want to see the herbal.

"Suit yourself, lassie. But you are welcome to visit if ye wish."

He began to repack the box. In the growing silence, Rose adjusted her dress. For the most part everyone had treated her as if she were a guest, she thought as she stared at the four poster bed more suited to royalty than a hostage. From the sapphire velvet hangings draping the bed to the blue-and-green throw carpet and painted ceiling, she could conceive of such places existing only in her imagination. Except for the fact that there were so few windows, she found no fault with her quarters—any more than she had with the people who had served her. They'd been kind.

"Thank you," she said after a moment.

"Those who live here be decent souls," he said as if reading her mind. "I can tell ye Lord Roxburgh is no' as bad as ye want to believe he is, lass. He is nothing like the man his father was."

For the hundredth time since her arrival, Rose thought of Lady Roxburghe and the horror of losing one's child to an unknown fate.

Rose didn't know why she felt responsible for Julia's son, only that she had felt a connection to the woman. Perhaps it was because of the way Roxburghe had held her that night on the stairs as if they were more than friends. The same way he had held *her* in the glade, just before Rose had turned toward him and laid her hand across his heart. And he had made her feel safe.

"Lady Roxburghe must have wed Lord Roxburghe's father at a young age," Rose said.

McBain shut the surgery box and clasped the lid. "Aye, but 'tis no secret that the betrothal should have been between his lordship and Lady Julia. But her father wanted his daughter married to an earl, and Roxburghe wanted a beautiful bride and more sons. That be the way it is, I suppose. A man needs sons."

The candid tone brought a flush to Rose's cheeks. "What happened?"

"What *could* happen?" McBain's eyes became blank as pebbles as they no longer seemed to focus on anything. "His lordship got it into his mind to save her from her fate. He would wed her and take her from Scotland, though where they would have gone . . . ? Young people do no' have the sense the good Lord gave a squirrel. Well, three days before the weddin' is to take place, he and Lady Julia run away together. Only, she balks and they never made it to the kirk where his lordship had paid the minister there to marry them.

"Duncan and his lordship's father caught up to them before they had gone a few miles. He might have killed his father if no' for Duncan stepping in. When his lordship woke up three days later, he found himself delivered to the old captain of the *Dragon*. The ship did no' add *Black* to the *Dragon* until a year later when his lordship took the helm. Lord Roxburghe married Julia a week after he sent his son off to sea as if naught had ever happened to forever estrange him from his only son and heir."

Rose pretended close inspection of her hands. "One hears gossip."

"Aye, and I'm only telling ye something everyone else already knows, lass. But if ye want to know more you'll have to be askin' his lordship."

Rose came to her feet and turned toward the fire. She held her palms facing outward against the heat. "Is it true that my father killed the former Lord Roxburghe?" she asked, dreading the answer.

"Aye . . . that's what they say. Ye and Jamie have been thrown into the middle of a fight that has nothing to do with either of ye."

"Do you know my father then?"

"Reckon his lordship knows him best." McBain's implacable tone was unmistakable. "They were business rivals, so to speak."

"Lord Roxburghe personally knows my father?" She had not meant her voice to come out so sharp, but the fact that Ruark and her father were *personally* acquainted had somehow escaped her. She didn't know why it should have seemed important, except that it felt relevant to her current situation. "Just what manner of commerce did my father and your laird share?"

McBain ran a finger beneath his stock while he cleared his throat. "Reckon ye best be takin' up that topic with his lordship when he awakens, lass."

Ruark heard the swishing of a petticoat first, before he became aware that the soft tread of slippers on carpet was not Mary Duff pacing a rut into the fine weave. Pushing up on his elbows, he gave his trespasser's back a frown even as he admired her lines and the way her skirts flared from her hips. With his hair falling over his forehead, Ruark could barely see more than shadows and shapes in the darkness, but he would know that enticing silhouette anywhere.

His first inclination was to check his weapons. His second was less refined. Just then, she lifted her head and saw that he was awake. "What the hell hour is it?" he grumbled.

"Late. 'Tis at least seven o'clock."

Turning her back to him, she stretched out her arms like Moses confronting the Red Sea and threw open the heavy velvet curtains that usually blocked out the light of the day.

Sunlight glared through the lead glass and he winced against the brightness. The master's chamber, though unmistakably masculine—dark furniture carved from solid oak, jade damask wallpaper, and plum brocade chairs—looked severe in contrast to Rose's soft, refined presence.

She placed her hands on her hips, giving him her full measure. "I have just come from a visit with McBain."

Ruark slept naked. The sheet covered the lower half

of his body, but that was all the modesty it afforded him. Her presence in his room had a predictable effect on him. Clearing his throat and turning on his side, he rested his head on his hand and his elbow on his hip, letting his arm hide the obvious. He admired the fit of her bodice. With her hair braided in a thick coronet around her head, she reminded him of a female Thor or the goddess Diana. Leaning slightly to peer over the edge of the bed, he saw that the hem of her skirt only reached her calves, exposing a well-turned ankle. She wore shoes the color of soft butter.

"Did you hear me?"

The glaring heat from those green eyes was enough to hold his attention. That and the hint of a blush staining her cheeks. "And that warrants a visit to my chambers. Why?"

"You *know* my father."

Ruark pushed himself into a sitting position against the carved oak backboard, dragging the sheet up with him. He pulled one knee to his chest beneath the sheet. It occurred to him that Mary or Jason would never have allowed her in these chambers. "How did you find my rooms? Have you done away with my staff while I slept?"

"And if I had, would I have spared you?" She raised her chin. "I think not."

Peering more closely at her attire, he wondered where the hell Mary had procured those garments. They did not belong to his mother. And he was damn sure they did not come from a modiste. "You look like something out of a children's ditty about lost sheep." But rather than a shepherd's staff gripped in her hand, he pictured a bolt of lightning. He almost laughed at the image until the look from her narrowed eyes stopped him.

"Mrs. Duff is in the kitchen," she said and continued

her limping pace back and forth in front of the window. "Jason is sitting outside my door and probably does not even know I have left the room. As for how I found you, 'twas simple. Mr. McBain said you were asleep, so once outside, I looked for the room with curtains shuttered against the light, and thus through a matter of deductive reasoning and pure luck, I ended here. Your *boundaries* be damned."

He allowed himself a small smile. It didn't surprise him that she had found another way out of her room. "And yet I doubt you are here to serve me breakfast."

She stopped in front of the plum tufted chair beside the bed. "Everyone knows my father served the admiralty before he retired to live at Kirkland Park. You were a privateer for the king. I want to know how you know each other."

Ruark should not have been surprised that she would have eventually confronted him over the subject. Then suddenly it didn't matter if she knew.

Scraping his palm over his bristled jaw, he gave her a direct look. "Almost two years ago outside Rotterdam, I came across a ship carrying contraband that Hereford removed off an East Indiaman. I impounded it."

"You mean you stole it."

"The wares were already stolen. I merely put it to better use."

She visibly swallowed. "Why did he never report the theft?"

"What is to report? That I took cargo Hereford had pirated a month earlier from an East Indiamen off the Azores? Cargo he was trying to sell in France, consisting of tea, China silk, and gunpowder. Also a hundred tons of opium, all owned by the venerable John Company. Aye, we know each other personally." As he began to feel the faint stirrings of a deep-rooted hatred, Ruark clenched his jaw. "We were well acquainted before he returned to England and accepted an appointment as the English warden."

Rose sank into the chair. The window framed her like a Holbein portrait. "Why France?" Her quiet tone pulled at him and he looked at her to find her eyes on his face, searching.

"The French are always fighting with the British. They need gunpowder. As for the other wares, Parisians pay a premium to support their vices."

"What did you do with the goods?"

"I kept the gunpowder. One never knows when it will come in handy. The opium went overboard, into the sea. As for the rest, you would have to ask Tucker. He used it to keep much of the good folk around Castleton and Carlisle from starving last winter."

Almost self-consciously, she looked at her hands clenched in her lap. "You *are* good friends with Friar Tucker."

"We were. Until you."

She smoothed her skirts, an action he noted she did often when uncertain. "My father was bound to have found me eventually," she said. "There is no sense in holding a grudge with one another . . . because of me."

"I think I can manage the friar."

It was his increasing feelings for Rose with which he found difficulty reconciling himself. He had returned late last night exhausted only to pass her room on the way to his and stop. She and Mary were inside and Ruark had stood outside listening as Rose laughed at something his housekeeper had said. Jason told him that Lady Roselyn had behaved ever the gracious lady while recovering from her serious injury, sharing tea and sewing with his staff. Today he had planned to conduct a search of her quarters because he did not trust her complicity—no doubt she had knives, forks, and scissors stashed in every corner of her chambers—but last night it had taken all of his control not to open the door and go inside because, Lord . . . he wanted to look at her. Now he wanted only not to hurt her.

She said nothing for a moment but the whitening of her knuckles revealed her tension. "Did people die? On that East Indiaman, I mean."

He could lie, but decided she'd been lied to enough in her life. "The ship was destroyed somewhere off the coast of the Azores. Rumor was it vanished during a blow. A storm. No one would have doubted the story had some of the East Indiaman's cargo not begun showing up two weeks later in various ports in Tripoli and Antwerp. And finally Rotterdam."

Her eyes were wide, refusing to believe the horror of the worst. "But is it not possible the ship did go down in a storm?"

Pulled by the braided piece of silver warming his finger, Ruark leaned his head against the backboard and studied the ring. It seemed to absorb not only the sunlight but also the darkest edges of his thoughts, as if to bring them into the light and into his focus. And for a brief moment, he felt exposed and vulnerable to his sins.

"You can believe what you wish, Rose." He curled his fingers into his palm as if that would make him less culpable for his own choices in life. "But that cargo was taken off that Indiaman before the storm."

"You are so sure . . . because you were there?" She looked at him closely. "You *were* there," she whispered, "Why? Because you were following my father or the East Indiaman?"

"We had been shadowing the East Indiaman for days. The letters of marque I carry gives me authority to aide and protect British economic interests. Before the ship passed the Cape, everyone within a thousand miles knew the real value of that Indiaman's cargo. There had been other attacks on our vessels so we followed. Then a squall caught us while we were under full press of canvas and snapped our mainmast.

"When we finally caught up to the Indiaman two days later, there was nothing left of the ship but the burned-out debris to tell the tale. After plucking four survivors from shark-infested waters, we learned that a British naval vessel had been responsible for destroying the Indiaman, which carried a crew upward of two hundred souls. We learned that a large amount of cargo had been transferred from the British naval vessel to another ship. I followed it to the Dutch port of Rotterdam, where we both put in for refitting. Later, I impounded the cargo in the open sea." He looked down at his hands. "The captain knew who I was when I boarded. He told us where the cargo had come from, then he hanged himself. Out of fear of retribution from me or Hereford, I will never know."

"Surely you could have told the admiralty."

"On that dead captain's word?"

What Ruark did not tell her, what he could not tell her was that the ship he had boarded, the ship that had accepted the stolen cargo, belonged to Roxburghe Shipping. His own family's fleet of trading vessels. He could not accuse Hereford without implicating his own family and casting the name of traitor to the Kerr name. He might despise his father, but he would not destroy Jamie or Julia. He did not know if his father was involved. He could find no proof.

"Without evidence, I had nothing. But I could bloody

make Hereford's life hell on the sea. He never got hold of another ship after that."

Now his father was dead and Jamie gone.

Her eyes swept to and fro from the floor to the wall. "And now in the past year my father retired from the admiralty to take his place as the English warden, your father is dead and your brother is a hostage." She shook her head as if mulling over these same observations and then coming to the correct conclusions. "What was the value of that cargo?"

A fortune by even royal standards. Yet, he was compelled to tell her the truth. Why not? He had spared no detail yet. "Ninety thousand pounds."

Rose's disbelief came at him. "That is what my father wants from you in exchange for your brother. Payment for what you took from him." She came abruptly to her feet, tension in every line of her body. "This has been your fight from the start? It is you personally he wants to destroy. Check and checkmate."

She spun away, folding her arms across her chest. "Have your actions been any different from my father's?" she cried, her voice distressed by emotion. "Are you not alike?"

He dragged the sheet off the bed as he stood and walked over to her. His mouth tight.

Ruark had told himself a thousand times he was not to blame for Hereford's actions. That he was nothing like Hereford.

But his own silence condemned him.

He had brought this upon himself. He could not pretend to shortsightedness, because in the back of his mind he had been perfectly aware of the consequences of his actions and had not cared—until his father died and Duncan played right into Hereford's hands and took good Kerr men across the border, maybe to die as well. Now suddenly Jamie's life was at stake.

And Rose had become the anchor around his neck threatening to drag him deeper into murky depths. Yet, it was not her worth in gold that caused him to inspect more closely his feelings, and why her presence in his life was blóody fooking with his internal moral compass.

He leaned his hand against the glass, so close to her he could smell the sunlight on her hair. "You tell me, Rose." Ruark spoke softly but his words cut deep. "Am I like your father? Are we the same?"

"I think . . ." She furiously scrubbed the heel of her hand across each cheek and turned bright eyes on him. She touched his face. "I think a man who can help Castleton and others survive a winter with smuggled goods at great peril to his own life, and someone whom Friar Tucker has clearly respected, cannot be malevolent," she said, with such conviction it stopped his heart. "Now I understand. Without me, you do not have enough with which to bargain for your brother's life."

She blinked back tears, but it was not hate he saw in her eyes, and he was shocked that one look could undo him so completely. Then she said something else he did not expect. "Thank you for being honest with me."

She turned and walked out of the room, leaving him with his palm pressed against the warm glass of the window, looking outside upon a rare sunny day and suddenly feeling much older than his thirty years.

Chapter 10

"Your solicitor arrived last night from Hawick," Mary said from the doorway of Ruark's bathing chamber.

He stood at the water basin, swishing soap from a razor as he raised his gaze and locked with Mary's in the glass. She stood behind him, her hands on her ample hips, her lips pursed in a straight line. Water dripped from his wet hair onto his bare shoulders. He wore a clean pair of leather breeches but little else and those he had dragged on after Rose left his chambers.

Ruark had gone to Hawick last week for many reasons, one being to assess Stonehaven's accounting books. Ruark needed to know his father's business transactions these past years. If there *was* a connection between his father's death and Hereford, it would be found in the accounting books, many of which were missing from Stonehaven, but which he had hoped his father's solicitor had copies. Most importantly, banking transactions were always duplicated. If he could find proof, anything to connect Hereford to his father's death, there may be another way to end this standoff with Hereford.

"Where is he?"

"I took the liberty of informing him you take your

breakfast in the dining room at eight and that he may await your presence there."

Ruark finished wiping the soap off his face. "Thank you, Mary. I will be down directly."

Mary remained in the doorway. Ruark finally turned, waiting for her to speak her mind. "I know the lass is no' the first woman to be used as a means to an end . . . and she be the warden's daughter—"

"Do I need this dressing-down, Mary?"

Recognizing that the tenor of the reprimand coincided with his mood warned her that even for her there were limitations to his patience. "Lady Roselyn has refused to see the modiste," Mary said before taking her leave. "I was just to see her and told her I have arranged one to visit tomorrow. After much searchin', I learned of a modiste living in Hawick and made provisions to bring her here. I would use that French highbrow Lady Roxburghe brings over from Paris three times a year. But I did no' think we have—"

"Why did Lady Roselyn decline the offer for a modiste?"

"She informed me that she was convent raised and would no' face her father being anything more than who she was, her father be damned. She asked me to thank you for your consideration, the gist of her comment bein' along the same sentiment. She does not need your charity."

Christ.

Ruark intended to see that when it was time to face her father, she would do so as *exactly* who she is: the daughter of an earl, not some impoverished supplicant beneath that man's regard.

Fifteen minutes later, he was trooping down the hall, adjusting the lace on his wrist. He dismissed Jason to attend to his breakfast as he passed the lad, then he was standing before her door. He reached for the knob, paused, then he decided to knock rather than barge inside. For a moment, considering this, he braced his palms on the door frame.

The door opened. Her eyes widened, and it was as if he'd stepped into bright morning sunlight. "My lord."

He had been wholly unprepared for her effect on him, only because she had not left his thoughts, and he already considered his mind and senses finely attuned to her. He was wrong. She stood in a bright patch of the sunlight filtering through the high window from her bathing chambers. Her plaited copper hair crowned her head in a wreath of red-gold glory. She had changed her clothes and now wore homespun, but the simplicity of the dress merely refined the complexity of the tall woman beneath. The common accented the uncommon.

After what they had already shared between them, Ruark was surprised anything could make Rose blush, but she did as she found his eyes on her, and suddenly he was remembering the journey they had shared in the glade. There wasn't a part of her he had not touched. A part of her that he did not want to touch again.

"Sunlight becomes you," he said.

"I was just thinking about you," she said not unkindly, reaching around to drag up something behind the door. "This is for you, my lord."

She gave him a knapsack made from a patchwork of wool and muslin. Curious at the clinking and odd weight of the thing he peered inside to find it filled with silverware, napkin rings, and a chalice as she informed him, "I have no more need of such as I have every intention of going to my father when 'tis time."

"Is that right?"

"I have not made the decision lightly. But you were

right when you told me that night at the river that there was nowhere I could go that my father would not find me. So I have decided to make this simple for all of us."

"If there is another way?"

"After what you have told me, I know there is not."

Her words banished the softness that had momentarily incapacitated him. Though he grudgingly admired her courage, he did not intend to hand her over to Hereford.

"I do not need your protection, my lord."

The steel in her words told him she did not *want* his protection. His first instinct was to parry her steel with his own. But he did not. He had forgotten his purpose for coming to her room but as Mary rounded the corner, he had not forgotten his solicitor was awaiting him.

"Our chaperone has arrived," he said, then leaned a hand against the doorway until his face was near hers. "You wish to meet your father on your terms? Give Mary one of your dresses to take to the modiste for measurements. Let her make you something . . . simple."

"Simple?"

Hell, he probably knew more about lady's garments than Rose did. "Something provincial. Silk. Velvet. Emerald in color," he said. *The color of her eyes.* He would have added, *with all the proper undergarments and accoutrements*, but he would choose to leave those details to Mary's discretion. "You wear *simple* very well," Ruark said. "You want to meet your father as you are? Never go into the wolf's den looking like a sheep, my love."

"Even with your infusion of gold, you still do not have enough to pay the ransom, my lord."

Ruark stood at the window across the table from his father's solicitor, who was tucked quite eagerly into a meal of bannocks spread with molasses. Ruark had been distracted for the last half hour, staring outside at the parkland, half reading Mr. McCurdy's pile of papers, half woolgathering before he'd forced his thoughts back to the task at hand unprepared for the news just delivered to him. What Ruark found on Stonehaven's balance sheets stunned him.

"You are telling me, Stonehaven's coffers are nearly empty?"

"Except for what you put there, my lord. You could sell the last of the Roxburghe fleet of ships. The *Black Dragon* itself would be of interest—"

"'Twill be a bloody cold day in hell before anyone gets his hands on the *Black Dragon*," Ruark said. "What has happened here in thirteen years?"

The lines of strain tightened around McCurdy's mouth. "This place has fallen on rough times. His lordship lost a fortune when other investments failed this past year. The crops and rents haven't produced enough to pay the debts. Then the village fiscal embezzled the rest, though we'll never know for sure where that went."

"Where is he?"

"Dead, my lord. Six weeks before your father died. He tried to leave here during a snowstorm. Duncan caught up to him, only to find him dead, frozen solid beneath his horse and no gold to be found. Thieves most likely got it all. He left a wife, three sons, and a wee lass behind."

Ruark didn't know the details behind the fiscal's death last winter, except the eldest son, Rufus, was one of the hostages taken with Jamie.

"Your father got himself involved with some shady dealings, my lord." McCurdy then remarked that in his opinion all power politics was apt to be dirty business as evidenced by the current situation involving his brother and the young woman held hostage at Stonehaven.

Ruark turned back to the window, his mind sifting through Stonehaven's financial problems to something more subtle. "Have you been able to find any information on Elena Kirkland Lancaster, Lord Hereford's dead wife, or on Kirkland Park, her ancestral home?"

He had not expected McCurdy to know anything given the time constraints from when Ruark had asked, and was surprised when McCurdy replied, "I didn't find much about the wife, but her ancestral home and the entire area around Redesdale sits on land that was once part of a larger crown charter of the barony granted to Lady Hereford's great-grandfather by Charles the First. The patent, the deed of settlement, has since expired."

"Then none of Kirkland Park is tied up in entail."

"The grandfather was a smart old codger, though. He put the family's wealth in trust just after Lady Elena gave birth to her daughter. All of the funds are vested in consuls, an annuity that pays its six percent to the estate yearly."

"Then someone has to know the girl is alive, or Hereford would not be receiving funds. Who controls the trust?"

"Friar Tucker does," a feminine voice said from the doorway.

Recognizing it, Ruark turned into the room. McCurdy clamored to his feet, nearly spilling a cup of tea on his shiny blue satin breeches.

Rose stood in the shadows backlit by the gray light coming through the corridor's window. He could not see her face, only the shape of her shoulders and waist, the curve of her hips and breasts perfectly feminine. Her hair seemed to pull color from the darkness.

"My apologies," she said. "Mary implied breakfast was

being served and you were in the dining room. I had not expected to find anyone else here."

'Twas a lie, he knew, since Mary had been the one to send the solicitor to the dining room to await Ruark.

McCurdy bowed clumsily over his arm. He looked first at Rose then at Ruark. "If you wish to finish breakfast, you may do so in the library, McCurdy," Ruark said without looking away from Rose.

The solicitor grabbed up his plate, and with a nod to Rose left the room by way of the glass doors that let out into the garden.

"Would you care to sit?" Ruark said when she joined him near the window, and then she took her place at the head of the table.

Ruark hesitated. Perhaps she didn't know that was his place. She folded her hands and peered up at him. Her eyes widened. "Have I sat in the wrong chair?" she suddenly asked.

He reassured her that she should remain where she was and took the one next to hers. She glanced down at her hands, gathering her thoughts, and he seized the moment to study her, to examine again the fundamental softness of her profile and his own desire to protect her.

"Rose . . ."

She inhaled deeply then gave him her full attention. "Friar Tucker controls Kirkland Park through a trust set up by my great-grandfather," she said. "His father was vicar there for decades. I have an aunt living in France on my mother's side who appointed him trustee. I learned about her a few years ago when I learned about my great-grandfather's will."

He studied her. "Go on."

"He told me that when my father found me, he would have taken me from the abbey. But Tucker convinced him my anonymity protected all our interests."

Every muscle in his body tightened. "Your father has always known where you were?"

She swallowed. "My great-grandfather's will states that if by one and twenty, I should . . . die, control of Kirkland Park and all its assets stays in the trust and everything is willed to the church. Father could never wed me to anyone for he would risk losing control of everything to my husband. He never feared I would wed for no union would be legal without his permission."

After a hesitation, she continued, "My father was promised that in exchange for leaving me at the abbey, he would receive the deed to Kirkland Park. For seventeen years, he kept his side of the bargain and left us alone. I accepted long ago that I would never know my ancestral home. Never touch my mother's things. Never know who she was. I had accepted all of that. But then you came along and shattered our well-laid plans.

"You would have to be willing to kill me to be any true threat to my father. Because when I am one and twenty, unless I am dead, he will receive Kirkland Park. My hope was that when this was over, he would have no more vested interests in me. I had hoped it would be enough to set me free."

"Why are you telling me this?"

"Because I saw the look on your face this morning. I was afraid you might try to do something honorable."

He sat back in the chair, his long legs crossed at the ankles as he pondered her impression of him. And he found himself looking away from her.

"All of my life I have wanted to be free of my past," she said. "If you can understand that. I think you can. Now I am looking for the courage to confront it."

"Why?"

He had no idea why her answer to that question was so pertinent to his future and to hers. Perhaps he was curious to see that they were more alike than different in many regards. Only he had not made the decision to confront his demons, merely to destroy them.

The only person he loved in this world was living in a cold, dark cell, garrisoned at Alnwick Castle.

"I am no martyr," she said, "but you will not see your brother again if you do not follow through with what you have started."

Ruark stood and walked to the breakfront. He removed the crystal stopper from the decanter and sloshed whisky into a tumbler. He viewed the tapestry in front of him of handsome lords and ladies riding and hawking in the parkland along the marshy banks, an innocent world he'd known as a child.

"If you could go anywhere, where would you go, Rose?" he asked without turning.

She must have realized it wasn't a rhetorical question. He turned to confront her silence now colored by deeper insight of his own motivations.

He only knew that no matter his future or hers, he could not, would not allow a monster like Hereford the chance to get his hands on her.

"I would find my mother's family," she said. "I would go to France."

He'd been to the cliffs of Calais. "France is nice," he said.

"Where would you go?" she asked.

The picture in the tapestry filled his mind, as did the white sands of the Indies, turquoise waters and warm breezes in the moonlight.

Aye, he understood Rose's want for freedom. "I am

still looking," he quietly said into his glass, then tipped it back and swallowed the burn.

For the next two days, Rose managed to avoid crossing paths with Ruark, which was not difficult on an estate the size of Stonehaven. She no longer spent her time in her room, but took walks in the garden. She had no desire to talk to anyone or see anything of Stonehaven. The courtyard below her window became her haven. With its unkempt flower beds long ago abandoned by loving hands, the place had drawn her and she spent time weeding the beds.

Even as McBain examined her leg this morning and pronounced her sound, she didn't feel sound.

And as another day closed in on her life, and she sat on her knees in the garden staring out across the reflection pool, she felt a sense of hopelessness taking root for reasons she could not account. She wondered if this was how Julia felt facing the world every morning.

Until Ruark had entered her life, Rose had been so sure of her goals, self-righteous in her courage. She could slay dragons. She didn't know what she was fighting for now. Ruark had muddled her heart. In her mind, a man who did bad things even for good reasons was still beyond pardon. Ruark had even admitted to his transgressions, all the while accusing her father of heinous crimes.

Perhaps the biggest crime of all was that she believed Ruark. He had no reason to lie to her. Her growing anger reflected her own fallibility. No wonder people hated her so.

'Twas one thing to be the daughter of a man guilty of using his power for political gain and another thing entirely to know he had ordered the destruction of a merchantman, killing everyone on board. For a man capable of such a cold-blooded act was capable of killing a young boy for vengeance.

How did one reconcile oneself to the reality that a mother she had idolized would not throw herself off a cliff rather than wed herself to such a man?

And as Rose worked on her hands and knees in the garden pulling weeds from the dark loamy earth, she thought her heart might burst from the constriction in her chest.

She wanted to hate her mother for being weak. Rose thrust her fingers into the soil, ignoring the first drops of rain, when suddenly the dark clouds churning in the sky opened. Sheets of icy water fell over her. Elbows deep in mud, she raised her face to the sky and let the rain wash over her, hating her father most of all. The sentiment was different from before, she knew, when a part of her had held out a deep-seated childlike hope that her father was not as people painted him. Different, for it was like a poison that seeped into her veins and touched even the most sacred, precious memories she held of her mother.

Rose didn't know how long she remained on her knees in the garden. No one came out to fetch her inside. Before she knew what she was doing, she found herself walking past storm-lashed trees, no longer aware of the dull ache in her leg or her heart. No longer aware of anything at all.

Her feet sinking in the mud, she pushed past low-hanging branches and entered the parkland, past sheep huddling against the rain, through a clove-covered field, and kept walking, farther and farther from Stonehaven. Even if she had nowhere to go. Even as a part of her mind acknowledged that Ruark Kerr might be a self-admitted pirate and smuggler, but at least he was an honest and courageous one.

By the time Rose made the long trek across the open divide and emerged onto the top of a small hill, the rain had spent most of its fury and so had she. She sat for a while and rested where the hill sloped away in a breathtaking fall of rocks that spilled into the head of a lovely glen. The fecund scent of wet earth and fragrant pine filled her nostrils. As the sun began to set, she pushed away from the rocks and continued walking.

Water sluiced over granite boulders, disappearing into mossy crevices. She crouched to avoid a low-hanging branch and as she maneuvered her way down the narrow footpath, she thought she heard the faint whicker of a horse. Through the mist, she could see an aged chapel ahead. A three-foot-high iron fence surrounded the chapel yard. She approached a cemetery, wet leaves muffling her footsteps. This was Ruark's family cemetery.

She followed the fence around the chapel. She could see Stonehaven's rooftop in the far distance through the thinning branches of the trees.

She almost laughed.

For all the time she had spent traipsing across the parkland and through the woods, she had somehow walked in a circle. It occurred to her then that no matter what she did, she could not seem to escape Ruark or her fate. Surely, there was irony to be found somewhere in that observation.

She peered at the chapel where moss had grown over the stones turning the entire north side a deep green. The building looked sad and alone standing among the stone monuments of the dead.

The mist began to thicken and she shivered as she looked around the empty yard. Her gaze fell on the horse tied to a wooden hitching post off to the side of the chapel.

Loki.

Rose looked around but saw no sign of Ruark. She drew back the iron lever on the gate, wincing slightly as it screeched on rusty hinges. She entered the yard and walked among the stones to where the horse tore chunks of grass from the wet ground, chewing thoughtfully as he eyed her approach. No one was near to prevent her from taking the horse and riding away. But something stopped her.

All her life, she had felt trapped by other people's decisions about her future, leading her about like a horse wearing a halter, telling her what she could do or not do, who she could be or not be. She found that even drenched as she was and with mud caking the hems of her skirts, she had never felt more in control of her own fate. Even if the illusion of choice falsely empowered her, 'twas her choice to not take Loki and run.

Behind her, the door to the chapel stood slightly ajar, and she found herself stepping inside. The interior smelled old and musty like mildew, beeswax, and a hint of incense that had been burned into the stone walls over the decades. A beautiful mural of angels colored the domed ceiling high above her head. She thought a candle burned in the loft. She turned up the stone staircase to her right. This was a crypt. The wall bore the names and ages of the various Roxburghe earls along with their wives, sons, and daughters for the last two centuries. A small, narrow room opened at the top of the staircase. A candle burned in a ceramic holder.

Someone had set it on a narrow table in front of an engraved stone built as part of the wall. Rose bent and read:

RUARK JAMES LINDSAY KERR
BELOVED FATHER AND HUSBAND TO JANELLE HIS
ENGLISH BRIDE
1650–1685
CHANCE NOT. WIN NOT.

A profane statement about one's destiny.

"He was my great-grandfather." Ruark's voice came from behind her and she spun around alarmed. He stood on the stairs. "I surprised you," he said. "I apologize. You were absorbed."

She had not seen him when she entered, but it looked as if he had been up here awaiting her.

She gestured to the angels floating against the ceiling. "This area looks newer than the rest of the chapel."

"The loft was added during my great-grandfather's tenure as earl, after a candle caught fire and burned the timbers in the old chapel roof. So he has been granted his place of prominence . . . despite the fact that he was presumed to be a traitor and distrusted by many on both sides of the border. He was a privateer in the service of King Charles the Second."

"Perhaps he was also a smuggler and pirate. I cannot imagine any relative of yours selling out so completely, no matter appearances."

Ruark climbed the stairs, stopping just before he reached the landing where she stood. He'd tied his hair at his nape with a leather thong. Soft leather riding boots hugged his calves.

His cloak and hair were damp as if he had not been long out of the rain. She could smell the clean scent of soap on him. He walked to where she stood and peered out the window as if to make sure Loki remained tied.

"I considered it," she said. "Escaping."

"I know." Leaning a shoulder against the cold stone wall, he folded his arms. "I was beginning to think you had got lost."

"You knew I would be coming here."

"I saw where you went into the woods and knew where you would be exiting. There is only one path."

"You left Loki unguarded?" she accused him. "I could have stolen him!"

"And yet . . . you did not."

She felt trapped by the fact that he had not so much left Loki in the open, but that he would have let her take him.

"I have been watching you, wonderin' how I should approach you," he said. "I know that learning about your father came as a shock—"

"Why would you care?"

He smiled briefly. "I could not rightly say," he admitted, scratching his head and eyeing her with bemusement. "You do not much like me—that is true, I think, and deservedly so. You have only tried to cut my throat and bash my brains with a rock. Maybe I do not like having the advantage between us, love." He paused, then said softly, "Maybe I have been where you are. Trapped."

Folding her arms, she dropped her gaze to her feet and swallowed past the constriction on her throat. The smell of burning candle wax made her nose itch. After a moment, she sat on the wooden bench in the alcove next to the narrow stairway. As if she'd invited him, he settled his large body next to her making her scoot a bit to accommodate him. She could not help staring, for his warmth burned through her damp clothing. He leaned forward with his elbows on his knees, and they remained thus in companionable silence. She could feel his eyes on her profile. His leg remained in her field of vision and she glanced at the stone engraved with his great-grandfather's name.

"He isn't buried here," she said.

"He perished at sea a year after Janelle died giving him a son."

"I . . . am sorry," she said, compelled to say something.

"Aye, but 'tis a fact of life. Loved ones die. Ships vanish."

Most ships that vanished remained so forever. No one ever knew the fate of the crew or passengers. Like her mother. Ruark could have so easily met such a fate. "You are his namesake. How is it you managed to follow in his footsteps?"

He didn't answer immediately and she sensed some kind of struggle within him. "My father made the decision for me," he said watching the candle sputter. "He and I did not have the best relationship. More often than not when it came to settling our differences, he won. One day after a particularly . . . violent disagreement, he shipped me off."

"McBain told me . . ."

"It was a long time ago," he said. "The reason no longer matters."

The tenor of those words told her that at one time nothing else had mattered more. But something had changed inside him just as something was changing inside her whenever he was near.

"Is it true then that you tried to kill him?"

Humor twinkled in his eyes, though his gaze was at once direct. "Aye. I was not known for my restraint in the tender years of my youth."

"But thirteen years ago you were barely an adult. How is it that you eventually became captain of the *Black Dragon*?"

"The captain was a drunkard and wieldy with a whip. One day while he was beating one of the crew, I decided I'd had enough."

"You mutinied?"

"I am guilty of smuggling. Perhaps even a bit of subversive behavior should anyone choose to mount an offense against me. But not a mutineer. The Roxburghe family owns a fleet of merchant ships. My great-grandfather's legacy to this family. The ship on which my father exiled me, the *Dragon*, was my own inheritance. My father possessed a macabre sense of irony when it came to doling out life lessons." He studied his clasped hands. "It took me a year of hell before I had the guts to claim the helm of that ship as my own."

"What did you do with the captain?"

He glanced sideways at her. "I dropped the bastard off in Workington with a note to my father, telling him to go to the devil. I then gave the crew a choice to stay or leave. Every single man jack stayed."

"Will they come to live at Stonehaven?"

"Maybe. I don't know. Most want to stay on the sea."

Do you? she wanted to ask.

"I came here to save my brother," he said, as if he could read his mind. "I never had any intention of staying. I've never been much of a farmer."

"You should stay, my lord."

She looked around the sunlit stairwell in hopes of diverting her thoughts. Dull early-evening sunlight broke through the clouds and filtered through a stained-glass window at her back throwing patches of red, green, and gold on the walls around her. "This is a fine loft that your grandfather built. You have kind servants. A beautiful home." She cleared her throat and stood. As did he, slowly, as he stepped down the stairs and once again took his place in front of her.

"Why should I stay?"

"Because you are looking for something, and if you have not found it already, then you have not been searching in the right place." Self-consciously, she looked down. "Now that I have rambled about, I think I should like to return."

He propped one boot against the landing to prevent her escape. They stood nearly eye to eye, and something hot and dangerous arced between them. "There is a hunting lodge an hour's ride from here," he said. She felt the warm assessment of that dark blue gaze. "I have been meaning to visit the place since my return. You are welcome to ride with me. Chaperoned, of course . . . if you choose to go back and fetch Jason to accompany us."

"A chaperone? Because you do not trust me. Or I should not trust you?"

"Both, perhaps."

This time it was her turn to laugh, but she sobered at the thought. "At least we are honest with one another," she said.

Honesty in and of itself was a form of trust. She had only truly trusted two people in her life. Friar Tucker and Mrs. Simpson. A hostage houseguest was not supposed to trust her captor. Or feel safe. Or feel this much desire. Yet she did.

And as the silence lengthened between them, he cupped her face with his hands. Her heart pounded against her breasts as if she had been running uphill, and then he bent his head and kissed her.

She stood on the landing, still holding tightly to the balustrade as if to catch some of her weight. Her mouth opened taking his tongue and giving her his. She wanted to touch him, to know him as she had that night in the glade, except in the light where she could see and feel him, where her mind could not lose him in the darkness. His kiss gentled, a contradiction to the raw desire she sensed in him and which coursed through her.

He pulled back, his hooded eyes surveying her as if to discern her thoughts. Strangely, she was no longer afraid of the future. She had at last found the capacity within herself to confront her future on her own terms. "Will everyone not wonder where we are?" she asked. "Are they not looking for us?"

He swept back a wayward strand of her hair and lent his mouth to the shell of her ear. "I am the only person who went after you today, Rose. If they wonder, they will not speak of it upon our return."

Chapter 11

The hunting lodge was a two-story, ivy-covered Tudor cottage in the woods with a yard overrun by bramble and bracken. Inside, the dusty floorboards creaked with each step. A forest of horns gleamed back at Rose from amid a variety of weaponry on the walls. They had barely made it to the cottage before the second storm hit them. Rain slashed at the windows and made a *drip-drip* sound in the fireplace.

Ruark knelt in front of the huge stone hearth, large enough to roast a spitted boar. Yet, somehow, he managed to build a roaring fire. A lightning flash illuminated the room. With the heavy rain, she saw nothing but rivulets sliding down the thick lead glass. Her teeth chattering, she moved nearer to the hearth. To Ruark.

He turned to look up at her from his position closer to the floor. He'd slicked his rain-black hair to his nape and it remained tied back. The silver ring in his ear caught a flash of light.

"It looks as if no one has been here for years," she said.

Crouched on one knee in front of the hearth, he looked around the room. Much of the furniture remained: a long wooden trestle table and chairs, an oak breakfront stacked with a plethora of porcelain ware, none of which looked to have been touched in years. "I used to come here when I was a lad."

Her clothes were soaked through and he dragged two heavy chairs nearer to the hearth for her to lay out her attire to dry.

He pulled blankets out of a cabinet set atop the breakfront. Standing in front of the hearth with one hand outstretched to the warming flames, she continued to watch the fire burn. She was neither coy nor demonstrative about her desire, but the newness of it all caused her to hesitate. She felt shy and nervous and did not know how one behaved in such circumstances.

He'd seen her before undressed by the pond, but stripping out of her clothes now had a different connotation. She knew it. He knew it.

She could see it in his eyes as he stopped beside her to give her a blanket. Thunder grumbled against the eaves of the house. He looked up at the ceiling as a burst of lightning illuminated the room. "I need to see to Loki," he said. "There is a stable behind this lodge."

They had left the horse tied near the front of the house. After the fire began to warm the room, he left her to secure Loki in a stall. She remained in the silence, her eyes closed, her senses opened to the pungent woodsy smells and sounds of the night surrounding her.

Then she set aside the blanket and struggled with the hooks and strings on her bodice and skirt. But her hands were freezing and it took her longer to remove her bodice, stays and petticoats. She laid her stockings over the back of the chair nearest to the hearth. Ruark still had not returned from the stable, so she wrapped a blanket around her shoulders and went in search of something to drink.

* * *

Ruark did not return until sometime later. Wrapped in the woolen blanket, she had waited for what seemed an eternity. She had found a flint box and lit a candle, then discovered dusty bottles of wine in the other room. Inside the breakfront were serving dishes. She set out two glasses for the wine.

She stood at the end of the table, next to the tall carved oak master's chair, watching nervously as Ruark stomped the mud from his boots and cursed the rain and the bloody chill. The rain had plastered his shirt against his arms and shoulders. "The storm looks like it might be here a few hours." His voice partially muffled against his sleeve as he wiped his face with his arm.

When he saw what she had prepared, he paused in his remonstrations. His gaze fell first on the pallet of blankets she had made in front of the hearth, then on the table. But as he dropped his arm to his side and approached, he had eyes only for her.

She clasped the blanket tightly to her bosom. "I found bottles of wine and brandy in the back room." Her chin lifted and her tongue seemed to move faster. "I do not think I misinterpreted your purpose for bringing me here."

He stopped near enough to her to touch. "Nay, you have not," he said quietly, reaching out to tilt the wine bottle into the light as if to check its contents.

She laughed, but he heard the tremble in her voice. "I have not had anything to drink, if that concerns you. I thought . . . so that we are both clear on the matter at hand, anything I offered you this day should be done with a sober bearing. I wanted you to know my mind 'tis sound as it ever will be."

He looked down at the pallet she had made in front of the hearth. "*Is* your mind sound?"

"Are you calling me a lunatic then?"

His low laughter sounded from deep within his chest, and he reached out to smooth the hair from her face. "Maybe."

She might be of sound mind, but she remained uncertain. The lines of his lips softened as he spanned his fingers over her cheek. "It was not my intent when I brought you here to ask why you agreed to come."

"Should it matter?"

"Aye, I did not think it would."

Just then, there was a patter of windblown rain against the sheaves and glass, yet neither of them looked away from the other. "I have discovered that I possess a certain honesty when around you, Ruark Kerr. 'Tis simple."

She eased the blanket off her shoulders, bearing pale shoulders in the firelight. Then she lowered her arms and let the blanket fall to the floor.

She stood before him wearing nothing at all but the golden glow of firelight. His eyes swept over her. She had never seen herself fully naked as she stood now before him. She had never seen herself in another's eyes as she saw herself now in his. Tonight it was as if she stood on the edge of the cliffs that bordered the falls, with all the rush and wild fury of the water churning at her feet and through her veins.

Only one small step brought his body against hers. His skin smelt of rain and sweet-scented soap, his hair smelt of cloves. The fire blazed hot on her back and on his arms where she raised her palms to the powerful cord and muscle that delineated his shoulders. Rivulets of water trickled from his hair to his chest.

He lowered his head. He traced the shape of her mouth with his tongue, parting her lips. "Lord, Rose . . ." His breath pushed hot against hers. "I am not myself around you. I need to slow down. Or I will hurt you."

She clung to his arms, her fingers digging into the rigid flesh. He was thick and hard against her stomach, and as the storm outside raged, another more powerful one churned inside her.

He tangled his fingers in her hair and dragged her head back, and still she had not breathed. The silver earring caught some of the firelight and it shimmered like a star. "What is it you want, Rose?"

She wanted never to be responsible for another person's pain again. She wanted this night with him. She wanted someone to want *her*!

"Open your eyes to me, Rose. Look at me."

She played no coy game of seduction and, with a blinding honesty she was not used to feeling, she knew that neither did he. He wanted her.

The pads of his thumbs stroked her lower lip, his touch feathered across her face. His warm mouth moved downward until it closed over the turgid hardness of her nipple. A shiver passed over her.

She melted against him and her head tilted back as his lips suckled the pulse beating wildly at her throat.

She felt something primal claw at him. Something that made him seek to narrow the space between them and do more than simply possess her body as he grasped the backs of her thighs and lifted her to the table, stepping between her legs.

She caught herself against her palms. The wine chalice on the table tipped, spilling wine over her fingers. He bent his head and kissed her nipple, rolling it between his lips, swirling the fiery lash of his tongue around the sensitive ruched flesh. Her breath caught and held.

"Ruark . . ."

His voice touched her senses. "Shh." His strength surrounded her, consumed her, sweeping her into a sea of desire. He kissed the underside of each breast.

His want explicit, he reached between her legs with his hand and parted her, the melting friction of his finger sliding inside her turning her to jelly. On a gasp, she broke from the kiss.

His hair askew and half falling from the thong that held it, a lock brushed his cheek. Her breath came in little pants. And she seemed to hang suspended with him.

He stepped back, his hooded eyes surveying her nakedness while he worked to free his shirt from his breeches. She half sat motionless, unable to take her eyes off his hands. As he pulled his shirt over his head, she smoothed her hand over the hardened planes of his stomach, the intense pleasure of watching him undress heating her.

He tossed the shirt behind him, his expression remaining impassive, and she watched him remove the rest of his clothing and carelessly drop all aside. She remembered the way he had looked by the pond, taut of waist and narrow of hip, his thighs exuding strength.

But now she could see all of him. His member extended thick and long from a nest of black curls. The pattern of his man's hair tapered upward in a narrow line that arrowed up his abdomen and sprinkled his chest.

His fingers closed on her shoulders as he eased her back never breaking the intimacy of his touch. He moved his palms between her thighs and with the gentlest of pressure nudged her legs apart.

"Bend your knees," he whispered.

She did as he bid. Then his lips took hers again. His kiss was thorough. Sliding one hand around her bottom, he lifted her, spreading her legs wider. And somewhere in that touch, he pushed inside her heated body.

He used both hands on her waist to hold her. A gasp of pleasure punctuated her groan. He was large, and she was tight, despite how aroused she was. He leaned his cheek against her hair, then kissed a warm trail down her temple to her throat. Dark, silky hair brushed her cheek.

"Better?" His voice broke on a gasp.

She adjusted her bottom, and closing her eyes, felt him more deeply inside her. The burning had passed. The pressure intense. She felt . . . "Much better."

He steadied her body with one hand on her nape, intensifying the pleasure with his fingers. "Brace on the table. Lift higher," he said between his teeth.

He used both hands on her waist to adjust her as he thrust. Slowly at first, his face fiercely beautiful in the firelight. His lashes, thick and dark, framed his eyes. "Open to me, Rose. Let me feel you." Sliding the tip of his tongue from the pulse at her throat in a seductive path across her shoulder, he kissed her flesh. "Let me be deep inside. Deep."

His mouth moved on down until it closed over the turgid hardness of her nipple. A shiver passed over her. When his hand parted her thighs and pushed her wider, she drew a sharp breath.

She savored the rasp of his flesh against hers. Where he led, she wanted to follow. In this, she trusted him.

Her hips moved with his. Against him. Like the melody and harmony that combined to make perfect music. "Come with me, Rose."

He pulled back to look down on her, her hair spread against the table.

Their gazes touched and locked briefly, his dark and searing. The pads of his thumbs stroked her lower lip, his touch feathered across her face. He watched her from behind a thick fringe of his lashes. Then his gaze was following the slide of his hands along the pale smooth curve of her waist to the place where his body was joined to her.

She was aware of the fullness of his sex within her as he thrust against her. Instinctively, she sought more of him.

Instinctively, she arched her back.

Her breaths became shorter. Then he was moving hard between her legs and she found herself absorbed with sensation. The friction of his movements. His scent as he leaned over her, slightly salty and definitely male. She could smell herself on him as well, the soap she'd used to bathe. All with every stroke as he rode between her thighs.

With a cry, she wrapped her legs around his hips, holding him close. Her head fell to the side. She felt liquid beneath him. Unbearable. Breathless. She cried out softly as he continued carrying her. Higher.

He pressed his lips against her throat. Yet each time his lips parted from hers, they returned for more, slanting across hers in an openmouthed kiss, swallowing the cry that rose at the back of her throat, and she drowned in his kiss. Drowned still clinging to him. Their breaths ragged as he found his release inside her. She refused to let him go until her heart's tempo began to slow.

Then, moaning something earthy and profane, he buried his face in the moist curve of her neck, and they began to breathe with more measure. She lay flat on her back, staring at the timber crossbeams in the ceiling.

He brushed the dampened hair from her face and kissed her brow. He stared at her with an expression she couldn't read. Then he lifted her into his arms and carried her to the blankets in front of the hearth.

* * *

Rose roused to half sleep when she felt Ruark rise some time later. Turning her head, she caught a glimpse of his taut buttocks as he padded naked across the room to where he had set his canvas saddlebag. She thought him beautiful, bronzed by firelight.

He stopped at the breakfront and poured water from a skin into a blue pottery bowl. She heard splashing. He must have found a rag among his things for he returned with both. He had not spoken more than a few words since he had settled her against him, and she had been too absorbed by what had just transpired to worry that something may be wrong.

He knelt beside her. His eyes dipped to where the blanket had fallen to her waist, making her conscious of the intimacies they had shared. Suddenly shy, she wanted to pull the blanket up to her shoulders.

"Open your legs, Rose."

She hesitated, then did as he told her.

"This will be cold."

The water *was* cold, but it was also cooling. His touch was gentle as he removed traces of semen on her thighs. "I was too rough," he said.

"'Twas different this time," she said. "Better even than before."

He raised his eyes, amusement touching her. She wanted to ask if what had just happened between them was always so special between a man and a woman.

He lay down beside her and, settling her into the crook of his arm, pulled the blanket over them. She lay with her cheek against his shoulder.

Splaying her fingers across his chest muscles and dark springy hair, she considered the strength of him beneath her palm as she collected such random observations about him. She could not help admiring his dark nakedness against her pale skin. She traced a fingertip down the thin line of hair over his abdomen, pushing the blanket ever lower.

His fingers grazed her cheek, drawing her gaze upward. As if sensing her mood, he pushed his fingers farther into her hair. "You will find more to explore if you keep touching me like that."

"I like touching you."

She traced her fingertip across a round indented scar just above his hip. "You've been wounded . . ."

"Grapeshot," he answered.

Remembering what McBain had said about the measure of a man facing a broadside, she touched another jagged scar beneath his ribs. "Rapier," he answered before she could ask.

"Truly." She rose up on her elbow as she found another thin line across his collarbone. "And this one? Musket shot or ax blade?"

"I fell out of a tree when I was ten."

Her mouth quirked. "I see."

"I was spying on the milkmaids bathing in the stream. The branch broke. If not for the fact that I fell on half the Kerr cousins on my way down, I might have broken my neck." She shook her head and fell back on the blanket laughing. He rose on his elbow above her. "Duncan made sure the lot of us could not sit for a week after that. We did no more spying to be sure."

"You are close to Duncan?"

He hesitated. "In every way, he was more a father to be than my own."

He pushed her hair back. "And what of you?" he asked when he had her attention. "Other than your thigh, have you any scars 'pon such lovely flesh?"

"As a matter of fact, I do."

She lowered the blanket to her hip and pointed out a small scar the size of a shilling where she had burned herself.

"Tell me about it."

"I am what Sister Nessa claims 'possessed of a curious nature.' I never understood if she was speaking about my mind or the fact that most who know me think me unusual. I believe now she meant both. She warned that curiosity would be the death of me. She was nearly right."

He twirled a strand of her hair around his finger. "Was she?"

"Aye, I blew up the watermill. 'Twas an accident, of course," she said in all seriousness, for at the time it had frightened her. "I had sought to make a lightning arrester. I thought a rod would divert the electricity, but instead it invited a strike. I still do not know what I did wrong. I was so sure . . . You are laughing."

"Nay, love. But what possessed you to think of such a scheme?"

She sat and settled the blanket about her hips, her long thick hair protecting the rest of her modesty. " 'Twas my intent to save the church tower in Castleton. Every year the tower is struck by lightning. Every year the villagers rebuild. Mrs. Simpson had given me a book about a phenomenon called electricity and some people were open to the idea, thinking they could better spend their time building other things. Others argued that I was attempting to circumvent divine will by placing such a rod on the tower in hopes of diverting destruction. They believed that if He chose to continuously throw lightning bolts at the church steeple, I should not interfere.

"So as an experiment, I took my rod and copper to the watermill, which sits at the highest point near the abbey.

Lightning *did* strike. It caught the mill on fire. It burned it to the ground in a spectacular bonfire that could be seen for miles. Friar Tucker was beside himself."

Ruark was laughing so hard, Rose glared down at him. "'Tis how I came to be in the vault and discovered the puzzle box that contained the ring."

He held up his hand. "This ring?"

She frowned as the memory of his theft intruded. He may not believe in its power, but she did, and she was not even the person who wore the ring.

Frowning, she held his hand, and traced her fingers over the ring, as if by touching it, she could know that much more about him. "'Tis an Arthurian relic. When you are granted whatever you want most, only then will the ring release you."

He tilted her chin with his palm. "Do you believe in magic, Rose?"

"Everyone needs to believe in something," she said.

He slid his fingers into her hair. He pulled her head down and, kissing her with unhurried ease, rolled her onto her back. "At the moment, I can think of wanting nothing more than you."

He set his mouth to her breasts, drawing first one budded peak, then the other between his lips. He lowered his hand and gently palmed her sex. "You are hot," he whispered against her throat. "How do you feel?"

His erection registered in her half-drugged senses.

A soreness burned between her thighs and a throbbing heat still lingered in her womb, as if he had permanently branded her with his touch. Yet she wanted to feel him inside her again.

She splayed her fingers in his hair, watching from behind half-closed lids as he explored her body with his mouth and his hands. "I feel as if I should ask if you are under some sort of mystical enchantment."

He smiled against her breast. "Aye, I am enchanted. Or I would not want you as I do. That is the truth."

She half believed he *was* charmed.

Or *she* was. For she was in danger of falling in love with him. "You could at least pretend you want me for something other than—"

"Desire?"

She had intended to say a political pawn, but stopped herself 'ere she spoke the words.

He pulled her into a kiss with the other hand, inviting her passion. Passion was safe. It asked for everything yet nothing at all. Passion was merely physical.

Thunder shook the rafters. Outside, the storm continued to blow, and he looked over her head toward the windows. Rain continued to beat against the glass but without the same intensity as before. "The rain is moving east."

Toward the sunrise and a new day. He leaned his cheek against her hair, then kissed a warm trail down her temple to her throat.

Their breathing ragged, he joined his mouth to hers, and seized her lips in a long, fierce kiss, and soon it didn't matter that the storm had moved away and would leave a starlit night.

He was moving between her legs, indulging her senses, and she did not think about anything else at all.

She was lost. But so was he.

Chapter 12

The ride to Stonehaven remained cloaked in a wet grayish mist that twined around trees and blanketed the glens and rocky slopes. Dawn had barely touched the mists by the time they reached the stable.

Aware of the man who rode behind her, his hands loosely holding the reins, Rose was almost sad to glimpse a structure rise from the sea of waspish vapor. Ruark dismounted in front of the stable and reached up to lift Rose from the saddle.

Even through the wool of his cloak protecting her, she felt the warmth of his hands around her waist. Her gown remained damp from the rains the day before, and the chill of the morn had done little to warm her.

He held her to him and she lifted her chin. The thick morning mist shrouding the countryside had wet his hair.

"Are you all right?" he queried.

Neither she nor Ruark had spoken since leaving the lodge. The shroud of fog made her feel more isolated, but not alone. "Aye." She shivered. "I am merely cold and wish to change."

Two groomsmen ran out of the stable. Ruark greeted the men and handed off Loki's reins. "Rub him down and feed him," he said, placing a guiding hand beneath Rose's elbow and turning her up the hill.

She could feel the groomsmen's eyes on her back and, pulling the cloak tighter about her shoulders, she kept her head down to better watch the path. "They all think I tried to escape," she said. "And that . . ."

"We spent the night together and that I ravished you? I dislike informing you, love, but most already think that."

Wet leaves muffled their footsteps. "I do not regret what happened between us," she said, momentarily lost to the tempest swirling around her heart.

"Your words have eased my conscience, love."

She stole a glance at him. He *did* look quite at his ease, she thought, somewhat perturbed that he could return to Stonehaven unchanged for what had occurred between them.

"I care naught what anyone thinks of me or you, Rose."

"You are laird. 'Tis not you they judge."

"I *am* laird. My opinion of you is all that counts."

She frowned up at his profile, but he remained looking straight ahead. "Truly your conceit is enormous even for a laird."

She saw one corner of his mouth slip upward. "Aye, 'tis," he agreed, slanting her a rakish glance that would bring ruin to Aphrodite herself. He drew her around. "But that does not change the facts. I am still laird, love. And you are still mine."

She caught her palms against his chest. His fingers dug into her upper arms. Then gentled. "And I have something to say before we go inside, Rose. I mean to say it now—"

She pressed a fingertip to his lips. His features were

lost in the shadows of the mist but she could feel tension inside him. Since the moment they'd left the lodge, he'd been silent in a restless manner that told her something weighed heavily in his thoughts. She feared what he might say.

She had made her mind up to return to her father. She was finished running from her past. She would not allow him to risk his brother's life for anything they might have shared last night. Not for her.

"I know what you are going to say . . ."

He pressed his lips to the inside of her wrist. "Do you? I doubt it."

He lowered his head and brought his mouth close to hers. A door suddenly slammed somewhere in the mist ahead of them and, before Rose could respond, before she could think of what to say, Mrs. Duff appeared, clucking toward them like an angry hen. Her bulk swayed with her stride.

Dropping away, Rose turned to face the woman, unsure if the anger in Mrs. Duff's demeanor was directed at her or the master of the manse.

"Half the staff has been awake awaiting your return, Ruark. Worried sick we've been."

She turned the force of her gaze on Rose. Ruark spoke first. "Before you think the worst of her, Mary, know that she was with me last night."

Rose felt the blood leave her face. Mary's eyes narrowed. "And are ye tellin' me ye ravished the girl, too? Her bein' helpless and under our protection?"

"I am telling you, her absence was not her fault. And that will be the end of it. Now . . . she needs a hot bath and sleep."

He reached for Rose only to find that Mary stepped between them and removed his hand from her arm. "Aye, she does. But you'll no' be the one takin' her, Ruark Kerr. Off with ye, now. Ye can order your own bath, too." She waved off Stonehaven's laird and Rose held her breath, afraid of what he would say to Mary. "Come, lass." Mary tugged Rose forward. "Let me get ye cleaned up and out of those damp clothes lest you catch your death."

Just before she entered the portico, Rose stole one last glance over her shoulder at Ruark standing in the wooded path, his gaze fixed on her, the feel of him still lingering in the soreness between her thighs.

Deflected by her own emotions, Rose could not help the softening of her lips as she turned away, remembering their night together, and, oh, so much more.

"Aye, I've seen that look in many a young maid's eye," Mary said, catching the flicker of awareness in her eyes. "And naught good ever came of it, Lady Roselyn. I assure you."

The forecourt bustled with activity. Because of the early hour, Rose had not expected to see so many already awake as she and Mrs. Duff emerged outside the walls of the courtyard. Rose followed the housekeeper down a gravel path that wound around a floral border stretching across the south side of the house and on past the kitchen and dovecotes, all the while listening to Mrs. Duff chat. Over the course of the last few days, Rose had accepted life at Stonehaven with no complaint. Breakfast was served at eight, tea at eleven, lunch at one, and so on and so forth. The evenings, she dined in her chambers and later she read in bed. True to his word, Ruark had allowed her free rein of the library and gardens.

"Do I have permission to send letters to the abbey?" Rose asked.

"I see no reason why ye can no'."

She had written to Friar Tucker, Jack, Sister Nessa, and Mrs. Simpson. She had written to Friar Tucker to tell him that she was well. To the others, she had been more succinct and told them who she was, apologizing for her lack of honesty and asking them to forgive her.

Ruark had left for Jedburgh two days ago and she expected she would be summoned any day now.

The housekeeper stopped and turned, nearly causing Rose to collide with her, and making her wonder if she had said something to displease the woman.

"Ruark told us we were to grant ye every courtesy, and so I will," the housekeeper said, a hint of steel—though not unkindness—underlying her tone. "Some here resent ye for being who ye are, but I learned long ago no' to judge a person by the blood running through his veins. After all, we are no' brought into this world with a choice of parents. So fer that you'll be findin' me more tolerant than the rest."

Thank you seemed incongruous.

"Now . . ." Mrs. Duff brushed her hands down the apron pinned to her ample bosom, taking Rose's measure, as if to say that would be all she'd speak on the matter. She pointed to the side gate. It hung ajar and opened to a wooded path leading into a grove of trees. "That be the way to Mrs. Fortier's cottage. Ye can no' miss it."

With that declaration, Rose was left standing in the middle of the path as Mrs. Duff strode up the incline toward a whitewashed outbuilding. From the pungent aroma of hops and yeast in the air, Rose guessed the place to be the brew house.

Not another person was around.

Suddenly uncertain, Rose glanced back at the large stone manse settled like a throne amid the jeweled landscape.

Stonehaven was even larger and grander than she'd first imagined upon her arrival. So different was Ruark's world from the one in which she'd been raised, she thought.

Mrs. Fortier's small cottage sat in a glade of dappled sunlight, surrounded by a white picket fence, the kind used to keep rabbits and other critters at bay. Rose eased through the wooden gate and relatched it behind her, looking around her at the earthen mounds overflowing with wintergreen, yellow dock and wild carrot mixed among a colorful array of flowers.

She found Mrs. Fortier at the back in the garden, a red scarf on her head as she knelt among the flowers. She looked up and saw Rose.

Rose ran to her to help her to her feet. "My lady." Mrs. Fortier dipped when she stood.

"Please, Mrs. Fortier," Rose said. "You must be careful."

Mrs. Fortier's hand went to her chest. "Heavens, every time I see ye, ye give my heart a start. Please call me Anaya."

"I wanted to meet you. You served my mother."

"I did, my lady. She was a kind one, she was."

Anaya brought Rose inside. She shared the room with two others who worked in Stonehaven's kitchens. Rose sat at a small circle table and Anaya made tea. They spoke for a while as Rose asked about Kirkland Park, what it was like, what her mother had been like, questions she had never been able to ask anyone. "Did you know my father?"

Shaking her head, she looked down at her hands, clearly too frightened to speak about Lord Hereford. "Nay, mum . . ."

Rose laid a palm over the other woman's hand. "I am

in need of a companion. You are widowed. I wondered . . . I am hoping perhaps you might want to accompany me when I leave here."

Anaya grasped Rose's hands. "I loved your mam, I did. I loved her enough to protect your secret and never betray ye. I will be accompanying ye to Jedburgh as a witness as is required. But Lord Roxburghe has given me the chance at a good life here. I ask that ye no' take it from me, lass."

Rose peered around her at the comfortable setting and understood what it meant to feel safe. "Nay, I would not."

Chapter 13

McBain, Jason, and Anaya Fortier arrived with Rose to the royal burgh of Jedburgh three days later, where she was sequestered in a remote red sandstone abbey on the banks of the Jed Water. All she knew was that Ruark was here and that her father was also in Jedburgh.

A single torch threw shadows against the stone walls as she paced the narrow confines of the room. She was vaguely aware of the soft swish of her patterned silk gown, the pad of leather slippers on the cold stone floor, and a bodice that was too tight to be comfortable when her wont was to breathe deeply.

Rose had been taken aback when Mrs. Duff laid out the dress yesterday morning before her departure. Rose knew nothing of ladies' fashions, and she had not thought herself capable of loving such a dress, with its beautifully decorated skirts and beribboned underclothes. 'Twas a silly vainglorious sentiment to think a dress held the capacity to transform her into something she was not, but Ruark had been correct when he had said that she should not be a sheep when walking into the wolf's den. Today, she felt every inch the earl's aristocratic daughter.

A knock sounded on the door in the other room. She had been expecting the summons since breakfast hours ago. She stopped her pacing. Making a determined effort to steady her breath, she seated herself upon the settee provided for the occupant's comfort. The worn piece of furniture that surely hailed from King James's day was the only luxury in the sparse room that contained a table and a narrow bed. She folded her hands in her lap in an act of forced serenity, as she heard the squeak of hinges as Anaya opened the door. Friar Tucker stepped into the dimly lit room. "Rose." No one had ever been so welcome.

They met halfway. He caught her against him and pressed her cheek against his shoulder, gently holding his hand to her head. His wooden rosary rattled at his waist.

"Rose," he whispered. "I didn't think I'd have a chance to speak to you."

"Do you know what is happening?"

"Aye. Someone will be arriving momentarily. We haven't much time."

He enclosed her hands in his much larger ones and sat with her on the settee, the action reminiscent of every other time he had sat her down for comfort's sake. "Is Lord Roxburghe safe?" she asked. "Is he well? Have you seen him?"

"Aye, lass. He is in the great hall."

He had been gone a week. What had happened during that time? Only her imagination could guess.

"These uncertain times have put us all in jeopardy to be sure, Rose. There are those among Roxburghe's own clan who want to use this moment as a rallying cry to continue their fight with the English. It is enough no blood has yet been shed. I must know, Rose." He tightened his hold on her hands. "Did he treat you . . . well?"

She didn't want to talk about herself when this was already too painful to bear, when she had so many questions to ask. Would her father release Jamie Kerr? But something in the tenor of Friar Tucker's voice pulled her focus to his face. "Aye, Father. But I am ready to have done with today."

More than anything, she hated the vulnerability that came with her next words. 'Twas Kirkland Park her father had always wanted. Not her, she knew. Yet, some part of her, the young girl she had once been, wanted to believe he could not be the monster everyone painted. Someone would come to her and say that 'twas all a mistake. *Your memories of him are true.*

"What of my father? What is he like?"

"He would foment the rift as best he could in the Kerr clan. He is not much different than he ever was when it comes to getting what he wants."

Friar Tucker gave her a colorless, edited version of the happenings of the last few weeks, and told her how he had been summoned to Jedburgh, just as Anaya Fortier had been, to confirm her identity. Jedburgh was between Alnwick and Stonehaven. But it was all for show, like a spectacle with dancing bears and colorful jugglers to awe the crowd.

Friar Tucker ended by changing the topic with news about Mrs. Simpson, Sister Nessa, and Jack. "The boy misses you," he said.

Her eyes lost their blankness and became brilliant again as she looked at him. "I would very much like to see both of them again. Will I, do you think?"

Approaching footsteps fell upon her ears. She turned her head toward the door. "Rose," Friar Tucker rushed to say. "There is still much I have not said . . ."

The footsteps in the corridor were suddenly in front of the door. A tall man appeared in the doorway, not much younger than Ruark.

"The name is Bryce Colum, Lady Roselyn. I served with Ruark on the *Black Dragon*."

Then she realized he had been one of the guards who had helped kidnap her.

He greeted Friar Tucker with a subtle nod, his blond curls brushing the broad width of his shoulders. "'Tis time."

Had he meant to make it sound like he was escorting her to the gallows? Rose thought some moments later after they had left her chambers.

The stone corridor was damp and cold beneath her thin leather soles. Though the sun slanted through tall arched windows at intervals. Rivulets of rain streaked down the dirty glass. Outside the cloud-laden sky was a dark gray. To Rose, it felt like night. She had been ensconced in a windowless room since yesterday, trapped by the thick stone walls. Yet, in spite of the cold, she felt hot and her temples throbbed. Earlier, she had blamed the tightness in her throat on the smoke from the brazier heating the room, but she knew now it was a lie.

"You are not Scots?" she asked Mr. Colum, concentrating on the scent of rain in the air, the sound of their steps on stone in the empty corridor.

"No, my lady. I am English. My family hails from York."

"You are a gentleman," she said, noting his cultured voice.

He pressed a hand to his chest. "My family would wholeheartedly disagree."

He suddenly stopped as they reached a fork in the hallway. She heard voices coming from a room at the end of the corridor.

"I am instructed to tell you that Lord Hereford has

been directed not to approach you, and that you should only speak to the questions put to you. When it is done I am to take you back to your chambers. Then tomorrow morning, I am to take you from Jedburgh, where we will await instruction. Hereford has agreed to Ruark's terms to see you safely escorted from Scotland to a place of your choosing. You will be free, my lady."

Her hand went to her chest. Ruark had done that for her?

"You will not be in the room long," he said.

Noting the sword hanging from a sling at his waist, she looked around the empty corridor. "Is Lord Roxburghe afraid of my father's men or his own?"

"He is watchful of all men, especially today."

Rose recognized the same ominous undertone she had heard in Friar Tucker's voice. "Is Lord Roxburghe in danger from his own men?"

"Pity the man who tests him, my lady. He is well able to take care of himself." Turning slightly, he offered a hand down the three steps.

She saw now why he had stopped. Where was her mind that she had missed seeing the stairs? Her hands were trembling.

The noise in the hall rose as two pages pushed open the heavy oak doors in front of her and Rose stepped into a tall, cavernous hall with wooden beams that stretched across the ceiling. Shock stopped her cold on the threshold.

Three or four dozen battle-hardened men, bristling with weaponry, filled the hall. Sitting around the long table and standing against the walls, all turned as the doors swung wide.

Her escort motioned for her to proceed. "My lady."

The heavy air reeked of wood smoke and unwashed bodies.

No friendly face looked back at her from among the sea of bearded faces. Somehow, more afraid of showing fear in front of this group than she was of what awaited her, she continued to move her feet forward.

Mr. Colum stopped, and the only noise that followed was the scrape of leather soles against stone as a path opened in front of her.

Then she saw the man sitting at the head of the room. Flanked by two of his own guard, he made a single abrupt movement of his hand as if silencing those around him, like an ax that severs the head from a body. And at that moment, her courage deserted her.

She could go no farther.

He wore a cut jacket with an embossed silver waistcoat, breeches tied just below his knees, the civilized refinement a stark contrast to his reputation. She could not tell the color of his hair beneath a powdered wig queued at the nape, but his brows were blond and flecked with gray.

There was no tenderness in his gray eyes as he sat back and perched his chin upon his steepled fingers with the casual indolence one might use when studying a problem that required too much thought and one wished only to be done with it.

Rose lifted her chin in a manner that told him she cared little if he found her lacking.

But it was a lie.

Perhaps something of him was buried deep inside her after all.

For she did not understand the intensity of her emotions.

And as if reading the thought in her eyes, Richard Jerome Lancaster, the fourth earl of Hereford, the English warden and former captain in the Royal Navy smiled. It was contrary to her one memory of him those years ago when he had put her on her first pony and told her she would one day ride like the wind. For 'twas not a kind smile. Yet one that asserted itself in his voice as he spoke.

"Come forward out of the shadows," he said, with the cultured arrogance of one used to obedience. At least he did her the service to stand. "Let me see you."

A hand on her shoulder stopped her.

Ruark stood behind her, his eyes hard on her father. Dressed as he was in leather breeches, white shirt beneath a leather jack clasped shut with a heavy buckle, Ruark looked far more disreputable than her father, and infinitely more dangerous in his boots and spurs and a sword belt fastened at his waist. She almost leaned against him, even dared to touch the fold of his sleeve before she stiffened herself to stand alone.

Rose had an image of the two men facing each other in much the same way across the bows of their ships. Whatever this meeting was today, it was personal between them.

"You will abide by our agreement, Hereford," Ruark said. "You have seen her as we agreed. Do you confirm her identity?"

Her father stepped around the table only to be stopped as a guard dropped the end of a pike in his path.

He laughed though his eyes bristled with umbrage. "Surely I am no threat, Roxburghe." Obviously, for the benefit of those standing around them, he spread his arms. "I am unarmed. As are my men."

"Aye." Ruark's smile was all teeth. "But not the three hundred you have awaiting your return outside the walls of this abbey. Or did you think you need such a force against forty men?"

The comment stirred the men to laughter.

"For it will take a siege to retrieve what is left of you should you break your word, Hereford. Answer my question."

Her father's gray eyes lingered on her and, for a moment, something inside her responded. Then his gaze shuttered as his attention moved to the hand resting possessively on her upper arm then to the man standing behind her. "You are more priceless than you know, Roselyn."

"Then you do not deny her?" Ruark asked impatiently.

"Nay, I do not."

Voices rose to a murmur around her.

Until this moment, she didn't know how much those simple words would affect her. No one had ever publicly acknowledged her existence.

She felt shaky, for as a part of her life had been returned to her, another part was now gone forever.

"Am I allowed to approach my daughter?" Hereford demanded. "Or will your man run me through?"

Ruark looked down at her, a question in his eyes. An infinitesimal nod signaled the guard to allow Hereford to pass.

Her father walked to where she stood but not so close that he could touch her or she him. Only slightly taller than she was, he was still a big man, remarkably fit for a man of fifty years. Remarkably ruthless, and she dared not forget it. She was not a fool to think he had ever cared anything about her. He wanted her ancestral home. He wanted her Kirkland Park. She had accepted long ago that it would be the price of her freedom. And now he would abide by his agreement and grant it.

"Do you remember your mother?" he quietly asked.

"Nay, I do not."

"You are more beautiful even than she was," he said.

"Beauty is a curse to women and a bane to men. Is it not, Roxburghe?" There was something sinister in his tone as he voiced the query. "Your mother was *also* a whore, Roselyn," Hereford said. "It appears her daughter is of the same ilk."

Ruark had gone stiff behind her. "Apologize, Hereford."

"Or you will do what? Defend the honor of my Sassenach daughter?" He laughed, his eyes like daggers as they pierced Rose through the heart. "Do you want to know the last words your mother ever said to me as I went off to serve my king and my country? She hoped God would have the foresight to send me to the bottom of the sea. I see a certain irony in the fact that it was she who was ultimately sent to die in the cold, black depths of hell. Irony and justice."

He looked past her. "And you, Tucker . . . is this what you think I promised you when I let you keep her? A happy ending?"

Friar Tucker stood in the doorway, his hands folded in front of him. "Tucker! *Lover* to my beloved wife. Man of God. The man who swore on his life to the world that my daughter had boarded that ship with my wife. Does she know your own part played in this melodrama?"

Friar Tucker did not defend himself. Rose met Tucker's gaze in confused accusation.

Her mother's lover? His own part?

"Enough!" Ruark said, handing Rose back to Colum, who stood behind them, and she stumbled on the uneven stone floor. "Our agreement was that you would see her, and then let her go. You do not need her to get what you want. Tucker has agreed to our terms. This interview is over."

"This interview has only just begun," Hereford shouted

above the growing din. "And what I have to say is best done in public for all to hear so there will be no mistaking what passed this day."

His eyes narrowed on her. "I would have you answer one question, daughter. I shall even phrase it for your comprehension. Did Roxburghe have carnal knowledge of you while you were in his care?"

With her color rising, she shook her head. She didn't understand what was happening. Her gaze sought Ruark's.

"Answer the question, Rose," Ruark said. "'Tis not your head he wants served to him this day. 'Tis mine. The consequences are mine to bear."

Even if those consequences entailed an accusation from her father of rape? Such a public indictment coming from the lips of the English warden himself was a dangerous charge, even for a Scottish peer. "Nay, they are not yours, Ruark."

She faced her sire. "You are mad if you think to provoke a fight this day over honor. I am your daughter . . . I have no honor in which to defend. Lord Roxburghe treated me with more kindness and respect than ever shown by you."

"Did he *fuck* you, Roselyn?"

She gasped at the man's crudity. "How dare you!"

Beside her, Colum's hand went to his sword. Ruark stopped him with a hand on his. "Answer the question, Rose," Ruark said.

"These things are easily discerned by an examination," Hereford said. "You can answer the truth now or bear it out an hour from now. I have a physician with me . . ."

Rose's gaze flung to the short, stubby man standing behind her father. He wore a priest's robe, but she would wager her soul he was no priest. Her thoughts swerved dizzily through her options. What options? her mind screamed.

"You . . . you would not dare have a man touch me in that way!"

"I bear the consequences of my actions, Hereford." Ruark said. "Now let her go."

Rose stepped in front of Ruark. "He did nothing without my consent," she said. "Nothing!"

Hereford laughed. "Consent? You foolish girl. The law does not give you the right to *consent* to anything."

Her father raised both brows and confronted Ruark darkly. "Aye, you will bear the consequences, Roxburghe. You will marry her, and take a Sassenach bride home to your precious clan, and if you want to see your brother alive, you will give me every damn thing I ask for. Including Kirkland Park and the *Black Dragon* for your debt to me that remains unpaid."

The room erupted. All around them, the shouting escalated.

Rose whirled and clutched her hands in Ruark's shirt, standing as if she was a wall between him and her father. "Nay!" She gave him a shake. "You must refuse. I beg of you. Refuse. If he wants Kirkland Park, he will take the trade. Ruark . . . I will go with him. Please," she whispered in desperation. "I will not let you do this."

"Cunning, Hereford," Ruark said. "Bloody *fooking* clever."

"Ruark . . . please," she whispered, holding herself against him.

He studied her upturned face. "Go back to your chambers, Rose."

Then he nodded to someone behind her, and a hand came to her elbow. Colum stood beside her. "Come, my lady."

"Nay." Furious, she turned to her father. She had no idea what would happen should she not agree to this foolishness, she certainly knew what might if she did. "You will free Lord Roxburghe's brother or I swear I will throw myself off the tower in this place and dash myself on the cobbles. If I die before the age of twenty-one, everything I have goes to the church. Including Kirkland Park. You will get nothing!"

Clap. Clap Clap. Hereford brought his hands together. "Capital show, my dear. Do you hear that, Roxburghe? She would rather die than wed you. Aye, she has my blood in her veins."

The hiss of Sheffield steel against metal silenced the room as Rose drew Colum's sword from its sheath and with one violent move closed the distance between the blade tip and her father's throat.

He fell backward against the table, momentarily blinded by shock and an overconfidence that failed to allow him to perceive the danger to him. Rose tightened her grip on the hilt, her palms sweaty as she held the weight of the sword. "Do not tempt me, *Father*. I care very little about you. Even less than what might happen to me should I run you through."

A hint of color shaded his ruddy face to a darker hue and his eyes narrowed to slits. "I swear you will pay for this, Roselyn."

"Pay? With what? Something has to matter to me first. You have seen well and good to strip me of all that was ever important."

"Tell me the life of every man in this room does not matter to you then? For if anything happens to me . . ."

The sword began to grow heavy in her hand. She had lost the momentum of an attack that came with surprise, and she knew if he fought her, he could escape before she did too much damage. Still, even a little blood would make a terrible mess of his fine clothes.

Ruark laid his palm against the blade. "Not this way, Rose. He is here under a flag of truce."

Tears blurred her eyes. "Men speak such fine words of honor," she said, "when it suits their interests to do so. Your truce. Not mine."

"Wanting to kill is not the same as killing," he said softly. "I promise you nothing said today is worth the price you will pay for that deed. And I am not speaking of the consequences that will befall every man here. There is not a man who does not wish Hereford dead and who would not defend your actions."

She swallowed against the increasing tightness in her throat. Ruark cupped his palm over her face, forcing her to look at him. His eyes embraced hers. "You will have to trust that I can take care of us both."

She saw him through a blur of tears. A hand at her elbow tugged her. "Come," Friar Tucker urged. "Let us be gone from here, Rose."

Ruark's eyes told her in more than words to trust him. She did trust him. He was the only man in her life who had ever truly been honest with her.

Finally, she lowered the sword and returned it to Colum.

Not a man around her moved. Her eyes passed over one bearded countenance, then another. A pin dropped could have been heard in the room. Without a word, Rose strode from the hall, leaving Friar Tucker and Colum behind. Once in the corridor, she lifted her skirts and ran. She didn't stop until she reached her chambers, slammed shut the door and slid the bolt home.

Chapter 14

"**C**ome now, my lady. Open up. The good abbot will not appreciate the loss of a door should we have to break it down."

Ruark heard pounding on the door before he rounded the corner and saw Colum coaxing the panels.

"She has barricaded herself inside her chambers," Colum said, stepping aside. "I didn't reach her in time. She is fast."

She was also capable of eluding them all.

Ruark stood glaring at the door as if his will alone would unbolt it. Three other men milled behind him. He'd passed two others on his way here. The door was three inches thick and solid oak. Short of using an ax to break it down, no one would gain entry until Rose opened the door.

Ruark turned to two of his retainers behind him. "Find the abbot and make sure there is no other way out of the room." He gestured to the third man behind him to follow before returning his attention to Colum.

"Who is inside with her?"

"Only Anaya, the maid with whom she arrived."

"Where is Tucker?"

Colum shook his head. "If you were a priest, where would *you* go after what just occurred?"

Ruark's gaze found the lancelet window that overlooked the inner courtyard outside. A light cold drizzle fell on the garden. He saw a gate in the exterior stone wall and the chapel beyond. He hadn't set foot inside any church in years.

Rose found the chapel dark except for the soft red glow of the sanctuary lamp. The air smelled thickly of incense and wax. A small table beside the door was covered by a cloth and bore the stoup of holy water. A few clear white votive candles burned near the back beneath a shrine of the Blessed Mary.

"I was expecting you." Tucker's even voice pulled her around.

A scarred wooden railing divided the chancel from the rest of the chapel. She walked forward and saw the brown-robed figure rise from where he had been kneeling at the front and slowly turn toward her.

"How *could* you?" she demanded. "How could you not tell me you and my mother were lovers? Is it true?"

It was far easier to escape her room that it was the questions she needed answered.

"'Tis not that simple," Friar Tucker said.

"Then make it simple."

For a heartbeat, the lines of age softened before he looked away. "I loved her."

Tears burned behind her lids. They scalded. Then she grabbed his hands. "Are you . . . ? Does he hate me because you are my father?"

He raised his gaze and she thought tears touched his eyes, and for just a moment, she hoped. "Nay, lass. I am not your father. He hates you because you are hers. You are Elena's."

Rose covered her face with her hands. Why could he not lie?

"Your mother, we grew up together at Kirkland Park. I lived every day watching her," he said into the silence, "with her fiery hair and love for life. How could I not love her," he said simply. "When she was eighteen, she met your father and fell in love. He was dashing and titled and all the things she thought she wanted in a husband. All he wanted from her was an heir and Kirkland Park.

"In the beginning, your mother and I shared only our friendship. In time, it became more. I am making no excuses for us. Hereford was not a kind man on the rare occasion he came home.

"It was a relief the months he was away at sea. One night after he had returned, in a fit of melancholy, Elena told him we were lovers and that she wanted to leave him. She never told me what Hereford did to her that night, but afterward, she was desperate to get you out of England. She thought she could take you to France and you would be safe. A storm that night delayed the ship, so she sent you and Anaya to me to care for you both until she could return."

Tucker lowered his head. "The rest you know. Today presented him with the perfect opportunity upon which he could not pass. By wedding you to Roxburghe, he wanted me to know that despite everything, his is the final word over your future. And unlike my agreement with him, because he holds Jamie Kerr, he knows he can ask for and will receive anything he wants from Roxburghe."

Rose could only shake her head. She didn't understand any of this.

Tucker folded his hands. "Upon your marriage all that

you have will go to Roxburghe. He will then deed Kirkland Park to Hereford."

"And Ruark? What of him and his life? What of his *Black Dragon*?"

Tucker lifted his head and looked over her shoulder toward the door. The wooden beads at his waist clattered softly. "Tell me that she is not equal to any bride worthy of your title and your ship, my lord."

He stood in the shadows backlit by the gray light coming through the corridor's window. She could not see his face, only the shape of his shoulders, the swing of his cloak, his sword beneath. He had not removed the weapon before stepping into the inner sanctum, which said more clearly than words he did not trust in a higher power to protect him even on holy ground.

She wanted to run to him.

"My lord," she said.

"Lady Roselyn." His gaze turned on Tucker. "I would have a word with her," he said. "Alone."

Tucker turned to Rose and tried to take her hands. But Rose did not want him to touch her. Not yet. She felt too raw. Betrayed by everyone close to her.

"Very well, Rose," he said.

After he left, she turned to Ruark. They stood still and looked at each other, though what flowed between them like a fast-moving river current remained unspoken.

"I feel . . . I feel nothing," she said. "Not even anger. Do you think that is bad? I suppose in time, I will feel a great deal more than indifference and a great deal less than anger at my mother."

He had walked to where she stood and she looked up and saw him through a sheen in her eyes. "You cannot mean to give him the *Black Dragon*?"

He looked momentarily startled that her worry was for

him and not for herself. "Aye," he said. "I was thinking of retiring from the sea, anyway."

"Truly, you lie."

He said nothing.

"I am sorry—"

He touched a fingertip to her lips and stopped the words. "Do not apologize to me for anything. Do you understand?" Their gazes held for a heartbeat and his touch softened. "You have nothing for which to be sorry."

Seeking refuge in the shadows, she folded her arms over her chest. "When I was a little girl I had a fascination with the stars," she said, raising her eyes to gaze at the painted golden angels on the ceiling. "The constellation Andromeda was my favorite because she gives the appearance of a female warrior holding a sword. Or other times a maiden held by chains. The dichotomy intrigued me. I told myself I would always be the warrior who held the sword. I don't believe in anything anymore."

He leaned against the scarred wooden railing that enclosed the chancel and sat his hands on solid wood to brace himself as if he didn't trust himself to touch her. Then Rose moved in front of him, so close, the fabric of her gown brushed his thighs, and he did touch her then, pulling her nearer to him. She laid her head on his shoulder. "We do not have to do this my father's way. I cannot be the woman you were forced to wed to save your brother." Her chest rose and fell. "I would have you promise . . ."

He placed his forehead against her temple. "What?"

"If we manage ourselves correctly, the marriage can be annulled. Or you can divorce me," she said. "'Tis been done before, by England's own monarch. You and I then can be free to live our lives as we choose."

He held her casually imprisoned between his legs, his fingers splaying her cinched waist. "Aye. 'Twould be a simpler matter severing the vows than merely removing your head."

She pulled back. "I am trying to be logical about this."

"No sane Scot would dispute that you are an unsuitable wife for the Roxburghe laird, Sassenach."

She frowned at his jest. "Then you understand," she said. "Right?"

"Aye, but you are foolish to think either of us has any choice in the matter," he said, his growing anger more refined than hers but no less visible in his eyes as he spoke. "If Hereford wants to drag you back to Kirkland Park, he can. He can marry you to any man he chooses, and you will have no say. The fact that he even allowed Tucker to raise you speaks to something inside him at least."

"Aye, it speaks to his greed." She stepped away. "I am trying to give you an honorable exit."

He silenced her with a look. "Where is the honor in divorce, Rose? And there can be no consideration of an annulment. When we leave Jedburgh tomorrow, there can be no question in anyone's mind as to my claim on you. You will be wedded and bedded well and good. My wife in full."

She could feel the heat rise in her cheeks. "But this is only a game to my father? Is it to you as well? Check and checkmate?"

He came to his feet and she fell back a step and bumped the bench. Her melodrama might have been amusing coming from another, but she truly did believe something inside her would perish if she wed him. She *was* frightened, just as he said. Not of him, but of what she perceived of her future as his wife. She did not wish to marry him. She was not standing before him under any pretense of nobility. She stood before him with the intent to bargain her way out of an intolerable situation.

"Please . . . do not touch me. I do not think I can bear any more of this."

When he felt her trembling, he silently cursed. He used his arm to pull her to him. "I am not the ogre you wish me to be in this." He tilted her chin, then held her to him and some intangible part of him flowed into her. "Where else do you have to go, lass? I will no' treat ye unkindly. You have my word on that."

She sniffled and leaned her face against his sleeve, forgetting that he was Scots sometimes. "The word of an outlaw?" she asked.

He sensed more than felt his smile. "The word of a border lord, Lady Roselyn."

"A privateer."

"A Scots."

They both laughed for this brought them back to her first morning at Stonehaven, familiar camaraderie. Then tension of a different sort returned to fill the void.

He put his hands on her shoulders. "I have learned that what is spoken in a moment of heated passion holds more truth than that which is spoken deliberately and with calm. We can agree that ours is not an optimum marriage. But it will begin with a modicum of honesty between us."

He lifted his gaze to a point over her shoulder and she saw two men standing at the door. Rose backed away through a circle of sconce light. She was a wreath in the darkness no longer able to hide. And suddenly she did not want to.

Ruark watched Rose turn on her heel, the wordless action indicative of the uncertainty in her heart, and as she left the chapel, Ruark realized what these last few weeks had cost her in pride and in the loss of her independence forever and the total betrayal of those she loved. Yet, when she had looked up into his face, he had seen the unwavering trust and commitment to him in her eyes.

Ruark understood her reticence. He understood her feeling of helplessness spilled from her erroneous perception of his own reasons for marrying her. He allowed that she had a right to own those feelings.

What she did not know—what she did not understand—was that no one could have forced him to wed. No threat or bribe would have been large enough to sway him had he not *wanted* her.

He leaned his head against his hands, resting the weight of his thoughts in his palms, before he pulled out the special license he held in his shirt, the license he had gotten in Hawick weeks ago. He had received special dispensation to wed her from the authorities there.

He even owned to the nefarious fact that his intent to wed her was not one born from any *noblesse oblige* he might possess, which he did not. His purpose had been born from vengeance pure and simple and the unwillingness never to lose a fight. *Check and checkmate*, as Rose had told him. Just as it had been the first night he had taken Rose in the glade.

He had not thought of her feelings. Nay he had been driven to have her.

And when Ruark had learned from Rose that Hereford knew of her existence, he had set this day in action. He'd even made a contingency plan for the *Black Dragon*.

Check and checkmate.

He could read Hereford's black soul because in many ways they were the same. Ruark was not nice. He was not kind. Or gentle. Especially to a man who would abuse a twelve-year-old boy.

Ruark had not come to be known as the *Black Dragon*

because he hosted teas and picnics on the deck of his ship. He may not have been chasing the East Indiaman that fateful day she crossed paths with Hereford's ship but he *was* guilty of piracy on the high seas.

And then something had happened to him that afternoon Rose had come to him in the chapel. He knew instinctively what battle did to a soul, and he'd seen the pain in her eyes. He remembered it himself at seventeen. He had taken her to the lodge because he had wanted her. And then he had tried to do something unselfish. He had wanted to find a way to set her free. Truly he had.

Ruark didn't know how long he was alone in the chapel. One minute. Five. He sat back, crossed one hand over the other in his lap, and his gaze fell on the ring where he sensed the low hum in his body. Pulling his thoughts.

A week ago, when he'd left Stonehaven, he thought he'd been prepared for this day. But when he had seen Rose in the hall facing her father, he knew he was not.

He had not been braced against the slam of his emotions, or the realization that he was trapped by an emotion he had sedulously avoided for thirteen years and had fancied himself immune to. Even less prepared for the violence of his own reaction to it, all the while, as he was working over in his mind how he was going to manage to save Jamie if he took Rose.

And then Hereford had granted him his greatest desire in a move so spectacularly executed that he could not have planned it any better had it been more premeditated.

Tell me that she is not equal to any bride worthy of your title, Tucker had said when Ruark entered the chapel.

Aye, she is of great worth.

She was beautiful and spirited. Equal to him in every way. Ruark did not want her handed to him trussed up like some fabled sacrifice. •

But he wanted *her.*

Now that the shock had worn away, Ruark wondered if he could be dreaming, so perfectly had everything transpired.

Then he wondered why he felt as if he had just stabbed Rose through the heart when she had lost everything, and he had lost nothing at all.

Chapter 15

Rose's marriage to Ruark was arranged to occur before the sun set on a day that was as gray and damp as her mood.

There was no dearth of qualified persons to perform a wedding ceremony, even on short notice. But somehow, Ruark had a special license. All that Scottish civil law required was mutual agreement between partners followed by consummation.

And witnesses to both.

But English law required the special license. Her father was not present. Two of his representatives were. On the morrow, Ruark's brother would be delivered to a field just across the river, and Ruark would ride outside the stone walls of this abbey and retrieve him.

No one seemed to consider that nothing would prevent her father from reneging after the exchange. Forty men, even Scotsmen, were no match against three hundred.

Still, she stood with Ruark in the same chapel they had been in earlier as a strip of white linen was wrapped around their hands linking them together. She wore a froth of lace that her maid, Anaya, had turned into a beautiful veil when pinned to her hair and topped with a wreath of pearls. The lace was beautiful and Rose felt beautiful wearing it.

She listened as Ruark said two sets of vows, the litany of Gaelic interspersed with English and Latin. He knew the language and his fluency surprised her for she had so rarely heard a brogue in his voice, and hearing one now reminded her of their differences.

She looked up at his face bathed in the pale amber light of the chapel, his dark lashes framing his eyes. It was the first time since she had entered the chapel, carrying a small bouquet of pale roses, that she had even looked at him. She felt something stir deep within her.

More than the vivid memory of his possession pressed on her mind.

He was not some farm boy or simple layperson who had never ventured beyond the boundaries of his village she was marrying.

She was marrying the laird of clan Kerr, and the earl of Roxburghe. Then a ring was placed on her finger. A delicate band of silver. Its very simplicity drawing her gaze to her hand, for the circlet held more meaning to her than the grandest of jewels. She wondered how Ruark had managed to come up with both a veil and a ring in so short a period.

Then again, she should not have wondered, for Ruark Kerr showed much ingenuity in all that he did. What was a wedding to him when compared to battles he had fought?

Now facing him, she quietly repeated something in Gaelic, something about the spirit and union of souls bound until death.

She felt her senses reeling, heightened by his closeness, the heat of his body, and the clean masculine scent of him. He'd combed his hair into a queue at his nape that swept off the collar of a fine lawn shirt with a lacy jabot. The small earring in his ear so opposing to the scant civilized mien of his attire.

And in that moment, she had eyes only for him.

Aye, I could easily love him, she thought, more afraid of what her own vulnerability would do to her.

She held still as the linen cloth was removed from around their wrists and he was told he could now kiss the bride.

As he lowered his head to kiss her, without realizing, she moved instinctively toward him. The touch of his breath, which carried the sweetest taste of wine, was still warm on her lips as he slowly pulled away.

The ceremony was over and she was now his wife.

Moonlight threw shadows on the floor around where Ruark stood against the wall. God only knew his impatience, as the faint sounds of feasting came from the empty corridor behind him.

"Dammit, McBain. Where are you?" he mumbled.

The last place he wanted to be at this moment was standing outside looking out upon a mist-shrouded courtyard.

Ruark had not expected this night to be filled with joviality, but ale and the promise of Jamie's release tomorrow did much to lift spirits. It didn't seem to matter to anyone that Hereford had an army camped across the river. Ruark liked that about the Kerrs. None of them lacked for courage. Their skills, honed by generations of border raiding, made them all at ease with the long odds.

Surprisingly, most of these same staunchly fierce clansmen had accepted the Sassenach Rose as his bride. But as Ruark considered that fact, he suspected their acquiescence to his circumstance had as much to do with the flow of abundant drink as it did with Rose's willingness to skewer Hereford like a kabob that afternoon. After witnessing that event, many of his men would have lain down their lives for her.

Rose had not spoken to him all evening except to say her vows and an occasional polite thank you as he handed her wine. He had managed to slip her from the noisy hall, and now she was on her way to the chambers they'd be sharing this night.

The crunch of pea gravel alerted him to someone's approach, and he straightened. He recognized McBain's elfish form as he rounded the corner. Three taller men walked behind him. Ruark could not make out who they were. When they passed through the torchlight and into the corridor, Ruark stepped out of the shadows.

"Lord Almighty!" McBain blasphemed, a hand pressed to his chest. "I've a mind to die of heart failure. 'Twould serve ye bloody right for all the trouble you've put me through this night."

As the most circumspect of his men, McBain had been the logical choice for arranging the witnesses needed for tonight. Ruark assessed the three men standing uncomfortably behind McBain, two distinguishable by their priestly robes. They belonged to the kirk in the village. The third man was the mayor's brother-in-law, a solicitor and known English sympathizer. Many of the borderland families championed the king, so finding such an individual had not been difficult.

"Hereford rode out of the abbey this afternoon and is encamped across the river as he said he would be," McBain said. "Jamie is there."

"You have seen him then?" Ruark asked the three men.

The shorter robed priest answered for the three. "Aye, my lord. The boy be in . . . temperate spirits and is ready for ye to fetch him home."

"What of the two men who were taken with him?"

"Rufas and Gavin Kerr will be turned over along with the boy in the morn."

A cold unsettling gust fluttered the torchlight, and Ruark glanced up at the clouds rolling across the moonlight. The night had turned waspish. "You have been apprised of the entire situation then?" he asked, pushing right to the point.

McBain sniffed, insulted that Ruark had to ask. "They have. And trust me, they would rather be anyplace else, which is why I picked them." He rocked back on his heels and laid his palm across the hilt of a wicked-looking short sword at his waist. "They will confirm that consummation took place and will make an oath of it afterward. The marriage has already been properly recorded."

The shorter robed man cleared his throat. "We are preparing papers now as per Friar Tucker's instructions. Mr. Colum will have the necessary documents drawn up by morn, my lord."

There would be no doubt as to the legality of this marriage, Ruark thought. Tonight was a necessary path to that end.

With McBain's curt order that the three were never to gossip about anything witnessed tonight on threat of slow torture and death by dismemberment, they shuffled away, properly horrified by McBain's threat.

Ruark was momentarily amused by McBain's protectiveness. "Are you going soft on me, McBain?"

"'Tis not for ye I'm thinking," he said with a disapproving sniff, "but for that girl. She has been through enough."

"Any word yet from Duncan?" he asked.

The word had gone out as Duncan rode west and north to bring more men into Jedburgh. Ruark had been expecting the arrival of more clansmen by that evening. Duncan had not come.

McBain seemed to think over his next words carefully.

He scraped his palm over his bewhiskered jaw. "No one has dared say anything . . ." he said after a moment. "And no one would be sayin' anything to me. But there are some who believe Duncan wouldna' mind if somethin' were to happen to you and Jamie tomorrow."

Ruark might believe Duncan held a certain animosity toward him, but not toward Jamie. "Then I will have to make sure nothing does."

"Will ye really be givin' him the *Black Dragon*? You'll no' be returning to sea?"

"Is Tucker off?" Ruark asked, avoiding discussion of his future plans.

"Aye. But he oughtn't to have left without telling the lass good-bye."

Tucker would not take an escort, though Ruark would have spared him one. Ruark had agreed it best he leave as well but for different reasons than he told McBain. "If tomorrow does not go well, I cannot guarantee anyone's safety. Least of all Tucker's."

McBain sniffed. "Aye, and who does Tucker think he is to think only of himself at a time like this?"

"He is someone who has loved and cared for Rose for most of her life. He did not make the decision easily, McBain."

Dear Rose,

> *By the time you read this letter, I will already be on my way back to Hope Abbey. Lord Roxburghe and I both agreed that it was best to leave tonight.*
>
> *You and I were not able to speak much today, and I did not want to depart with discord still between us. Before leaving for Jedburgh, I went through your room at Hope Abbey. I knew that, after tomorrow,*

you would never be returning, and I wanted you to have that which you had always held close to you. I wish I could have given you more. In time, you will decide if the years at the abbey were happy ones.

Now I will tell you in writing what I should have told you in person today, my precious Rose. Since the moment God saw to bless me with you, there has not been a time that you have not brought joy to my life. Never a moment you have not brightened the lives of all those you have touched here at the abbey. I wish I could have always kept you safe. But know that I have always held your best interests in my heart.

You may not agree with your choice of husband, and you may find what was done to you unjust for you both. I wish you could have had more time to prepare, but someday you will come to know Ruark Kerr as I know him. I truly believe that fate brought you together. Now it is up to you both to open your hearts.

The letter in Rose's hand had neither wafer nor wax. He signed the letter only as *Father*.

Friar Tucker rarely went by Father, though many called him such. She looked down at the box delivered with the letter earlier in the evening.

"Is there anything more ye need me to do, my lady?" Anaya asked Rose.

The maid stood in the doorway that separated the small sitting room from the bedchamber. Rose absently smoothed a stray wisp of hair from her face as she turned from her place on the stool.

Anaya folded her hands in front of her. "I have added a feather tic to the bed."

Rose forced a smile. "Do you have a place to sleep tonight?"

The woman dipped slightly in reply. "Lord Roxburghe said I was to stay in Friar Tucker's room, now that he is gone. He said Mr. Colum will fetch me when ye are ready to leave in the morn."

"Did he say anything else? About Friar Tucker, I mean."

"Nay, mum. All his lordship said was that I am to be prepared to leave here with ye before dawn, my lady."

Anaya looked about her as she worried that she had forgotten something. The woman had helped Rose remove her dress and comb out her hair. She had packed Rose's one small trunk and laid out tomorrow's attire, which was the same traveling dress in which Rose had arrived. The blue-and-yellow beribboned garment was a bright spot on the droll seventeenth-century settee.

Rose had no idea the time that had passed since Mr. Colum had left her at the door that evening, but she wanted to be alone now. "You have done enough for me, Anaya," Rose said, liking the woman but uncomfortable with her over-willingness to please, and unused to servants. "Go seek your bed and hopefully some rest. Tomorrow will be a long day for us all."

"Yes, mum."

Before she could leave, Rose stopped her. "Anaya . . . thank you."

"Yes, mum. Thank you. His lordship asked if I wanted to stay with ye once we returned to Stonehaven, my lady. I said 'twould be an honor. I will see you in the morning."

Rose heard the door shut behind Anaya in the other room.

Wearing a simple nightdress and robe, she had been awaiting Ruark's onerous arrival in a place of warmth.

A single candle on the table and the coals in the brazier provided the only light and warmth in the room.

Returning her attention to the plain wooden box on the floor, she rose from the stool where she had sat to read Friar Tucker's letter. She folded the letter and laid it aside, then knelt and worked the lid off the box.

It contained her mother's threadbare purple-and-green plaid wrap. The one Rose had worn most every day of her young life. A palm-sized Bible Friar Tucker had given her when she was five, various silly trinkets collected over the years. Her entire life contained within a plain wooden box the size of a turnip basket.

Nothing was as she had once imagined it would be.

With a false sense of bravado, she left her place beside the warm brazier and walked to the table, where she poured sweet red wine into a goblet. She nursed the rim of the cup, unable just to tip it back and drain the contents. Her stomach would not allow it, any more than it had allowed her to eat that evening.

She did not want to be intoxicated tonight. However unplanned this marriage had been, 'twas still her wedding night. She wanted to remember it.

The door opened a crack, as if someone had turned the latch but was not yet ready to enter. She heard Ruark speaking to someone outside the room, probably Colum. He entered the room, not seeing her at first. He hesitated, then shut the door behind him, and slid the bolt home. He carried himself with ease.

His leather boots, turned down at the cuffs, gave him unnecessary height. Whoever had built these rooms had not had tall men in mind. Her new husband's head was mere inches from the wooden beam that braced the ceiling. His gaze wandered over the room before finally coming to rest on her.

Her white dressing gown afforded her little protection from the heat of his gaze. A blue ribbon closed the robe and tied beneath her breasts. Anaya had seen to her appearance. She didn't have to look at herself to know the low décolletage revealed the soft rounding of her breasts above its scalloped lace. Her hair, falling softly to her waist, had been brushed to a sheen. She had not the least doubt that she was beautiful. She had wanted to be beautiful.

Ruark braced his back against the door and folded his arms. She could not read his thoughts, but her heart raced as if she had consumed more than a few sips of wine.

"You would test my mettle further?" she asked, wondering why he was not moving toward her.

She also noted that he wore no sword or dirk.

"Nay, love. I know your mettle. But since my life depends on my caution these next few days, I am merely taking note of my surroundings."

Their old repertoire returned some of her verve. "Surely you do not think I would attempt to murder you?" she said with nonchalance.

Subdued amusement played on his face. "You have only attempted to do so twice. I am hoping now that you are wed to me, you are of a different bent, especially since we already know one another well."

"I thought you were not coming," she said after a moment, her quiet tone filled with emotion she did not want to feel.

He unbuttoned his waistcoat and stepped forward at last. "You thought wrong, love."

She forced herself to breathe evenly. "Who will serve as witness?"

He set the waistcoat atop her trunk against the wall. "Does it matter?"

She looked about at the walls, attempting to spy cracks

or holes in the stones. Then she remembered the hidden door, the way she had escaped that afternoon. Ruark's hand came alongside her jaw and stopped her from searching. The odd bit of lace on his cuff fell around his finely shaped hand that seemed to belie its strength. He had moved without a sound to stand beside her.

"'Tis no one you know or will ever see again, Rose."

She tightly hugged her torso, drew in her breath on the heel of a pause and nodded. "I suppose that is no mean feat. I know very few people."

His eyes swept her. "Are you chilled?"

She should not be cold with him standing beside her. "A little."

He walked over to the single brazier in the corner of the bedchamber, where he knelt and added more coal. She watched the way his shoulders pulled at the fine lawn of his shirt.

After a moment, he braced one elbow on his knee and saw the box. He fingered the faded plaid, then turned the letter over in his hand and skimmed the script. "Tucker was here?"

"Clearly, he had an idea that I would not be returning to the abbey," she said jutting her chin toward the box. "'Tis all I had that was truly my own. Strange, I am an heiress, yet it still feels as if all I am is in that box."

She had not meant the words to sound so cold, but they did, and then she realized she didn't have to care what anyone thought of her. At least her thoughts were hers and hers alone.

Ruark walked over to the table and poured a glass of wine. "Wine?" he asked, holding out the bottle to her.

Her hands trembled a little. "I have drunk enough. If we are to have an audience, I will remember what I do this night."

Yet, her heartbeat tripped over itself. How fast her resolve crumpled. "Did you see Friar Tucker before he left?" she asked.

"Nay, I did not. Colum handled the details." He studied her over the rim of the goblet, then drained the glass. "Is it necessary to talk about this tonight?"

Perhaps he was telling her he was in no mood for conversation or that particular conversation, or perhaps he was only telling her that nothing they said was between only them. Privacy was an illusion. The stone walls gave the false impression they were alone.

Rose cast about for something relevant to say but could not seem to wrap her thoughts around anything solid.

He turned his head. His glance took in the rest of the simple quarters including the narrow bed hardly large enough to fit her much less the both of them. "Have you been comfortable here?"

"This room is better than most in which I have stayed," she said.

She could have said the mattress was hard and lumpy and the ropes squeaked, but the look that passed through his eyes told her he already assumed as much.

"Certainly 'tis better than spending this night bivouacked outside with your men," she said.

And just that fast, the matter between them suddenly wavered and shifted to the forefront.

He seemed to recognize this as well.

A small shiver slipped under her skin as she fixed her gaze on his. He framed her face with his hand. "There can be no doubt when this night is gone that ours is a legal marriage, Rose."

The tenor in his voice told her he was not referring only to her father but to questions that might be raised by his own people later. He was not so much protecting her as he was securing the future for any children they might have together.

Children.

Of course, she would have his children.

"You need not fear this night, Rose."

In other words, he would make it quick. She nodded her comprehension. Her next words, though faintly uttered, conveyed resolve. "I understand."

She would do what she thought was expected of her. She wanted to feel no shame this night. Not tonight when this was supposed to be her wedding night. It mattered little that there were people who listened, even watched from the alcove behind the walls. She would not let that fact intrude. She had the power to block them from her mind. She had power.

Turning away from him, she began removing her robe, bending her head to pluck at the ties.

Ruark came to stand at her back. She felt a tingling awareness of him along her spine as he placed his hands on her shoulders and turned her slowly to face him.

She finished untying the ribbon laces, then lowered her arms and let the robe fall in a pool around her bare feet. Her night dress, though thin, was not sheer, but it revealed the soft peaks and curves of her breasts and hips.

"We are of the same bent to see this night over and done with, Ruark."

She pushed to the balls of her feet and tried to kiss him, but he stopped her. He raised his palms to her face, touched his thumbs to the rise of her cheeks, but not so far that she did not feel his breath on her lips.

For a moment, she lost herself in his gaze. And 'twas not difficult to find pleasure in his touch as he brought his mouth down on hers. It was not a scorching kiss.

Yet, by its very gentleness, possessed and burned just the same.

The backs of his hands whispered down her arms and, twining his fingers through hers, he raised them to his shoulders.

She was hardly aware of his palms on her waist.

Hardly aware that he spoke her name as he shifted and closed the distance between them until his hips aligned with hers. He scored the soft underside of her breasts, rekindling more than the spark inside her. In the glimmering candlelight, he became like the solitary flame that burned in the room. She resisted her feelings for only as long as it took to draw in her first breath.

And then she was aware of nothing at all. His touch was liquid, and it was suddenly simpler to abandon herself to him.

She threaded her fingers into his hair, loosening the queue, and letting the action define her desire.

She wanted him to touch her as much as she wanted to be touched by him. She wrapped herself in the fragrance and heat of him. She held him and was held in return.

Only when he pulled away did she remember they were not alone. But as if sensing the thorn in her thoughts, he whispered soothingly, telling her to look at him. To feel only him, know only him.

He gently and persistently kissed the fear away, turning her head so that her mouth shaped more firmly to his, increasing the unrelenting pressure of his lips, compelling in their promise. Then he reached around her and blew out the single candle in the room, descending the room into a colorless shadow realm revealed only by the burning coals in the brazier.

She became like the whisper of his voice, ethereal and

otherworldly, yet there was not a part of her flesh that did not feel alive.

She drew in a deep uneven breath. His mouth grazed hers. "Come."

She opened heavily lidded eyes as he lifted her in his arms and carried her to the bed, where he laid her atop the covers. She watched as he undressed.

Unlike her, he stripped down to flesh and muscle. Then he dragged an eiderdown from the settee and climbed beside her, tantalizingly warm as he brought his mouth back to her lips. She cradled his face, taking the weight of him against her body as he moved atop her, but not inside her, though she felt his member heavy against her thigh. It was as if he, too, recognized this moment for what it would mean to their future, and that her elemental desire came as much from her need for him as her need to trust him.

He drew back, his expression one of tender desire, controlled yet not completely restrained. He would not hurt her, nor see her hurt. "Keep the eiderdown over our heads," he said.

"But then no one will know . . ."

She felt his chuckle. "They will know."

Then he raised up on one elbow and looked down her body, his hand pulling up the nightdress. She adjusted her body, helping him as he pushed the gown higher and over her head, letting it flutter to the ground beside the bed. His lips closed on the tip of her breast. He kissed her then suckled first one rigid peak then the other, taking his ease with each as he laved her with his tongue. Lower still, he moved, across the underside of one breast, his lips fluttering hotly down her stomach, pausing over her naval to dip his tongue and taste.

Wrapped in an eiderdown cocoon, she wanted to touch

him, but could not and still hold the blanket over them.
The quandary frustrated her. Her restless mewling came
as much from frustration as bliss, and drew him back to
her mouth, where he explored deeply, swirling his tongue
around hers and wresting another cry from her.

His kiss was as intoxicating as it was unrelenting and
anchored her to him in the humid darkness beneath the
covers. "Shh, love."

With no warning, he shifted his body. His hair brushed
her chin. His lips her breast. He moved lower. His tongue
a fluttering caress.

He drew on her flesh and gently kissed her naval.
"Ruark . . ."

Her tone questioned his actions. While her body wanted
to know more. Tension heightened her tactile senses.

Then he kissed her.

There.

Lightly at first. His humid breath teasing.

He slid an arm beneath her thigh, splayed his fingers
over her buttocks and, with the other hand he parted her
moist flesh, exerting a gentle pressure. She whimpered
at the first touch of his mouth.

Unprepared for the shock of that contact and the first
stroke of his tongue. The impact on her senses was acute
and pervasive.

He gently plundered her with his lips and his tongue.
He drew on her flesh. Lapped it. Suckled it. Her fingers
left the nest of the eiderdown and curled in his thick
hair. Loosing herself to sensation, she cried out, arching
her pelvis so he could take more of her into his mouth.
Quivering beneath him, she had ceased caring what anyone
saw or heard. When she came, she shattered.

She gasped for want of breathing, boneless as he rose
to his knees above her, and steadied her with gentle kisses

and softly uttered words. She did not notice the cover slide to his waist. Only that his features were set.

Braced on his elbow, he took himself in hand and guided himself easily inside her. She wrapped her thighs around his hips and held herself to him as he settled firmly between her legs.

"Aye," he said against her lips, his voice heavy with inflection, his unruly hair brushing her forehead. "You are well and truly wed this night, my love."

Then he raised himself against his palms, his gaze veiled and remote in firelight, his every thought focused as he rocked against her. Again and again and again. The powerful flux and flow of his lower body guiding her.

And she momentarily disliked that he could so easily own her body.

That he knew how to pleasure a woman so thoroughly. That she was more his than he was hers.

For at the back of her mind, niggling like splinters in her thoughts, were all the reasons he had wed her, none that would ever include love.

She was valuable and courageous. She could wield a sword and a dirk with skill, but she could not wield her own future in her hands.

And while he'd etched his touch on her body and mind, he had also reminded her of her place in his life.

Reminded her . . . that she should not want this. Or him.

Yet, fulfillment came again when she did not think it could.

Then his mouth came down hard on hers. This time when she shattered, he was with her all the way.

Chapter 16

The knock on the chamber door came too early for Ruark. He stirred the coals in the brazier. He had dressed hurriedly and his shirt hung loosely out of his leather breeches. His long hair was unbound and he was unshaven. His crimson-and-green plaid was draped over one shoulder, and he held his sword belt in his hand.

Rose stirred, but did not awaken completely until he bent and kissed her. Not even the brush of his morning stubble on her soft skin drew a protest when he kissed her again.

"Anaya will be here in a moment," he said, leaning over her pliant form. "You have a long trip ahead of you."

As if still drugged by last night's passion, she opened her eyes and looked into his. He waded through a whorl of his own hazy thoughts as he watched her stretch and look around her. Though he was not one given to fancy, he thought she smiled as she turned her cheek into his arm and sleepily murmured something.

Anaya arrived in the room. Two of Ruark's clansmen stood behind her. Rose saw them as Ruark brushed the hair from her cheek. "I have to go now, love."

She wrapped her fingers around his wrist. Their gazes locked. Emotions passed between them just as last night had come, then gone. A flash in the darkness. "Wait."

The bed ropes creaked with her movement. He patiently remained on the edge of the mattress as she sat up, her hands clutching the eiderdown to her breast. Her tousled red-gold hair tumbled over her shoulders but did not cloak the swell of her breasts. She couldn't wriggle out of the bed with him in the way, and he wanted it that way.

"You should not have allowed me to sleep."

He brought her hand to his lips as if her worries were inconsequential, when in fact they mattered more than she could know. "Now, why would I have been so cruel as to awaken you?" He unfurled to his full height before she could speak. "Colum and McBain will be escorting you to Stonehaven, Rose."

She flung her legs over the mattress. Dragging the eiderdown with her and working to clutch it around her bosoms, she followed him barefooted into the other room. "Ruark!"

She grabbed his hand, but it was not the strength in her grip that stopped him. It was the desperation in her voice.

He was not a man prone to whim.

But two things happened to him concurrently as his gaze fell first on the hand that held so tightly to his and then the rings—on her finger and the *wishing* ring on his. His tactile senses hummed.

And he had the most incongruous thought that no matter what happened hours from now, he would remain unharmed. He could jump off a cliff and would not die this day.

Then he laughed, because despite what the morning might hold, his brother would be coming home and Rose would be at Stonehaven when they returned there late tonight.

Aye, what more could a man want in one day?

"Another kiss to send me into battle, love?"

He held her hand fast as she tried to pull away. "This is my fight, too."

"Nay, Rose. In this you have no say."

He nodded to Anaya, who stood behind Rose. "Colum will be expecting you outside in a half hour. See that she is ready."

He released his wife. Gripping the blanket tighter, she stared at him with eyes widened by fury. "And while you might think it highly improbable that I should care what happens to you . . . what happens to *me* if you are killed out there today? At least I should be with you."

The men standing behind him in the corridor chuckled, but she silenced them with a glare. "You are outnumbered. I do not trust him."

"Considering the warden's nature, aye, in that we agree. But trying to kill me and doing so are not the same. Now *you* listen to me. If you have a care for my safety, you be in that carriage and gone before I meet Hereford."

Halfway down the corridor, Ruark slipped the sword baldric over his shoulder. A half dozen of his clansmen walked beside and behind him, rapidly relating details of their preparations. The men were mustering, the horses being saddled now. Their spurs and weapons clanged in the stone corridor.

"Think Hereford's men are nervous yet?" another said, a tall, bearded clansman as stocky as a rough-hewn log.

"Some of us saw Rufus," a man in the back said, and Ruark recognized Angus's voice. "Takin' a piss at the latrine. Turned and waved to us on the hill afore the Anglish bastard what was guardin' him pulled him back inside the tent."

A ripple of laughter followed. All were in rousing fighting spirits.

Ruark adjusted the dirk at his waist. "Any word from Duncan?"

The men walking with him grew silent. He could feel the air chill, like the draft that twined around his calves as he stopped and faced them. Angus spoke first. "He'll be here with the others," he said, a slight edge to his voice. "Duncan would no' miss this fight."

"How many men have we?"

"Gavin's family came in last night with fifty men. Ninety men now," Angus said. "We've seen worse."

Ruark looked at each man's bearded countenance, knowing they awaited some signal to his mood. He gave Angus a hearty slap on the arm. " 'Tis better than forty standing against three hundred, eh?"

They all laughed as Ruark turned on his heel, pushed through the doors, and walked out into the pungent dawn mist.

Smoke and morning fog layered the air like ghostly tentacles stretching out from the fields surrounding the old medieval abbey, an eerie contrast to the serenity of the morning. This was Scotland's graveyard. A dozen major battles had been waged over these grounds across the centuries.

Ruark didn't anticipate starting a war today. Nor did he expect Hereford would want to take a chance on losing any monetary gain he hoped to make in this trade, especially if he wanted the *Black Dragon*. But tension remained high on both sides, and today was as much about show of strength as it was about national pride and a little blowing off steam. He would not want one of Hereford's men thinking that just because the Scots were outnumbered on their own green earth that it meant a single one of them was easily defeated.

Ruark also knew that his own men looked to him for leadership. Allegiance in the Borders was earned, as much by resolve and action as by birthright and sometimes a great deal of gold.

The three men who had served as witnesses to the consummation of his marriage last night stood uneasily in the open awaiting him. Two were robed clerics, the third, their resident English sympathizer, a dandy this dull morn if Ruark had ever seen one. He wore a lacy jabot and breeches, and brown periwig slightly skewed as if he'd been dragged from sleep. Next to them, McBain carried a sheaf of folded papers wrapped prettily in red ribbon.

Ruark thumbed through the contracts and marriage papers. Copies of everything had been made. More formal papers would be delivered by his solicitor later. "Has someone read these over?"

"Colum did, m'lord," McBain said.

Ruark held out his hand. McBain presented a quill as Angus held a small jar of ink. "Which one of you is serving as emissary?" he asked the three men without looking up as he scrawled his signature across the bottom of each paper.

Acute silence answered Ruark. No doubt the three would rather be subjected to a tooth extraction than go down that hill and across that bridge into Hereford's camp. White flag or nay, no one wanted the task and didn't consider the job part of their original agreement. Unfortunately, for them, Ruark did.

He raised his eyes and looked at the three, returning the papers to McBain to see that they were properly dried.

"I will go down there, my lord," the taller cleric said.

"'Tis the least I can do after a rather . . . invigorating night. Lord Hereford wants confirmation. There will be no denying the truth from my lips."

One corner of Ruark's mouth quirked. "What is your name?" He gave the quill over to Angus, who handed the pen and ink to someone else.

"Father Samuel. I am English," he said almost defiantly. "Come to visit my brother."

Ruark drew on his heavy gloves, eyeing him with interest. "Well, Father Samuel, you have done enough this day, and I have another emissary in mind."

Sensing the bent of Ruark's mind, the dandy straightened his brocade waistcoat with a jerk. "But I don't ride a horse," he protested.

"Then get the man a cart," Ruark told Angus.

Angus shouted across the yard for a cart. The call went down the line of men saddling horses until the order reached the stable.

"But my lord . . ." the man rasped, justifiably terrified. "What if Lord Hereford makes me swear to something that is not true?"

"Then we will have a problem."

On this precariously diplomatic note, the cart arrived, equipped with a white piece of linen tied to a hoe but no place to put the pole. Angus drew his dagger with a flourish, cut a piece of rope and bound the hoe to the wooden bench. In just as efficient a manner, he lifted their emissary into the cart. Before Ruark made the suggestion, the second cleric volunteered to accompany the man, and he too made his way onto the bench beside the first. The man holding the pony's halter walked the cart and riders to the hill's edge to await the signal from the other side of the river.

They would meet Hereford's representative on the

arched stone bridge, exchange the necessary words and agreements as came with such dialogue, and then Ruark and Hereford would meet. Ruark would give Hereford the signed documents. In return, Jamie, Rufus and Gavin would be allowed to go free. Such was the way of negotiations.

Loki was brought forward. Ruark stepped into the stirrup and swung a leg over the saddle. He tossed a bag of gold to Father Samuel. "When the other two return, you will be free to go as well. I will trust you to share equally."

McBain approached and returned the papers to Ruark, once again bound in red ribbon. "I do no' think 'tis right ye sending me away," he groused. "Ye may have need of another sword."

"If we do, one more will make no difference."

Ruark told him it was time to take Rose and leave. "Tell Colum he is not to allow her from his sight. Now go."

Watching him hurry away, Ruark shoved the papers in his shirt.

"I'm tellin' ye it makes no sense," Angus said a moment later, coming along beside him and riding a large black barb. "Duncan . . . he'd no' turn from a fight. Not this fight."

A breeze stirred the grass. The morning sky had begun to lighten and as the last shining star in the northern sky faded, Ruark's gaze slipped past the stone walls overgrown with larkspur, beyond the chapel to the stables, where dozens had followed his lead and mounted. He rode his horse to the highest point overlooking the river, where the men began to line both banks, their accoutrements winking in the sunlight. Firelight dotted the landscape, and in the awakening light of dawn, he saw Jamie across the river. The boy sat on a roan next to Hereford's large barb.

It was the first time Ruark had ever glimpsed his younger

brother. His hair was not dark, like Ruark's or their father's as he'd expected, but the bright blond color of Julia's. He was not large, but fine boned.

Loki restlessly curveted beneath Ruark.

"He looks well," someone beside him remarked, swinging the glass in his hands and noting that Rufus and Gavin did not look nearly as pampered, but at least they were walking on their own volition as they were led from a tent.

Their long tangled hair looked as if it had not seen a comb in months. They wore no boots. Their trews, and what once had been white homespun shirts, were torn and ragged beneath old plaid rags. Then they raised their chained hands and a cheer suddenly went up in the crowd, followed by another that began farther down the river near the watch. Like everyone else, Ruark turned his head and looked west. A low grumble strengthened in the earth beneath him, the thunder growing louder as a line of mounted men roared over the distant hill.

Four hundred men exploded into view and across the rise. They were a wild-looking bunch, bearded, hair long and unkempt, fearless, enough to dampen the enthusiasm of even the most confident enemy.

Duncan rode at its head. Seeing Ruark, he broke ranks and turned his horse up the hill to where Ruark reined Loki around to meet him.

Raucous cheers continued to greet the newcomers as they jostled for space beside those already lining the riverbank. Heckles and jeers on the other side followed and soon swords were raised as taunts were lobbed from both sides. This went on up and down the river for as long as it took Duncan's men to move their lathered horses into place.

Loki, perhaps sensing Ruark's mood, sidled away as

Duncan's arrival was met with jovial backslapping by those on the hill. Duncan looked at Ruark. Scraping a hand across his bearded jaw, he leaned slightly in the saddle. "Sorry we are late, nephew. Nothing occurred while I was gone?" His gaze swept the gathering troops across the river. "I would hate to have missed the excitement."

Showing yesterday when expected would not have had the same dramatic effect on the clan and its foes as his arrival this morning. No doubt, Duncan preferred the more substantial role as this day's hero, especially considering the part he'd played bringing about these events in the first place. In some way, whether advertent or not, he had played a part in all the events, including yesterday's events that led up to Ruark's marriage to Rose. Had Duncan arrived as planned, the proceedings might not have progressed as far as they had, and Rose might not now be his wife.

But the effect of Duncan's arrival on morale was palpable.

"Your presence is welcomed, Duncan," Ruark said.

It seemed appropriate that he should smile.

The first time Rose heard the raucous voices raised in cheer had been shortly after the carriage left the market square north of the abbey. The coach had not stopped but continued to career over cobbled streets as if the devil himself were on their tails. But now the black coach came to a grating standstill in the middle of an ill-maintained road five miles outside Jedburgh. In the silence that followed their unexpected halt, Rose heard the faint crack of musket fire.

She moved aside the heavy curtain and peered outside, unable to see any part of the outskirts of the town through the dull gray mists. McBain climbed down from the coachmen's roost to join Colum, who had dismounted

and walked off the road away from the clank and creak of
the coach as it settled. The ten outriders, the coachmen,
Rose, and Anaya all bent their attention apprehensively
toward the sounds floating faintly across the valley on
the awakening breeze.

Without waiting for the step to be lowered, she swept
aside her heavy skirt and exited the coach to go and stand
beside McBain.

"Were those *shots* fired?" Rose asked, hoping he would
tell her this was a positive sign that everything had gone
to plan and not the bloodcurdling sounds that preceded
battle and the spilling of blood.

Anaya was leaning her head out the window. "Aye,
mum," she said.

McBain exchanged a telling glance with Colum that
she did not understand. "Does this mean the trade is
completed?" Rose asked.

The fact that no one could answer her only added fuel to
an already heated temper. Then Colum pointed his finger.
Rose followed his gaze. She felt the low reverberations
beneath her feet just as she watched riders materialize
from the mists. They were miles away and would pass
them at a distance. But the sight was impressive as the
mass continued to grow into hundreds strung out along
the rustic river valley, high spirits all. She would not have
wanted to be in their path.

"Duncan must have arrived with the men just after we
left," Colum said.

"Aye, he'll fancy himself the hero this day to be sure,"
McBain replied.

Rose cared little who was the hero this day as the
thunder of their passing faded, leaving only a handful of
slower riders, their horses following at an unhurried lope
as if they knew the others would have to eventually slow.

Halfway across the valley they stopped and seemed to look in Rose's direction. One rider broke away and turned his horse toward her. She did not have to recognize Loki's deep red coat to recognize his rider.

She started to follow Colum and McBain down the rocky incline to meet him, but he was not looking at her as he reined in the horse in front of the two men. Dust darkened his handsome countenance.

"Is the boy well?" McBain asked cautiously.

"Aye, he will do fine for now. He has gone on ahead with Duncan."

"You would let Duncan arrive at Stonehaven in your stead?" McBain asked. Again, Rose was reminded of the earlier look he had exchanged with Colum.

Ruark laughed. Leaning forward with one forearm on his thigh, he said, "'Tis a day's ride to Stonehaven. I have no doubt I will catch up to him in a few hours."

Then his head lifted and his eyes found her. She was standing some distance away. But not so far that she couldn't hear every word he spoke or feel his gaze touch her. "Would you care to join me, Lady Roxburghe?"

Indeed, she had more than earned her place to ride to Stonehaven at his side.

Chapter 17

By the time the first stop was made at an inn to eat and rest the horses, most of the riders had broken away and pressed onward in different directions. Later the boisterous group passed the outskirts of Hawick and stopped for supper before the last stretch to Stonehaven. The men, bristling with all manner of arms, took over the common room, running off anyone who did not belong to their crowd, and compelling the poor innkeeper and his wife to feed the unruly throng.

The two rescued Kerr cousins, Rufus and Gavin, found it amusing to have Rose look over their wounds. Since McBain remained in the slow-moving coach, he was not expected back at Stonehaven until tomorrow. So it was left to her to see to the injuries the three incurred while in the warden's care. She should not have bothered with concern or kindness, or worried that the injuries already showed signs of corruption, because the two considered them badges of honor to be bragged upon and displayed. Perhaps if they were not so drunk they would have taken her more seriously or felt more pain. She wondered what they would think when a foot or an arm rotted and dropped off.

Ruark said nothing over his ale as the men backslapped

one another and guffawed as if the three-month ordeal had been naught more than a test of their precious Scottish manhood. The young Jamie was now newly initiated among their ranks. Though far less boisterous.

"McBain should be here tending you," Rose had said with some asperity, frustrated with their nonsensicality.

"But this McBain, he is not here, lass," said the younger of the unruly louts as he attempted to pull her onto his lap, perhaps not fully grasping that she was his laird's bride.

Though Rose understood a person's need to release pent-up emotions like a heated tea kettle spouting steam, they also needed baths, haircuts, and someone to shake them.

One glance at Ruark told her she needed to contain the situation quickly. He seemed to be allowing her to handle it for now, but the last thing she wanted was for Ruark to rescue her from his own family. She snatched her hand from the grip holding hers.

"I'd be careful if I were yournself," Angus said casually from a wooden bench across the planked table from the two cousins. He held a drumstick the size of his fist and ripped at the greasy flesh with his teeth.

Chewing evenly, he grinned at the pair, who beneath all that black hair were probably only a year or two older than she. "The lass 'bout skewered Hereford through the gullet with a claymore." The words were spoken casually with many an "aye" echoing from the crowded tables around them.

Rose felt her throat tighten, realizing the public comment was as much a declaration of their allegiance to *her* as it was to protect the lads from their own stupidity and arrogance. Not because she would harm them, but because Ruark would. Of that, she had no doubt.

Duncan leaned forward on his elbow, the bench creaking

beneath his weight. "Did ye now, lass?" he asked, interested. "Was that before or after ye married our laird?"

"Before." Ruark raised the tumbler of whisky to his lips, his eyes on the unkempt cousins. "I would have let her split the bastard's gullet if he had not had the lot of *you* in chains."

Sitting beside Duncan, Jamie was watching Ruark cautiously through a lank fringe of blond hair, then he quietly tended to his meal. She had not seen Ruark and his younger brother exchange one word, though Ruark was always near and the boy seemed to steal an occasional glance his way. Rose felt strangely akin to Jamie. Perhaps because he and she both were out of place in this room filled with oafish bewhiskered men. Or perhaps because he seemed a little lost despite the manly show of bravery he'd exemplified all day. Or maybe in some small way he reminded her of Jack.

Then, bellies full, they were horseback again.

A rain-dampened, subdued and smaller group arrived at Stonehaven near midnight. Rose had never been so glad to see a structure as she was to see the old baronial estate. It rose from the sea of fog that hovered over the countryside, a brilliant amber beacon visible only at first as small dots of light through the red ash trees. Lights burned behind every window. Torchlight up and down the drive glowed dimly in the mist.

She looked over at Jamie, riding just ahead of her on a dun-colored gelding, his blond head bobbing listlessly with the horse's slow gait. He was barely staying in the saddle. Every time he'd nodded off, she'd wanted to reach her hand out to him, but the boy, for all his twelve years, considered himself a man and like most men, she suspected, would not appreciate interference from a woman. A Sassenach woman at that.

As she rode through Stonehaven's arched iron gates surrounded by darkness and fog, the reasons for her feelings did not matter. He'd got sick shortly after leaving the inn, and hadn't kept anything down for two hours. Now, he looked as if he would fall off his horse. Clearly, something was wrong. Then suddenly he was toppling.

"Stop!" She dropped from the horse to catch him, but Ruark was already off Loki and running toward Jamie.

Ruark caught him before he hit the drive. Rose dropped to her knees on the ground beside him, testing his face for fever. His skin was chilled to her touch. She stripped off her cloak and wrapped it around him.

She swung around and glared at those who had climbed down from the horses and stood around dumbly. "Get some water, for pity's sake," she ordered.

A skin of something liquid was thrust into her hands. After pulling off the stopper and smelling the contents, Rose was satisfied she was giving the boy water.

"I do no' feel well, Ruark," she heard the boy say as the first shouts from the direction of the house sounded.

"Aye," Ruark said gently, a chuckle in his voice. "'Tis probably the ale ye drank at the inn, *a'bhrarhar.* Can ye walk?" Rose glared at Ruark. *How can you be so heartless?* she wanted to shout. She did not believe Jamie suffered only from the drink Duncan had given him at the inn. The boy was exhausted and ill nourished.

"Aye, he can walk," Duncan said, coming up behind her, a dark looming shape in the darkness. "The lad is no babe to be shamed."

Rose pushed herself to her feet. "Do not be ludicrous. Can you not see he is ill?"

"He is a Kerr. He does no' need your coddling, woman."

Ruark gave Jamie a hand up to stand. "He may be a

Kerr. But he has proven himself enough these last months, Duncan. Sometimes even a Kerr needs the help of another." He looked down at the boy, who stood on legs as wobbly as a newborn foal's. Angus put a firm warning hand on Rose's shoulder, stopping her from moving forward to help him.

"Your mam will be down the drive at any moment," Ruark said to the boy, an unspoken question in his voice.

Over Ruark's shoulder, Rose glimpsed those filtering out of the house, now hurrying down the drive toward them. Julia's heavy satin gown flared about her like a peony as she ran.

"Mam," the boy whispered, newfound strength in his voice.

Throwing off the cloak, Jamie struggled up the hill on his own volition to meet the human onslaught coming toward them. Jamie had recovered for the moment anyway, and for now, he was twelve years old again and in his mother's loving arms. Watching the happy reunion, Rose felt a surge of bittersweet feelings, yet comforted to note that there still existed loving families in this world. She should not be jealous but she felt exposed and awkward.

The other men who had ridden through the gate with them began to move toward the stables, taking Loki, leaving the more intimate reunion to closer family members, which Rose was not. Angus remained behind with her, and from their place in the shadows said, "Ye did right not interfering, lass."

Only because he'd prevented her from doing so, Rose thought. "In my world, a person is not afraid to give or accept aid from another," she said. "He is only a boy."

"The lad is old enough to be hanged for his misdeeds. Ruark, more than most, understands. In our world, no

Kerr should be carried on his back to his own front door unless he is dead. Especially in front of the men."

Rose didn't much care for Ruark's world and thought it in need of compromise. But she understood.

"Strength lies as much in perception as action," she said quietly.

Angus clapped her on the back as if she were one of his clansmen. "Aye, ye be remeberin' that yourself, and you'll do right among us, lass, even if ye do come from Hereford's stock."

Rose glared up at his gruff face, but he was already looking to the needs of his horse and bending down to reach the reins.

She turned to look for Ruark and found him on the drive in conversation with Duncan, though conversation might be the wrong word. Ruark jabbed a finger in the middle of Duncan's chest, their harsh whispers growing in strength.

"What happened this morning with Duncan?" she asked worriedly, remembering the exchange between Colum and McBain earlier.

Angus saw where she was looking. "Hmpf. There be history between those two, lass," he said. "You best stay clear of it and go inside. Ruark will find you when he's done with Duncan."

Rose decided to take Angus's advice to heart and not involve herself in Kerr family matters. Now that Jamie had confirmed himself to be a man to everyone's satisfaction, she hoped she would be allowed to examine him.

Rose sloshed water from the ewer into a bowl and rinsed the rag. Jamie sat in his bed, his legs drawn up to his chest, his chin on his knees. He had been stubbornly quiet all day, not making a fuss, never complaining. She had come here to give him her aide, but she knew 'twas more personal.

Mary had given her permission to enter the room and see him. Something was going on outside between Ruark and Duncan, and had taken much of the staff's attention, leaving the few who remained busy running off in every direction to get food, water, clothes, and medicines. Mary had sent Julia out of the room while Jason finished helping Jamie wash his hair and check for lice, but as Rose looked at the wounds and injuries, she knew Julia had been sent out for a reason.

He wore a long white nightshirt unlaced over his chest and rolled up to his elbows, revealing scrapes and cuts on his arm, a head injury that should have had sutures. His shoulders bore signs of a whip.

At that moment, she had never hated anyone more than her father.

She needed medicine or a tonic to soothe Jamie's stomach. He had a fever and had vomited again. Her heart ached for him. Her soul cried.

A sniffle sounded. She pushed back a strand of blond hair. He had eyes the color of Ruark's, the same shape nose. Ruark must have looked very much like his brother at twelve. Was he ever as vulnerable? He held a gold doubloon in his hand that he had picked out of a drawer filled with seashells and other treasures young boys collected.

"You are very brave, Jamie."

He lowered is chin. "Nay, I was no'." He swiped at his cheeks with the heel of his hand. "If Da ever caught me crying, he would have taken a strap to my backside and give me a reason to cry. I did no' weep once while . . . while I was away . . . even though I was scairt of the dark. Rufus and Gavin . . . they didn't seem scairt."

"Believe me, they were."

His voice barely audible, he asked, "You are his bride?"

She looked away to wring out the rag. Water dribbled into the bowl. "Aye."

"They said he married ye to save me."

"I suppose he did," she said quietly to the saucer-eyed boy, who seemed to have inquired more out of compassion, not judgment. Perhaps his feelings weren't for her, but they did hold for his brother.

"You're no' like him . . . your da." He blinked wet eyes at her. "People were afraid of my da, too. Duncan says Lord Hereford killed him."

Telling the boy that she was sorry seemed inadequate. "I know."

He studied the scraped fingers that held the doubloon. "Da made Ruark go away before I was born," he said after a moment. "I did no' even know I had a brother until I was nine. When I was older I heard Da shout at Mam that it was her fault, he made Duncan take Ruark away."

"You must have communicated somehow. That is a gold doubloon in your hand. That must have come from him."

"Mary gave it to me. She has family in the village and Ruark would send letters to her with gifts inside, and she would send my letters to him. I liked having a brother everyone called the *Black Dragon*."

The creak of a floorboard turned her attention to the door. Ruark was standing in the doorway, Julia behind him. She carefully folded the rag and draped it over the bowl. Then stood as he approached his brother and as Julia swept past.

He was a master at hiding his emotions, but for one instant she glimpsed the bleakness in his eyes as he looked down at his brother.

Rose walked out of the room. Mary stood in the corridor. "Look at ye, lass. Your dress is damp and ye look in need of supper yourself."

She had been barely conscious of her damp gown for the last hour, but as she looked down at her skirts, she saw that grass stains and dirt from the ride also marred the beautiful fabric.

But she didn't care as her feet carried her down the corridor. She heard someone call her name but her flight had already taken her down the stairs and into the entry hall. Her heart began to thump faster as she swept past a dozen servants and hurried toward the kitchen, nearly toppling the cook in her haste to throw open the door and walk out into the night. But she wasn't walking, she was running, scattering dogs and geese that slept outside the scullery. She had wanted to go to the surgery, then realized she did not know where it was, and McBain wasn't here to show her.

She heard the sound behind her a moment before a hand came down on her shoulder and spun her around. Startled, she stumbled and tripped over her skirts. Ruark stood before her, the concern visible on his face in the pale, misty moonlight, silencing her struggles.

"I . . . have to do something for him, Ruark. I cannot just dismiss the fact—"

"That your father is responsible?" he quietly asked.

"Aye, he is responsible," she whispered with passion. "He is responsible for that boy's . . . care, for your father's death . . ."

"So you think you can fix everything he broke and make the world a better place for us all," he said dispassionately.

She shook her head, spilling her hair over her shoulders.

She didn't know how she could begin such a task; she didn't know where to begin.

Ruark took her against him. "I would like to lay the blame of everything that has occurred in this life at your father's feet, but I cannot, Rose. He does not bear all the responsibility. There are many here who are culpable."

She didn't believe it. Not anymore.

"He has a fever, Ruark," she said. "He could be ill. And he's scratched and bruised and scared. You cannot just wash him and put him to bed and think everything will be all right. He is just a boy. He needs . . ."

"The person he needs most is in the room with him, Rose."

"I am so sorry—"

He gave her a shake. "I will not let you apologize or martyr yourself. Do you understand?"

She tried to step past him but he caught her hand easily, turning her. She pressed her palm against his chest. "I do not understand how you went through with this ordeal, when this marriage could easily have been annulled."

His low voice challenged. "Truthfully? I wed you because you were compromised beyond all hope, Rose. You have proven beyond a doubt that I am a gentleman."

She stared at him aghast. She was attempting to talk to him and all he could do was make light of her efforts.

"And there is always this to consider, my love."

His mouth covered hers.

He parted her lips and drank in the tension that came as she spoke his name. The long fingers of his other hand framed her jaw and turned her face. The kiss deepened with mutual desire and need. But despite the wave of longing pulling her under, uncertainty wracked her mind and her heart.

Perhaps it was the way he knew how to touch her that made her feel important to him. Only after a few moments did she seem to realize the magnitude of her doubt. Then as the weight of the last few hours began to crush her, she leaned against Ruark and kissed him with everything that was inside of her.

His hand came under her chin to lift her face. He caught a tear at the corner of her eye and his mouth curved downward. "Tears?"

A cold shiver shook her. She was afraid of speaking, afraid she would say something she'd regret later. "I swear I will be a loyal wife to you."

"I want more than loyalty."

Loyalty was the only offering she could make him that came from her heart. "I do not know what else to give you that is my own, Ruark."

She didn't understand him enough to know what he expected from her, and she pushed past him in the darkness seeking . . . seeking what?

She never saw what tripped her, a tree root perhaps, but she hit the ground hard. She came to in Ruark's arms with the light around her, her head resting against his shoulder, his voice distant. A door slammed somewhere behind them. Its staid symbolism not lost on Rose in her murky state of mind.

An hour later, Ruark finally let Mary convince him that Rose was not seriously injured, but merely exhausted. Mary had bathed her and seen she was not bruised, not even a bump on her head. Later, his hair still damp from his own bath, Mary found him standing in front of his window. She reassured him Rose had dined on soup and Mary's own hot toddy and was now sleeping soundly. She reassured him that Jamie was also sleeping.

"The lass was vexed that she had caused so much trouble and told me that I should be with Jamie, not her," Mary said as if that should surprise Ruark.

"Did you tell her we have fifty servants who are attending to Jamie?"

Mary replied that she had said as much, but Ruark sensed Mary was of a mind to speak more. "The lad will be all right. Do not think ye are to blame. Ye are not."

He continued to stare out the window, seeing nothing but his own reflection in the darkness, and not liking the man staring back at him.

"I know who is to blame, Mary."

"Some believe your taking an English bride will cause opposition among those who have yet to swear their fealty to ye, that Hereford intended such."

So she had heard about the disagreement he and Duncan had had on the front drive. "I know, Mary."

"Ye knew, and ye wed her anyway. Then went and sealed it so ye can never annul it."

"I wed her because I chose to." Now, impatience to have the housekeeper gone forced him to soften his tone as he spoke, "Go, now. 'Tis late. And I have a wish to be abed."

Her expression softened. "Ye are a decent man, Ruark Kerr. Despite what ye may think at this moment."

He laughed. "Am I now?"

Ruark had never held illusions about his character. But even at his worst, he'd always known there were consequences to his actions. Despite the wealth and privilege in which he'd been born, he had made his own way and survived. Not because he knew *when* to fight and when to retreat but because he knew how to fight.

Until now.

After Mary left the sitting room, Ruark walked to

his bedchamber. The firelight revealed Rose in his bed. Her even breathing told him she was asleep and not unconscious.

He unknotted the belt on his loose-fitting black robe, removed the garment, then crawled beneath the blankets and pulled the soft down over his shoulders. He felt her shiver as the cold air touched her. He adjusted her head to rest on his shoulder, gently smoothing silken strands of hair from her cheeks. Her tranquility in sleep contrasted with the turmoil inside him as he lay in the warmer darkness of the damask-canopied bed listening to her even breathing. And for the first time since he'd left his old life in Scotland, he felt something stir deep inside him he'd thought gone forever. Passion that did not rise from the darkness inside him.

He didn't understand his need to possess her; he only knew that when she was near him, he could think of little else.

She clouded his brain, and as he turned her in his arms, he knew he wanted her even now, when he should be too exhausted to want anything but sleep. Even now, when his brother weighed heavily in his heart.

Her hand slowly splayed his chest and she murmured sleepily. "Tomorrow will you show me the herbal?"

"I will take you myself, love."

"*Thank you*," she breathed and kissed his cheek, then settled her cheek against his shoulder before he could touch her, before his arms could respond and wrap her to him.

Before he could take her mouth and turn the kiss into something more than an affectionate act of gratitude.

"I thought aristocrats slept in separate beds from their wives, my lord."

His hair was not tied back and when he rose on his

elbow above her it fell over his shoulders. "Ye must be thinking of the English, *m'eudail*. In Scotland, we are not afraid of our women."

In the darkness, he could feel her eyes searching his face. He made a gentle pass over her collarbone with his thumb and around the curve of one breast. "Are you afraid of me, Sassenach?"

Her breath grazed his cheek. Hesitation? "Nay, Ruark."

He'd not shaven, and he was careful not to scratch her pale skin as he kissed her throat. "Then you were not running away from me tonight."

"I am your wife."

"Aye," he said against her neck.

His hand slid to her waist, turned her slowly and spread the front of her nightdress. "You are mine."

But she had not told him she was not running away from him when she had tried to escape him in the garden. He dipped his head lower and suckled each nipple, willing her to stir. The darkness hindered all but a soft inviting mew as he curled his fingers in her nightdress, pushing the hem to her hips. Her breath quickened as his hand went between her legs and spread her for his exploration. He wanted her in a way he'd not wanted anything before. He wanted more than her acquiescence or gratitude or obedience.

He wanted to be inside her body and her mind, he needed to taste her passion, to see himself in her eyes when he made love to her. In the darkness, he would settle for her desire as he dragged her hand to his erection. "You can touch me, Rose," he said huskily. "I am not delicate."

Her fingers closed around him. His skin was warm and taut, the shape of him well defined by her palm. Her touch whet his pleasure beyond the quickening of his blood. Her breathing slightly ragged, she found the base of his shaft and, with her responding inhalation, he felt as if he had won a victory, slight as it was.

Her life was his and she was here because he willed it of her. He should feel guilty that he wanted this from her as well. But this time the sound he heard was his own.

"How do you say in Gaelic . . . ? 'That pleases me, Ruark.'"

"Tha sin a' cordadh rium," he said on a breath and braced himself on his elbow as he moved between her thighs and let her guide him. A hot shiver shot through him as he buried himself inside her hot sweet passage until he no longer cared where she ended and he began.

"Tha sin a' cordadh rium," she whispered, wrapping her legs around his hips.

"This pleases me, too," he said.

Then he unerringly found her mouth in the darkness and set about showing her just how much.

Chapter 18

Thumbing through a packet of correspondence on his desk, Ruark finished the last of his tea. He disliked tea immensely, but today he didn't notice. The glass doors behind him were open to the mid-morning breeze that billowed the curtains. Birdsong filled the air on one of those rare hot days when the sun had already burned away the garden mists before he'd returned from his ride.

But early a riser that he was, Rose was even earlier. For the last two mornings, she had awakened before him, dressed and was gone by the time he stirred. Yesterday, she'd found him in the stable after she'd spent the day with Mary and his household staff. He'd been with Angus talking over a late spring foal and he'd not been able to share her day with her. Today she had invited him to see what she had done in the herbal, and again, he'd found something else to keep him occupied. He sat forward with his elbows resting on his desk, the correspondence surrounding him all but forgotten as he twisted the silver ring on his finger, more an unconscious result of thought than a need to remove it. Besides, he had already attempted and it would not come off. No amount of greasing or soap would remove it.

Rose had asked him only yesterday if he had ever made

a wish on it, and he had laughed at her foolishness, but later he began to think what one would wish for if that *one* had a restless soul and a heart he did not know.

The door swung open and Mary entered carrying a breakfast tray. He had told her he wasn't hungry, but as usual, the woman ignored him.

Her pale pink shell earrings bobbed with her movement as she set down the tray. Nearly all of the servants working and living at Stonehaven had been a part of the household for generations, but he was closest to Mary, which accounted for his tolerance of her boldness. He leaned back in the chair.

"What do you know of Arthurian relics?" he asked, the question more rhetorical than literal, and he did not expect an answer.

"Ah," she said, her enthusiasm for the topic obvious. "There was an archeological dig near Stonehaven some fourteen years ago. Naught of significance was found, as is usually the case." Mary talked as she laid out the serviette, stating that she was still friends with the archaeologist's wife, who had conducted the dig. "Mrs. Simpson continued her husband's work after he passed some years ago."

"Does she still live in Scotland?"

"She lives outside Castleton, on the English side of the border. In fact, if ye suddenly have a hankering for artifacts, your new bride knows her. She sent Mrs. Simpson a letter during her first few days here. They are friends."

If this Mrs. Simpson person and Rose knew each other, then Ruark suspected Rose had believed the ring to be an authentic relic for a reason. She'd received expert advice on the subject. It was such a silly trinket for him to give much thought, but it had been *her* trinket, and he had carelessly taken it from her. And his mind more and more was diverted to it.

As Mary poured coffee the conversation shifted. Mary told him that Rose had asked to see Jamie. "I said she need no' ask *my* permission but his mam's."

Ruark looked up as she busied her hands on his tray. "I see." What Mary did not tell him, what she didn't have to tell him, was that Julia had already objected to Rose's visit to Jamie's room.

But his first instinct had been to protect his wife. "Has someone else made a comment to you?"

"Not yet. But Julia is awaiting Mr. McBain's return and your young bride has taken it upon herself to care for the lad until he arrives."

Ruark mentally groaned. Three days he had been back at Stonehaven, but McBain had yet to return. Yesterday one of the outriders accompanying the coach McBain and Anaya had been riding in from Jedburgh arrived with a message from Colum, explaining that the carriage axle had broken outside Hawick. This morning a message arrived saying the axle could not be repaired and that McBain would skewer the first man who attempted to get him on a horse. Colum said he would remain with McBain and Anaya until such time a new carriage would be delivered. Ruark had business with his solicitor in Hawick, and he needed to pick up Colum before traveling south to Workington to sort out the *Black Dragon* business with Hereford. But this he did not tell Mary.

"McBain is stranded outside Hawick until I can get another coach to them," he told Mary. "The family has three in service—and at least I can fetch McBain and Anaya back to Stonehaven." He dropped a dollop of sweet butter into the porridge Mary had served him. "I have to visit the Roxburghe Shipping office in Carlisle and on my way south I want to ride the southern section of this property."

Mary's hands froze. "The southern edge? Ye would go alone?"

Without looking up as he ate, Ruark told her he wanted to check on the planting. "The crop was planted late due to the weather," he said. "I do not need an army behind me to speak to the tenants, Mary."

"We both know ye are not going down there to speak to the tenants about their crops. This has to do with what happened to yer father down there. Ye should take Duncan with ye."

Even if Ruark currently knew Duncan's whereabouts, he would not take his uncle with him. "Aye," he said, dabbing the serviette against his lips. "My visit south does have to do with my sire and I will speak to the tenants without Duncan present."

Ruark would piece together for himself what happened the night his father was killed, and in the process he had unfinished business with Hereford.

"Is it so important to ye that your father is dead? Duncan has already said that Hereford killed him. Perhaps ye should leave it at that."

Ruark tossed down the serviette. "Why, Mary?"

"Because your da was not a kind man. Whatever happened to him . . ."

He deserved. She did not say the words, but they lay there between them in the silence. "Everything happens for a reason," she said without looking at him.

"Aye? I could not agree with you more. But since when have you become so fatalistic, Mary? I am only going to speak to the tenants. I have to go anyway. I have not been there since my return from the sea, and, as I said, I have business to dispose of farther south."

Mary sniffed and lifted the tray. Ruark barely rescued his coffee she had just poured. "Then ye best be talkin' to

Julia first before ye leave Stonehaven," she said. "Assure her that yer new bride has no designs on the life of her son." Mary then abandoned him to ponder that task.

With a quiet oath, Ruark downed the last of his coffee. He stood and made his way upstairs to Jamie's bedchamber. Then stopped. He leaned with his hands against the doorjamb. Ruark had never pretended to be any good around children, even older ones who could actually talk. As Rose had noted last night, he had not spent much time with Jamie since his return. But his reasons were complicated even to himself.

He found his brother asleep and Julia sitting in the high-back chair beside him. Upon his entrance, her expression changed from one of worry to one of relief. "How is he?" he asked.

Clutching a woolen plaid shawl to her breast, she rose in a swish of wrinkled muslin and hushed him out of the room, quietly shutting the door behind her before facing him and saying in a low voice, "She was here again this morning, Ruark. In my son's chambers."

He felt a burst of irritation at Julia. "What happened?"

"She came in while I was asleep and sat on the mattress beside him," she whispered, shaking her head. "I was asleep in the chair. She could have done *anything*, Ruark, and I would not have seen it. I will not allow that woman to give my son any more of her medicines. I want McBain or Mary up here."

Ruark understood the ramification of Julia's fear in a way that sent a chill over him. If something happened to Jamie while in Rose's care, he would never be able to protect her from his family's wrath.

"You have hardly slept since his return, Julia. You are exhausted. I will send Mary up. Go wash. Change your clothes. Sleep. I will talk to my wife. She will not go near the boy again unless you say so."

Julia touched his forearm, her long slim fingers feathering across the crisp white of his sleeve as if unsure. In the end, she withdrew her hand. "Will ye not come inside and see Jamie?"

"I have to go to Hawick and fetch McBain," he said, inexplicably annoyed with both himself and her at the moment. "Have you seen Duncan since our return?"

She shook her head. "Nay."

Julia's hands tightened in her shawl. She made no other move to touch him. She had kept her distance since his return, even taking her meals upstairs. She was avoiding him, almost as much as his own wife was avoiding him, and last night he had dined downstairs alone. "Nay. I have not."

He started to turn, then stopped. His impatience gone, replaced by something less discernible.

"Did my father treat you well?" he asked, because he had not asked yet, and because for some reason he needed to know.

Her mouth softened as if she understood the turmoil her forced marriage to a man like his father had once caused within him.

The light from the diamond-paned window at the end of the hall captured her blue eyes. "You did not fail me, Ruark. It is I who bears the shame for then and for now. I know what ye did for me and for this family now. And I will never forget it." She moved toward the door.

"Julia." He curled a hand over the doorknob to prevent her leaving.

Her shoulder brushed his, and she raised her chin without moving away. She was still as beautiful as she had been at seventeen. But he knew now he had never loved her. "Rose is my wife."

"Mayhap, but she is not Jamie's physician. I have no idea what motive she would have for continuing her visits, as if we would want her near him."

He dropped his hand from the door knob. "Maybe you should ask her, Julia."

An hour later, Ruark reined in Loki at the top of a barren rise broken only by a stretch of twisted rocks. Cattle grazed in the distance. He'd ridden past the manicured parkland through the orchard above the northern field oft used as grazing pasture in summer. The hillside had been cleared of trees generations ago when reivers still roamed the countryside and warred on their unprotected neighbors. Thistle and tansy, with its strong-smelling foliage and flat-topped yellow flower heads, grew in abundance among the rocks. Loki stomped in impatience, snorting his displeasure as Ruark tightened his grip on the reins.

He'd been to the surgery only to find Rose gone and had come this way after one of the groundskeepers saw her walking toward the fruit grove, carrying a large empty basket on her arm. The ground was still soft in places after last night's rain and a small print marked someone's recent passage. He followed the tracks down a path to the open field.

Summer days might be long in Scotland, but warm weather could oft be short-lived. Today the sun shone high in a flawless blue sky and a warm breeze caressed his face, bringing with it the faint scent of pine from the distant wood grove that led to the falls. He spotted her walking out of the woods, Jason beside her. The two were engaged in conversation as Jason helped her negotiate a creek. Ruark nudged Loki forward.

Rose's laughter died while Jason greeted Ruark's arrival

with a wide grin. "We have been to the falls. I was just telling her about the art of tickling trout."

Ruark shifted his gaze from the delicate hand resting on Jason's forearm to Rose's flushed face framed by her unbound hair.

She wore a dark blue apron over a brownish homespun dress that could have been a burlap sack for all he cared or noticed, when she was more beautiful to him than sunlight at dawn.

Ruark smiled, his tact considerable when he found himself perversely stirred and annoyed at the same time, first by her unsmiling response to his arrival and then by her proximity to Jason.

"I will see her safely returned," he told Jason. The lad nodded, but before he'd taken three steps, Ruark called to him. "Thank you for seeing her safely about."

Jason seemed to recognize the inherent message in his words: *She is never to leave Stonehaven's walls without an escort.*

To Ruark's surprise, Rose laughed. He'd never heard a gladder sound than her laughter. "Truly, Ruark," she scoffed after Jason started jogging toward the house. "I did not go far. Besides, this has been a most productive morning and I have taken full advantage of the bounty your lands offer. I found exactly what I sought."

Indeed, she looked as if she'd been crawling on her knees in the dirt. The hem of her skirt showed evidence of mud from the stream.

She offered up the basket for his approval. Inside it laid assorted plants and roots. She tapped a pile of field fungi. "*Bolg losgain.* Frog's pouch," she said proudly. "Used to stem bleeding, counter boils and abscesses."

She caressed a muddy root ball like a mam admiring her wee babe. "Mallow root. 'Tis for stomach ailments.

And this?" she held up a handful of . . . something—"is for fever. This will help Jamie."

Lowering the basket, she held the handle with both hands and squinted in the sun as she peered up at him. "What are you doing all the way out here this fine day? Are not lairds supposed to be occupied with their lands and serfs and not worried over their brides' whereabouts?"

He leaned his elbow on his knee. "I came to tell you I have business to attend to in Hawick and the shipping offices in Carlisle."

He didn't tell her he would be leaving her for a few weeks, and she didn't ask why he was going. He wouldn't have told her anyway. She would have tried to stop him.

"I see." She turned on her heel and walked through a patch of meadowlark, leaving him to follow on Loki. "I bid you have a good trip then. When you return, you must show me this 'trout tickling' business of which Jason spoke."

He reined Loki in front of her and blocked her path. "I will return you to the surgery."

"I prefer to walk, my lord."

Was she challenging him? Daring him to *force* her to do this as well? He breathed out a sigh and swung down from the horse. One battle lost was a small concession. He took the basket from her, and he was surprised she let him. He carried it as they walked side by side like a young courting couple. Despite himself he grinned at the image.

"What is so amusing?" she asked, obviously watching him from the corner of her eye.

"I was trying to decide how long 'twould take you to acquit me of my sins and decide you will ride the horse." He grinned down at her. "Boots are tortuous when walking, *leannanan*."

She was unmoved. "Have you been to see your brother, yet?"

Looking across the pasture, his eyes squinted in the dazzling sunlight. The only sound was the soft thud of the horse's steps beside him. "As you say, I have been occupied. I plan to spend time with him upon my return. I need to ask you not to see him, either, until I return."

She stopped and faced him. The breeze stirred her hair and she tucked a red-gold strand behind her ear. "I see. Julia spoke to you."

He saw the hurt in her green eyes. His voice gentled. "She is feeling protective, as any mother would. There are some who do not know you as I do."

"They are suspicious of me? Do they think I would murder the boy? Why in heaven would anyone think me capable of—?"

He stopped her with a finger that went to her lips. "No one thinks you capable of murder."

"Not even you?"

He chuckled. "Aye, admittedly you have attempted to bash my head in." He placed his fingers under her chin and tilted her face. She was putting on a good show of indifference. "But not even I think you capable of harming a child. Swear to me, Rose. Do not go near that boy for now."

"I will stay away then, if that is what you want, Ruark."

"Only until my return."

They walked in silence until they reached the cart path. The left branched into the fruit orchard, the right back to the main house.

"What business do you have to attend to in Hawick?" she asked when they reached the top.

"My solicitor is there." He slanted her a glance. "Now that I am a married man there are certain legal matters which I must settle."

The surgery was not far now and she stopped. "You mean you have business to finish with my father. Swear to me you will not provoke him."

He laughed, unsettled by the ease in which she could read him. "I live life just to provoke the bastard."

But his mood was a nebulous thing and he looked away from her to the grove unable to reconcile the need to gather her into his arms and protect her and his want to kill her father. His gaze found hers. "I have business with Hereford's solicitor and with Roxburghe Shipping in Carlisle. I will be gone a few weeks."

"You will stay safe?"

Just looking at her, he experienced a fleeting sense of vertigo he got whenever he was taking her—possessing her. "Always, love."

She reached for the basket only to see the ring and pause. Her expression changed. "You have got what you want. Your brother is home. Have you attempted to remove it yet?"

Apparently, she, too, had assumed that his brother's return was what he most wanted. As had he. "Many times," he said.

"'Tis a shame," she said sadly. "I had so believed it to be authentic."

"Why do you think it is not?"

She looked around her, then toward the house spread across the horizon like a huge stone labyrinth amid the jeweled landscape. A number of chimney pots smoked over the gray roof tiles and mingled with the morning mist.

"You have everything. What else could you possibly want?"

He had always been a man possessed of a sense of his own purpose and the wisdom it took to achieve a goal. He had returned to Scotland to save his brother, a noble-enough task, and now he didn't know quite what to do.

Yet while he had never believed in the ring's magical properties, he *had* found himself of late pondering the elusive questions of what he truly wanted most in this life. A question he had never contemplated and one he could not answer. He only knew that until recently, he had never cared about his future.

Indeed, if he believed in such whimsy as magic and wishing rings, he might put such power to his use and figure out a way, how *not* to want her.

Ruark left Rose standing on the narrow path that would take her up the hill and through the fruit orchard to the back of the surgery. Holding her basket filled with the wonderful offerings she had gathered from the woods and fields, she watched him mount Loki and ride away.

With the presence of two groundskeepers and a few others who had looked up from their tasks at Ruark's approach, his farewell to her had been brief and fraught with formality. He hadn't kissed her. After the sight of him had grown small and faint in the distance, Rose stared around her at a world that was as unfamiliar to her as the part of her trying to escape the walls of her heart. She found she wanted very badly to be accepted at Stonehaven. Whether she resented that desire or nay, she had become Stonehaven's mistress.

Despite herself, she felt relieved that her husband would be gone for the next few weeks.

Once inside the surgery, she set the basket on the counter at the back of the room, unpinned the apron from her skirt and raised it to cover her bodice. She wrapped a red headscarf around her hair and went to work preparing and drying what she had found near the falls.

That a boy would suffer because of people's dislike

of her did not seem fair. She would honor her promise to Ruark to stay away from Jamie, but that didn't mean someone else couldn't help him.

She worked the rest of the afternoon shaving bark onto a drying shelf, then mixed it with licorice to mask the bitter taste. The mallow root balls she tied with a string and hung in a special area in the orangery McBain used for such things. This was not an overnight process and could take days. She checked the progress of some of the leaves and roots McBain had already gathered before he'd left for Jedburgh. Some looked ready for preparation and she removed them from the drying line. When she finished, she slapped the dirt off her hands and returned to the surgery without realizing how long she had been working. She had a dreaded appointment at three o'clock with the dressmaker.

Rose shivered at the mere thought of sitting down to select her wardrobe. She knew nothing of fashion.

The thought of having to choose between a silk, linen, muslin, velvet, floral or striped morning or walking dress paralyzed her, almost as much as sitting down with someone at a formal dinner, where all silverware and glassware looked the same to her.

Mary found her an hour later, near the hearth in the back of the surgery as she finished drying the last of the willow bark. "Have ye no ken the time?" the woman demanded, her round face flushed from the heat in the room.

Rose scraped the bark into a tin. "I know. But this is important. You should not have come all this way. I am almost finished."

"Should no' have come? Are ye daft girl? The dressmaker will be here shortly. Ye cannae' be seen lookin' like a sheep herder's wife."

Aye, I can, Rose thought stubbornly, perfectly comfortable in her present attire. Jamie's health was far more important in her mind than her wardrobe.

She presented Mary with the tin. "'Tis willow bark and licorice. You make it as a tea. This will help with Jamie's fever. If I must drink a cup to prove I hold no ill will toward that boy—"

"You've no need to prove yerself to me."

Rose was astonished. Never had she thought to find an ally in this woman. "His lordship forbade me to see him, Mary."

"I know, lass. 'Tis for the best."

"Why?"

"Have you considered what might come to pass should something happen to the lad under yer care? Nay, I will care for Jamie until McBain's return." Mary squeezed her hands. "Now, I have my cart outside . . ."

Rose withdrew her hands, picked up a rag and returned to clean the countertop. "I will come as soon as I am finished cleaning in here."

Mary didn't argue, but sniffed. "Verra well, lass."

"Remember, a decoction, not an infusion," she said as Mary reached the door. "Boil the ingredients in a pan, then strain. Not simmer in a cup."

The woman crinkled her face and placed one plump hand on her hip. "I'd no' be worth my weight as a housekeeper if I did no' know the difference between a decoction and an infusion. Now hie yerself off to the house as soon as ye can and clean up for the dressmaker, lass."

A half hour later by Rose's estimate, she had finished cleaning McBain's surgery. She removed her apron and dropped it in a basket, snuffed the candle and had just put away the flint box when the door banged open. Duncan seemed to blow in on a sudden gust of wind. The narrow doorway made his large size more formidable. His long hair fell uncombed below his shoulders.

He stopped short when he saw her. "McBain is no' here?"

Alarmed by his tone, she peered past him, expecting to see men carrying in a mortally wounded patient. "He is in Hawick. Ruark left today to see that he gets safely back. Are you injured?"

He looked at the cupboard behind her filled with all manner of insidious surgical instruments. "Nay, lass." He shut the door behind him, and she thought he was walking toward her until she realized his destination was the cupboard. "I've been with Rufus these past days. The wounds on his foot are festering."

"Did I not warn the lot of you at the inn? This is what comes from foolishness. He should have been tended to at once."

Duncan turned to look down at her, his shoulder nearly brushing hers with the movement. But rather than note his proximity and move away, she stood her ground. He smelled surprisingly like soap for looking as if he had not bathed in a week.

"Aye, ye did, lass," he said, his teeth white against his beard. "Now, I have want of a blistering iron, saw, and McBain's scalpels."

Her eyes widened. "You cannot mean to remove his leg?"

"Not the whole of it. I came for McBain, him being a ship's surgeon." His eyes narrowed speculatively on the shelves stacked with jars and tins, then on her. "But you'll do well enough, lass."

Chapter 19

After barely giving her enough time to gather her supplies, Duncan forced her to accompany him outside and strapped her bag to the cantle. She rode on the back of his horse clinging to him for at least an hour by the sun's placement in the sky before he finally reined in his horse in front of a large stone cottage at the foot of a picturesque hill.

She glimpsed a barn and a shed for silage. Summer roses grew in abundance in a walled garden. Beyond the barn was a small stone *doocot* fluttering with cooing pigeons. Even with the stench coming from the hog pen, this was a well-kept farm.

She shoved against Duncan as he lifted her off the horse onto legs stiff and chafed from the mad ride. "Let go of me! Oaf! I am not baggage."

He opened the cottage's front door and politely held it for her. "He is upstairs, lass."

Rose remained annoyed with Duncan's highhanded treatment of her, and told him so, even as he waited for her to follow him into the house.

She stepped past him.

The room was filled with large men who looked as if

they had spent the day cattle lifting. It smelled of wood smoke and beeswax and looked much bigger on the outside than on the inside. Three oak beams stretched across the ceiling. Most of the men were tall enough to touch the beams. A lone woman in long skirts and a dirty blood-stained apron paced in front of the hearth. She looked up as Duncan entered, her anxious expression falling as she glimpsed Rose.

"Where is McBain?" the woman demanded, giving Duncan a look that would turn a smaller man to stone. "Ye said ye would bring back a doctor."

Duncan wrapped his beefy hand around Rose's upper arm and drew her deeper into the room. "He is no' at Stonehaven, Kathleen. This is our own Ruark's new bride. Her ladyship's come to offer us her aide should we have to remove Rufus's leg."

Rose had *never* pretended to be a surgeon. She was an herbalist if she was anything at all. Aye, she knew something of medicines and she had assisted Friar Tucker when he visited the unfortunates who had been injured in farming accidents. However, looking into the suspicious, hostile faces of those standing around her, Rose elected to reveal none of this.

"Have ye lost yer brain?" the red-haired woman said sharply to Duncan, her color high. "And where is our laird that he would allow ye to steal his bonny Sassenach bride from beneath his nose to come out here and nurse the likes of us? Will he be bangin' down this door?"

"Now, Kathy . . ."

"Och! Do no' *Kathy* me, Duncan Kerr. Is there no' enough bad blood between ye already . . . ?"

"He's no' at Stonehaven . . ."

The rest of the argument was lost on Rose. Content to remain out of the family dispute, she shifted the bag in her hand, looking around her. Behind her, the stairs led upward to the room where Rufus lay.

A tug on her skirts drew her gaze downward. A small towheaded girl stood next to her, her eyes wide and serious as she stared up at Rose. "Are ye here to save me bruther?" she asked.

The arguing stopped as Kathleen stepped around Duncan to scoop up her daughter, sizing Rose up with one frank glance. "We've no cause to trust ye, any more than you've cause to trust us," Kathleen said. "But if Duncan says ye can help my son, then we'll trust ye will and let it be at that."

Indeed, Rufus Kerr, a distant cousin to Ruark, and one of Lord Hereford's former hostages, was not doing well. Rose made that diagnosis the instant she entered the sickroom and smelled the putrification in the air. He lay on a narrow bed in a closed-in room that sweltered from the heat of a fire blazing in the hearth. At least he had been washed and bathed and much of his tangled hair shorn from the last time she had seen him at the inn. She had thought him to be in his twenties. Now she could see he could be no older than seventeen.

Shabby brown curtains were shut tight over what Rose presumed was a window. Many who fancied themselves experts on the human condition and the humoral balance in the body believed keeping cool air away from ailing patients to be essential. By the look of the lancet and bowl on the nightstand beside the patient's bed, he had been bled.

The first thing Rose did was throw open the curtains and the window, if only so she could see. The sun, though low in the sky, still provided substantially more light than the single candle on the nightstand. Then she turned to

Duncan and told him to get everyone out of the room. She might not like Duncan, but she trusted him to be capable of removing everyone, including the reluctant Kathleen.

"And bring me a bottle of red wine," Rose said.

Friar Tucker had oft touted the healthful benefits of red wine when taken internally as libation and when used as part of a dressing. She had never put either remedy to a test, but she would now.

Outside in the corridor, the arguing started again, low voices that faded down the hallway. Rufus's eyes were open and he was watching her. "You'll have to forgive me, mum," he said in apology. "We've enough troubles without bringing our laird down on us." A grin cracked his chapped lips. "He'll kill Duncan if something happens to ye, to be sure. Then my kin will probably kill him."

"Humph. Are you not all kin?" Rose tilted his face into the candlelight. His pupils were dilated. He'd been given laudanum. "All this talk of everyone killing everyone else. I thought families were supposed to love one another."

"Aye, we do, most of the time. But some are thinking Duncan should be chieftain. There is grumbling and some do no' like that a Kerr has taken hisself a Sassenach bride."

She focused on the lad's face. "I see."

She wondered why, if so much was at stake for Ruark, he had ensured that their vows could not be easily annulled. "Then let us make sure nothing happens to me."

Rose walked to the end of the bed and removed the blanket covering her patient's lower legs.

Her breath caught like a hot iron in her throat, and, looking away, she knew it was all she could do not to betray her expression to the lad.

He had been wearing shoes at the inn when she had examined the wounds left by the ankle chains. Now as she pulled a stool to the end of the bed and sat, she wondered how the boy could ever have stood or walked at all. Three of the toes had been broken within the last week of his incarceration and had attempted to heal. The irons that had bound his ankle had left raw wounds that had healed over open sores. The newly healed-over scabs would have to be cut away and the wounds beneath lanced and drained to rid the body of the oozing infection.

Nausea clenched her stomach. Closing her eyes, she breathed in slowly, drawing from the fresh air coming through the window.

The enormity of the task ahead suddenly paralyzed her. She could not do this. Sensing Rufus's eyes on her, she found him watching her from beneath half-closed lids. "Will I lose my foot?"

"Nay," she lied.

He could very well loose his leg if gangrene set in. He would surely lose his life if sepsis poisoned his blood. His body was warm to the touch, which meant he was already fighting infection.

She stood and, turning her back to him, retied the red scarf on her head to give her trembling hands something to do. She wished she could faint about now and be spared what she knew needed to be done.

"Gavin and me, we should no' have laughed at ye at the inn," Rufus said.

Her back to him, she bit her lower lip. "I am sure it was the ale that gave you your courage," she said, her voice even.

The door opened and Duncan entered carting two bottles of wine.

"May I talk to you?" she asked, wanting to step past him into the corridor, but he put his arm on the door.

"Speak in here," he said.

She glanced over her shoulder at Rufus. "I think we need—"

"In here," Duncan said again, his voice losing the ever-present humor. "The lad has a right to know what it is ye have to say."

Duncan wasn't going to allow her to tell him she couldn't do this. He wasn't going to allow her to leave this room. Panic filled her.

"Sometimes we have to do a thing we do no' want to do, lass, because it must be done. Now I will be in here with ye. And Rufus there"—he tipped his chin toward the bed—"he is no' afraid as ye are. Are ye lad?"

Rose saw a faint smile twitch at the corner of Rufus's lips. Duncan was wrong. As she looked into the wounded boy's face, she could see someone in this room more scared than she was.

Duncan handed her the bottle of wine. "Let's get on with what needs to be done, lass."

Rose lost all sense of time.

She had never noticed when the sun set. The fire died sometime in the night, but the cool air from outside kept her focused on her task.

She worked by candlelight, snipping and slicing away the infected layers of skin to clean beneath until fresh blood oozed. She picked debris from both the ankle wounds and the toes then washed the wounds with water and wine as fresh blood oozed over her fingers. Somehow, she held onto the small pincers that grew heavier in her hand with each passing hour. The toes were not the worst, though she was worried she would not be able to save the smallest one. Once when Rufus screamed, Duncan kept the lad still, his voice as calming a balm as the dose of laudanum she had given him.

She took a grip on herself, concentrating only on each task, and when that was done, she moved on to the next. Duncan spoke soothingly to the young man, his voice also soothing her. The painstaking work lasted until dawn.

When she finished, she cleaned the blood from her hands. She stirred the fire until a small flame leaped from the peat, and she heated water and used burnt alum on the deeper wounds. Then she wrapped the foot in strips of cloth that she boiled in garlic and witch hazel. There would be terrible scarring, she thought and, though she had done her best with the toes, they might never heal straight.

At last, she loosened the leather Duncan had used to tie the lad's leg to the bedstead and sat back on the stool. She looked up to find Duncan's eyes on her, and he gave her a nod of approval.

"Ye did fine, lass," he said. "Real fine."

It was all that he said, and she doubted he was speaking about her work. She still did not like Duncan, nor did she trust him. But the words made an impression on her. One that followed her to bed as Kathleen led her to a chamber down the hall.

"You've seen to my boy," Kathleen said, clearly grateful. "I've no' a right to ask you to remain any longer."

"I do not mind," Rose said just before her head hit the pillow and she slept.

Over the next two days, Rose took turns with Kathleen and Duncan, sitting beside the lad, reading to him, bathing his face and waiting for his fever to break. Rose felt an inner peace and confidence that it would. She didn't know where such an emotion came from.

Kathleen had made sure one of her other sons delivered a note to Stonehaven the night of Rose's arrival, reassuring

Mary that Rose was safe, so she felt at ease remaining with this crowded family.

Though she could not tell exactly how they were related to Ruark, on her fourth morning, she felt comfortable enough to ask.

She sat in the stone-paved kitchen boiling water for chamomile tea while Kathleen worked on that day's meal. A few copper pots burnished to a rosy glow hung overhead, and fresh-cut flowers sat across from the hearth on the same countertop Kathleen was using. The rhythmic slap of her palms shaping the bread dough stopped abruptly as she considered the question. She thought her husband came from an offshoot branch of one of the former earl of Roxburghe's grandfather's cousin's uncles who had married more than one wife, "whilst the others still lived," Kathleen said and laughed.

"Though there was some discrepancy in testimonies depending on how much silver was involved. If ye wish to learn about the Kerrs, find the family Bible. All the births and marriages are recorded there. At least the legal ones are."

Rose liked this family. Kathleen was in her mid-thirties and mother to three sons and one small girl, Rufus being her oldest. Her husband had died less than five months ago. For some reason, she had thought her Duncan's wife.

"If no' for Duncan, I do no' know where the lot of us would be," Kathleen said, working her hands into the bread dough, raising a small cloud of flour. "We have no' always been poor, ye ken.

"My husband was the village fiscal," she said. "We had a nice home in the village. Then one day, people accused him of running away with their money and embezzling funds and were ready to tar and feather his family. If no' for Duncan . . . we might never have learned the truth."

"What happened?" Rose asked as Kathleen's voice faded.

"Duncan found my husband's body. He'd been caught in a snowstorm and died of injuries when his horse fell. No gold was found but by then the damage had already been done to this family. This house was once Duncan's, but he's no family to speak of, least no' any children. He gave us the house and has taken it upon himself always to make sure our larder is full."

"Is it not the laird's responsibility to see to his tenants' care?" Rose asked.

Kathleen turned the bread dough over on a wooden block and began beating the other side with equal intensity. "Aye, 'tis. We shall see if the new lord Roxburghe is of a different mettle than his father," she said, and though she would say nothing more to denigrate the former earl of Roxburghe, her stiff shoulders stated her feelings eloquently.

Rose grabbed a hand pad and removed the tea kettle from the fire bringing it to the countertop where she had set out a teapot and a cup on a tray. "His lordship does not speak of his father."

"Humph," Kathleen said. "You have met Jamie's mother?" she asked after a moment, slanting Rose a glance, before resuming her kneading. "Ruark may not have thought so, but Duncan did him a service back then when he shipped Ruark out of Scotland."

"Because Duncan got him away from his father?"

"With lady Julia between them, one of them would have killed the other to be sure."

Rose pretended close attention as she poured hot water into the teapot. A spur of doubt nudged her, for her heart would not completely let go of the rationale that real love did not die easily.

"How did Lord Roxburghe die?" she asked after a moment.

"Hereford killed him," Duncan said from the doorway.

Rose and Kathleen turned at once. Duncan leaned with his big shoulder against the wall, his arms folded across his chest. He did not look nearly as fearsome as he did in the darkness of a mist-shrouded night. He wore leather trews and a loose-fitting white shirt, minus the usual baldric dangling with all manner of weaponry and muskets. His wild russet hair had been tied back from his face.

He grinned, though his blue eyes wore a less amused expression as they settled on Kathleen. "Are ye telling stories about me, lassie?"

She sniffed and returned to her kneading. "As if anyone could tell a story about ye, Duncan? Who would dare?" Her shoulders worked as she folded and squished the dough with her fist, then she turned and rolled her sleeves back to her elbows and faced Duncan. "Why don't ye tell the lass why you believe Hereford killed your brother?"

When Duncan did not reply, Kathleen answered for him. "Rumor is that a valuable cargo in which Hereford had monetary interest went missing from one of Roxburghe's merchantmen outside Rotterdam some years ago." She set her hands on her hips. "What is it Hereford accused him of? Collusion with pirates?"

Duncan narrowed his eyes, none too pleased with Kathleen's assessment of the former earl of Roxburghe's character. His gaze on Rose, he straightened. "Come lass. Say your good-byes. Ye are the laird's wife and belong back at Stonehaven. You've been gone long enough as is."

He turned on his boot heel, and after his heavy steps had faded on the planked floor, Kathleen said, "He's right. You need to be returnin'."

Rose unlaced her apron and folded it. She had done all

she could for Rufus. But she was not thinking of him as her mind mulled over the details of Kathleen's conversation. "You said Hereford made the accusation of collusion after a cargo went missing on a merchantman outside Rotterdam?"

She was remembering the story Ruark had told her about the ship he had boarded outside Rotterdam some years ago. The ship had carried contraband that he believed Hereford had taken off an East Indiaman sunk off the Azores. Ruark did not tell her he had taken the cargo from one of his father's own ships.

"Was it true?" Rose asked. "The accusation."

"No one will ever know," Kathleen said. "The cargo was never recovered. Ruark's father accused Hereford of attempting to ruin his reputation. Accusations went back and forth. Then last spring, our former laird decided he would confront Hereford over the issue. Duncan was a day late reaching the meeting and found his brother with a musket ball in his head. Ruark oft docked in Workington, but it took two months to get him the news." Kathleen brushed at a loose curl. "Even then I do no' think he would have returned to Stonehaven if no' for Jamie. Some of us did no' think he would be staying."

Kathleen squeezed Rose's arm. "I have no' meant to distress ye. We owe ye a debt of gratitude, and Duncan well knows it." She smiled. "Otherwise, he would no' care how ye got yourself back to Stonehaven."

Rose answered with her own weak smile. She examined Rufus one last time and gave instructions to Kathleen for his care, promising that she or McBain would return in a few days. "If the bandages stick to the wounds, fresh lint dipped in sweet butter will help loosen the dressing so as not to tear away the scabs."

Carrying her young daughter, Kathleen hugged Rose

and took her outside, where Duncan had hooked up a cart. He was crouched in the dirt, scratching the ears of a shaggy sheepdog. He saw her and stood.

In the bright sunshine, he looked almost cheerful as he presented Rose a courtly bow and placed her in the cart. "Nothing but the best for my nephew's bonny bride," he said.

"Duncan!" Kathleen chastened from the steps. "She'll no' be able to stand straight by the time you get her to Stonehaven."

"Aye," he agreed, and patted the rolled-up blankets he had placed on her side of the bench, "which is why I have gone out of my way to see to the lass's comfort." He winked at Rose, "I would have used the chariot had Kathy's miscreant young brother not taken it carousin' last night and run into a ditch."

Kathleen laughed. "Do no' believe Duncan, lass. Jason has never caroused in his life and we've no' a chariot to our name."

"Jason is your brother?" Rose asked.

"A fine lad he is," she said fondly. "Do no' let Duncan tell ye otherwise."

Duncan told her nothing. They did little conversing on the return trip to Stonehaven, which to Rose's mind had as much to do with the occasional teeth-rattling pothole as it did with the scenery. Daylight revealed a beautiful terrain, glens, and distant pines stretching into a stark blue sky. Occasionally, they passed an ancient ruin of an old church or cottage, and she asked about its historical significance, finding herself engaged by his answers, even as she reminded herself why she did not like him.

After a long bout of silence, he turned his head, as if he read her thoughts. His shoulder jostled hers with the cart's movements. "Did ye enjoy your little talk with Kathleen this morning?" he asked, amused.

She kept her hands folded tightly in her lap. "Which part?" she said casually. "Where my father killed Ruark's? Or the part where you delivered his son to a cruel sea captain—?"

"It was either that or see him hang, lass. Ruark is stubborn when he gets it in his mind to murder someone. I could no' allow him to fight his father."

"What about Julia, Duncan? What of her life?"

"Why would ye feel sorry for Julia? She has everything," he said with a lack of gallantry. "She has been spoiled and self-indulged. Now the young lover of old has come home to roost and take his place as laird. You should be concerned with yourself."

Heat burned her cheeks. "And what flight of fancy leads you to suppose my husband holds a *tendre* for another woman?"

"Oho!" He laughed. "Ye feel passion for our laird, do ye no'?" Duncan said as he studied her. "Maybe ye will do after all, lassie. If ye feel passion enough for him, then you will come to feel the same for Stonehaven. She needs a strong mistress. Someone who wants to be here. Someone who is no' afraid of a fight. But ye are no' her mistress yet."

Left speechless by the man's barefaced effrontery, she disliked that he could glean an emotional response from her when she was so certain she disliked him. Perhaps she disliked him because he had tapped into her deepest doubts with no effort at all.

They arrived at Stonehaven an hour later. "You'll no' have any more problem seeing Jamie, lass," he said. "I'll talk to Julia."

Rose didn't know what to say. When the staff hurried

out to greet them, Rose quit to her room for a bath, and left Duncan to contend with Mary's scolding on his own. Evidently, she was upset that he'd taken Rose away from Stonehaven and allowed her to be gone for days. But much like Ruark, his uncle did not mind being admonished by Mary.

Anaya greeted her upstairs in her chambers, surprising Rose.

"I returned this morning, mum," she said brightly. "McBain is in the surgery with a head bump. The roads be terrible, mum. We almost broke another axle and himself not having another carriage to bring us. Told Mr. McBain, he would see him back at Stonehaven when he finished his business."

"Is that all he said?" she asked, wondering at once how she could ask a servant such a question, as if Ruark would tell Anaya anything.

"Aye, mum. McBain is a fretful sort. His lordship did no' want him to vex."

Rose took her supper in her room. Later, in the growing darkness of her bedchamber, she sat in her shift at the window seat, her chin propped on her hand as she stared outside. Her window overlooked the front of the house and the garden. She could hear the babble of voices below, and a moment later Duncan appeared with Jamie and Julia, resplendent in blue watered silk. At supper that evening, Mary had said that Jamie was recovering nicely.

Rose watched the threesome from the darkness of her bedroom.

At least she was capable of admitting to herself that her turmoil had as much to do with her doubts about herself as it did with Ruark's absence. Duncan's observation of her character had been correct. She *did* feel passion for Stonehaven's laird.

If ye feel passion enough for him, then you will come to feel the same for Stonehaven. She needs a strong mistress. Someone who wants to be here, lass. Someone who is no' afraid of a fight. But ye are no' her mistress yet.

The unfortunate circumstances behind her marriage did not change the fact that she was Ruark's wife. That her sons and daughters would be born and raised at Stonehaven, and she would one day be buried here, not at Hope Abbey, not at Kirkland Park, or France, but here. Rose could accept her *fate* as a victim. Or she could shape her fate as a victor.

Suddenly a visit from the dressmaker was no longer akin to subjecting herself to the inquisition. She may not know the difference between a day dress and morning gown, but she could certainly learn.

To find she was still capable of an honest fight, even if the antagonist was herself, restored some measure of equanimity to her disposition.

Anaya entered carrying her robe. She looked over Rose's shoulder outside. "Poor wee fatherless lad," she said. "Sometimes 'tis simple to forget he is not yet thirteen."

Not yet thirteen . . .

A sick feeling twisted her insides. She suddenly knew what was bothering her . . . what had been bothering her since her conversation this morning with Kathleen.

Drawing on her robe, she left her chambers. She padded barefoot along the shadowed corridor through the narrow gallery, where centuries of Kerrs stared down at her as she passed. Downstairs, she found the library.

Moonlight spilled through the windows. She looked at the rich paneled walls and ornate bookcases. Her gaze paused on a rostrum. The family Bible sat on that stand. Kathleen had said that all marriages, births, and deaths were recorded in the family Bible.

Rose found a tinderbox in the desk drawer and lit a candle. She brought the heavy leather-bound book carefully to the desk. She flipped the ornate cover open and peeled back page after page. She ran her fingernail down the list of inscribed names and stopped when she saw hers, surprised to see that her marriage to Ruark had already been entered. Her finger paused over her name. Pushing the Bible closer to the light, she recognized the penmanship as similar to that on her marriage documents. Ruark must have made the entry.

She flipped the faded pages backward to see when Ruark's parents were married, then his birth, May 10, 1725. He had only recently reached his thirtieth birthday. She had not even known his age, she realized. For some reason, she had thought him older. His mam had passed when he was six, just two days before another entry and death, an infant brother, was recorded. His mam had died in childbirth. His father had remained unmarried for eleven years when Julia's name was listed, then James Marcus Kerr was born eight and half months later. *Eight and a half months.*

A fist went to her stomach. She thought she would be sick.

Rose closed the Bible. Back when she had first come to Stonehaven, McBain had told her that Ruark and Julia had run away together. Today, Duncan had said they had been lovers.

After a moment, Rose returned the Bible to its place. It was a long time before she could sleep.

Chapter 20

Ruark sat outside the Lusty Mermaid at one of four trestle tables that looked out on the Solway Sea, a treacherous body of water that eventually became the headway for the River Eden. A thin layer of mist had formed on the water and was now drifting inland, and encapsulated the sounds from sea: the faint sound of a ship watch bell, the lap of water on the beach. Two black-and-white mongrels milled at Ruark's feet, supping on scraps he had fed them earlier from the trencher the little barmaid had set in front of him.

Colum sat at the table behind him. "Do ye think Hereford will attempt to kill ye now or later?" he asked.

A soft chuckle conveyed Ruark's response as he had just been thinking that very thing. Lounging with his legs stretched in front of him, a mug of ale in his gloved hand, he and Colum were watching the progress up the street of Hereford and his entourage. The warden had rumbled into this small seaside hamlet with forty heavily armed men and attempted to find space in the narrowly confined square for all the horses and men.

After leaving his solicitor in Hawick, Ruark had traveled more than a week to get here. Fifty other men from his ship were also with him, though a person would be hard-pressed to spot the infiltrators among the scruffy-looking residents of the village. They looked busy, moving casks and hogsheads of rum from offloaded flats on the beach a short distance away and flirting with prostitutes, casting lots on a blanket spread near the street.

Out on the water, stark masts bobbed in the cove, a six-teen gun-privateer, brigantine, and a sloop, all sharing the inlet waters of Solway Firth, where coasters could unload their cargo. Goods landed here would be carted inland into Carlisle and from there, dispersed. Her silhouette visible against the sunset burning into the sea, the *Black Dragon* pulled against her anchor chains.

With its raised quarterdeck and forecastle, and carrying thirty-six guns—which had now been removed—the frigate was a substantial vessel, too large to come into the shallower waters except during higher tides. This was smugglers' country and Ruark knew the waters well.

Hereford scanned the thatch-roofed buildings up and down the street before fastening his eyes on the lopsided placard bearing the inn's name and the carved image of a buxom mermaid. Nothing of his dark attire caught a gleam of the fading sunlight that glinted off the glass behind him.

Ruark hadn't shaved for today's meeting. He'd clubbed back his hair, but little else about his appearance would pass for civilized. Hereford looked at him and chuckled. "You look at home with every other cutthroat present."

Ruark lazily sipped his ale, noting the dozen men standing near the warden. Hereford was a leader at ease with his perception of power.

Hereford turned and looked out at the *Black Dragon* floating languidly on the calm surface of the sea. "Aye, she's a beauty, Roxburghe." His gaze went to the packet of papers lying next to Ruark's elbow and he smiled, an unsubtle gloat. "You brought the papers, I see."

Hereford sat and snapped his fingers for the barmaid. She hurried to him with ale. He sent her off for vittles. "Don't mind if I celebrate this occasion with supper and drink." He tossed his gloves on the table and reached for the packet of papers.

Ruark dropped his hand over the bundle, preventing Hereford's taking possession of it. "One question," he said, disinclined to engage in small talk with the bastard. "We both know Roxburghe Shipping has profited from certain illegal enterprise. What I do not understand is how my father could have been in league with you."

A minute change in Hereford's eyes betrayed his surprise and Ruark wondered if it was at the question asked or more so because of what Ruark had not asked: Had Hereford killed Ruark's father?

The chair creaked as Hereford sat back and relaxed his weight. "Roxburghe was a man who understood politics," he said with a bored air. "Your *father* outwardly supported Scotland's independence whilst secretly supplying the king's armies with the weapons to fight against the Jacobites at Culloden. I know this because I supplied him with the firearms."

It was all Ruark could do not to stand and grab Hereford by the throat. Ruark's father was many things, but his loyalty to Scotland had never been in doubt. "Is that right?"

"The Roxburghe ships now carry a dominant share of Scotland's trade because of *my* help. In exchange, I would give him a tax-free cargo of which to dispose and he would give me the enormous profits. And in so doing, I kept my family name clean. A business arrangement that benefited us both. But not once in all those years did we meet. He had an emissary. Why would I kill your father? For all that he owed me, I should have *owned* the Roxburghe fleet of ships."

Ruark studied the mug of ale. "Who was the emissary?"

"Your village fiscal handled the monetary transactions and all the arrangements. He is now dead. Ask your uncle how that might have happened. No one was more adept at safeguarding your family honor, including committing a bit of murder, if he thought someone was robbing Stonehaven's coffers."

Even as Ruark knew the warden wanted to foment discord within the Kerr ranks, his comments were not easily dismissed.

Perhaps because Ruark recognized truth in Hereford's interpretation of Duncan's character. A loyal Kerr and a Scotsman, Duncan would not hesitate doling out clan justice to a traitor.

Hereford's supper arrived in a trencher, roasted chicken and potatoes, steaming in the cooler air outside the tavern. Hereford forewent the eating utensils and tore the breast in half with his hands, observing Ruark with interest as he ate.

"You and I are alike," Hereford said over a mouthful. "We've done a bit of pirating." He swallowed the ale and dabbed at his lips with the back of his sleeve as he observed Ruark. "We can each share the *largesse* of what is fast becoming the wealthiest empire on earth. We can enjoy a profitable partnership or I can become Roxburghe Shipping's biggest rival."

"Your generosity overwhelms me, Hereford. But I would as soon lie with a warthog as partner with you."

Unaffected by the insult, Hereford shoved away the trencher and reached across the table for the papers. This time Ruark did not stop him as his greasy fingers snatched up the packet.

"All is in order then?" Hereford popped the wax wafer on the packet and unfolded one sheet after another of blank paper. "What is this?"

"You did not think I would just hand over the *Black Dragon*."

Hereford's face darkened a shade. Ruark leaned an elbow on the rickety table. "The ship was not mine to sell."

"What do you mean? Not yours?"

"I sold it to an associate a week before I wed Rose." He opened his arm to encompass Colum, sitting comfortably behind him seemingly enjoying the cool breeze. "If you want the *Black Dragon*, then you will have to negotiate with the new owner."

Hereford sputtered. "That . . . that is *mad*. You signed—"

"Mr. Colum is Cambridge educated. He is a lawyer. He informed me the documents I signed are worthless and took great issue that I attempted to sell you something that belonged to him. I only wish I held the same power to stop you from taking Kirkland Park."

"If you renege on our arrangement, I will consider all agreements voided."

"Do tell, Hereford. Rose is my wife and that is something you cannot undo."

"Except by your death."

Hereford sprang to his feet in a brash movement, his hand on the hilt of his cutlass. But before the weapon cleared its sheath, Ruark had the tip of his own blade at Hereford's throat. From every direction, a hundred men suddenly drew sword and pistol, the clatter of imminent warfare sounding in the street, sending innocent bystanders to ground and behind the safety of doors.

Ruark met Hereford's furious glare. "Tsk. Tsk," he said. "Do we kill each other now or later? 'Twould be a shame if you died, Rose being your heir and all."

"Fuck you, Roxburghe. There is naught a thing I will—"

Ruark used the tip of his cutlass to trace a circle over Hereford's chest. "I should kill you for what you put Jamie through. For putting my family in chains."

"I was within the law to hang the three of them."

"No profit in hanging," Ruark said flatly. "You are an opportunist. Know now, the only reason you are still alive is because I have no proof you killed my father. I have asked enough questions this week of people around Chesters to know you were nowhere near there the day someone shot him. I had no great love for the man, but his murder almost caused a bloody war between us. I have no want to watch other men die for a lie."

A tic was visible in Hereford's jaw. "What is it you want?"

"You already gave me what I want, Hereford."

Hereford let loose the hilt of his sword and the blade slid back into its sheath. His men followed suit. A man rarely bested, he took the loss mildly. "You always did have the bollocks of an ox. I had heard grumblings that you had a *tendre* for the girl, that she had charmed Stonehaven's laird. Though I didn't expect that Elena's daughter would have half her mother's fire . . ."

"Do you like fire, Hereford?"

Let him have the *Black Dragon,* Ruark thought. He was impatient to be gone from this place.

"Colum, would you be willing to trade your ship for another? Roxburghe Shipping has a few in need of a good captain."

Colum scratched at his whiskers as he contemplated

the *Black Dragon*. "I was hoping you wouldn't ask me that, Ruark."

"Colum—"

"Aye, 'tis a fair trade."

Ruark withdrew a packet from inside his waistcoat and tossed it onto the table. "Consider all debts justly paid. The ship is yours, Hereford."

Colum followed Ruark as he turned abruptly on his boot heel. The slight warmth of the day had fled quickly in the darkness. Ruark could not see the moon as he strode past the stable, the clang and jangle of sword and spurs at rhythm with his stride. At the edge of town, they met twenty of their men and mounted horses. The others had scattered. Some would be returning with Ruark to Stonehaven, perhaps to begin new lives. Others would go on to Workington, find new ships belonging to Roxburghe Shipping on which to serve. All of them reined in their horses three miles outside the village and turned to look toward the water.

He could already smell burning pitch on the breeze. Loki pranced in a circle as Ruark held tight to the reins. The ship was already full ablaze. The inferno lit up the sky. Flames climbed high, choking the heavens.

Aye, his heart and his life had once been there.

But no more.

"Bloody hell," Colum murmured, his eyes narrowing on the slow-growing orange glow in the distance. "He will kill you for what you have done this day. Hell, he will kill me. I owned the *Black Dragon*."

"You still do. The papers I gave him were worthless."

Without comment, Ruark reined his horse around. He had already said good-bye to his crew and no one wasted breath on sentimentality now. It was best they all got across the border.

His thoughts were already turning to the more pressing matter of the weather moving in. And home.

Six days later, Ruark and Colum crossed into Scotland, and two days after that he reached Stonehaven's border, weary, disheveled, and saddle worn. A full moon sat just above the tree line as they rode past the gatehouse and up the long, winding drive toward the cobbled courtyard at the back of the house. He'd been gone almost three weeks.

Now as he slowed Loki to a lope, he felt his pulse accelerate. Until now, he hadn't let himself think. He'd been driven by the powerful need to get home. The need to know Rose was safe. The thought sank in now and set its claws deep as he looked up at the ivy-encased stone house. Every window was alight and blazing. "At least no one is abed," Colum observed from beside him, his mind clearly set on a hot meal after Ruark had bypassed the last inn in favor of continuing onward. The men who had traveled on with him had veered off hours ago to the village.

Ruark nudged Loki with his heels. They reached the cobbled courtyard and Ruark dismounted as Mary burst from the doorway to greet him. Two groomsmen rushed past her and down the stone stairs to take the horses.

"Heavens, Ruark," Mary said, coming forward to greet him, her round face warmed by a smile. "We did no' expect ye back so soon."

Amused, Ruark removed his gloves. "So soon?" His gaze touched the windows. "Is there a sound reason you are burning every candle at Stonehaven then, if 'tis not a beacon to guide me home from England to your lovely self?"

"Och, Ruark." She giggled and turned in a crackle of

petticoats, clearly expecting Ruark and Colum to follow. "Today is Jamie's birthday. Or have ye forgotten ye used to send him a gift every year?"

He *had* forgotten.

"Our Julia and Lady Roxburghe have been entertainin' the local gentry and their families for most of the day—"

"*Julia* and Rose? Together?"

Mary stood against the door to hold it open as Ruark and Colum passed ahead of her into the entry hall. "'Twas silly that her ladyship was not allowed to see the boy." Mary shut the door and waddled ahead of them. "Duncan told Julia 'twas time to accept the new lady Roxburghe as Stonehaven's mistress if she wanted to continue living beneath the same roof. Now, I dare say, they are at least speaking to one another. Julia helped her ladyship and Kathleen plan the celebration for Jamie."

She glanced sideways at Ruark. "Ye remember Kathleen. The fiscal's wife. Rose saved her son's foot from rot. Though, he did lose part of a toe, poor lad . . . Last week, McBain had to remove—"

Ruark set both his hands on Mary's shoulders and forced her to stop talking. "What the bloody hell are ye talking about?"

"Our own Lady Roxburghe labored the night to save Rufus and his foot. He had a wretched infection and McBain was not yet back from Hawick. Duncan took her to Kathleen. McBain said she saved the boy. 'Tis simple as that."

"You allowed Duncan to take my wife from Stonehaven?"

Mary jabbed a finger at his chest. "Do no' use that tone with me, Ruark Kerr. You've been away a long time. Things are different. Ye may be laird here, but *she* is Stonehaven's mistress."

He laughed. "Hell, I have been gone all of twenty days."

Mary sniffed. "She accompanies McBain every other morning when he visits the tenants. There is no' a person who would harm her. Ye can thank Duncan for that as well. He would skin alive the man who dared touch her."

She stepped past Ruark, leaving him to follow as she continued down the corridor. Colum brought Ruark out of his fog with a nudge.

"Kathleen came to live here last week," Mary tossed over her shoulder as they turned a corner into another corridor dimly lit by sconce light. "We were in need of a cook. Bessie can no' hardly walk anymore. Gout ye know. Always comes on when the weather starts to grow cold." She hesitated mid-stride to allow Ruark to catch up to her.

"Now Kathleen lives at Stonehaven with her family, so her children can be properly schooled with the other local children. Duncan found an unused structure and everyone turned out this week to make the thing into a school. 'Tis that old hunting lodge between here and the village. Ye remember the place. No one has used it in years."

Aye, Ruark knew the place. He and Rose had spent a blissful night in that lodge.

Mary continued walking. "Everyone is there now. Our mistress wanted to include the tenants' families in the final hours of the celebration, and so Duncan and Angus and some of the other lads hunted a boar in the western woods and brought it back this morn. They've set up a bonfire from the wood they cleared around the new school."

Mary turned at the bottom of the stairs and placed her hand on the newel post. Ruark stopped in front of her. "Is there anything else I should know before I go in search of my wife?"

"A week ago, Mrs. Simpson arrived toting with her a lad named Jack. She heard of our ladyship's marriage and wished personally to meet her Scot's husband."

Ruark turned on his heel but Mary snatched his sleeve. "But no' lookin' like an heathen Pict from the North Country."

Colum's chuckle ended in a throaty cough as Mary turned her fierce look on him. "Ye look worse, Bryce Colum. Now upstairs with ye both. You've been gone three weeks. Another hour will no' matter."

But to Ruark another five minutes was longer than he was willing to wait to see Rose. He'd bathed yesterday in an ice-cold river, and at least the clothes he wore had been washed three days ago at the last inn where he and Colum had stayed. Last night, he'd even removed the silver hoop from his earlobe.

Leaving Colum to deal with the horses, Ruark walked through the crowd, aware that as he passed, people stopped what they were doing and stared. He vaguely recognized Stonehaven's blacksmith and nodded. Rushlights dotted the fields where jugglers and ropedancers, probably left over from the *Lammas* celebration in a neighboring shire, entertained the children. A dozen tents filled with what remained of someone's apple or peach harvests, pies and other goods were closing as most had clearly been here all afternoon. He could smell Duncan's roast pig on the breeze and hear the faint strands of the fiddle coming from farther away. A shimmering orange glow from the bonfire brightened the nighttime sky. As he drew closer, he could hear the strains of laughter and cheer.

"Lord Roxburghe!" someone called.

He turned on his heel. His first glance fell on Duncan, but it was the woman dressed in bright yellow beside him who was smiling. The fiscal's wife. He had not seen her since he had been a lad in short pants. "We did not expect you for another few days," she said. "You remember me?"

"Kathleen," he said. She was six years older than he was. "Who can forget the prettiest girl in the shire?"

Then he straightened and acknowledged Duncan with a curt nod. Both Duncan and Kathleen carried an armful of wooden trenchers.

"Do you know where I can find my wife?" he asked Kathleen.

She shifted her load and pointed to the lodge. "She was with Julia in our new soon-to-be school, but that was an hour ago. You might try the bonfire, where dancing has started. Have ye seen the school?"

"Perhaps later," he said politely.

Through a narrow break in the crowd, he glimpsed the high-stepping dancers. People clapped to the fiddler as they watched a spirited reel. He did not see her at first among the dancers. He had been looking at the spectators. Ruark shouldered through the onlookers encircling the line of the brightly lit dancers and stopped at the circle's edge.

She had told him once she did not know how to dance. And he wondered when she'd learned. Jason danced across from her. Gavin stood at her side. He didn't know the names of the other dancers young and old alike.

She wore nothing more elegant than a simple blue muslin sloping from the wide neckline to a point at her narrow waist, yet the front-laced bodice clung to high curves of her breast and her skirts flowed around her slender form. With each sprightly step, she revealed a pair of shapely ankles. Giving her right hand to Jason, she changed places with the female on his right, then the male on her left. The steps went on until Jason grabbed her hands and, laughing brightly, she and Jason danced up the middle of the line toward him.

Heat emanating from the bonfire seemed to burn through Ruark's clothes and into his blood.

He had ridden days to get back to her, worried as hell, only to find she had not only survived perfectly without him but that she had thrived.

He stepped forward just as a hand clapped on his shoulder. He thought Duncan had come up on him. Already in a killing state of mind, his first instinct was to grab the arm and turn with just enough pressure to break the contact. But the owner of that firm grip belonged to Angus.

"She's no' done anything wrong, lad," he said, his voice mild. "We've been with her the night. All of us."

On the other end of the circle, he glimpsed Duncan's hard gaze. He saw Jamie and the boy next to him Ruark remembered as Jack.

The fiddlers stopped playing abruptly. The dancers groaned. Confused by the sudden halt of music, shouts of encouragement to continue playing rose among the crowd. Breathless, Rose turned. She was hot and flushed, her nape damp beneath her hair. She shoved aside a wayward lock of hair, her laughter dying as she met Ruark's gaze.

He stood at the circle's edge. His name went over the crowd like a whisper of wind as his presence began to draw more attention. He felt the tension leave his muscles. His sanity returned. Maybe 'twas the way she looked at him. But he felt that touch to his soul.

Her gaze dropped in confusion to Angus's hand on his shoulder. By her expression, she must have guessed what he had been about to do. "My lord," she said, and left him to close the short distance between them, which he did, but not without seeking a reward for the effort.

The dust of the road still clinging to his clothes, he

pulled her into his arms and kissed her. The crowd exploded in cheers. Their laird was back, business settled. Now he wanted his wife to himself. Her hands closed into fists against his shoulders.

Against her lips, he said, " 'Tis time to leave."

"I will *not*," she said between her teeth. "Kathleen and Julia went to a great deal of trouble tonight. 'Tis rude merely to leave because you . . . I . . . have not even eaten supper."

"I will feed you upon our return."

"This is your brother's birthday, have you taken the time to wish him well? Since you have returned from your twelve-year-and-nine-month hiatus on the sea, have you spent any time with your tenants? Visited the village?"

"I have been a bit occupied, love. As you well know."

"Aye, so occupied you could not wait to leave Stonehaven after Jedburgh. I know these people better than you do. Your people. Your family."

"I am glad, Rose." He touched his lips to her ear. "But as much as I enjoy these moments together, I have not changed my clothes in days, and I have slept little these past weeks. All I want is to bathe and take you to bed." He turned her in his arms so that they both faced the crowd.

Angus raised a mug in toast. "To our laird and his bonny bride."

More bantering went around. "We'll not be mindin' if ye wish to take the lass from us tonight," someone shouted over the laughter.

Ruark waited for the drinking to finish. "Aye, lads, we were just discussing our possibilities. She's missed me."

More laughter. Rose squirmed from him. "You cannot

be gone for weeks, then return and with the snap of your fingers think I will jump."

"Looks to me like she's already forgotten ye, my lord," another barked from the back of the crowd, and laughter followed as other men and women alike joined in the good-natured ribbing. "Maybe ye just have to remind her a bit harder."

Rose looked shocked and he almost felt sorry for her. But the Scots were an earthy bunch and less inclined to a civilized fight when it came to their patriotism, their home, and their women. What she did not understand was if they did not truly love and care for her, none would have raised their cups in toast.

Everyone expected him to take her from here, and never one to disappoint, Ruark picked her up and threw her over his shoulder, to the eruption of applause. "Now if you will all excuse me, it has been a long time and I would like to take my bonny bride home to bed."

Chapter 21

Lying across Ruark's shoulder, her fists pounding on his back, Rose stopped shouting only when he slowed to instruct Colum to see that the boys and Julia got back to Stonehaven safely.

Deaf to Rose's fury, Ruark swung her up on Loki, then mounted behind her. He settled her across his lap. He placed his palm across her stomach to hold her firmly against his chest as he bent to secure the reins. Then he galloped away from the celebration she had helped organize. He rode for a mile in his estimation before he felt her shuddering inhalation, as if the effort would calm the race of her heartbeat that thumped so heavily against his palm. His mind was too awash with whatever she was feeling to define his own emotions.

Her full mouth, inviting his gaze, remained neither flat nor pursed, hinting only of the intensity of her control.

"Are you planning to remain silent all the way home?" Ruark asked.

Apparently, she was. He could kidnap her. Twice. Wed her against her will. But he could not make her talk.

He waited until he had ridden a suitable distance from the lodge, until he could no longer see the glow of orange in the sky from the bonfire. Then he reined in Loki. "Dammit, Rose."

His hand swept along the taut curve of her waist, and he turned her in his arms. A gust of wind snatched the hem of her dress. She did not resist him, not because his physical strength made escape impossible, but because her power against him lay in submission.

He rubbed his thumb across her cheekbone. The moonlight revealed her eyes, wet with hurt. In the charged silence, all he wanted to do was kiss her.

The magnitude of his desire had reached proportions startling even to him. Desire he was only beginning to understand.

He had wanted her since the first time he had seen her at the abbey. A passion that had slowly grown and fed upon itself, that had awakened him at night these past weeks, that had stopped him in the middle of a meal or a conversation as he remembered her touch, the scent and texture of her hair, the taste of her on his lips, and why he had wanted to get home to her.

He caught her chin with two fingers. "Rose . . ."

"Let go of me. Please."

"Tell me you did not miss me," he cajoled.

He could read the answer in her eyes. She would be lying if she told him nay. His hands came over her breasts to undo the laces on her bodice. "You would force me, Ruark?" The question was a wounded whisper.

He stared at her upturned face. She was his wife. She must know there could be no question of force.

He paused. His eyes closed briefly, then opened.

"Tonight 'twas a bit of good sport for all, Rose. We are just wed. I have been absent nearly a month. No one thinks less of you."

She looked surprised that he understood her feelings.

'Twas not only *his* actions that injured her. It had been the ribbing and laughter from everyone else. Claimed by her Scottish laird. She felt betrayed by their ribaldry as their laird carted her off like a sack of grain. The conquering hero comes home to his bride, and everyone has a wonderful time at her expense.

His statement galvanized her. "How dare you arrive home after being gone three weeks and show such disrespect. I worked weeks cultivating trust and what I believed to be friendships. I met the tenants, visited the village elders. I had so wanted to show you my school when you returned. I do not want to care, yet I cannot pluck the hurt from my heart as if 'tis a splinter easily removed."

Indeed, she had seen something different in his actions from what everyone else recognized. She knew his actions for exactly what they had been as she'd first seen him in the cemetery when he had forcibly taken her from Hope Abbey. And she was correct in her assessment.

From her point of view, his behavior only reinforced a long list of grievances and hurts. Her entire life had been bartered away by another, her worth calculated by her value in gold and lands and political power, not by what she could give from her heart.

Her tears started sliding down her cheeks and he knew she blamed him for that as well. The startling honesty of her hurt finally settled against him. He didn't reply to her. Not for a long time.

Then he kicked his heels against Loki and they rode the rest of the way to Stonehaven in silence. She didn't wait for him to rein in completely before sliding off the horse. Catching up her skirts, she walked up the stairs to Stonehaven's front door, as regal as royalty, as if she'd been born into the role of countess, not stopping as the butler appeared. She swept into the entry hall past an openmouthed Mary and Mrs. Simpson, who had remained behind to enjoy tea with an old friend. The two of them sat in the parlor and came to their feet as Rose walked past them and up the stairway.

Ruark remained on the horse, one wrist crossed over the other on the pommel for a few minutes, watching the whole thing through the tall window. Then he dismounted and gave the reins over to the startled stable lad who stood with his mouth agape.

He followed Rose's path up the stairs to the door. Rose's icy silence back to Stonehaven was not the only source of his surly mood. He stepped into the entry hall as the distant slamming of a door reverberated through the house.

The butler made no comment as Ruark handed him his riding gloves. "I will need a bath and supper brought up to my wife."

"Aye, my lord."

Ruark stopped in front of the small parlor where guests usually awaited the master of the manse's leisure. It was a brightly colored room unlike the darker-paneled entry hall. It was simply fitted without heavy tapestry and finished off with blue upholstered furniture. He rarely used the front entrance of the house and had not been to this room in years. It had been his mother's entertaining room.

He found Mary standing. "I left Colum to see that Julia and the two boys are returned home safely. Where is Duncan sleeping these days?"

"He stays at the gatehouse."

His gaze briefly touched the pert gray-haired woman next to Mary, and he accepted an introduction. Sophia Simpson wore fine gray linen that despite its severity made her look regal. She looked to be in her sixties and better-dressed than one would have expected of someone he had imagined living in a simple thatched cottage outside

Castleton. "Mrs. Simpson is the expert on Arthurian legend of which I spoke," Mary said.

The woman did not curtsey but seemed to be studying him, her opinion of him not visible in the blue eyes that held his. "'Twas my husband who was the real expert," she demurred after a moment. "Rose herself had an interest in a particular relic. Though she informed me 'twas no longer in her possession. I wonder if the person wearing it now has found his life greatly changed."

This woman had brought Jack to Stonehaven, someone clearly special to Rose, and she knew about the ring. Who was to say his life would not have changed in the same manner without the ring? But something had indeed changed inside him, touching on emotions and hopes and dreams he'd buried so deeply he thought them forever gone.

"I am pleased to make your acquaintance," he said.

Strangely, he *was* pleased. He saw a lot of Rose in Mrs. Simpson's demeanor. She politely inclined her head. "Likewise, my lord. Welcome home. Rose has missed you despite what you might think."

With a detached sort of amusement, he considered that after she had witnessed Rose's entry a moment ago, she also surmised Ruark would be receiving no proper homecoming tonight. "Perhaps I will see you at breakfast," he said, a corner of his mouth turning up.

Mary cleared her throat. "Her ladyship has given me leave to accompany Mrs. Simpson tomorrow to visit old friends of her husband's in Hawick. In the Roxburghe coach. We will be gone a week."

Ruark raised his brow, unsure if he was more surprised by the obvious respect she paid Rose as mistress of Stonehaven, or that Mary was actually taking a holiday. "Then I wish you both a safe journey. Ladies . . ."

"My lord . . ." Mrs. Simpson's voice brought him back

around. "A captured butterfly might be beautiful, but is still captured. If you want what you seek most in the world, then open the cage and let the butterfly find *you*." She smiled. "I have known Rose since she was a child, my lord. She is special to my heart. To many hearts."

Irritation pricked him but left as soon as he felt the sting. Mrs. Simpson had not said anything more or less than what he already knew himself. "What is it *you* think I want, Mrs. Simpson?"

"I could not say, my lord."

But she was sure *he* knew what he wanted.

Aye, he could charge upstairs and force himself on his wife.

But tonight was suddenly not nearly as important to him as tomorrow and all the other tomorrows to follow.

Rose had very little that was hers, and what she did have she fiercely guarded. Her heart was hers alone to give away. He would never own it completely if he did not first win her trust.

Chance not. Win not.

He remembered the inscription on his great-grandfather's empty tomb, the other pirate in the family, the one who had found his life and his peace with his English bride.

Audace fortuna juvat. Fortune favors the bold.

If he did not risk his own heart, he would never find hers.

Rose awakened to morning light spilling into her room and over the soft white eiderdown comforter that wrapped her in warmth. While Ruark had been away, she had moved her belongings into the blue damask bedchamber, with its flamboyant rococo-style furnishings, but she had continued to sleep in her husband's bed. Last night she had barred the doors and slept in the blue bedchamber.

With her mind still weighted by slumber, for a heart-beat she'd forgotten her angry tears last night and only remembered that Ruark was home.

Memories of last night banished the warmth she felt. She sat upright, her hair tumbling over her shoulders.

Sighing, she threw off the covers and rose from bed, the hem of her pale cotton nightdress tumbling to her calves.

She padded barefoot across the thick Brussels carpet to test the position of the walnut writing cabinet she had slid in front of the panel door in the wall. She then tested the main door to make sure the key remained in the lock. To her utter disappointment, he had not attempted to break down doors to get to her. She had awaited him to try, too, in a fine, hot temper, daring him to come to her just so she could throw something at his head. How dare he not come to her chambers so she could have the privilege of throwing him out?

Feeling disappointed but secure, she retired to her dressing room to wash. She splashed water from a pitcher into a large delft basin sitting on the washstand against the wall. She cleaned her teeth with teeth powder that she had sprinkled with mint leaves to mask the wretched taste, then began to unbraid her hair. Voices outside drew her to the window. She walked over, pulled aside the mulberry brocade curtain and looked down at the yard. No matter where she slept, her window was always left cracked open at night. A climbing rosebush that wrapped an iron trellis filled the morning air with perfume.

Her melancholy began to ebb as she watched Jack and Jamie playing near the reflecting pool. She had told Mrs. Simpson only yesterday that she loved it here at Stonehaven and she wanted Jack to remain.

"Will your husband abide by that wish?" Mrs. Simpson had asked.

Truthfully, Rose did not know. She suspected that despite his unforgivable behavior the night before, Ruark would allow her the freedom to do most anything within reason.

Then she thought of Jamie Kerr and the possibility that he could be Ruark's son, and she decided she would find a way to keep Jack with her here.

The two boys were dressed in loose-fitting brown frock coats and breeches, their silk stockings of the finest quality. The silver buckles on their shoes glinted in the morning sunlight. The lads would be accompanying her and McBain today on their rounds.

When Jack looked up and saw her, his face split with a gap-toothed smile. He waved vigorously and she waved back. Jamie, though more subdued, also returned her wave with a smile. The two boys were not quite friends, but Jamie seemed to follow Jack everywhere.

"Look what we got to take with us," Jack called up to her.

He and Jamie were eating buns from a basket that Jack had gotten from the kitchen. Buns supposed to be going to the pastor's wife at the village kirk.

She called back for them *not* to eat another bun. She would be down momentarily. After they ran off toward the stable, she found herself glad the two were at least getting along.

She decided to ring for Anaya. With her new wardrobe having arrived only two days prior, Rose had learned *why* a lady's maid was not only appreciated but practical, to overcome the complications of dressing.

Rose yanked shut the curtains, turned and nearly ran into Ruark. She gasped, stepped back and bumped the edge of a chair. He was leaning with his back against the washstand, his arms folded, amusement in his eyes as if he had been watching her for some time and enjoying the show. Her gaze flew around the room trying to detect how he had got into her dressing room.

"Kathleen set up a table outside," he said as if he had not walked through locked doors to get inside here. "I thought 'twould be nice to take breakfast in the garden with my wife."

"How did you get in here?"

"I grew up in this house. There is not a secret passage-way or servant's walkway or door I have not discovered or opened." Their eyes locked and a few beats of silence passed between them. "I missed you last night," he said softly.

As if to escape his gaze, she scooted around the chair and hit the wall. He followed her retreat and trapped her, his hand braced against the wall behind her. "Rose, I behaved like an insufferable boor."

"Aye!" she flung at him. "You . . . you did!"

But his admission had snatched the wind from her sails. Last night her anger had formed around a tempest of fury.

This morning, in daylight, the storm had weakened.

She had wanted to speak to him about Jack. She had wanted to talk to him about Jamie. Ever since she had read the entry in the Bible, she had questioned if Jamie could be his son.

Last night was simply too silly to fret over, she told herself. Yet the tears came. "You have apologized," she said, and attempted to step past him. "And I have another engagement this morning. Now if you will excuse me."

She'd never questioned the existence of desire but she had never experienced it in its primal form, never reckoned with its power until his hair brushed her cheek and his words touched her ear. "Last night is an excuse, love. Because that is not why you are angry now."

"Move aside."

"Like hell I will."

His own anger shot her gaze back to his eyes. "Do you remember our first meeting at the abbey, Rose? You asked me after I had been standing outside during a lightning storm—aye, you guessed correctly about that—you asked if I feared death. Or defied it. At the time I could honestly tell you, I feared nothing.

"You told me lightning is the most powerful force on earth. 'It intrigues, tempts, and taunts you. You cannot master it but it makes you feel something powerful. Only a man who cannot feel life seeks to find ways to destroy his own, if only to define his own existence,' you said. Do you remember those words?"

She did remember and he had repeated them verbatim.

"You told me I am a man without purpose. I am not that man any longer."

So conscious of his gaze, her mind lagged in catching up to his words.

"Aye, you are a bonny bride worth much. Tucker told me that from the beginning you were an heiress. But in Jedburgh, I was willing to let you go if I could find a way to get you out of England, because that is what *you* wanted.

"Since the first day I met you, I have wanted you, love. Do you truly believe Hereford could have *forced* me to wed you?"

She looked up at him through a hot veil of tears. His words, everything he was saying left her momentarily bereft of thought.

"Ah, love. I have injured you," he said, and gathered her in his arms. "I have apologized."

She nodded. He did not need to apologize. "I know."

He let her pull away from him.

"Now tell me about your school, love."

He produced a towel that had been lying beside the washbasin for her nose. Welcoming the change of topic, she told him of the school and the plans she had for the tenants' children and how she hoped the lodge was close enough to the village to draw children from there. She blew her nose and ceased sniffling. "I have written to Friar Tucker and asked if he would talk to the older girls to see if one or two might be interested in teaching positions. I told our kirk pastor that I would go over the applicants with him this morning." She peered up at him. "You do not object?"

"Nay, love."

She dabbed at her eyes and regarded him suspiciously. "You are being very humble and cooperative."

"I am trying." And the words went straight to the warm pit of her stomach.

His dark hair was still wet from a recent bath and tied back at his nape, emphasizing the handsome sun-touched features.

Dressed as he was in leather breeches and a simple white cambric shirt open at his throat, he looked neither aristocratic nor Scots today. He looked like he belonged on the sea. She slid her finger over the shell of his ear. "Where is your earring?"

He wrapped his fingers around hers. Turning her palm upward, he pressed a kiss into her hand. "I removed it, Rose."

"Why would you do such a thing?"

"If you do not know, then it matters little why the thing is gone."

Before she could respond, a knock sounded on the door in the bedchamber. "That is Anaya," he said. "I took the liberty of sending for her before I came up here."

Gowns and petticoats, shoes, hats, and sundry feminine articles lay on the settee, floor, and her dressing table. She had not finished looking at the beautiful things the modiste had brought her and not everything had been put away. A glance around at the abundance brought sudden amusement to his eyes. "I will have to compliment the modiste. Shall I send up another maid?"

She never knew quite what to say when he teased her. It made her feel young because she did not always understand his mood. "I should not have ordered so many gowns."

"You are not that extravagant. I can afford to purchase you gowns."

Another timid knock sounded. Ruark strode out of the dressing to open the bedroom door and allow Anaya into the room.

"Ruark . . ." Rose hurried to stand in front of him before he could turn the key in the door. She grabbed his sleeve. "Wait!"

Despite his current cavalier demeanor, she felt the firmly muscled flesh beneath the sleeve hard with tension. She wanted to ask him what he meant about the earring and to understand him, but she suddenly found she wanted him to kiss her more than she wanted anything else at all at the moment. But he did not kiss her, and Rose withdrew her hand from his arm.

"Perhaps I can prevail upon you to join us in church," she said. "We will be picking peaches afterward."

He arched a brow, and she could see the amusement in his eyes. "A visit to the holy kirk and a day in the peach grove? Enticing, but the only peach I want to pluck is standing in front of me."

And just that fast, he rescripted their dialogue, redirected her emotions and made a mockery of her will.

His thumb stroked the line of her jaw, and with the gentlest of pressure, his other hand closed in her hair, pulling her head back, exposing her neck to his hot, moist mouth. Her nostrils flared wide and she inhaled the clean scent of him. Then he lowered his head and seduced her mouth with a kiss that invited her to wrap her body around his and let him take her down to the grass.

A kiss that reminded her of all the days he had been away. She resisted for a moment, because the simple pleasure of being in his arms was doing disastrous things to her heart and will. How easily she surrendered.

He raised his head to look at her, and with the pads of his thumbs, he traced the curve of her throat. "I want more than your surrender, Rose."

He lowered his hands. Let her think about the words.

He bent around her to open the door. "Anaya awaits, love."

Chapter 22

Loki shied nervously at the darkening clouds and the brilliance of a distant crack of lightning. His gloved hand keeping a firm grip on the reins, Ruark soothed the horse as he awaited a man to catch up to him. He'd seen him from a distance, a small speck against a turbulent sky. Ruark had been twice to the gatehouse looking for Duncan and thought the rider might be he.

Duncan's continued absence weighed heavily on Ruark, and he was not in the most restrained of moods, having spent the last three days searching for his uncle to talk about what Hereford had told Ruark, which was beginning to prove a fruitless endeavor.

Yesterday, Angus told him that Duncan was not with the others bringing in sheep from the northern pastures as he had first thought. Today he had sent Colum to Hawick to speak to the coroner who supposedly had viewed the bodies of both Ruark's father and Kathleen's husband.

Angus approached and, seeing Ruark, reined in his horse. "A bit restless are ye, lad," he quipped as his eyes narrowed on the sky. "Out on an evening like this."

Ruark looked beyond the wild glen, then across the fells. "Aye, that I am. Are you not supposed to be escorting McBain and my wife to the village today?"

He scratched his heavy beard. "They returned some hours ago. Ye have no' been back yet?"

Ruark told Angus to return to Stonehaven and thumped Loki into a gallop. He would be late returning home that night. Aside from the quick trip to look over the new foals yesterday morning, Ruark had spent little time at Stonehaven.

For the last three days, Ruark had settled into a routine of normalcy as much as was possible with Rose in the adjoining chambers and him playing the celibate monk.

His wife had gone about her business as mistress of Stonehaven, overseeing Mary's duties during her absence. He barely saw her unless it was late at night and he stood in the doorway between her chambers and his, trying to remember all the reasons why he should turn away.

And so he kept himself occupied learning what it meant to be Stonehaven's laird. Yesterday he had gone with Angus to look over the new foals and discuss next year's acquisitions. Before that, it had been the barley fields that occupied him, and learning that some of the fields had not seen crops planted last spring. Tomorrow he would go south to the mill on the river and meet the foreman.

After a while Ruark quit thinking. The air was cool and crisp, as heady as rum punch as he rode Loki across the field. He rode up on the lodge, his gloved hands keeping a firm grip on the reins as he dismounted in front of Rose's school. The scent of larkspur and juniper mixed with the smell of earth and rain and familiar memories as Ruark looked up at the high roof. All but the watchman had left for the evening, leaving Ruark to walk the empty rooms in the fading light of the day, freshly painted with whitewash and windows newly glazed and the smell of plaster in his nostrils. He was impressed with his young wife's accomplishment. The building would make a fine school, and he felt pride knowing Rose was responsible.

Ruark walked around the grounds. The wind caught his hair. Dusk had left the countryside bathed in the deep magenta that mixed with the swirl of dark clouds as if the tempest came from within him. His head came around at the sound of a horse. He looked to where he had left Loki hobbled and grazing on a patch of grass.

It wasn't until he was nearly upon the stallion that he saw the second horse hobbled nearby. Rose stood beneath the branches of a large oak looking at him, her hand gripping her copper hair to keep it from whipping the air around her. She wore a cloak over a gown, the color of the surrounding tempest.

And he walked to where she stood, the sudden sharp stab of desire worse than when he had seen her dancing at the bonfire.

Worse even than last night, when he had returned home late to find her asleep on the settee in his library, the lamp burning low on the table beside her, a book upon her chest as if she had been trying to stay awake and wait for him. He had carried her to bed and she had not even awakened when he set her beneath the covers.

He stopped just beneath the branches.

"Angus said he saw you coming this way," she said.

"You were following me."

She made the smallest nod. Neither took a step toward the other though he could feel the pull between them.

"I have always considered myself judicious and balanced in my outlook," she said. "Quite above it all. I do not know about the kind of love hailed by poets. No one in my life has ever born witness to such."

Her voice wavered. "I only know that ever since I found the puzzle box in the abbey's crypt with the ring inside, my life has not been the same, almost as if a hole opened in my heart. Mrs. Simpson warned me that I was tampering with something beyond my ken. Yet, I opened the box without fully understanding the power. My heart is like that box.

"Until you, I had never looked at a man and felt anything beyond a need to exercise patience. Even you have tried mine immensely.

"Until you, I had never gone to sleep dreaming of some handsome face I might have glimpsed in the village or awakened feeling lost and confused, wondering if my heart would stop in my chest, it beat so soundly and painfully in panic. Until you, I had never known what 'tis like to know I would lay down my body to protect yours. I would do so for many, Jack, Mrs. Simpson, Friar Tucker—these people are my family. But I do not awaken in the morning with this feeling that if anything should happen to one of them I would rather die than live another day alone."

She scraped the heel of her palm across her cheek. "If this is love, then I love you so much it frightens me into wanting to run away as far as I can. Every time I look outside my bedroom window, I want to run back to the abbey where I once felt safe. To allow something so powerful into my heart and my soul scares me as nothing ever has. Does this manner of cowardice make me a self-contained, ignorant girl? Aye, probably. I am quite proficient in thinking only of myself."

His hands flexed. He had no defenses against the surge of emotions that trapped his words in his throat.

"I have missed you," she whispered.

His heart was pounding so loudly it sounded like an ocean's roar in his ears. Before she could say another word, draw another breath, his mouth covered hers. His hands glided from her hips to her neck and cupped her face. A low moan escaped him. In answer, her slender arms rose around his neck and she pressed her body against him, drinking in his kiss, and he never realized just how sensitive his tongue was, how it could distinguish so vividly the textures of her mouth. Above them, wind gusted through the branches.

Closing a fist in her hair, he drew her back. The intensity of her eyes was a caress. "I have missed you as well, love."

He looked up at the sky to measure the clouds and need to get the horses inside. "Come." He grabbed her hand as the first plop of heavy rain fell. "We may not want shelter from the storm. But the horses do."

The stable had stone floors and stone walls much like the one at Stonehaven. Straw littered the floor. A door and window balanced each end with stalls in between. The slatted window near the pitch of the thatch roof let in the early-evening air mixed with sounds of the storm.

Up in the hayloft, Ruark and Rose lay on her cloak in a cozy nest made warm by the rasp of their bodies and the measured tempo of their breathing. Her dress was somewhere behind them in a crumpled heap, near his shirt and boots that lay like crumbs leading to where they had finally fallen in the straw.

"Have you ever made love up here?" Rose lay with her legs wrapped around Ruark's thighs, his weight resting on his elbows as he pulled back to look into her face.

He chuckled against her lips. "Pray tell, why that question now?"

"You seem to be familiar with the stable and this loft in particular. And I find I am jealous of any woman from your past."

Her petticoats cradled her head, pale against the spread

of her hair. He brushed his lips against hers. "Nay, love. You are the first."

With a subtle deepening of her sirenlike smile, she came back for a second taste of his lips and lingered. "I like being the first," she said as he settled his hips more firmly against hers, knowing the tension inside him was because of her.

The inevitable effect of her words spread through him like liquid heat, and he was no longer content just to feel her. He drew back and thrust.

She gasped slightly when he moved. Their kiss deepened into a luxurious and mutual exchange that crowded all other thoughts from his mind, until only their breathing filled the small space in the loft. Until it was she and him and the rumble of thunder above their heads. He rolled onto his back, taking her with him, her body sheathing him, even as her hands braced her weight against his chest.

A low moan escaped her as he cupped her breasts, swirling his tongue around the sensitive ruched flesh of her nipples. Instinctively, she arched her back so that her breasts rose to meet his caress. He slid his hands into the silken tangle of her hair and brought her mouth down to his, parting her lips under the growing pressure of his, nibbling, seeking the response from her that was burning in him. He found it. Her fingers wound in his hair. He slid both palms down her shoulders over her waist and hips.

Her body yielded easily to his touch. He clasped her bottom, holding her against him, watching her rock in restless abandon. This was not the first time she had willingly come to him, but this was the first time more than willingness lay between them, more than desire.

Then she was climaxing around him. Her eyes, heavy lidded, watched him until he drove into her, shuddering in release.

They both smiled at the same time, concurrently—their emotions easily surrendered. Strangely enough, she was his, but suddenly he began to wonder how he could hold on to her. He didn't understand why the thought struck him as it did, as if it was a premonition.

Her hand touched his face. "What is it?"

His kissed her. A gust of wind slapped rain against the slats as he gathered her in his arms. "The storm looks like 'twill be a long one. I am thinking neither of us has had supper."

She smiled. "Do you think the watchman minds that you stole his wine and bread?"

Ruark chuckled. "He should feel grateful I allowed him to remain on his cot bed in your schoolhouse."

Rose snuggled her head against Ruark's shoulder. The remains of a meal lay beside them on the cloak. He sat propped against the wall, his knee drawn to his chest, one hand dangling a wooden cup over his knee and his other arm casually draping her as she leaned her back against him. He had found a flint box, and a small lamp now burned in the corner. The dim light fell in a circle around them. She wore his shirt. The rain drumming against the thatch roof provided a cozy backdrop for the intimacies of their quiet conversation in the twilight of a fading day. Rose closed her eyes as thoughts of a darker nature began to intrude upon her peace.

"You have been silent for a full minute." Ruark pressed his lips to her hair. "What is it?"

She raised her head from his shoulder and twisted around to look up at him. "I have been plagued by a question I feel I need to ask that concerns us both. I will still stand by you no matter what your reply, but I need to know. I hope you will be honest."

Lanthorn light defined his nearly black eyes under thick lashes. "I will try, Rose."

Yet the tenor of his reply told her he was not certain of his honesty, and she realized, despite everything, there were still many aspects of his life that he was not ready to share.

Drinking from the loosely held cup in his hand, he awaited the question.

"Are you Jamie's father?"

He nearly spewed his wine. He snatched up an edge of her cloak and pressed the cloth to his lips. "Madam," he gasped. "Please warn me before you accuse me of fathering a child on another woman. I am in danger of strangling."

"I read the entry of his birth in the Bible. He was born eight months after Julia's wedding to your father. I know she was with you shortly before that and that you had taken her to a kirk to marry but that she balked."

His eyes amused, he said, "Then there is nothing else I can tell you. It seems you have mined all there is to know about my life."

"Can you deny you were in love with her?"

"I will not deny that when I was seventeen, I was willing to elope with her. But please, you cannot hold me responsible for the actions of a rash youth."

"Then you and she . . . you must have . . ."

Ruark raised a brow. "We must have what?"

He was going to make her say the words. "You must have been intimate with her."

"I will admit I have not been a virgin since I was fifteen . . . but she was different. She and I had known each other since we were both in swaddling. Our mothers were close friends. I loved her, I thought."

"And did she love you?"

"I thought she did." He studied the wooden cup in his hand. "But looking back, I know now she was not *in love* with me.

"I had always believed we would one day be wed if only because of our families. I had little respect for most everything else in my life, but I did have respect for her. She was fragile. She reminded me of a delicately painted glass doll and I wanted to protect her from breaking. If I had pressed her into an intimacy, I knew she would have been the one hurt."

"You must have felt betrayed by both her and your father."

"Strangely, never by her. My father. Always." Ruark leaned his head back against the wall. "I can think of no time in my life where he ever reached out to me or my mother. When she died, he was with his mistress. He was not so much physically cruel as he was indifferent and self-involved, except when it came to Stonehaven.

"I rebelled against everything for which he stood. I cared little for the lives of those who lived there. By fifteen, I was a dissolute heir already intent on drinking and gambling away my heritage and forcing him to claim note after note against my markers. I believed in nothing.

"One could say Duncan took exception to the direction of my life when he decided to send me on a new path and rescue me from destroying myself."

"After you fought your father."

"I have since lived almost as much time out of this country as I have in it." Ruark was silent a moment, then his eyes met hers. "I brought a lot of misfortune upon myself and others caused by anger and pride. I have been no better than a smuggler and much-cursed pirate with little difference between Hereford and myself, or my father, 'twould seem. Cunning and ruthlessness kept me alive."

He finished off his cup and set it at his thigh, and as he peered at her some of the cold left his eyes. "'Tis only recently I have learned the value of compassion."

"Yet, you still feel guilty in your failure to save Julia."

Ruark met her gaze steadily. "How is that, love?"

"You have not spent any time with her son, your father's son, the brother you worked so hard to save. As if you think that you also failed in saving him. He is home and safe because of you. And he loves you."

"Perhaps," he said thoughtfully. "Or it is not knowing quite what to say to a brother I have only known through letters." After a moment, he asked. "What of you, love? Have you any regrets you wish to rectify?"

The question begged an honest answer even to herself. "I regret not remembering my mother," she said. "Nor did I treat Friar Tucker as well as I should have. I have never told him I love him."

She sighed softly. "I think, a part of me blamed him for the choices he made for my life. I do not know why I felt the way I did—he has been nothing but patient and loving. I was never outwardly angry but I must have been angry . . . for I have always been searching . . . for something. I do not know for what, but it is there on the horizon." She lowered her head, and her hair fell over her shoulders. "I have learned resentment no matter how small and seemingly insignificant is like a smoldering ember. It burns at the edges of a person's soul and eventually blackens all that it touches."

She had not meant to be so honest or allude to her restlessness as if that took away her newfound feelings for him. His arm tightened around her and he pulled her close to his heart.

She looked up at him with a wobbly smile. "Perhaps we

are both still looking for a place that feels like home."

Just then, there was a gust of wind against the slats. Ruark lowered his head took her lips in a kiss, slowly turning her in his arms until she was across his lap. Her fingers slid through the wisp of hair on his chest as he pressed her down into the cloak. He pulled away to look down at her, the expression on Ruark's face unreadable. But he needed no words, as he loved her.

They remained in the loft until dawn, when the rain finally stopped and she was forced to rouse from her languor. Forced to admit as she smiled up at her husband that if this was what it meant to be in love, this need to be near him, this all-consuming passion, then she wondered how one survived it.

She dressed while Ruark saddled the horses, then climbed down from the loft for a bit of privacy outside. The sun emerged from behind the clouds as Rose pushed open the stable doors. She looked out across the field, empty save for a few brown shaggy cattle, and approached the nearest tree when she spied a horse hobbled nearby. She walked around the stable.

Duncan sat on a rock, both feet on the ground. He was bent over his knees whittling at a stick with a sharp knife. He looked up at her, squinting against the sun at her back.

She and Duncan had reached an understanding these past weeks. She still disliked much of his bullishness, but she had seen something behind his gruff exterior that made her more tolerant of the man himself. Only a week ago, she had watched him literally give the shirt off his back to one of the drovers injured after a horse threw him. McBain had had to rip it up for bandages.

A breeze fluttered the red ash trees and dappled the ground briefly with light. "Why are you sitting here?"

Duncan braced both elbows on his knees and regarded her levelly for a moment. "I do no' think you would rather I have interrupted you last night."

"You have been here all night?"

"He's been lookin' for me. I suspect he's thinkin' many unflattering things about my character after seeing Hereford in Mawbray. Business with the *Black Dragon*, ye ken. He did no' trust me to go along with him."

She had not known what business had taken Ruark from Stonehaven this past month. Then Ruark no longer owned his ship.

"Good men could have died because of you, Duncan," Ruark said from a place behind her, cold deadliness in his voice. "Come here, Rose." He held out a gloved hand to her. She walked over to him and took it.

Rose looked from Ruark to Duncan, and didn't understand the danger she sensed. More than long-standing animosity that stretched farther back than merely the incidents of the past year vibrated the air between the two.

"Aye, she will stand at your side, lad," Duncan said in amusement. "She is no white-knuckler pissin' herself over a wee thing like fear. I'd wed the lass myself if she was no' already mistress of Stonehaven."

"Stay away from my wife and from Jamie. Stay away from Stonehaven."

"Ruark," Rose gasped.

Duncan held up a hand to stay her. "Leave off, lass." His eyes remained on Ruark. "No matter what Hereford might have claimed or hinted, I did no' kill your da, lad, though he deserved killin' for the man he was."

"And Kathleen's husband? Did he deserve killing as well?"

Duncan rose to his feet and slid the knife into a sheath

at his belt. He was a big man with large shoulders and hands. Dirt and dead leaves clung to his shoulder-length hair and worn plaid. "I would have done the deed had his horse no' fallen and done the killin' for me. Him leavin' her and his youngest bairn bein' just four. Procurator fiscal, principal public prosecutor, a regular limmer he was." Duncan spat. "Your da sent me after him for stealing from him. He was no' dead when I found him trapped beneath his horse, and gold in his saddlebags. He begged me to save him and told me what he'd been doin' all these years for your da and for Hereford. Had a mistress in Carlisle he was swiven'. It took him a day to die in the cold with his injuries and trapped as he was beneath the horse. If he had no' killed himself with his stupidity, I would have, for what he did to Kathleen."

"Christ, Duncan . . ."

"You told everyone he was innocent," Rose said.

"Aye," he tossed out in defiance. "Kathleen loved the bloke. Why destroy that with the truth. I've no' much honor left in me, and I'm no' denying I'm guilty of plenty of sin in this life, but those bairn of his would have carried the stigma of their father's crime to death."

"And yet you kept the gold," Ruark said.

"It stuck in your da's crawl like a burr when I said I did no' find any gold. That gold was supposed to have gone to Hereford to pay a debt caused when you took that cargo ship outside Rotterdam. They were to meet in Chesters in late spring. Aye, I learned then he and Hereford were partners."

"A devout Scotsman who had devoted his life to protecting and dealing out justice for Stonehaven's chieftain might also take exception to finding the earl of Roxburghe an English sympathizer and in league with Hereford. If one thought Hereford to blame for the laird's betrayal of the precious Kerr honor, one would want revenge against Hereford. What better way to rally the family than Jamie's capture in a bout of cattle lifting."

"I'll no' deny my actions nearly started a war, lad. And I'll no' deny Jamie has had a bit of a hard time of it since his return. He is no' you to be sure, a big strappin' lad come home to take your da's place with a bonny Sassenach wife like yourn to warm a man's bed. But I would no' ever harm the lad."

A breeze fluttered the red ash trees and dappled the ground briefly with light. Ruark swore and looked away. "What should I do with you, Duncan?"

"I can find my own way, lad."

His glance touched Rose then he strode past her to his horse. After he tightened the cinch on the saddle, he mounted and, swinging the gelding around, nodded to them both and rode away.

"Oh, Ruark. You cannot mean to let him—"

"Christ, Rose!" His voice cut across hers. "Do not defend him to me again." He started to step around her.

She wrapped her arms around his waist and drew herself tight against him, to keep him from walking away from her. She wanted to hold on to him forever to protect him. After a moment, he wrapped his arms around her. Gradually, the heavy thump of his heart eased.

He pressed his cheek to her hair. "Duncan will be fine, Rose."

" 'Tis not for him I am worried."

He set his hands on her shoulders and gently pulled her away. "Your concern is appreciated but not needed."

"Yet, I am concerned. You told me you were to see my father's solicitor." She dropped her gaze because tears suddenly veiled her eyes. "You should have told me you saw my father. That frightens me. What did you talk about?"

Cupping her chin, Ruark raised her face to his searching gaze. "'Twas just business with the *Black Dragon*."

She didn't believe his inane response. "'Tis never just business with him. Or you. Have I not already learned that?"

"Come," he said. "I will get the horses."

Chapter 23

Ruark sat at his desk in the library, where he had spent the last few mornings dealing with business. He held a quill pen poised above one of the sheets of foolscap spread out before him. The scratching of the quill pen continued for a bit longer as he finished the letter to his banker. Then he replaced the pen in the silver inkstand and sprinkled fine sand from the pounce box onto the letters. He opened the top drawer on his desk and pulled out a signet ring. He folded over each of the four corners of the foolscap, then folded it in half, poured wax over the joint and impressed his ring before returning it to the drawer. For a moment, he turned the signet over in his hand and rubbed a callused thumb across the crest. He had never worn the signet ring. It had remained in this desk since his father's death.

A knock sounded and Julia peered around the door. Ruark stood as she entered. Something seemed to turn over inside him, and the unfinished chapter in his life had suddenly become a book that he had yet to close.

She looked lovely today in pale blue that matched the color of her eyes. Her fine blond hair was knotted in a thin ball at her nape. She had not changed much in appearance from the girl she had been. The years had bruised her heart immeasurably, though only her tightly clasped hands gave away her feelings.

"You requested to see me?" she tentatively asked, as if any request from the laird of Stonehaven was something to be feared.

Ruark closed the space between them, his steps quiet on the thick carpet. He indicated the upholstered chairs in front of the desk. "Sit down, Julia."

The ease of her compliance annoyed him. He hesitated, then sat in the chair across from her. "I am not going to bite you."

She stiffened. "We have never really spoken since your return. What do you expect me to make of this summons? Especially when I have heard you have asked Duncan to leave Stonehaven."

"Duncan is free to go where he wishes," Ruark said, having no intention of discussing his uncle with Julia.

She lowered her gaze to her lap.

"Julia," he said. "As the Dowager Countess Roxburghe, you have a special place here at Stonehaven, and I am obliged to see you cared for. I am giving you a monthly allowance that is yours to do as you please. I am responsible for Jamie's care but I will not presume to take him away from you. You may remain here. Or the Roxburghe family has holdings in Edinburgh and Carlisle if you wish for a more social climate some of the year."

She paled. "Are you asking me to leave?"

"Nay, Julia. When is the last time you made a decision for yourself?" Ruark raised a brow. "Never?"

He was wrong of course. Thirteen years ago, she'd made a decision to elope with him. And she had made the choice not to go through with it.

She must have read the thought in his eyes.

"Did you ever think about me at all?" she asked.

"Would it make a difference if you knew that I had? Aye, I thought of you."

She considered this. "That is something at least."

He leaned forward. "I am giving you permission to be free, Julia. To make your own choices about your future. Fall in love. Marry whom you choose."

Tension seemed to leave her shoulders. "I would like that very much."

They spoke a little more about the uncommonly warm weather for September. The new pony he had given to Jamie and the lad Jack, who would be remaining at Stonehaven. "Your wife does seem to hold great affection for the little urchin," Julia replied, less than pleased at the prospect of someone of Jack's birth sharing the same tutor as Jamie.

Ruark reassured her she would grow accustomed to it.

Later, he gave Mary the letter he had written to post to Friar Tucker. She and Mrs. Simpson had returned from their "holiday" last week, as Mary so brightly put it while displaying a new pair of paste earbobs upon her return.

At the door, Mary said, "Herself has instructed that I tell ye she and the lads and Mrs. Simpson are aboot to go to the village, but that lunch will be served outside upon her return. She expects ye to join her to make up for missing supper with her last night."

Ruark recalled last night in a rather different light after he had returned late to find her in a bath. She had balked at him joining her in the tub as he stripped off his dust-worn clothes from working with the horses all day. But he could be most persuasive when he wanted something and he had presented his case quite convincingly.

The braided silver ring on Ruark's finger drew his focus as he pondered its relevance to his current state of mind.

For therein lay the crux of his problem.

Whether by seduction or violence, he had not survived as captain of the *Black Dragon* and as a man without the power to persuade, influence, or crush. Too much of his life had been spent as a marauder, taking by force that which he could not gain by determination and diplomacy alone.

Including Rose.

The very thing he wanted most had not come to him by her choice or free will. He had taken her first by force at the Abbey, used seduction to get her to the lodge, and in Jedburgh . . .

He was a stranger to uncertainty.

Not since he had been a boy had he felt vulnerable to emotions and doubts that were not fueled by anger and hate. He understood the helplessness that came when choice is stripped from your life, when the dictates of others control your fate.

It wasn't enough that Rose had given him her heart. For he was plagued with the reality that she had not yet found peace, or the home to which she had referred. He didn't want even a small ember of resentment left inside her.

He only knew that when he was with her, it was as if a hand reached into his heart, removed the dark and cold from his past and let free that which was once inside when he had been a young boy . . . before his mother had died, and taken what remained of his world with her.

Lord Hereford's two emissaries arrived a week later, riding onto Stonehaven land carried by a black coach, drawn by six black horses, the Hereford crest emblazoned on the lacquered door—two swords crossed against a blood-red turret—and eight liveried outriders.

His hair wet with sweat and tied back in a queue, Ruark came from the other side of the house still wearing his fencing gear: thick leather jack that protected his shoulders and chest. Boots. Black leather wrist guards that reached up his forearms. He didn't bother changing before he strode into the dining hall, where twenty of his clan had followed the carriage through Stonehaven's gates and dozens of servants had gathered to receive the men. Both men stood nervously against the wall awaiting Ruark's arrival. Colum remained at the door to see that no one else entered.

The properly bewigged emissaries announced that they had come in the official capacity as representatives of the earl of Hereford, their fancy red velvet coats, gold satin waistcoats and dark orange breeches incongruous in a room filled with bearded, tartan-clad Scotsman. The two made their carefully rehearsed presentation to Ruark then stood back and awaited his reply.

The hall grew silent as everyone turned eyes on him, as if awaiting the word from him to remove Hereford's two jackals from Stonehaven and have them dipped in tar and feathered. Ruark leaned forward with his hands on the table, his leather jack creaking with the movement. "Just what *exactly* does Hereford want?"

The elder cleared his throat. "He wants to visit his daughter."

"Like hell he will."

"He has brought her a gift. Many gifts, my lord. Her mother's belongings."

From the back of the room, he heard a commotion and looked up as Rose came running into the hall, the mumblings of her entry turning everyone's attention toward the door. Before Colum could stop her, she'd swept past him, her skirts hiked to her ankles as she came to a stop below the window, her eyes bright with emotions. Her gaze came to a halt first on him then on her father's emissaries.

She started forward. He was quicker than she was and stepped around the table and into her path. "Rose . . . you should not be in here."

"But is it true? Did my father send my mother's things?"

"Yes, my lady," answered the elder spokesman. "We have brought only a few trunks with us. The rest will be delivered"—dark eyes turned to Ruark—"as soon as Lord Roxburghe agrees on an arrangement."

Her eyes turned to Ruark. Again the elder spoke, "Your mother's belongings, my lady. He thought you would want to have them."

To his disbelief, Ruark saw that after all her father had put her through, this would be the thing to put hope in her eyes.

And Ruark struggled with the burning awareness of his emotions sweeping through his veins worse than fire.

Worse than yesterday, when no one could locate her for half the day, and he had finally found her at the falls with Duncan—*Duncan!*—her herb basket looped over her forearm as his uncle cut lichen off the upper reaches of a tree for her. Enjoying herself as if she had not a care in the world, as if he had not asked her to stay away from his uncle.

And Ruark knew then that he loved her beyond all reason, and his anger had come as equally from jealousy as it had from fear for her.

Then she made them sit down together and share lunch with her.

He could no more destroy the hopefulness in her eyes

now than he could yesterday. Though in the end, he and his uncle had talked and perhaps even begun to heal, he saw no similar good ending here. She would know that.

But Hereford had found his single weakness.

Yet, with a nod to Angus, Ruark sent him to deliver the trunks to his wife's chambers.

Mrs. Simpson smoothed the hair from Rose's damp cheeks. She sat on the floor, her pink-petal skirts spread around her, her head in Mrs. Simpson's lap as the elder gently spoke.

Rose sat amidst her mother's finery, porcelain figurines, etchings, portraitures, silver ewers, gowns, and laces. She clutched a gown with silk blond lacing that resembled spun gold.

Her mother's hair had been the color of gold.

"I remember so many of these things." With eyes closed, she breathed in the faded lilac and knew now why she so loved springtime. "I thought I had forgotten. Everything."

Mrs. Simpson held a small portraiture of her mother cradled in her palm. "You have her face, my dear. She loved you so."

Rose lifted her tear-stained face. "How can you know?"

"How can any mother not love her child, lass?"

The door opened and Ruark entered. Even at this later hour, he still wore the thick leather jack and boots she had seen him wearing in the dining hall, though he had removed the fencing gloves. His hand on the doorknob came to a sudden halt.

Rose came to her feet, as did Mrs. Simpson. "I will see you in the morning," the elder said.

After Mrs. Simpson left, Ruark walked over to her,

his deep blue eyes filled with gentle concern. "You are crying. Why?"

She shook her head. "I am happy."

The back of his finger caught a tear. "Is this happiness, love?"

"We must get the rest of what he has," she said. "We must. If it entails him visiting here, what can be the harm if he will bring the rest to me?"

"This is the harm, Rose. To see what this is doing to you. He is not here for your happiness."

Unable to bear the intensity of his gaze that came with the tender brush of his fingertips against her cheek, she laid her hand over his and looked down at all her mother's beautiful things. "I know. I know."

She did know. More than anyone, she knew her father never did anything without a reason, without intent. But what could be the harm in allowing him to see her just one more time if it meant . . .

She looked up into Ruark's face, beseeching. "He did not have to do any of this. Yet he did. Why? Why would he do this? Why now? I don't understand. I don't deserve this from him, Ruark. How *can* he . . . ? This has something to do with your visit to him."

He wrapped her protectively in his arms. "Rose . . ."

She ignored the hard, flat tone of his voice. Stepped out of his arms and faced him with her palms on his face as she forced him to look at her. Her courage wavered. He had done something. Once again, he had brought this fight to his doorstep because of his actions. But whatever it was he had done, he must have passionately believed it was the right thing to do. She knew that much about her husband.

She pulled his face down to hers and kissed him equally as passionately.

"What happened in Mawbray?" she asked.

He stared at her. A finite second. A heartbeat no longer. "The *Black Dragon* is sitting in the shallows of the Solway Firth burned to her waterline," he said. "I sank her rather than hand her over to Hereford."

Rose's jaw dropped open. She couldn't begin to form words around her thoughts and looked away.

Sadness engulfed her. She looked around her, then back up at him.

She leaned her cheek into his palm. She felt the ring on Ruark's finger and felt more than the warmth of his flesh, and then she remembered what Mrs. Simpson had said about the ring that long-ago day in her cottage. *"What you think you want may not be what your heart wants, and nothing great is ever accomplished without sacrifice."*

She kissed him. Wrapping herself to him. He spanned her chin with his long, hard fingers. "Hereford thought that by trying to take the *Black Dragon*, he was taking what meant the most to me," Ruark said into her open mouth, walking her backward into the wall. "He was wrong. I needed him to know that."

He bracketed her with his hands. "I needed him to know what he threw away. I needed him to know that he had no more power over you and that you were mine."

He laid his palm against her chest. "I feel your heartbeat, Rose. Here. As if it were my own, as if something has been returned to me that I lost many years ago. I have struggled to understand. I only know I live in fear of losing it."

Rose wound her arms around his neck. "Have I not convinced you that my heart is freely given?"

'Tis only a ring, she told herself as his mouth slanted across hers with an urgency that equaled her own, and he gave her his own brand of magic that shimmered around her and made her float.

Picking her up in his arms, he carried her into his bedchambers.

"You have been in the fencing room," she said, attempting to unfasten the jack so she could touch the warm flesh beneath.

He lowered her feet to the ground. "Aye, Colum needs the practice."

His hands moved along her spine. He undressed her as quickly as he undressed himself. He bared her breasts and fell with her to the bed. Both of them seemed to disappear into the soft silken folds of eiderdown and fur.

She clung to him, knotting her fingers in his hair, then cradling his head against her breast, feeling his tongue against her hardening nipples, and she gave herself to his touch. She was very wet. Then the hardness of him was against her flesh and he was pushing inside her. He pressed up on his hands to look down at her, watching then catching her cries with his kisses and filling her with sensual fire.

"Ah, Rose," he pressed his mouth into her hair. "I do love ye so, lass."

Rose awakened late, which was not her usual custom. It had still been dark outside when she had awakened earlier to find Ruark sitting on the edge of the bed fully dressed. "I have to go out, love," he told her, pressing his lips to hers. "I shall be back soon. Do not fret. Go back to sleep and dream of me."

She had walked to the window, wrapping her arms around herself for warmth as she watched him and a dozen other men ride out. "That is the problem," she said. "I am always dreaming of you."

Then she crawled back beneath the covers, yet worried as she somehow managed to sleep away the rest of the morning, when she and McBain had their rounds to attend.

Rose splashed cold water over her face, brushed out her hair and plaited the length before Anaya arrived and helped her dress. The first big chill of September had arrived, and as Rose looked out her window, she saw a layer of frost on the ground. Grabbing her plaid wrap, she opened the door.

Colum sat on a chair, his arms and ankles crossed, his chin against his chest as if he were asleep—as if he had been there since Ruark left just before dawn. She gritted her teeth. She had promised her husband she would not contact the emissaries staying in the village. And he *still* put a guard on her. His lack of trust in her gnawed.

Rose saw that Colum was awake, pulled her shawl tighter about her shoulders and walked past him. He caught up with her at the stairs. "Madam," he complained. "'Tis too early for jaunty exercise."

"Does he think I would seek out my father? Is he *mad*?"

"Ruark trusts you fine, my lady. 'Tis your father he does not trust. Ruark has gone to send away the emissaries."

Rose turned to face Colum. "He told me he sank the *Black Dragon*."

Colum scraped a palm across his cheek. "Went up like a Viking funeral pyre. A person could see the glow for miles."

"I know he didn't want my father to have the ship. But why . . . ?"

"He was retiring from the sea anyway," Colum said philosophically and she glared at him in disbelief, unable to believe the man could joke.

She turned on her heel. Colum stepped in front of her. "I am to keep you company today, madam."

"Is Stonehaven under threat?"

"Your father is encamped twenty miles away. Nowhere near Stonehaven. However, I am still to keep you company."

Some of the tension left her shoulders. "Still, if he is concerned enough to sic you on me, then I am concerned enough to make sure the boys stay in today."

Ever since Ruark had taught Jack to ride a horse, he and Jamie were off every morning to the falls.

Clouds had formed by the time she reached the stable yard fifteen minutes later. "We were beginning to think you had forgotten us, dear," Mrs. Simpson said. "What is it?"

"Have the boys been down this morning?"

Rose walked past Mrs. Simpson into the stable and saw that both of their horses were gone. She clutched her shawl and walked back outside. "How long have you been down here?

"Thirty minutes. You did say we would be leaving at eight."

Rose looked over her shoulder at McBain knobbing it down the hill like a pirate with a wooden shank. "Tell McBain that we need to postpone today," she said, and looked up at Colum. "We need to fetch the two scoundrels back."

Before she knew what she was about, she was riding out of the stable on a feisty dun-colored mare. She knew the location of the falls, as she had gone there many times to collect plants for the herbal. But Ruark had warned the boys on more than one occasion not to go up there alone as 'twas dangerous to swim in the waters beneath the falls. The two had become good friends but together they caused naught but mischief.

Colum rode beside her. Rose was not wearing a riding habit and the wind pulled the hair from its braid. She sat with her cloak and blue muslin skirts tucked beneath her legs and stout leather half-boots in the stirrups and kicked the mare to a run, leaping a low stone wall and scattering a flock of tits foraging around a stream. Water sprayed around her.

They galloped for three miles before reining the horses back to an easy lope. The sun emerged from behind the clouds. She spied the two horses walking free some distance from the wooded path leading up to the falls. Her heart suddenly pounding with heightened physical tension, she pulled up short. A puff of fog rose from the mare's nostrils.

"'Tis a goodly climb to the top, and cannot be done safely with a horse," she said to Colum, as she tried to make sense of the apprehension that struck her like a heavy rock to her chest. "The horses probably got loose from their reins." One horse she recognized as the dragoon captain's horse Ruark had stolen the night he had pulled her from the river. The horse was Jack's favorite.

She started to ride forward, but Colum grabbed her arm. "Those two lads know enough to hobble the horses, my lady."

Her mare danced sideways. Rose had to reach down to calm the horse. Her glance went to the pine trees that disappeared into the low-hanging misty sky. And she knew something was wrong.

Colum eased his sword from the scabbard, then they heard a slow ominous hiss. An arrow flew past. "Go back now," she heard him say. "Go!"

The first arrow missed them both, hissing past Rose's head. The second and third hit Colum directly in the ribs, another somewhere else, she could not see. Her horse reared up, saving her life as a fifth arrow struck the mare in the throat. The horse screamed and faltered and went down in a flurry of hooves. Rose hit the ground hard; searing pain exploded in her head, driving her momentarily into unconsciousness.

When she stirred and tried to push up on her elbow, she saw Colum unmoving a few yards away, blood pooling around his head. She called his name. She struggled to pull her leg from beneath the fallen mare. "Colum!"

A pair of heavy black boots appeared where she leaned her hand against the ground. She looked up.

Geddes Graham!

She had not seen him or thought about him since she had held a blade to his bollocks and demanded Jack's coin returned. He could not be here.

"Milady Countess," he mocked as he squatted beside her, "ye ain't so big now without my knife in yer hand, are ye?"

She glared up at him through a tangle of hair. "What have you *done*?!"

Had Geddes killed the boys, too? Rage filled her and gave her strength.

From behind her, brutal hands dragged her to her feet. She cried out with the pain, then faced Geddes, that traitorous carnivore, with hissing fury, and kicked out at him, nearly striking him in the bollocks. Her foot hit his stomach instead.

"Bitch!" He backhanded her and split her lip. Only the rough hands gripping her kept her from falling.

Geddes gripped her hair, forcing her face back. "Your

dear da is payin' us to see ye delivered to him. He did no' tell us in what condition you had to be."

Rose tried to hang on to consciousness. Her swollen mouth stumbled to form her next words. "Why would my father do this?"

Geddes laughed. "'Tain't you Hereford wants, my thorny Rose."

Chapter 24

Rose came awake in slow stages, aware of the rocking movement of the wagon, and felt sick and momentarily disoriented.

She turned on her side, attempted to see through the slats in the wagon, and saw that the sun had nearly set. A lazy twilight had settled over the sky. She saw two of Geddes's henchmen trailing the wagon on horseback.

Ruark would know she was gone by now. She fell back and let her eyes adjust to the dark.

She lay atop smelly furs and blankets in a gaily painted trader wagon, filled with an assortment of wares. Pots and pans dangling from the roof clanked and rattled along with crockery, teacups. Nostrums and remedies jostled in their glass and tin containers, all neatly set in wooden brackets near the tailgate.

Though she was bound, Geddes had tied her hands in front of her this time, not at her back as he had all day yesterday, since she had worked up a few tears and pleaded for his mercy today. Geddes enjoyed her groveling. *Bastard*.

She was confident in her ability to outwit her captors, who seemed more nervous today and less attentive to her, and ignored her still tender and bruised mouth, now chafed with rope burns as she had gnawed through much of the knot. But in her exhaustion, her mind touched on Colum, and her throat tightened as she squeezed her eyes shut and tried not to think about him.

She was sure the boys had survived. Geddes had not bragged about finding anyone else at the falls, and he didn't have time to search, taking the extra horses instead.

Jack must have seen Geddes in time, she realized. Jack would know him and was smart enough to take Jamie and hide. Ruark would have already found the boys safe. She knew even now Ruark was coming after her.

Ruark had been correct when he'd told her they were connected. She could feel his heartbeat inside her as he must feel hers.

Aye, he was coming for her.

Geddes Graham and her father would rue the day they had been born.

The clatter of dozens of horses alerted Rose. She knew Geddes sometimes left the group to scout ahead for a hidden place to camp. After a while, the wagon lumbered to a halt. She felt it dip, then heard footsteps in the dirt as someone walked to the tailgate. A bolt slid back on the thick wood, first on one side then the other. A creaking sounded. The door came down and the canvas covering slid back to reveal Lord Hereford. She could not sit straight for all the goods hanging above her. He took one look at her.

"Get her out of there," she heard her father say to someone just out of her vision.

The mountebank appeared. She scooted, desperate to be free of the tomblike enclosure. He pulled until she could sit on the tailgate. A chill wind hit her. As the rough hemp on her ankles was hastily removed, she glanced briefly at the mottled magenta and amber-stained sky before focusing on the hand that helped her stand. The mountebank wore the same tatty loose-fitting frock, waistcoat, and greasy leggings she'd seen him wearing in Castleton.

As she struggled for balance, she faced her father. He captured her chin between his thumb and his forefinger and tilted her face. "Who struck her?"

When no one answered, he dropped his hand and turned to face Geddes. Without warning, her father's arm swung in an arc and backhanded Geddes across the mouth. "I don't care what you bloody do to the other women in your life, but this one is my daughter, and you will not lay a fucking hand on her again."

Geddes's lank brown hair hung in his eyes as he pressed the back of his hand to his bloody mouth. "She ain't te be trusted," he said.

"Of course, she isn't to be trusted! But I want Roxburghe cooperative. See that she is fed and cleaned up."

Geddes grabbed her arm. "Why are you doing this?" she demanded of her father. "Why did you go to all the trouble to send me my mother's things and ask to visit Stonehaven . . ." His actions were so cold. So utterly . . . cold.

Hereford's gaze swung back around to her, his smile unpleasant. "Roxburghe reneged on every agreement we made. A week ago, I received notice from his solicitor that he has made a legal claim upon Kirkland Park on your behalf. No one. I mean *no one* betrays me."

"Can he do that?" she whispered.

"Oh, aye. 'Tis called blackmail. He can tell the world I am a pirate, I can tell the world he is a pirate. We can both produce proof against the other and most probably be hanged for it all. And he can face a tribunal for kidnapping and raping you."

"But you *forced* our marriage."

"No jury will deny a father's need to protect his daughter any way he can. And I will see it annulled."

More powerful at that moment even than despair was fury at her father as he turned on his booted heel and strode across the camp, where he conversed with two red-coated dragoons setting up a tent.

She shouted after him. "It cannot *be* annulled!"

Geddes tossed a blanket on the ground at her feet. His contemptuous gaze swept her tangled hair and crumpled clothing. "Many pardons, m'lady, that we cannot offer ye a more accommodating bedchamber. One I'm sure you've grown accustomed to these past months."

"My husband will come for me," she said casually, as one might announce a change of weather. "He will hunt the lot of you down. But you, Geddes Graham . . . he will take special pleasure in killing. And if he does not, I will!"

She derived enormous satisfaction as she watched a momentary flash of doubt in his eyes. "My father will not protect you. Let me go now and I will see that at least your life is spared."

Geddes sneered. "If only I could, me thorny Rose. Lord Hereford and me . . . ? Let me just say we got us a special understanding."

Her eyes swept his swollen mouth. "I can see how much that *special* understanding means to him."

Geddes walked away, leaving her to sit on a rock and absently rub her ankles where the ropes had burned into her skin.

The mountebank presented her with a bloated skin that looked as if it had been recently filled in the stream. "We've stopped fer the night, Miss Rose," he said. "So ye can rest now."

Rose numbly accepted the skin. Her hands remained

bound and they trembled despite her best effort. As she drank, she looked over the rim at the mountebank. He had a face like a shaggy brown cow with large sad eyes and an underbite that made his lower jaw protrude. More so now with his emotions in his eyes. Wiping his greasy hands on his frock, he shifted from foot to foot. "I'll bring a bowl and a rag fer ye to clean up."

She watched him rummage through the back of his precious wagon filled with nostrums, throwing items this way and that. The sun was almost gone for the day. Rose looked up at the indigo sky and could not help the path of her thoughts as she thought desperately of Ruark.

He was trying to get back Kirkland Park for her. He must know the effort would fail.

Her father stood across the camp outside a tent, directing men to the watch detail. She studied his harsh profile. She glanced briefly at Geddes's men as they unsaddled horses and prepared a small cooking fire.

She could see about three dozen men sprawled out over forty yards. A wood of trees sat to her right and at her back. In front of her, mist rose from a field stretching into the darkness that ended on a high ridge a half mile away.

Rolf returned with a ceramic bowl the size of a cocked hat. "Why are you involved with Geddes and my father, Rolf?"

"I travel. Know things, Miss Rose." He looked away. "I've seen things, too. Things a man oughtn't see."

After he left her, Rose dipped the cloth in the water. The rag was fraught with some questionable sticky substance and she dropped it in the bowl without using it. Pulling experimentally at the bonds on her wrists, she looked toward the woods. Men walked the perimeter of the camp. Would she get far if she ran? Maybe. Dark was upon them. She threw one last glance at the clearing.

Standing and making a pretense of cleaning a spot on her ankle, she let the blood circulate in her feet. Then, with skirts lifted, she ran twenty yards and she was in the trees. Shouts followed her escape.

Fear seized her body and with it the sound of pursuing men crashing into the woods after her. She tripped when her skirts caught on a branch, then she ran head-on into a bear.

A huge beast. Or at least to her it seemed that way. She screamed and recoiled as two giant clawed hands clamped down on her shoulders to keep her from falling backward. She screamed. Her eyes swung upward past thickly furred arms and hit Duncan's face. He wore a bearskin cloak fastened at the neck with a wooden clasp.

Behind her, twenty men crashed into the clearing, some armed with dirks and daggers, others with pistols. Geddes was the last through the ranks, breathing hard as he found her. He thudded forward with murder in his eyes, was nearly upon her before he noticed the bear and stopped.

Duncan nudged her aside but kept a firm grasp on her arm. He looked casually among the group. "Have I interrupted somethin', lads?"

"Who be ye?" Geddes demanded.

"The name *be* Duncan Kerr," he said slowly and deliberately. "I've come to offer my services to Hereford. I am Roxburghe's uncle."

Rose could not breathe.

Then another voice said, "I had heard you were no longer living at Stonehaven." The group parted for Lord Hereford.

"Then ye are aware, my nephew holds no high regard for me, me bein' accused of murdererin' my own brother and all." He spat. "Though I do no' mind the credit. But a man who kills his own brother so he can be laird can no' be trusted no' to murder the two who stands in his way." He let the words land against Rose like a blow. "I am no longer welcome at Stonehaven."

Geddes laughed. "*You* killed your brother?"

Hereford peered with interest at Duncan. "Geddes here might take insult to your boast, Duncan. Mightn't you, Geddes?"

Duncan's eyes narrowed on Geddes. "I did no' say I killed my brother. I said Ruark thinks I did. Though I would have if he were no' already dead when I arrived."

Hereford glared at Geddes. "Check him for weapons. Go."

Duncan let Rose loose. She stumbled backward as he blatantly opened his arms for anyone brave enough to approach and lay his hands on him.

Geddes finally stepped forward for the task. He removed a knife, two pistols, a sword, and a dirk, handing each off to a man behind him. "Why are you here, Duncan?" Hereford asked when it finally looked as if he was clean of weapons.

"I came to do ye a favor, your lordship. I came to warn ye to prepare to fight or leave. Ruark knows where ye are."

Rose watched her father's expression change. "None of my spotters have signaled. How many men?"

"A hundred."

Hereford laughed. "Is *that* all he could muster?"

"A hundred men . . ." Geddes said worriedly.

"Are you an idiot, Graham?" Hereford said. "Roxburghe isn't going to let those men ride down that hill with their weapons blazing. We have *her*. Why would you tell me this?" Hereford asked Duncan.

"I have no loyalty to Ruark." Duncan's teeth shone white in his beard. "But I do want Stonehaven and all that

belongs there. When this is over . . . when ye have Ruark
. . . you'll give me this one as my prize."

"Nay!" Rose whispered. "How can you do this?"

"Because he is no' deservin' of ye, lass."

And she truly believed Duncan. "And you are?"

"Aye, that I am."

"Bastard!" Rose flung herself at him, pounding his
chest with her bound hands. "I believed in you! I . . . I
believed . . . you were decent."

Duncan ducked the blows against him. She struck him,
and much to the amusement of all landed a double-fisted
blow against his chin before he could wrestle her body
around and hold her against his chest, one big arm over
her shoulder. He laughed. "Need I say more? The lass is
in love with me."

"Duncan's in place," Ruark said as he handed the glass
to Angus.

He swung Loki around and faced the horseman. Strung
out for a mile in the meadow behind him, four hundred
Kerr men were amassing along the ridge. They wore no
flashy accoutrements to catch the moonlight, and they had
ridden the last pair of miles silent and under the cover of
darkness. Dark like the mist.

Beside him, Colum said, "I estimate forty." His voice
was not strong.

With icy calm, Ruark's gloved hand tightened on Loki's
reins. "Are you sure you aren't still seeing double," he said,
perturbed that Colum had insisted on coming, even with
the head wound McBain had sutured. The thickness of
his clothes, and a leather jack had saved him from three
arrows. The two boys were safe as well.

Ruark's gaze was riveted to the center of the line behind
him. He had already given everyone instructions. He kicked

his heels and sent Loki to the ridge. For a savage moment horse and rider were motionless, a silhouette in ebony framed against the round lantern moon behind him. He came forward just a few feet, his horse restlessly pawing at the ground as if he knew Ruark's mind and his heart. Then four hundred men followed him onto the ridge. Their horses stretched out for as far as he could see into the darkness. Ruark raised his sword high. All around him, a battle cry went up that resounded across the sky.

He would not give Hereford time to amass or organize. And he was trusting Duncan to guard Rose's life with his own.

Ruark's arm came slashing down. And four hundred screaming Scotsman thundered down the ridge.

Rose had once heard that same bloodcurdling battle cry in Jedburgh. But this time her heart soared at the sound. Duncan grabbed her arm before she could go two steps. She fought him. "Nay, my lady Rose," he said, pressing her head to his chest. "I am here on Ruark's command."

She heard her father shouting orders. She caught his furious glare from across the camp where he had run to retrieve his pistols and sword. He had expected her price as hostage to bring easy surrender. Instead, it brought hell down upon him. Men scattered. Some on horseback. The others on foot.

Duncan pulled her to a tree and threw her on the ground beneath its boughs. He unclasped the wood broach and with a twist of his hands, it opened into a deadly knife. He cut the bonds on her wrists, then dropped the bearskin cloak over her. And she became a shadow in the night. Warm and protected by its thick pelt.

But no shot was fired, no arrow flew, no knife was thrown.

Only the mountebank, who had crawled beneath the wagon, was still present in the camp when Ruark reached the glade. He dismounted while the horse was still moving, already at a run when he hit the ground. His spurs jangled with each step and Rose was suddenly in his arms, where she remained. Duncan beside them ever watchful.

Within ten minutes, the Scots had routed the small group of reprobates and scattered the lot into the woods, and the skirmish was over. Still, Rose did pull away from the bristled cheek pressed against her temple, and he did not force her. No words were spoken between them.

His eyes on his uncle over Rose's head, Ruark asked, "Where is Hereford?"

"On foot," Duncan said. "I saw the one called Geddes following on horseback. There is only one way out of these woods for anyone looking for the border. I will take some men . . ."

Rose pulled away and looked up into Duncan's face. He touched her shoulder. "I should no' have hurt ye earlier with the lies, but I had no choice. I needed ye to believe I was against Ruark."

"Oh, aye," she said, gently indignant. "You convinced me well enough."

While Ruark's men gathered up the horses, he remained with Rose beneath the trees. He gently tilted her chin, looked at her face and examined the dark bruise on her swollen lip. "I would have been here sooner, but I had to find a way to get someone into this camp. Duncan would allow no other."

"How did you know where to find me?"

He laughed softly against her hair. "You ask that, love, when you have my heart and I have yours? I will always find you."

He *had* found her, she realized.

Or she had found him, he might argue.

"Will we ever know all the answers, Ruark?"

In the end, it was Rolf, the mountebank, who told Ruark everything.

Rolf confessed that it was Geddes who had murdered Ruark's father for the gold Hereford paid him to do the deed, a dissolution of the partnership after Ruark's father could not pay the enormous debt owed to Hereford.

If Ruark would have surrendered tonight as Hereford had wanted, Hereford would have made sure he never made it to England alive.

But Ruark would never allow Hereford the chance to threaten any of them again.

Before Ruark would ever find peace, he had to first find Hereford. So Ruark and Duncan left Rose at Stonehaven.

Three days later, they found him dead at the bottom of a hollow near where he had vanished in the woods. He had apparently fallen or been pushed, as Duncan surmised, as it looked as if a fight had taken place on the ground above the drop.

Geddes was found two days later outside Castleton, riding the black cavalry horse Ruark had stolen some months prior from the captain of a dragoon regiment, and was promptly arrested, which was why he was in custody when Ruark found him. Ironically, the horse had been the one Geddes had taken the day he took Rose. It had been the horse Jack had ridden to the falls. Ruark did not linger long but returned to his wife and family and found Rose in the sitting room, her hands clasped in Mrs. Simpson's, for she had already received the news about Hereford's death. But that wasn't why she was crying.

"I thought it time to reveal everything," Mrs. Simpson said.

Ruark stared as Mrs. Simpson turned to him and told him she was Rose's great-aunt, sister to her grandmother. Using a lace-edged handkerchief, she dabbed at her eyes. "I married quite young, you see, and quite outside the expectations of the family. I did not care a whit. Marrying my husband gave me a freedom in my life I could never have had with the strictures of my family." Her eyes on Rose, she said, "After your mother died, Friar Tucker and I knew you were in great peril. No one could know about me."

"But if you are still alive, then I am not the sole female heir to the barony or to Kirkland Park."

"Nay, you are not. Friar Tucker held the trust because I asked him to. I am the one who agreed to trade Kirkland Park for your future. If Hereford knew I was alive . . . you were important to him only as long as he thought you were valuable to him. In my role to you, I could always be near you without threat to either of us."

Mrs. Simpson told her about Friar Tucker and the deep abiding love Rose's mother and he had shared, and that Elena had made the mistake of telling Hereford. "Friar Tucker loves you as his own, Rose. It was his idea to let you find the puzzle box in the crypt."

"I . . . I do not understand."

"My husband and I uncovered the box at the Arthurian site in which he was working years ago, not far from here. It was one of the many trinkets and relics he had discovered in his travels and it sat useless in my home for years. Friar Tucker thought you needed something to believe in, to occupy your mind and your heart. He and I wanted you to have it. You were so desperate to believe in something, and the mind is powerful when it sets itself on a thing. We never expected the box to open, much less have anything inside."

"Then 'tis an authentic Arthurian relic," Ruark said.

" 'Twas found in an ancient grave along with another ring that has since been lost to us. No one truly understands what power, if any, the relics hold."

But deep inside, Ruark did.

His gaze caught and held Rose, who had taken his hand in hers, and for a man who had believed in very little his entire life, he had come to believe in something powerful. Whether by magic or by fate, his life had changed.

As Lord Hereford's only surviving heir, Rose inherited Kirkland Park on the fourth of October in the year seventeen hundred and fifty-five. Ruark had seen that the estate would remain hers in a special trust and would pass to their daughter just as it had done to all the Kirkland daughters for generations.

She had not wanted to visit the estate in the beginning, but Ruark had asked her go with him. She needed to go.

During an unusually warm week that followed, as if he had willed it himself, Ruark gathered up Jack and Jamie and brought Rose to Kirkland Park. There they met Friar Tucker at the gates. Ruark took the boys and let his wife and the friar walk through the gates alone as he remained outside a few moments more. The gray stones of the manor, covered in leaves and vines gilded by the cooler temperatures of fall, stretched against a bright, brilliant blue sky.

That night the ring came off his finger as Ruark was washing his face. He looked into the porcelain bowl and saw the piece of silver glittering in the clear water beneath. Rose found him and saw the ring as well.

She picked it up. Their eyes met over the silver circlet. Was it real?

He knew only that whether it was by fate or enchantment his life had changed. What he wanted most in the world touched him like a velvet sunrise on a warm dawn, imprinting itself upon his heart and his soul. Rose was the magic in his life.

That the ring had fallen off only now was surely a coincidence.

"Are you tempted?" he asked her, wondering if her life was complete, for despite everything he could not entirely banish all doubt.

He loved her so.

"Is there anything you want, Rose?"

She wrapped her arms around his neck and kissed him, then took his hand to lay it against her abdomen. "Nay, my love. I believe you have given me all that my heart could want."

She was going to have his child.

Before the thought could fully register, she kissed him again, and he knew a power such as he had never known.

Love had many faces. But like the circlet of silver, love was endless.

With no beginning and no end. It was both darkness and light. Opposite the other yet coexisting, like day and night. Happiness and sadness.

Love holds no expectations but simply is.

Ever changing. Yet forever constant.

And the Scottish lord had claimed her heart.

Unforgettable, enthralling love stories,
sparkling with passion and adventure
from Romance's bestselling authors

PASSION UNTAMED   *by Pamela Palmer*
978-0-06-166753-4

OUT OF THE DARKNESS   *by Jaime Rush*
978-0-06-169036-5

SILENT NIGHT, HAUNTED NIGHT   *by Terri Garey*
978-0-06-158204-2

SOLD TO A LAIRD   *by Karen Ranney*
978-0-06-177175-0

DARK OF THE MOON   *by Karen Robards*
978-0-380-75437-3

MY DARLING CAROLINE   *by Adele Ashworth*
978-0-06-190587-2

UPON A WICKED TIME   *by Karen Ranney*
978-0-380-79583-3

IN SCANDAL THEY WED   *by Sophie Jordan*
978-0-06-157921-9

IN PURSUIT OF A SCANDALOUS LADY   *by Gayle Callen*
978-0-06-178341-8

SEVEN SECRETS OF SEDUCTION   *by Anne Mallory*
978-0-06-157915-8

At Avon Books, we know your passion for romance—once you finish one of our novels, you find yourself wanting more.

May we tempt you with . . .

- **Excerpts** from our upcoming releases.

- Entertaining **extras**, including authors' personal photo albums and book lists.

- Behind-the-scenes **scoop** on your favorite characters and series.

- **Sweepstakes** for the chance to win free books, romantic getaways, and other fun prizes.

- Writing **tips** from our authors and editors.

- **Blog** with our authors and find out why they love to write romance.

- **Exclusive content** that's not contained within the pages of our novels.

Join us at
www.avonbooks.com

AVON

An Imprint of HarperCollins*Publishers*
www.avonromance.com